If you love Patricia Rice's Magic series, you must read her new contemporary addition to the series:

The Lure of Song and Magic

AVAILABLE NOW FROM SOURCEBOOKS CASABLANCA

*Sparks are still flying between the Ives and Malcolm families…
in the twenty-first century!*

"Even if you have never met a Malcolm before, you will be enthralled by this tale. Rice brings you great characters, a dynamite plot, and plenty of magic… Don't miss it."

—*RT Book Reviews*, 4½ stars

"[An] enchanting concoction of magic, suspense, and an unlikely love. Patricia Rice writes stories with so much attention to detail the characters truly seem to come to life."

—*Booklist* starred review

"Fans of Rice's original Magic series will enjoy reading of the Ives and Malcolm families' modern offspring and be intrigued by how the computer age has shaped how they hide and use their magic."

—*Publishers Weekly*

"Awesome. A story that I will read over and over again."

—*Night Owl Reviews* Reviewer Top Pick, 5 Stars

"*The Lure of Song and Magic* is different and refreshing."

—*Bookloons*

MUST BE MAGIC

PATRICIA RICE

sourcebooks
casablanca

Published by Sourcebooks Casablanca, an imprint of Sourcebooks, Inc.
P.O. Box 4410, Naperville, Illinois 60567-4410
(630) 961-3900
FAX: (630) 961-2168
www.sourcebooks.com

Originally published in 2002 by Signet, an imprint of New American Library, a division of Penguin Putnam Inc.

Library of Congress Cataloging-in-Publication Data

Rice, Patricia.
  Must be magic / by Patricia Rice.
    p. cm.
  1. Scientists—Fiction. 2. England—Fiction. I. Title.
  PS3568.I2925M87 2012
  813'.54—dc23

                              2012002340

        Printed and bound in the United States of America
              VP 10 9 8 7 6 5 4 3 2 1

To woman's intuition and to everyone
who feels a little different...

Author's Note

The second half of the eighteenth century was a time of burgeoning interest in all things scientific, although the word "science" was not defined as it is today. Reading bumps on heads was considered as scientific as staring at the skies through telescopes. Although this was also a time in Great Britain of great experimentation in agriculture, the word "agronomist" had not yet come into use.

For the sake of the modern reader, I have ignored eighteenth-century definitions and confusing phrases and used words like "scientist" and "agronomist," as we do today.

For the disbelievers among us who may be tempted to scoff at my heroine's gifts, let me remind you that it has been scientifically proven that smell can evoke memories and influence mood, emotions, and choice of mates. It can predict death and detect illness. In a primitive manner, man can communicate by smell. Just don't expect characters from the eighteenth century to recognize this as a science!

Prologue

London, 1735

"Pick little Christina if you must, but don't pick Leila for our team," a fair-haired adolescent warned her equally fair younger sister. "She has no powers. She's *useless*."

"But Uncle Rowland favors her," the younger girl replied. "He says Leila's just like him."

"That's because she's not like the rest of us," Diana, the elder, said with an arrogant toss of her blond curls. "Leila's hair is *black*, and she has no gifts. She's not a Malcolm. Even her baby sisters have more abilities than she does. Let her play on the babies' side. They won't know the difference."

On the staircase above, ten-year-old Leila cringed and backed up the way she'd come, her heart breaking with every step. She'd anticipated the joyous romp of the scavenger hunt her aunt had arranged. She'd been thrilled to have the company of her beautiful older cousins with their fascinating abilities to find lost objects and to paint pictures of what wasn't there.

She hadn't anticipated scorn at her own lack of such gifts.

She'd known her sister could see odd colors around people that she couldn't, but Christina was a *baby*. No one cared what babies saw, and what good were colors anyway? Leila was the eldest, and her mama said she was the best little helper she could have. Her papa called her beautiful. The little ones clamored for her company.

But her cousins thought her *useless*. Wide-eyed with shock, Leila quivered at the top of the stairs, not fully comprehending her cousin's antipathy.

Her cousins thought she wasn't a *Malcolm*. She might be *adopted*. She didn't want to be thrown out in the snow and left to die because she didn't belong here.

Panicking, Leila grabbed her black curls and threw a glance over her shoulder to see if the portly butler might already be bearing down on her, prepared to heave her out the door. Relieved to see no immediate danger in sight, Leila raced for the only comfort she knew—her very blond, very Malcolm mother.

Tears forming at her cousin's cruel dismissal, Leila rushed into the workshop and dived into Hermione's welcoming arms.

"I *am* a Malcolm, aren't I?" she wailed against her mother's plump bosom. "My hair will lighten to be just like yours someday, won't it?"

Sitting down on a low bench beside a cluster of candle molds and jars of herbs and fragrances, Hermione wrapped her beautiful firstborn in a hug. "Of course you're a Malcolm, dear. You're just *different*. You should be proud of your lovely black hair. Someday men will swoon over you."

"I don't want men to swoon," Leila declared, tears still in her eyes. "I want to make people smile like you do with candles that smell like happiness. I want to find lost things like Diana can. I can do anything I want, can't I? I'm a *Malcolm*." The last word came out almost as a plea.

Hermione stroked Leila's long curls. "It's up to us to make the most of what we're given, dear. You have beauty and grace and intelligence, and someday you will make some man very happy. Just don't let that man be an Ives," she added with a wry chuckle. "Your ancestors would rise from their graves."

Momentarily distracted from her grief, Leila gazed at her mother's serene features. "What's an Ives?"

"Only the downfall of all Malcolms, dear. We are creatures of nature, and they are creatures of science. Disaster results when the two come together. But you are much too young to worry about that now."

Disinterested in future disasters, more concerned about

the current one, Leila eyed the glittering array of equipment on her mother's workbench. Inhaling the bouquet of scents exuded by the mood-enhancing wax candles and soaps her mother made, she bit her quivering lip and straightened her shoulders. She understood very little of the nasty Ives discussion, but she knew she was smart. Smarter than Diana. She already knew how to play the harpsichord and sing far better than her older cousin. She could make her father cry when she sang, and smile when she played.

She had better things to do than play at a stupid scavenger hunt. Heart bruised but pride intact, Leila lifted her chin. "I shall go down and see if Papa wishes to hear me play. I'm much too big for baby games."

"And take the chess set to the boys. They always behave better when you smile at them."

Racing to do as she'd been told, Leila vowed to smile and sing and make everyone happy and prove she was better than her cousins so her mama would love her.

As the laughter of her sisters and cousins rose from the entrance hall, Leila stopped at the top of the stairs, scrubbed at a wayward tear, and sniffed back the sob forming in her throat. It didn't matter if they wouldn't play with her. She didn't *need* them.

But she needed to be a *Malcolm*. She didn't want to be left out and all alone.

One

London, April 1752

"He's mine," Lady Leila Staines announced, studying the imposing man at the entrance to the ballroom who scowled at her guests as if he were deciding whose head he might sever first.

Her sister, Christina, drew in a sharp breath as she followed Leila's gaze. "*Dunstan Ives?* Don't be absurd. He's an Ives and a *murderer.*"

Fascinated, Leila watched the formidable gentleman dressed entirely in black except for the immaculate white cravat at his throat. This Ives possessed the power to put her world back on course. She had to have him. "He's not a murderer; Ninian says so."

"He could snap your neck with a flick of his wrist," Christina whispered, watching with fascinated horror as Dunstan's companions were announced. "Look, his aura is black as night!"

Ignoring her younger sister, Leila observed the entrance of angelic Ninian beside her handsome husband, Drogo, Earl of Ives and Wystan. Then her gaze followed the towering man who was dissociating himself from his companions by lingering behind them. Both Ives men exhibited their scorn of society with their sun-darkened visages and lack of powdered wigs. The lean earl possessed an air of intellect and refinement, but his broader brother glowered with hostility as he scanned the glittering throng. In his tailored coat, with shoulders strong as those of an ox, Dunstan Ives made the rest of the lace-and-silk bedecked company appear effeminate.

"I don't know about his aura, but his clothes are certainly unfashionably black," Leila observed as she studied the brooding looks and powerful physique of the man she meant to proposition. He was definitely not the usual sort of London gentleman. But then, Ives men never were.

"He must still wear black for his wife," Christina murmured. "I suppose if he did not murder her, that would be tragically romantic."

"If he ever loved her, he fell out of it," their cousin Lucinda said, hearing this last as she joined them. "Of course, one shouldn't assume his lack of love means he intended harm," she added.

Since Celia Ives had been murdered most violently more than a year ago, Leila knew her cousin hastened to correct any impression that Dunstan might have had something to do with his wife's death. Lucinda possessed a gift for revealing true character through her paintings, and people tended to pay particular attention to even her most casual comments. She was careful, therefore, not to misstate her opinion and leave the wrong impression. Like all Malcolms, she had acquired a keen sense of responsibility along with her gifts.

Gifts that Leila didn't possess. All her life, Leila had searched for a similar gift in herself, but she had never discovered the magic that would prove her to be a true Malcolm. Still, even with her limited perception, she could see that the arrogant man standing in the doorway despised the parrot colors of fashion and wore black out of disdain for the society over which she prevailed. Love and grief had nothing to do with it.

He was an Ives, after all—cold and unfeeling.

Fanning herself as she admired his stature, Leila thought of her own dark attire and smiled faintly. They were soul mates in matters of dress at least. Black gave her an authority her age did not, and it set her apart from the common herd so she might better wield that authority. She was smart, as her mother had always said. She'd focused her intelligence on understanding society, and had applied what she learned to make a place for herself and her late husband in fashionable circles.

At least she'd made her husband happy.

What her intelligence couldn't master was what her family did without effort: see beyond the obvious, dabble in the supernatural, and help those around them through those gifts. All her life, Leila had been excluded from the whispered consultations of her younger siblings and cousins, simply because she could not see or hear what they could. Behind her, she could hear Christina and Lucinda whispering about their insights into Dunstan's character, excluding her as usual. Despite knowing everyone in this room, she still stood alone, the solitary cuckoo in her family's nest.

Until she discovered some special ability in herself and proved she was a Malcolm, she would always feel like an ostracized child—alone, unloved, and a failure.

She'd spent her entire life meeting her family's expectations of her. She'd married well, raised her husband's social and political standing, acquired wealth, made others happy, if not herself. Widowed now, and finally free of all expectations, she stood on the brink of opportunity, if she possessed the courage to take the risk. With the help of an Ives, she might discover who she really was and of what she was capable.

Leila allowed a tendril of hope to creep through her usual restraint as she watched the commanding presence of the tall man in the doorway. Nervously, she waved her fan, bouncing a loose pin curl in the breeze. After a year of planning and dreaming, she'd made her choice. All she need do now was approach Dunstan Ives and state her proposal. Even if he was immune to her charm, he should succumb to her monetary largesse, and then she would have England's most learned agronomist at her disposal.

"He's an Ives," Lucinda whispered in warning, apparently noting the direction of Leila's gaze. "Don't forget what happened to cousin Ninian."

Leila was aware of the danger Ives men posed to women, and to Malcolm women in particular. The attraction between them must be as powerful as legend said if even Ninian had risked disaster to fall for one of the logical, passionless men. But Leila was prepared to take her chances with the fire of physical attraction. Although men habitually flocked around her, she had never felt passion for them in return.

Her only dilemma lay in whether she dared retire to the country in the company of a man whose adulterous wife had been found with her neck snapped. No evidence confirmed Dunstan's guilt. None confirmed his innocence, either.

Leila offered a practiced trill of laughter at her cousin's warning. "I seduce men, not the other way around. An Ives is no match for me."

"Leila, you cannot tell what he's feeling as Ninian can," Christina warned. "He looks incredibly dangerous."

"Shall I go closer and see what I can learn?" Leila snapped her fan closed and, forgetting everyone else in the room besides Dunstan, left her sister and cousin.

Progressing through the crowd of London's wealthiest and most powerful, she stopped often to meet and greet her guests, never losing sight of the man she intended to trap in her net. *Mother of goddesses*, but he was built like a mountain, a smoldering one. She chattered and exchanged mindless gossip, but she couldn't look away as Dunstan Ives glowered at a footman and ended up with two glasses of champagne in his huge fists.

"Isn't that the Ives who murdered his wife?" one countess whispered. "Honestly, Leila, even *you* can't expect us to acknowledge a murderer!"

"Dear, dear Betsy." Leila patted the woman's gloved hand without paying her much notice. "I invited your current lover, the father of your son, and your husband, and I'm still speaking to all four of you. Be a good girl and don't spoil my fun."

She left the rouged and powdered countess with her mouth open.

"He looks as if he might murder someone any minute," Hermione, Marchioness of Hampton, murmured worriedly, sidling up to Leila and fiddling with the gossamer scarf about her throat. "I cannot think why you invited him."

"Because he is the best agronomist in all of England," Leila assured her mother. "Even Father says so. Since Dunstan has come to work for him, the estate has improved tremendously. Is that not so?"

"Yes, but your father is a *man*, dear. It is not at all the same thing. I do wish you would reconsider offering him a position."

"But the opportunity is perfect," Leila explained. "You know Father means to put Rolly in charge of the Gloucestershire estate. Rolly loathes Dunstan, says he does not take orders well. Why should I let Rolly drive him away when *I* can have him?" Leila did not slow her progress across the drawing room. Tugging at shawls and scarves, her mother trailed in her wake.

"Leila, you know nothing of these things—"

"Ninian does, and she says he's innocent." Ninian was years younger than Leila, but she possessed a gift of empathy and a talent for healing that had saved lives and fortunes—including Drogo's. Ninian was the one her whole family turned to because she *understood* things without being told. Leila bowed to her greater gifts, even as envy devoured her.

"You know perfectly well that Ninian is not herself when she's in town with so many people around to disturb her gift," Hermione whispered. "She could be wrong about Dunstan—"

"I'm not changing my mind, *Maman*," Leila said. "He's mine."

A sensual shiver rippled down her spine as she repeated those words at the same moment that Dunstan turned his brooding gaze on her, and the implication of her arrogant declaration raised its serpent head.

She wanted an agricultural expert, not a lover, but Dunstan's hooded dark eyes and prominent nose stirred long dormant feelings in her. Uneasy with the sensation, she reminded herself that no man had *ever* wielded the power to tempt her.

Safe behind a shield of indifference, Leila brushed a kiss on Ninian's cheek. "How good of you to come." Murmuring polite nonsense, she flirted with the impervious Drogo, then turned the full brunt of her attention on the imposing man standing slightly distant from his family.

Oh, my. His presence hit her with all the force of her mother's lust-scented candles.

"Black becomes you, sir," she murmured, drawing her black-gloved finger down Dunstan's lapel, resorting to her practiced role of flirt to hide the sensual impact this man had on her. Was it her imagination, or did his air of disdain conceal a slight whiff of loneliness? Perhaps his lack of artificial scent distorted her perceptions. Fascinating.

"Black's not fashionable," he replied, staring past her powdered curls.

"So flattering of you to mention that." She immediately retracted any sympathy she might have mistakenly offered. "Shall I run upstairs and slip into something more to your liking? In red, perhaps?"

Dunstan glanced down at her wide black skirts, then focused his gaze on the expanse of bosom exposed by her low-cut gown. "Scarlet seems appropriate."

The lady's sensual perfume of roses and jasmine wafted around him, and Dunstan stiffened. He didn't want to notice her at all, but she stood taller than most women, reaching past his chin in her heeled shoes. His gaze fell in direct contact with her lacy black cap, forcing him to notice how her tight, powdered curls accentuated her rouged lips and darkened lashes. Despite the white powder, he knew she was a Malcolm, and she'd have sun-kissed blond hair like all the rest of her kind, along with eyes that could ensnare and bewitch. He refused to look down and fall into the trap.

Nodding curtly in dismissal, ignoring Ninian and Drogo, Dunstan spun on his heel and strode blindly for what he hoped was the card room.

The lady's exotic perfume clung to his senses as he departed, and raw hunger clawed at his insides.

It had been that way with Celia.

Never again. He would put a bullet through his ear before he became enthralled with another aristocratic, conniving female.

Especially a *Malcolm.* He had enough disaster in his life without courting more.

Two

WOMEN PULLED THEIR SKIRTS ASIDE AS DUNSTAN PASSED. MEN scowled. Card tables emptied when he showed an interest in the play.

The clawing at his insides became a hot anger he could taste on his tongue. He didn't *need* this pack of rats and jackals. He had only put in an appearance because Drogo requested it, and he owed his brother far more than he could ever repay.

Loosening his confining neckcloth, Dunstan located the door to the balcony and stepped outside to let the familiar elements feed his soul. He'd never been a part of the fashionable London scene that his wife had adored—the scene that should have been his by birthright. Instead, his spoiled earl of a father had chosen to hide Dunstan's rustic mother and her uncouth sons in the country while the earl dallied in London with his aristocratic mistress.

His father's neglect had taught Dunstan to live without society. He'd grown up in the village vicarage of his mother's brother, had learned from his maternal grandfather to respect the land and nature. London's decadence had never called to him.

Of course, if he'd made even the slightest effort to enter society, Celia might be alive today.

Guilt joined the cold damp of the London fog permeating Dunstan's bones. Behind him, through the brilliantly lit glass, he could hear the poignant notes of violin and flute. Couples executed elegant dance steps and whirled about in colorful silks, laughing, flirting, arranging trysts. Celia had become a part of that world without him.

His innards writhed in an agony of discomfort. He had no place here. His abilities related to the land, not people. Experience had taught him he could only hurt people.

The land his grandfather had left him was little more than a useless bog he couldn't afford to drain, but Drogo had offered a few acres of solid ground for Dunstan's experimental crop—a fodder that would revolutionize farming by growing large enough to feed a flock of sheep all winter. This was the hope his future turned on, not this glittering artificial world.

He didn't have time to plant the seeds before returning to his tedious duties as estate agent for the Marquess of Hampton. The marquess's heir demanded his presence in Gloucestershire two days hence. Even dealing with the marquess's foolish son, Rolly, was far better than enduring an entire city of brainless fribbles.

Leaning against the cold balcony rail, Dunstan fretted over the lack of time to plant his valuable crop, concerned about leaving it in the dubious care of Drogo's steward.

Now that his brother had married and produced a son, Dunstan was no longer heir to an earldom or the entailed estate he'd thought would someday be his. He must find his own land and his own place in the world. He couldn't expect Drogo to support him for a lifetime.

His brother had paid Dunstan's way through school, provided for his illegitimate son, and loaned him enough to keep Celia in style. After Celia's death, Drogo had paid the debts she'd left behind. He'd even offered to take on the expense of investigating Celia's murder, but Dunstan had insisted that responsibility must be his. Until his name was cleared, there was little sense in wasting money on improving his boggy land.

Voices at the door intruded on his musings, prompting him to retreat into the shadows.

"The man should be hanged," a deep voice uttered in vicious tones. "We hang paupers for stealing bread. It's no wonder the lower classes don't trust their betters if they perceive us as getting away with *murder*."

"There's no evidence on which to try him," a calmer voice said. "There's no call for Ives to shove him in our faces, though. The man hasn't the political sense of a squirrel."

A flame flickered, and the aroma of a rich cigar drifted through the air. Dunstan cursed beneath his breath and considered his choices. Leaping off a balcony onto a flagstone terrace would either crack every bone in his body or split every stone in the terrace.

The first voice grunted. "Ives doesn't give a fig for politics. Shoving his criminal of a brother down our throats will ruin him."

"Polite society has standards," the second voice agreed. "Ives have always been a ramshackle lot, at any account. Shut them all out, keep them away from our daughters, and the world will be a better place."

The smug satisfaction in the lout's voice decided the matter. Dunstan had no doubt that Drogo could fight his own battles, and that his witch of a wife could hex the entire city if she were so inclined, but Dunstan wouldn't allow the taint of his reputation to harm his younger brothers, either the legitimate or the illegitimate ones. With no titles or wealth, they would have to fight the painful battle for survival with several handicaps. Dunstan refused to add one more.

With what he considered to be remarkable aplomb, he stepped into the light pouring through the glass doors. Towering over the elegantly bewigged and silk-coated gentlemen who stood frozen at the balustrade, Dunstan plucked the cigar from the speaker's mouth, dropped the lighted tobacco on the man's silver-buckled shoe, and mashed it with his massive foot.

"Polite society might consider adopting Ives standards," Dunstan said in his most courteous tone. "We crush stupidity and ignorance when they stand in the way." With one last grind of his heel on lordly toes, Dunstan stalked off.

❧

"Leila, Leila—hurry! I think your Ives has murdered someone!"

Leila stiffened as Christina pushed through the crowd of

suitors surrounding her. Trusting her sister's ability to detect strong auras, she didn't doubt there was a problem. She was merely annoyed that she didn't possess the ability to see it herself.

Hearing the commotion near the balcony doors, she directed her steps toward the gathering crowd.

"I say, let us hang Ives from the ramparts!" the younger son of an aging roué announced gaily, following in Leila's wake, as did his fellows. "It's not done, murdering a guest of Lady Leila's."

"Lord John, you…" *Have the wits of a gander*, she refrained from saying. She hadn't climbed this far in society by insulting those who had helped put her there. "Go find Drogo, will you? He'll listen to you." Appeal to the young man's pride. He had too much of it, but she could put it to good use. *That* was how she'd gained her position, by knowing the weaknesses of others.

"Of course, my lady." Full of self-importance, Lord John sauntered off, his closest gambling companion, Sir Barton Townsend, trailing along for security.

"Grown men, yet they're still children," Leila muttered to herself. What she would give for a *man*. She'd thought she'd married one when she'd wed Theodore. He'd been forty at the time, and it had seemed a reasonable assumption. But he'd been more child than his school-age nephew.

Henry Wickham stayed at her side, reeking of determination. A man of shallow character, he had his own grievances against Dunstan. She did not mistake his company as tenacity in her defense.

"This is a family matter, sir," she informed him haughtily, keeping an eye on the scene outside the balcony door. Drogo had arrived. And Ninian. Where was Dunstan? "Find Viscount Staines and apprise him of events."

That offered Wickham a dilemma—to cultivate her interest or that of her nephew, the much more impressionable young recipient of her husband's title. Wickham surprised her by actually choosing the wiser course. Leila smiled when he disappeared in search of the new viscount.

Her late husband hadn't been particularly disappointed that she hadn't produced a child to whom he could pass on the title.

He and his nephew were two of a kind, and he'd known the odds against a Malcolm bearing a boy when he married her.

Leila had been disappointed, though. Not bearing a child had been one more proof of her failure as a Malcolm.

Despite her lack of Malcolm abilities, she knew she possessed an astute understanding of human nature. If Dunstan wasn't in the midst of the shouting on the balcony, she knew precisely where to find him—providing he had not already escaped.

Damn the man. She couldn't afford to let him get away.

Veering from her original path, Leila swept past velvet draperies into the conservatory, a room providing a second exit from the balcony.

Humid warmth enveloped her as she opened the lattice-work doors. The servants had lit a few wall sconces, but the towering plants threw the jungle into heavy shadow.

"I am not a patient woman," she announced to the greenery. "You can't turn my party into the talk of the Season, then lurk in the shadows until we all go away."

"I'm not lurking."

Indeed, he *could* not. Dunstan Ives was much too broad in the shoulders to disguise himself as a palm or a lemon tree. She'd misjudged the density of the shadows.

She shivered in apprehension at the sepulchral sound of his voice. She should have recognized the scent of bone-deep isolation permeating the chamber, but she'd become too accustomed to her own. She entered, letting the door close behind her.

"I am debating wasting another cigar by shoving it up their arses." Blowing a curl of smoke, he leaned against a sturdy table, arms crossed, staring upward toward the glass ceiling. "Is that jasmine?" he asked, gesturing toward a towering vine with his obnoxious tobacco.

"Yes, it makes a delightful perfume." Gathering her panniered skirt to navigate the narrow path between them, Leila sucked in a gasp at the impact of raw male fury and an underlying current of—lust?—that he exuded. How could a man who looked so cold stir her with such heat?

"What cigar and whose arse?" she demanded, ignoring her passing fancy.

"No idea. Obnoxious old fart. Why aren't you out there with the rest of them, pouring witchy unguent on his wounds?"

"If I had any idea what the devil you were talking about, I might be. It seemed prudent to locate you first and be certain you didn't pull the house down around my ears."

"Or that they didn't form a lynch mob and hang me from the chandelier?" he asked shrewdly, turning in her direction.

"That caused me no concern whatsoever."

It did now. She had wanted to use this man's knowledge, but his isolation reverberated upon the untried chords of her own heart. Leila grappled with the odd inclination to comfort his wounded soul—then decided Dunstan Ives had no soul and was quite capable of handling anything that came his way.

He shrugged and ground his cigar against the dirt in a pot. "Where's your bevy of cicisbeos? Aren't they afraid I'll snap your neck?"

Amazingly perceptive of him, but she would not admit it. "I threatened them with hysterics if they did not leave me alone. Most gentlemen are instantly cowed by females who disturb their equanimity."

"Not cowed. Impatient. Blathering and dramatics are irrational and ineffective. If you will give my regards to my brother and his wife, I believe I shall depart for the country, where I belong." He pushed away from the table and loomed over her, waiting for her to step aside.

"Not yet," she commanded.

Leila shivered at the masculine aromas flooding her senses as he crossed his arms over his massive chest and glared at her. Someone—most likely Ninian—had tucked a carnation into his lapel. The combination of his male musk and the sweet perfume unleashed an unexpected hunger in her. In imitation of him, she crossed her arms beneath her breasts and shut out the sensation.

"I want you to work for me," she said, going straight to the point.

He remained impassive.

For the first time in memory, anxiety enveloped her. Wearing the guise of society coquette, she had persuaded dukes and princes to do as she wished—or rather, to do as her husband wished. She had never attempted to act on something she alone wanted, because she'd never thought that what she wanted was attainable.

Now, with the opportunity of a lifetime at her fingertips, she was terrified of losing her one and only chance.

"I need a garden." How could she explain that she didn't want just *any* garden? And that she didn't want it for the usual reasons? "I need flowers that no one else possesses. I want to propagate varieties that exist only in my head."

He snorted. "Female heads might be fertile ground for cotton, but flowers do better in soil."

She tightened her lips against a spurt of anger at his insult. She might have laughed at his riposte had he been another man or had this been another occasion, but it was her future he scorned. "You will discover my head contains far more than cotton. I wish to grow flowers that produce special scents. I will start with varieties I've already located, but I need someone who knows how to propagate them. My father says you are an expert."

"With vegetables. Flowers have no purpose."

Mule-headed wretched stone wall of a… *wall.* For whatever reason, Dunstan Ives had erected a barrier between himself and the world. She hadn't attained her position as society's leading matron by ignoring the nuances of male behavior. A man who resisted had something to hide. In Dunstan's case, she would prefer not to know what, but she needed the blasted man too much to allow his boneheaded stubbornness to stand in her way.

"You may grow all the vegetables you desire," she offered generously.

Had he just drawn in his breath, as if she had touched a raw nerve? She would have explored the possibility, but he stepped back, his emotions impenetrable once again. She flirted with danger by stepping closer, running her fingers up and down his chest. "Or are you holding out for a more… *personal* offer?"

She had no idea what possessed her to say such a thing, but his heat nearly set her gloves on fire.

Though she could barely see his face in the darkness, Leila felt him stiffen, and seeking the crack in his armor, she pressed her case. "You may name your terms," she said in a seductive tone that had brought generals to their knees, "as long as they can be measured in coin." She paused for effect, then took a gamble. "Unless you prefer something less tangible than coin."

He removed her hand from his chest with a strength that could have broken bones and with a gentleness that didn't.

"That's about the most inane thing anyone has said to me all evening. Go away before I chew you into little bits and spit you out." Dunstan flung her hand away and retreated from her reach. He'd been without a woman for so long, he'd forgotten their alluring scents and softness, the sway and rustle of tempting curves, the hot bloodlust that throbbed through him when the need was on him.

He couldn't afford passion any more than he could afford women. Whatever she offered, she would take too much in return.

"I am not an empty-headed twit," the lady replied with scorn. "You can't frighten me with exaggerated threats and intimidating stances. If you are the best agronomist in all England, then I need your services."

Intimidating stances. Dunstan almost chuckled at the way the irritating scrap of fluff stood there with her hands on her hips in her own version of intimidation.

"I *am* the best agronomist in England, but I am already employed," he avowed. "The last person in the world I'd work for is a Malcolm witch."

Even though he could barely see the lady in the darkness, she was still working her witchy Malcolm wiles on him. A part of him wanted to show her he was far more than the best agronomist in all England. He wanted to prove he was first and foremost a man—but that pathway led to hell, and he refused to take it, no matter what enticements she offered. *Name his own terms!* Gad, the woman had parsnips for brains if she didn't know the power of her own seductiveness.

Lady Leila had the most luscious curves created in the eyes of God and mankind. He was far better off out of her presence, and she was far better off understanding with whom she toyed.

Dunstan wrapped his hands around her corseted waist and lifted her to the potting bench, knocking plants out of the way with her wide panniers.

She gasped and got in a well-placed kick with her heeled shoes, but Dunstan merely grunted and staggered away.

Name his own terms, indeed. She would scream and have his head cut off if he told her exactly what terms he'd choose.

Three

Wiltshire, April 1752

THE LAST PERSON IN THE WORLD I'D WORK FOR IS A MALCOLM *witch*. Famous last words. Taunting a Malcolm was as witless as teasing dragons.

Cursing and wiping the filth of the road from his brow, Dunstan halted at a crossroad near Swindon and let his aging mount nibble grass while he debated his route.

Dismissed. The best damned agronomist in the land, and he'd been *dismissed*. For insubordination. Imagine that. And not another fat-headed lordling on the horizon seemed interested in hiring him.

Dunstan returned to pondering the crossroad. He could take the route east and crawl back to Drogo, but he'd rather eat his own foot than ask for help. The fiasco in London had proven he was a detriment to his noble brother as well as to his own son, whom he was determined to take under his wing one day.

Years ago, Celia had been horrified when he'd suggested bringing his by-blow, Griffith, into their household. Celia's death and the subsequent rumors had effectively destroyed his hopes of developing any filial relationship with the boy. Until Dunstan's innocence was established, Griffith was better off with his mother.

Dunstan might be a failure at his social obligations, but he knew he possessed an encyclopedic knowledge of experimental agricultural techniques. He wasn't too proud to work, provided someone would let him.

The cursed Malcolm witch had seen to it that no one would let him.

You may name your terms. Had she really said that? Was it a trap?

He glared up the road leading west, toward Bath and the Staines estate. He had no proof that Lady Leila was responsible for his current situation. After Celia and London, his reputation could be the reason that no man would hire him. But it had been the lady's half brother who had sacked him, even though Dunstan had tripled the estate's profits over the past year. It certainly looked like the lady's doing to him.

Of course, to be fair, Rolly was a prig of the worst sort, and Dunstan might have let the lordling know that a time or two. He didn't tolerate fools gladly.

Dunstan leaned against his horse's neck and considered his alternatives. His saddlebag still contained the experimental turnip seeds. He could crawl back to his brother—and the few acres Drogo had promised him—and never earn enough to pay his recently hired investigator to seek the truth of Celia's death, much less make a life for his son.

Or he could turn toward Bath and accept the lady's offer. *His terms.* The possibilities intrigued him.

He had catered to Celia's whims for years. Like a blithering fool, he'd showered her with fripperies and jewels he could ill afford, placating her with the dream of someday becoming a countess, since Drogo had no heir. He hoped she would be patient and learn to love him.

The instant Drogo had married and had a son, Celia had danced off to London and a round of lovers, and never looked back.

Dunstan would rather rot in the Tower than play carpet for a woman's dainty feet again.

He particularly wouldn't play the part of carpet for a seductive Malcolm. Lady Leila was too attractive and determined. She could walk all over a man, if he let her. Then again, no one said he had to let her.

She'd said he could name his own terms.

Crawl or fight. Friggin' hell of a choice.

Reining his gelding to the right, he set his jaw and hunkered down for the battle ahead.

❧

Dunstan pounded on the door of Lady Leila's rural mansion until a stiff-necked butler answered. Accepting Dunstan's hat, the servant led him toward the back as if he'd been expected. The witch had probably read of his arrival in her tea leaves.

Entering what was obviously her late husband's masculine study, he watched as the woman he thought of as the Black Widow paced before a sunny window. Or at least, he assumed it was she, given her black skirts. The bright light threw her features into shadow, and he had deliberately avoided looking closely at her in London.

At first, this female appeared every bit as tight-laced and haughty as the woman he remembered from the ball. But noticing the way she clasped and unclasped her hands, he sensed in her an uncertainty that he hadn't discerned earlier.

"I've come to inquire if the estate agent position is still available." Clenching his jaw, Dunstan focused on the cap covering her tightly pinned and powdered hair, avoiding any contact with her provocative Malcolm eyes. He didn't believe in fairy tales, but if even Drogo could be tempted by a Malcolm witch, he would take no chance that there was truth in the legendary attraction between Malcolm women and Ives men. He figured the legendary disasters between their families were to be expected of any Ives who was foolish enough to fall for a witch.

He wished the devil she'd sit down.

"As I told you before, I need someone who is willing to help me develop new strains of flowers, ones grown for fragrance," she announced, as if they were continuing the conversation begun in her home weeks ago.

Her perfume, which he remembered from their earlier encounter, smelled sweeter than the jasmine in her conservatory. He concentrated all the more on the lady's white curls.

"I know nothing of flower breeding." He tried not to bite off his stubborn tongue for flapping when it shouldn't. He *needed* this position.

"Learn." Advancing from behind the desk, she gestured with long, beringed fingers at shelves of books behind him. "I wish to start with propagating roses and progress to the development of other varieties. I mean to produce perfumes from my own distillations."

Standing there beside him, she absently patted his arm. "I have discovered that growing things is very"—her voice caught—"difficult."

Beneath the sizzle of her caress, Dunstan lost the power to focus on the hitch in her voice. He had the distant notion that she'd just hired him without question or interview, but the headiness of her perfume and her stirring touch blurred his brain.

As if sensing that, the lady tilted her coiffed head to regard him carefully, and Dunstan steeled himself, refusing to look down any further than the cap beneath his nose. If he tried hard, he could watch the robin in the bush outside the window.

"Flowers produce no income," he insisted, gritting his teeth. "My usual salary is based on the income I produce. How will you pay for my services?"

He thought she glared at him before she swung on her high heels and click-clacked away.

"I believe I told you to name your price," she said. "I have use of my late husband's entire estate. Take a higher percentage of sheep sales for your salary to make up for the non-income-producing acreage."

Use of her husband's estate? That did not sound very permanent. Dunstan debated questioning her, but he had no real choice. He needed money. His seeds needed immediate planting. He was here. She had land. It galled him to be obligated to a woman, but he knew he could prevent some other man from robbing her blind while doubling her income—if she'd allow it.

"I can do that," he said, testing the waters. "But I'll need a field of my own for my experiments."

"Take whatever fields you need, drain fens, plant crops, whatever you wish outside of the flower gardens. Start as soon as you like." Leila swung around to see how the arrogant son of an earl accepted her offer. She tried not to clench her fists and show her despair. This past month living in the country had sorely tried her patience. The few flowers she'd planted were dead or dying. She needed Dunstan Ives and his knowledge more than she'd imagined.

Standing in front of her accounting desk, frowning at her as if she were some form of insect, Dunstan seemed to steal all the air in the room. He wore muddy boots, his tailored wool coat and vest were unfastened in the warmth of the spring sun, and he vibrated with male energy and hostility. She opened a casement to let a spring breeze enter, but the masculinity of his fragrance made him impossible to ignore. Restlessly, she picked up her fan and opened and closed it while pacing behind her desk.

These past weeks had taught her how little practical knowledge she possessed, despite all her reading. Dunstan's unexpected arrival had revived her hope, but now she understood the difficulty of dealing with the strong attraction of an Ives. How annoying that she must learn to face temptation at this late date.

If only she could surrender her role as a pillar of society to explore these feelings… But circumstances didn't allow that yet. She still had appearances to keep up and her authority to maintain, or her nephew and his fellows would run all over her.

"I'll need a house with an adequate cook and housekeeper," Dunstan asserted.

Leila lifted an inquiring eyebrow, but the thorny Ives refused to look at her. More experimentation in managing his prickly exterior was called for.

"The farmhouse down the lane is already prepared," she answered, testing her strange perception of this angry man. "Have my butler give you directions. I've ordered more roses and will need to begin planning their location soon. I'll expect you to return this evening so we may discuss the best approach."

Dunstan rested an insolent shoulder against the bookshelves and crossed his arms over his chest. Thin lines creased either side of his set mouth, and she could read refusal in his dark eyes as if it were printed there. Therein lay the problem of hiring an aristocrat to do a servant's job. They simply didn't know their place.

In the sunlight, she thought him wickedly fine. His well-endowed nose suited his rugged features. Blue-black highlights gleamed in his raven hair, and a frown added to his dangerous appeal. He might not be handsome in the conventional sense, but he possessed the Ives maleness that spun a woman's senses.

She shuddered and turned away. She dared not place herself in the power of a man again, and definitely not one as commanding as this one.

"As you suggested," he answered her calmly, "I'll ask a higher percentage to compensate for non-income-producing fields. That could be costly, so your paying crops should be planted first. The roses must wait."

She could get angry and crisp him to ashes. Instead, she donned the deliberate smile with which she'd conquered society. Granting him a smoldering look from beneath lowered lashes, an expression that always conned men to do her bidding, Leila glided closer, until she could tell he was holding his breath. She could smell the sensual awareness on him. Seductively scratching a manicured fingernail over his jabot, she detected the rapid beat of his heart.

"The rose garden," she insisted, "comes first. If your income does not equal what my father and Rolly paid you by year's end, I will provide the difference as a salary."

"I'll study roses," he agreed, not really agreeing. He abruptly turned his back on her and scanned her bookshelves. "I'll take a few of these books with me," he added, "and go back to the inn to fetch my things."

He selected a few sturdy volumes and walked off.

May the goddesses rain toads upon his head!

Leila wasn't certain if she should laugh with relief or fling books at his stiff spine as he departed.

She wanted to hate the man for being so obdurate. Instead,

she longed to be just like him. She wanted to know her abilities and where they could take her with full confidence, as he did.

Releasing her disappointment and puzzlement, Leila let an almost giddy excitement renew her resolve. *Dunstan Ives, the best agronomist in all England, had come to work for her.*

Finally she had what she needed to explore her interest in scents. She could only pray that her explorations would lead to the discovery of her Malcolm gift.

The extraordinary gifts her sisters and cousins possessed all related to their more common talents. Lucinda had the gift of revealing character through portrait painting. Felicity, the bookworm, picked up images of the past from old maps and letters.

Surely, *surely*, her own gift must be related to her talent for scents. Perhaps someday she might discover in herself a gift capable of saving a life, as Ninian's had saved her husband.

Ripping off her cap and shaking a cloud of powder from her tightly pinned curls, Leila massaged her scalp and sighed in relief. Now, if she could take off this damned corset and gown and slip into the fields to see how her newly planted roses had fared through the night…

Glancing out the window, she watched Dunstan ride away, and an odd excitement possessed her. Could it be possible to work side by side with a man who might respect her for her talents rather than for her position in society?

Then again, how could she possibly work with an Ives? Whom was she fooling?

A carriage rolled up the drive. Running a hand through her hair to loosen it, she wrinkled her nose in distaste. She didn't want to put her hair up again for visitors. She'd invited several of her younger sisters and cousins to stay, but that wasn't one of her family's coaches.

She crossed to the study door to listen as the butler greeted her unexpected guest. She heard no feminine laughter, only a single male monotone. One of her suitors, then, hoping to beat the competition. Fie on him.

If that brat of a nephew of her husband's had some idea

that she would marry and thus give up this land as stipulated
in her husband's will, he had another lesson or two to learn.
She intended to wear widow's weeds into eternity.

She hurried up the back stairs to her chamber and rang for
her maid. "Who has arrived?" she demanded as soon as the
maid entered.

"Lord John Albemarle, milady." She sounded scandalized,
as well she should be. It was highly improper for a gentleman
to call without a family member in attendance.

"Lord John, the presumptuous twit." Leila glared at her
reflection as the maid brushed off her black gown and pinned
up her hair again. She hated black, hated powder, hated the
trappings of this woman she'd become to suit her husband.
But she wore the guise for good reason. It gave her the
authority she needed to wield her wealth and assets, and the
approval of society required to do so.

"He is most handsome, my lady," the maid whispered.

"And he's gambled away this quarter's allowance," Leila
replied in irritation, well knowing the company the gentleman
kept. She hoped her nephew avoided the gaming tables that
Lord John frequented.

"Ahh, but a gentleman like that could be *très* amusing. And
what pretty children he would give you."

Leila ignored the swift shaft of pain to her heart and, feigning
lightness, replied, "Oh, I'm much too busy for children."

She allowed Marie to pin her hair beneath the black lace
cap. Lord John was the spoiled younger son of a nobleman
and would not leave without a personal reprimand. His kind
always thought their charms irresistible.

Brushing away her maid's offer of earbobs and necklace
to match her rings, Leila descended the front stairs without
hurry. She'd performed the role of society beauty for so many
years, she could do it in her sleep.

She'd disdained panniers for this encounter and merely
brushed her petticoats aside as she entered the guest parlor.
Lord John leaped to his feet, made an elegant bow, and offered
his gloved hand.

"My lady, London has been forlorn without you."

"Fiddle-faddle. What are you doing here, sir?" She removed her hand from his. He smelled of horses and gaming tables, odors she found particularly repugnant at the moment. She produced a handkerchief to ward off the scent. "Did my nephew not tell you I have tired of the city and wish to rusticate a while?"

"I could not bear the thought of another evening without your presence. The lure of the countryside, and you, drew me onward."

So, the young viscount had not given him the message. The little brat. He was up to his childish pranks already. She would never be rid of these encroaching mushrooms. "I am sorry you have come so far without reason," she said. "My sisters have not arrived to entertain you. But I understand Bath is lively. Perhaps you could seek lodging there."

"Do not send me away so soon," he pleaded. "I will be all that is circumspect until your family arrives. Let us take time to know each other better."

Marie was right—he was a handsome man. Beneath his elegant wig, Lord John revealed a high, intelligent forehead, eyes of pleasing bronze, and curved lips one could contemplate with pleasure. She had dallied an evening or two tasting those lips, but they had not inspired her to more. In fact, his fawning courtship had shown her the shallowness of the seductive powers she'd wielded these last years.

"Remember my heritage, my lord," she said. "My father may be a marquess, but my mother is a Malcolm. I know you far better than you know me."

She rarely flaunted her ancestry. Her husband had frowned upon it. Most men didn't wish to be allied with a family that was commonly rumored to include witches, but Malcolms were wealthy and powerful, and men couldn't resist the alliance any more than they could like it.

It was a measure of Lord John's desperation that he hesitated only briefly. "I do not court your family," he informed her boldly. "It is you I desire. Let me beg just a few days of your time."

He kissed the back of her hand and gazed upon her

soulfully, as if he truly meant the depth of his devotion. Had she been an innocent eighteen, she might have believed him.

The loss of that innocence pained her, but it was too late for regret. She'd chosen to do her duty as a Malcolm should. Although she'd failed to produce more Malcolms, she'd accomplished the main objective of adding to the family coffers. Now that that duty had been fulfilled, she needn't marry again.

Leila removed her hand and rang for the butler. "Homer will show you out. I believe there is time to reach Bath before nightfall. It was good of you to stop and visit, and if you will post your direction after you are situated, I will see that you receive any invitations we offer this summer. Good day, my lord."

She held her capped head high, clasped her fingers in the folds of her black silk, and remained inflexible while the butler escorted her guest to the front doors.

With Lord John gone, the house echoed in emptiness.

Her nose twitched in irritation at the scent of horses and leather and cowardice lingering in the air after he departed.

It was almost sunset. She could slip into the garden to fill her senses with fresh fragrances and erase the stench of decadence. The most recently planted roses had been healthy last time she looked.

Flinging off her cap and shaking loose the pins for the second time that day, Leila raced up the stairs, gleefully anticipating the sight of those first rosebuds.

Four

"DAMNATION."

Garbed in an old red wool gown left from her unmarried days, Leila collapsed on the muddy ground in the middle of a garden of ruined rosebushes, fighting back tears.

"Hellfire."

Row after row of distorted rose leaves and withered buds stretched out around her. Propping her elbows on her knees, she sought every curse word she knew.

It seemed the only appropriate response to this latest in a succession of disasters. The horses had eaten her lavender seedlings last week. The geraniums had been frosted upon the week before that. Mites had infected the seedlings in the greenhouse. And now, her precious roses were dying.

She swiped furiously at a tear trickling down her cheek. "Bloody damn hell," she continued in such a tone that even her cat looked askance at her. "My gift has to be related to fragrances, Jehoshaphat. I can tell the scent of a Celsiane rose from a Celestial, a damask from an alba. And if *Maman's* gift is for creating happiness with scented candles, I don't see why I can't do the same or more."

Jehoshaphat jumped in her lap, crumpling the dead rose leaf in her hand, the useless product of years of study. Leila swallowed a sob, and feeling cast adrift on stormy waters, she stroked her only companion.

She'd spent the empty days of her marriage examining

every rose in England so that when the opportunity arose, she would know the varieties required to create the fragrances that danced in her mind. She'd kept notebooks, written down names and gardeners, and researched growing habits, pretending that someday she would have a chance to use her knowledge and ease the pent-up frustration of being a useless nonentity in her own family. Every time she flashed another false smile as she spun around a ballroom, she thought about the scents she could create from the flowers she studied and imagined how she might bring joy to people's lives.

With every blink of her eyelashes, she had longed to rip away her social mask and reveal the woman inside, weeping to get out.

These gardens were the life she'd never lived; the roses were the children she would never bear. And now they were *dying*. Something new and precious inside her withered with them.

"Friggin' filth." Feeling another tear escaping, Leila set the cat aside and dug at the roots of a plant, trying to discover some sign of life. But there was no sign of anything she could understand. She didn't know enough. All her book knowledge and learning were for naught.

Pounding the ground with her fists, she shouted, "Hell's bells!" At least out here in the privacy of her garden, she had the freedom to curse and rail at the heavens.

She smacked at a wayward tear and choked back despair.

Perhaps she was an anti-witch. Perhaps her every touch brought death instead of life. Maybe she really *wasn't* a Malcolm.

Horror struck her at the possibility. She would not think that. Ever.

She scrubbed at her eyes with the back of her sleeve, smearing her face with mud. "I just want to be useful," she muttered, scrambling to her feet.

She refused to believe she was without any ability at all. She *knew* she had a talent for scents. Her sisters loved the ones she'd created for them before she married. Perhaps she could buy the flower bases from other growers.

But other growers were simpleminded jingle-brains who didn't know how to pick what flower under which full moon, and they mixed varieties and scents indiscriminately. She wanted everything to be *perfect*.

Looking at her pitiful rows of distorted roses, she felt panic plucking at her heartstrings.

She'd married a man who could give her this fairyland setting of farmland, and then he hadn't let her plant it. She'd ignored his objections, and Teddy had run his hounds and horses through her tender plants. She'd moved her flowers elsewhere, and he'd ordered those acres turned to sheep. She'd been frustrated in every way by her husband, and now it seemed that even nature had turned against her.

Grabbing her hated black curls, she tugged and scowled at the threatening sky. In response, thunder rumbled in the distance.

She wouldn't give up. She *wouldn't*. Now that Dunstan Ives had arrived, she would pay him to do what she could not. She would risk whatever spell Ives men had over Malcolm women to find the gift that she must possess.

Wiping her hands on her skirts, she stalked from the field to escape the approaching storm.

Climbing the stile near the road, she watched a rider top the crest of the hill, silhouetted against the backdrop of boiling thunderheads. Cloak flowing over wide shoulders, thick dark hair swept back by the wind to reveal a square jaw, he appeared to be lord of all he surveyed.

Dunstan Ives.

Now, there was a throat she'd like to slit—a nice, strong throat. If he'd only taken the position when she'd first offered it, these disasters might have been averted.

But no, the goddesses forbid that a proud and worldly man submit to the command of a lowly female.

The servants had informed her that he'd moved into the steward's cottage. He must have been out surveying the land he meant to plant without consulting her.

Hands on hips, thinking bloodthirsty thoughts about her new hire, Leila watched Dunstan's progress with a far higher degree of interest than he deserved.

He kicked his mount to a gallop down the hill, apparently attempting to outrace the approaching storm. Surely he was not riding back to tell her he could not take the position after all.

More likely, the prancing jackass had just viewed her blighted gardens and come to rub her nose in failure.

Letting the wind catch her black curls and blow them off her face, Leila waited to hear his opinion of her multifarious disasters.

Lightning struck in the distance, and thunder crackled. If Dunstan had been a true gentleman, he would have offered her a ride back to the house before the storm broke. But the all-male households of Ives men offered few gentle influences. Barbarians, the lot of them. The damned man was practically upon her and hadn't slowed his mount yet.

Her red skirt billowed in a sudden gust of wind. Another crack of thunder rolled across the sky. Dunstan's horse whinnied in fear and balked. Leila admired the man's skill in bringing the huge gelding under control.

Reining in his frightened mount, Dunstan finally looked at her as she stood on top of the stile, wind whipping her hair and skirt—until a stronger burst of wind and a crack of thunder blended with an ominous snap above her head. Leila caught his look of horror but didn't have time to react before the branch whipped across her shoulders. With a scream, she lost her footing and plunged forward.

The horse reared, and Dunstan, reaching out to catch her, lost his balance just as the cloud burst open, unleashing a torrential rain. With a yelp, he rolled on his shoulder and landed in the lane with Leila on top of him.

He lay still, spread-eagled in the mud, staring up at the clouded sky, rain pouring in rivulets down his chiseled cheek-bones, mixing with the dirt in his raven-black hair. Sprawled across his sturdy chest, Leila thought she'd killed him.

Frantically, she slapped both sides of his jaw, trying to jar him back to life. She didn't have the slightest notion what she should do. She just knew this man exuded the most exciting aromas she'd ever known in her life, and she *needed* the wretch. "You can't die on me now," she yelled into the wailing wind. "Stop playacting and get up. *Get up!*"

Slowly, his gaze swiveled to focus on her. She knew the

instant she had his attention. The element of lust shot sky-high. Fascinated, she didn't bother moving from her unladylike position across his chest.

"I *am* up," he said solemnly, although with a touch of bewilderment. "I daresay if you would care to oblige by moving a little lower, I'll be more *up* than I've ever been in my life."

Heat suffused her face and spread lower. Annoyed, Leila smacked his face again, but he only smiled with the dazed look of a man who'd been unexpectedly offered heaven. The wretch was absolutely irresistible, even if he was an accursed Ives. Daringly, she propped her elbows on his broad chest and inspected him as if she were a common wench and he, her inamorata. "I think I've cracked your brainbox."

"I doubt that's any cause for alarm." His glance fell to her soaked woolen bodice. "Maybe I had to hit bottom before I could look up. Are you all right? Did the branch hurt you?"

Leila tried not to laugh. Surely she'd rattled his brains, at the very least. This was a side of the brooding Dunstan Ives she'd never imagined. Perhaps he was not entirely all male arrogance and prickly thorns.

She wriggled experimentally, and his sinewy arm shot out to wrap around her waist and hold her still. Heat and strength poured into her, and she eyed him with some measure of awe. "My, you're a brawny one," she said teasingly.

"Is that rain, or are we lying under a waterfall?" He squinted skyward again. "I suppose in a countryside where red ravens swoop from the trees, one could have waterfalls from the sky."

She laughed aloud at that. Minutes ago, she'd been feeling miserably sorry for herself, but all that had changed with a bolt of lightning. Hope filled her fickle heart with joy, even if she was lying on top of a madman in a muddy lane during a torrential downpour.

"I think the water is now seeping through the crack and soaking your brain. Come, you must get up." She attempted to slide off, but he wouldn't release her.

"Why?" he asked with perfect sincerity. "I am already soaked. I've ruined my best breeches. And I believe my horse has run off without me." He crooked his neck to look around her and verify the lane's emptiness, then returned to scrutinizing her breasts. "If I must live at the bottom of a barrel from henceforth, the view from here is much better than any I've seen for a while."

She had so many plans she wanted to talk about, so many things she needed to accomplish, so many hopes pinned to this impossible man—and his only interest was in her bosom!

She grabbed his long, aristocratic nose and twisted. "Let me go, oaf. I thank you for breaking my fall, but I'm not a water nymph. I want dry clothes and a roaring fire."

He removed her hand with ease and proceeded to nibble on her fingers. "Tart. Excellent dirt. I don't suppose you have a roaring fire nearby? Lady Leila won't exactly welcome me in this condition."

Leila's eyes flared wide. *The daft devil didn't recognize her!* He'd definitely cracked his brainpan. Was this how he behaved with all women other than herself?

But then, most men behaved more honestly with women of the lower orders, and that is how she must appear at the moment. He'd never seen her without powder or wearing anything less than the finest silks. How interesting that dressing in old gowns to play in the dirt liberated not only *her* but also the man in her company.

Mischief lurked within her, and she couldn't resist testing the theory. "I know a place where we can start a fire," she said brightly, without the studied purr she would have used in London. "It's just around the bend."

His expression was skeptical. "You're not saying that just so I'll release you, are you? I'm perfectly content to lie here until the moon comes out."

"And be run over by the next carriage? Up, my drowning sailor. I want a fire." She might be intrigued by the tantalizing effect of man and arousal and pure healthy sex, but she'd never succumbed before and saw no reason to do so now. Pleasure was short-lived, but her garden was for a lifetime.

She tugged her hand away and swung her leg over his broad torso the way a man dismounts a horse. She'd always wanted to ride astride, but this hadn't been her idea of a mount.

He grimaced when he was hit by the full brunt of the rain without her warmth to shield him. "I think I've broken every bone in my body. I don't suppose you would be inclined to help me up?"

She propped her hands on her hips and glared down at him with suspicion. "I don't suppose I would. I'd end up rolling in the mud again, wouldn't I?"

A smile of sleepy satisfaction spread across his normally taciturn face. "You're much too clever for a girl. Even my brothers fall for that one." With a grunt, he rolled to one side and heaved himself to a sitting position. This time, his gaze focused on her gardening shoes. "Dainty feet. Does the mud squish between your toes?"

It did. Her soles had separated from her flat kid boots, and the rain had soaked through. She kicked his solid thigh to pry him up, but he'd already succeeded in sending a thrill through her. Men didn't admire her *toes*. Dunstan Ives was too dangerous for her own good.

Dunstan Ives thought she was a country wench, free for the asking.

"Up, or I shall leave you here to wallow in the mud," she declared.

He staggered up, dripping mud and rivulets of water from hair and clothes as he towered over her. Leila caught her breath at the immensity of the man blocking her view of the landscape. A black ribbon dangled from the remains of a queue at his nape. His sopping brown coat hugged wide shoulders and powerful arms. A muddy, crumpled stock clung to dripping linen and a black vest that molded to his deep chest and narrow waist. He looked perfectly comfortable in the mess, and her heart did a jig. The gentlemen she knew would be bemoaning the destruction of their pretty attire, not looking at her as if she were a piece of tasty pie.

She wore no powder or perfume, her hair hung in straggling black hanks down a muddied woolen bodice, and she looked worse than she ever had in her entire life—so bad he didn't even recognize her. And still he stared at her with devouring hunger.

She definitely liked this man.

With a swing of her hips, she set off toward the cottage she'd had cleaned and prepared for the estate agent she'd hired——the best agronomist in the kingdom.

$\backsim$

Dunstan's addled brain seemed to tilt, then right itself once his feet found solid ground.

Feeling as if he truly must have cracked his braincase, he trudged down the lane after the woman in red. He'd *flirted* with the wench. Gad, he couldn't remember flirting since he'd sired his son on Bessie. He would have to further investigate the effects of blows to the head. Could one pound sense *out* of heads?

Rubbing his bruised skull and rounding the bend in the lane, he watched his playful companion walk up to a neat latched gate in a privet hedge. Beyond the gate, the steward's two-story stone cottage, which he'd moved into earlier, rose against a backdrop of larches and chestnut trees. How did the bedraggled female know to return him here—unless she was a servant he hadn't met?

Dunstan didn't waste much time studying people the way he studied crops and weather, but he had an odd notion that the impertinent bit opening the gate didn't have an ounce of servitude in her.

A pity. Given his clash with his last employer, he probably ought to take some lessons—

A sight down the lane, past the gate, distracted Dunstan's musing. Otto, his damnable horse, stood calmly cropping the grassy verge ahead.

Forgetting the woman waiting at the cottage gate, Dunstan strode past her to grab the horse's halter. Otto shook his shaggy head, splattering him with moisture. Amazed that he'd noticed those few drops in the midst of a downpour, Dunstan glanced up at the sky. The clouds had parted, and a rainbow pierced the sky.

He glanced back at the alluring figure tapping her foot, and something twitched inside him. He knew temptation when he saw it, and knew he must resist it at all costs.

Leading his horse, he stopped in front of her. Now that he wasn't blinded by rain, he could see that she had midnight-blue eyes lit with starfire and lush lips that didn't need the artifices of paint. No more golden-haired, deceitful aristocrats for him. A hearty country wench like this one was just the sort of woman he might one day hope to have at his side, and in his bed.

To his regret, that day wasn't today. He couldn't afford her or any other distraction until he cleared his name in Celia's death. It would be a long time after that before he could afford a wife, even a country one.

"I would offer you the warmth of a fire," he said politely, "but I cannot risk angering the lady of the manor by dallying where I shouldn't. I'll bid you good evening, and hope we meet someday under more auspicious circumstances."

Leading his horse through the gate, Dunstan turned his back on her surprised expression before she could destroy his illusion of loveliness by unleashing whatever female temper she harbored.

He was becoming very good at turning his back on temptation.

Five

After carefully covering his turnip seeds with damp linen, Dunstan jotted down a few notes in his scientific journal, then glanced out the cottage window to the freshly plowed field caught in the fading rays of the sunset.

The first pleasure and satisfaction he'd known in a long time rose in him at the sight. *His* field, earned with the sweat of his own brow, planted with his newly developed seeds—a root crop that with the proper care should grow thrice the size of all others. He'd been here only a week, but the weight of the world was already lifting off his back.

If all went well, he would have a thick crop of feed vegetables to sell next winter, the newly formed agricultural society would recognize his achievements, and he'd have taken a step toward improving the lot of small farmers everywhere.

Had he owned the land, his labors would be considered a gentlemanly endeavor to improve it, and he would have aristocratic visitors from across England. As it was, the snobs wouldn't step past their gates for him, and he would be fortunate to attract the interest of anyone except local tenants. So be it. He didn't crave recognition so much as a means of earning his living and a modicum of respect.

Self-respect would suffice, for now. It was hard enough to come by these days.

The vision of the broken corpse that had once been the bright-eyed, laughing girl he'd married still haunted him. He had a man's blood on his hands because of her. Guilt and shame and a gnawing horror at his own actions continually tormented him.

He didn't know if he had the ability to rebuild a life for himself in the aftermath of Celia's death, but he had a son to support. The challenge of surviving each day for Griffith's sake kept him occupied. The search for the truth of Celia's death kept him from wallowing in self-pity. Now that he had an income again, he had funds for the investigator with whom he would meet shortly.

He glanced at the daily written summons from Lady Leila that his housekeeper had left on his desk, which he continued to ignore. Allowing a seductive Malcolm to bewitch him was a certain road to madness. Better to remember Celia and the tragic results of passion.

He'd hired gardeners and ordered the ground plowed. What more could the lady ask? Visiting her would accomplish nothing.

A bright swirl of red dancing between the dirt rows in the sun's waning light distracted Dunstan from his thoughts. He didn't need some fool crushing the hills, destroying his seed. Furling his fingers into fists, he pushed away from the high desk, prepared to chase off the trespasser.

His eye caught the dancing red again as it drew nearer—the woman from the lane following a small black-and-white cat. She was like the moon, appearing at day's end to tempt a man to folly.

He wanted her gone—from his thoughts as well as from his sight.

He returned to leaning against the desk. With his reputation, an angry confrontation with a woman would not be an intelligent move.

If he was nothing else, he was an intelligent man—except when it came to women. Women infected his brain like green worms infected rotted apples.

There was something subtly erotic about the way she skipped among his carefully tended furrows, ruby lips flashing a taunting smile, as if she knew he was watching.

Dunstan turned away from the window.

He didn't need luscious lips tempting him to something he had no right to consider. Work must come first these days.

Retreating from his study to the front parlor, Dunstan grabbed his coat and hat. He strode to the stable, saddled his gelding, mounted, and spurred it into a gallop, leaving the figure in red behind him.

Fuming over the ability of women to turn him into a churning cauldron of lust, Dunstan rode to the pub where he'd agreed to meet the investigator Drogo had recommended. He'd spent this last year praying that the authorities would uncover Celia's murderer, but they all seemed to assume he had killed her.

He clenched his jaw and prayed that he had not.

Only idlers and travelers occupied the tables as he entered the inn. Dunstan accepted a tankard, nodded at the local butcher, and took a bench near the fire to wait.

"I say, you look familiar." A traveler in a silk coat pinned back at the tail for riding, and fashionable new spatterdashes to cover his stockings, spoke up from a booth in the corner. "Have we met?"

The speaker was evidently a London macaroni, and Dunstan made it a habit to avoid the city and its jaded residents. He sipped his ale before replying, "I doubt it."

"I'm Handel." The fop carried his tankard over to the settle. "I'd recognize an Ives anywhere," he said, taking a seat. "Those black looks and that long nose give you away. Inventive, the lot of you, I understand."

Dunstan shrugged. If this was the man Drogo had recommended, then his brother had made a rare mistake in judgment.

"I say, you aren't here to court the widow, are you? Not fair at all, I assure you. Drogo's claimed one fair Malcolm. There's no need for Ives to take them all."

"There are dozens of them," Dunstan informed him dryly. "The countryside is littered with golden-haired witches. There's scarcely enough of us to take them all."

The fop chortled. "It's the fair-haired ones who are dangerous, so they say. Now, the widow, she's different. Her late husband used to say her only power is that of seduction, and I've no objection to that."

That fairly well narrowed the topic of conversation, although Dunstan didn't grasp the difference between Lady Leila and the rest of her clan. They were all golden-haired, dangerous seductresses, in some manner or other.

He could still feel her fingers on his chest a week after the fact. He could easily see how a Malcolm could sink her seductive talons into a man, and he'd never be free again— although dying of pleasure might be its own reward. It just wasn't for him. He had other responsibilities.

"Her late husband's nephew is offering a bounty to the first man who catches her," Handel continued affably, apparently unconcerned that he was holding a conversation with himself.

The news about Lady Leila's nephew surprised Dunstan. He hadn't thought a young lad would be so astute as to offer cash to take the widow off his hands. "Why would he do that?" he asked, cursing himself for asking.

The macaroni shrugged his padded shoulders. "He keeps bad company? Perhaps he wants his estate back. The lady possesses only a life interest in it, and she surrenders that should she marry."

Dunstan struggled to hide his shock. All his hard work, the field he'd just meticulously planted according to the latest scientific recommendations—left to the whims of a woman who might marry and lose it all? Was ever a man so great a fool as he?

"For a man with no wish to immerse himself in the country, her lack of land would be no matter," the man continued, unaware he'd just dealt a blow to his listener. "She has wealth and position enough without it."

His seeds were planted, damn it. He couldn't leave now.

Raking his hands through his hair, Dunstan tried not to panic. How long would it be before she married and he was thrown out again by the heir? He'd only met the new Viscount Staines once and knew little of him, other than that he was an obnoxious adolescent just down from school, ripe for all the trouble London could provide.

"And your interest is?" Dunstan demanded, choosing belligerence over panic. The lady had hired him. He owed her the loyalty of protecting her from idle gossip, if naught else.

The fop grinned. "Just testing to see if you're interested in a wealthier wife this time around. Full appellation is Arthur Garfield, Viscount Handel. I believe you expressed an interest in hiring me."

An aristocrat! At the moment, Dunstan would prefer to plant his fist in the fop's breadbasket for his mischief-making, but that wouldn't convince the investigator that he wasn't the type of man to go about strangling wives. Why the devil would Drogo recommend he hire a *viscount*? Better yet, why would a viscount be available for hire?

"If you must test me before I hire you, I'm not interested in your services," Dunstan said, then drank deeply of his tankard and tried to disregard the shame and anger of having to prove himself to a coxcomb.

The viscount arranged himself elegantly on the seat across from him. "Of course you are interested in my services. You have the social grace of an ox. Your only hope of discovering the truth is to shake it out of someone."

Dunstan grimaced at these truths. "I can't afford a bloody viscount. Why the hell would you be interested?"

Handel fluttered his long fingers. "Naught better to do with my time. I only accept payment if I solve the mystery. It gives me a good excuse to poke my nose where it doesn't belong."

"Such as in Lady Leila's business?" Dunstan growled, still peeved at the macaroni for knowing more than he had about the lady's estate.

"Oh, Staines is informing all London of that. You really ought to visit the city more often. It's a hotbed of entertaining news. I can probably tell you far more about your wife and her lovers than you can tell me."

He was no doubt right about that. Grumpily, Dunstan sipped his ale and scowled. There were times when he wasn't at all certain that Celia deserved to have her killer brought to justice. And then he would remember the lovely child she'd been and know he was as guilty as she was. She'd thought he offered her a dream. Instead, he'd offered his surly self. More the fool, he. "I'd rather not hear the details," he said. "I simply want to know what happened that night."

"To know if you're capable of murder?" the viscount asked.

The possibility haunted him. If he had killed Celia—the thought curdled Dunstan's blood—then he was a danger to every woman he came across, particularly widows who annoyed him and barefoot country wenches who lured him astray.

Shoving his ale aside, Dunstan nodded curtly. "You'd best take payment in advance if you're inclined to accept potential murderers as clients."

Handel puckered his mouth in a frown of dismissal. "I'll rely on your brother to take it out of your estate. A handshake will do."

His estate—should he hang.

He would never have a life, much less an estate, if he had to live under a cloud of suspicion. A London macaroni would be far more adept than he at prying information out of the fast company Celia had kept.

Gritting his teeth, Dunstan held out his callused palm to the viscount's soft white one and sealed the deal.

✧

He'd been ignoring the flower gardens in favor of the income-producing fields—not a politically expedient choice, Dunstan could see now as he rode away from the tavern. He preferred logic to politics, but if Lady Leila was his employer, it might behoove him to ingratiate himself with her so she might give him a recommendation, should the time come when she married and her nephew took over the estate.

Disgruntled at the idea of groveling, Dunstan rode back under the light of the moon with an eye to looking over the land the lady wished cleared for her gardens. Contrary to what he'd led her to believe, he'd worked with his mother's rosebushes in his youth. He preferred a good solid feed crop any day. Turnips replenished the soil and fed livestock, and the strain he'd developed would help struggling farmers.

Flowers? Frivolous folderol that benefited no one.

He reined in his horse on the side of the lane, tied it to a tree limb, and climbed the stile to inspect the soil. Roses didn't like this rocky dirt, but he supposed the lady wouldn't be aware of how to measure soil quality. He would have the devil of a time developing a fallow field like this one.

He could bring in the horse manure pile from behind the stable, he thought as he followed a sheep path around the side of the hill. He halted abruptly at the sight that greeted him.

The woman in red knelt so still in the moonlight, she didn't appear to be breathing. Raven curls tumbled down her back and spilled over her slender shoulders, lifting occasionally in a light breeze as she gazed at something on the ground in front of her.

This woman never behaved in the manner of ordinary women—flying from stiles in thunderstorms, dancing in turnip fields at sunset. What the devil was she doing now? Worshiping the moon?

Common sense told him to turn around and come back tomorrow. Logic said she had no business being in the lady's field at night. Instinct warned of the dangers to an unprotected female from thieves and rogues wandering the roads. Torn, Dunstan hesitated a moment too long.

She turned. Moonlight flashed in her eyes, and enchantment moistened her ruby lips. Holding a finger to her lips, she gestured for him to approach.

Curiosity won over good sense. Striding as silently as he could across the rocky field, much too aware of his bulk and her slenderness as he approached, he crouched beside her. "Are you insane, woman?" he whispered, not knowing why he whispered.

"Shhh. Look there." She pointed to a clump of wild rose brambles sprawling across one of the many rocks scattered over the field. The branches bore the first green sprigs of spring.

Dunstan squinted through the moonlit darkness, feeling a fool. "I don't see anything."

"Brand-new baby rabbits," she whispered. "Look, they're no bigger than mice, and nearly as furless."

"You'd better keep your cat away from them, then." Rabbits! The woman had cotton for brains. He started to stand, but the mother rabbit twitched her nose and perked her ears, and he hesitated, drawn against his will. The newborns wriggled and squirmed, searching for warmth and food, helpless and unprotected against the dangers of the night. His fingers itched to touch them.

"Why did she make her nest here instead of in a rabbit hole?" she asked. "It's not safe. Do you think we could move them?"

"They're *rabbits*. They eat crops. And you want to *save* them?" Clinging to practicality, Dunstan regarded the fool woman with disbelief.

Hope welled in her eyes. "Could you, please?"

Her plea devastated his normal thought processes, and he struggled to find the logic behind her request. "You hate Lady Leila that much?"

She blinked in consternation and shook her head. "Of course not."

"Those baby rabbits will munch her seedlings to the ground and grow into great big rabbits that will mow down her entire garden," he pointed out.

"But they're babies!" she protested illogically. "It's not fair to hurt the helpless."

Bound by her lack of reason—or her tempting curves—Dunstan surrendered. He tugged at his sleeve to release his arm from his coat. "You want to raise bait for Lord Staines's hounds?" he suggested.

She shook her head and watched him with wide eyes that made him feel vastly interesting as he peeled off his coat.

"You have a fox at home that prefers rabbit stew?"

She chuckled as she caught on to his warped humor. Shaking her head, she checked the rabbits again, then watched with even greater admiration as Dunstan removed his vest.

"We could put them in a pen and fatten them for dinner," he offered, hoping to lessen the impact of her eyes and the spring night and the sweet scent of a woman's perfume. His gaze fell to her bee-stung lips, and he swallowed, hard.

"They're *babies*," she insisted.

His brain gave up on logic and focused on frailty and females and the desire to do whatever made her happy. Even in this poor light, he could tell her simple gown covered ample curves unhampered by a corset. He could reach out and touch her breasts with just…

He took a deep breath. "You have some suggestion as to where to move them?"

Leila beamed. She'd known she could trust Dunstan Ives, even if he was the most obstinate, irritating male alive. "Do you think you can? Mama Rabbit won't like it."

Dunstan touched his finger to his lips to silence her, then with surprising stealth for so large a man, he flung his coat over the mother rabbit and trapped her in its folds.

"Use my vest to carry the little ones." He clung to the struggling rabbit while Leila delicately lifted the mewling creatures into the silk of Dunstan's vest.

"Where to?" he demanded.

Rather than explain, Leila headed off across the field in the direction of the rocky hill ahead. Feeling freer than she had in ages, laughing eagerly at this chance to slip her bonds, she led the Ives a merry chase. She could smell his lust and disbelief and laughter, felt the astonishing rise of ardor within herself, and exulted in the newness.

"Here. There's a crevice here." She crouched down to show him the opening into the hill. "May I use your vest to soften the nest?"

"By all means," he answered with a dryness that would have done a desert proud.

She smiled at the return of his usual dour nature. Swiftly and methodically, she slipped the vest with its precious contents into the protected shelter behind a boulder. When she was done, she sat back to let Dunstan release the mother rabbit. She held her breath until mama sniffed and twitched her nose and located her babies, then hopped into the hill and out of sight.

The laughter of relief and joy spilled from her lips, and daringly, she leaned over to hug Dunstan's brawny neck. "Such a lovely man! Thank you, sir. Few others would be so kind."

Ah, the scent of him! He filled her lungs with the precious aromas of adolescent nights and stolen kisses, of a time when all things had seemed possible and desire was new. Her breasts tingled and swelled at just the brush of his shirt. His lust and the scent of a spring night aroused all her senses.

He stiffened and stood up quickly, breaking her impetuous hug. "Few others would be so stupid," he said gruffly. "The creatures will nibble Lady Leila's flowers as fast as they grow."

Stubborn man! Her flat boots brought her eyes to a level with his neckcloth when she rose to stand toe-to-toe with him. Leila contemplated strangling him with his cravat, but whimsy won out. She tilted her head and studied his locked jaw. "Then the lady will build a fence around the flowers. That's your responsibility, isn't it?"

Before Dunstan could react in his usual surly manner, Leila wrapped her fingers in his linen, stood on her toes, and pressed a kiss to his bristly cheek. "You're not nearly as wicked as you pretend, sir."

With a swiftness that caught her by surprise, he wrapped his big hands around her waist, lifted her from the ground, and captured her mouth. His kiss stole her breath, tingled her toes, and annihilated all ability to think. Parting her lips to his probing tongue, she clung to his shoulders for support as he accepted her offer.

Before she recovered her spinning senses, he abruptly set her back on her feet, grabbed his coat, and strode away.

Oh, my! Leila touched her fingers to her aching lips and let hunger flow to parts of her body long denied as she watched him walk away. He seemed to have no idea that he'd just awakened desires she'd never dreamed of.

Somewhere beneath the cold, controlled exterior of Dunstan Ives lay a wild stallion chomping at the bit.

It really wasn't healthy to keep all that passion reined in. What would happen should she unleash it?

Intrigued, she rubbed her fingers over the lingering man smell of him on her cheek and deliberated.

Six

In the rosy light of early morning, Leila happily studied the workshop she'd created in her late husband's dairy. Her mother had sent equipment and vials of perfume bases from her own stores. Leila had ordered workbenches and shelves built to her specifications. She'd also purchased expensive scents from other gardeners so she could begin experimenting before her own fields grew. Finally, after years of Teddy's disapproval, she had everything she needed to begin her lifelong dream.

Teddy must be rolling in his grave.

Crossing to the window overlooking the gardens that would flourish with flowers once Dunstan applied his formidable knowledge to them, she breathed in a sense of accomplishment.

She'd conquered society for her husband's sake. Now she was creating beauty for her own. And if all went well, she hoped to achieve far more than beauty.

Of course, all she'd accomplished so far was to plant a few struggling roses and make some scented soap. With a sigh, she returned to the vat of tallow and fat cooking on the stove. She'd adapted the family recipe to suit her delicate fragrances, but she thought a dash more lye would better befit a man like Dunstan Ives.

Remembering the manly chest beneath his worn linen, she smiled wickedly. She might not possess any Malcolm gifts, but she could recognize lust when she smelled it—the earthy

Dunstan Ives craved the equally earthy woman in red. His scent evoked memories of long-ago days when she'd thought marriage would be filled with passion and excitement.

She hadn't thought to find passion in widowhood. She reached for the oil of patchouli. She was thinking forbidden thoughts, but she couldn't help comparing the Dunstan who rescued baby rabbits with the arrogant gentleman who sulked in ballrooms and ignored a lady's requests. She'd deliberately worn a mask of happiness and sensuality all these years to hide her unhappiness and lack of passion. Could Dunstan be hiding in the same way? Was he even aware of it?

She touched her nose and gazed over her choice of scents, then seized the container of dried honeysuckle.

She had stirred the liquid soap to perfect consistency and was in the process of pouring the batch into molds when a clatter of light feet and a spate of feminine giggles in the stone corridor warned that some portion of her family had arrived.

She almost felt irritation at being thus disturbed. She loved her family and she loved company, but right now—

"Leila, we've brought presents!" a sweet voice called—her younger sister, Felicity.

"Leila, was that an Ives we saw on the road?" Willowy and fair, Christina danced into the room. "No one has an aura like an Ives. I swear, the man exuded male—"

"Christina!" Leila reprimanded. "Felicity is too young to hear that."

"Felicity is a dull bookworm who may not *wish* to hear, but she's certainly old enough."

Ignoring the petty squabbling of her sisters, Felicity wandered along Leila's workbench, pushing her spectacles up her nose to inspect labels, refraining from touching anything with her gloved hands. "This is so much nicer than Mama's workshop. Could you make a scent for me?"

"It can only be a common scent," Leila warned. "I don't have my own distillations yet."

Felicity poked at the soap molds and wrinkled her nose in distaste. "I trust we will not bathe with these. They are very strong, and not very pretty."

More experienced in scents, Christina bent to smell, too. She threw Leila a roguish look as she straightened again. "Musk. These are for a man. Not the Ives, surely?"

Impatiently, Leila discarded her apron and strode toward the door. "I assume Ives men must bathe as others do. Come, let's have some tea, and you can tell me of your journey. Will you stay long?"

"Mama wants me to debut this year," Felicity called, clattering ahead of them, stopping occasionally to inspect decorations in the dairy's tiled walls. "But I don't think I shall marry. Surely we have wealth enough by now. The family coffers do not need my contribution."

Leila laughed at the old complaint. "You have not yet been kissed, have you? You'll change your mind."

Felicity favored her with a disgruntled look and raced ahead. Leila's nose twitched at the scent of anxiety Felicity left behind, reminding her of her own first come-out. The scent summoned vivid memories of moonlit nights and overeager suitors. She'd been brash enough to try their kisses. Felicity wasn't.

She missed her sisters and the hurly-burly of society. She ought to be with her family for their debuts and triumphs, not plodding through muddy fields. But muddy fields might produce the means of truly becoming part of her family. She had to try.

She refrained from rubbing her nose and let memories of past glories fade. Candlelit balls and glittering jewels didn't equate with happiness.

Christina dallied behind, swinging her beaded reticule. "Lord Harry Hollingswell has asked Father for my hand," she said casually. "I've known him all my life, and even if he is only the duke's younger son, Aunt Stella says we will suit."

"You know better than any of us if he's a good man," Leila replied cautiously. Love had little to do with Malcolm marriages. They all knew that. Men seldom understood the Malcolm gifts, and where there wasn't understanding, there couldn't be love. Still, the deeper knowledge of character provided by their gifts allowed them to arrange solid marriages that provided wealth, more Malcolms, and a higher level of satisfaction than most.

Ninian had unexpectedly thrown over all expectations a few years ago by marrying for love, and minor rebellion had occasionally rippled through the younger set ever since. If Leila could save her sisters from the boredom and resentment she'd suffered in her marriage, she would, but without the gifts the rest of her family possessed, she did not feel wise enough to make that judgment on her own.

Christina shrugged. "Harry is good, but dull. He is only a few years my elder. We may be married a long time."

Leila nodded sympathetically. "Then he had best be a man who allows you to go on as you wish. Tell *Maman* that. She will understand."

"I can't read *that* much into his aura."

"Does Harry know you read auras?" Leila asked, knowing how difficult it had been for the logical Drogo to accept Ninian's empathic gifts.

Christina glanced away. "He laughs and calls me his imaginative little creature." Indignation tinged her voice. "Men are always pleasant and accommodating when they want something. Once they have their way, they're impossible."

Leila chuckled. "A duke's younger son has no need to provide an heir, and Harry already knows to expect only girls from Malcolm women, so he must be marrying you for more than your looks. He will be fascinated for many years if you play your cards well."

"I'd rather play my cards with someone exciting, like an Ives," Christina grumbled.

"As a rule, men like that make very bad husbands. Drogo excluded, of course," Leila warned with amusement. "Drogo has the title and wealth. The other Ives are all poor and dangerous."

Felicity burst back upon them before Christina could reply. "There's a grand carriage coming up the drive. Are you expecting visitors?"

Leila groaned. More of the eager suitors her nephew encouraged, she supposed. Drat the brat, she had wanted to plant her new roses today, not entertain unwanted suitors.

And she wanted to see Dunstan in his shirtsleeves again. The man's immense knowledge captured her imagination, but there was something about a man in dishabille…

Foolish thought. She'd best concentrate on her guests. For the sake of her sisters and their introduction to society, she must don her smiling mask and welcome her nephew's guests.

✑

The lady had demanded his presence—again.

Dunstan tugged down his overly tight vest—his good one now lined a rabbit hole, thanks to a foolish woman, or his foolish lust—and prodded his gelding toward the rose garden rising out of a rock field.

He couldn't believe he'd rescued a damned rabbit because of a woman, but it certainly served as a reminder of her different manner of thinking—and of his inability to resist her wiles.

Tying his horse to a branch, he cut across the lawn to the field where he'd found the girl in red last night. He stopped short at the sight he encountered past the hill.

Lady Leila, wearing a black gown accented with a lacy white neckerchief and a swooping black hat that concealed her face from the sun, stood watching over gardeners digging at the skeletal remains of her blighted roses.

The laborers Dunstan had ordered to clear the field worked around her, carrying rocks to a wall meant to prevent the flock of gamboling ewes and lambs from grazing the flower beds.

Dunstan glared in annoyance at the stack of brown rose canes piling up beside the workmen. He hadn't ordered anyone to touch the roses. He'd been waiting to see if any of them were still alive. Lady Leila was a damned incompetent gardener, but a determined one. Even as he watched, she shooed away a curious lamb while pointing out another blackened bush to her crew.

Fool woman was bent on building this garden, with or without him. He'd best teach her how to do it properly. Stripping off his coat and flinging it over the wall, he lifted the lamb out of the rows, gently carried it to the other side of the wall, then stalked across the remains of the rose garden.

Aware of her stare, Dunstan recognized the impropriety of appearing before a lady in his loose shirt. She'd have to get used to it if she insisted on visiting the fields. "What the deuce do you think you're doing?" he demanded as he approached.

"What do you care?" she replied, scrubbing at her cheek with the back of her gloved hand. "You have not bothered to tend them."

"I've had men out here every day—" Coming close enough to see the tear tracks staining her fair skin, he stumbled over his tongue. "What the devil are you crying over?" he inquired, realizing even as he said it that he only made matters worse.

The lady jerked down her veil to hide her wet cheeks. "They're dead! All those magnificent flowers and magical scents—*lost*. Don't you feel *anything*!"

"They're certainly dead once you rip them out of the ground." Not wanting to care about damned useless roses, Dunstan glared at the workmen, who were watching him warily. "Leave the bushes alone," he snapped. "Harness the oxen to the plow. Once this field is turned, use the wagon to carry the stones over to the boundary wall."

He didn't bother checking to see if they obeyed. From an early age, he had taken it for granted that men would follow his orders. Men followed orders. Women, on the other hand...

Dunstan wrapped his fingers around the lady's elbow, steering her away from the stack of uprooted bushes. "I'll dig out the dead ones. They were planted too early, and the change in weather damaged them. Some might still live if they're treated properly."

"Really? You can save them?"

Her sob of relief pierced an unguarded chink in his armor.

Dunstan didn't have the words or the time or the *patience* to talk to elegant ladies, particularly ones smelling of roses and jasmine. "Maybe. If you'll stay out of my way."

"You're a big fraud, you know." Not moving away, she tilted her head so he could see the smile forming on her lips.

Startled at being told something similar for the second time in twenty-four hours, Dunstan dropped her elbow and glared at her. She was but a shallow flirt, and he should take no notice of her foolishness. But a small voice in the back of his head warned that she was also a Malcolm. What was she trying to tell him?

At his thunderous silence, her smile widened. "Beneath that prickly exterior of yours is a man who cares."

Fool woman! Having expected something much more momentous, Dunstan growled, "Not about roses," and stomped away, trying hard not to hear her laughter.

Locating the first heavy stone available, he hefted it to his shoulder and heaved it in the direction of the wall. Hard physical labor had helped ease his sexual frustration these past years. He would probably kill himself if the damned Malcolm insisted on polishing her temptress talents on him.

❧

In the shade of evening, after donning her old gardening gown and slipping away from her guests, Leila examined the results of Dunstan's efforts. The wall was almost high enough to keep out the sheep, and the roses had been pruned back to tiny shoots of green. Her heart leaped wild and free with excitement.

Letting her cat scamper after a field mouse, she stooped to test the quality of the soil as she'd seen Dunstan do, and didn't realize she had company until a lengthy shadow fell across the furrow.

The scent of smoke and cards and an underlying tension told her who it was before she glanced up. Henry Wickham. He'd appeared with the other guests earlier, apparently apprised by her nephew that her sisters were on their way. She didn't remember him as being so nervous when he'd courted her in London, but he wasn't much older than herself and probably new to the activity. Annoyed that he'd caught her with her guard down, she remained kneeling.

"You have some interest in fields?" she inquired dryly, knowing he seldom left the city. Wickham wasn't a large man, but the kind of languid, lace-and-beribboned gentleman who spent far too much time at card tables and too little outdoors.

"Only in what grows in them, if you are any example," he replied suggestively.

Leila narrowed her eyes. In the fading daylight, he stood over her, swaying slightly. She wouldn't call his words the polite flattery he usually bestowed on her. He'd no doubt spent too much time imbibing liquid courage after dinner.

She bit back the insult that leaped to her tongue and started to rise.

Wickham caught her elbow and dragged her upward. "Come here, and let me have a better look. I have a shiny coin for you, if you suit."

Leila gaped at the insult. The light must be poor, or he was too besotted to recognize her voice or see anything but her unbound, unpowdered hair and rough clothes. She had dressed casually in hopes of catching Dunstan here, not some drunken rake.

She ought to be afraid, but mischief won out. "And I have a shiny knife for you, if you don't let go," she warned in her best tavern wench manner.

"Now that's no way to speak to a gentleman. I know the lady of the manor. I could have you turned off this land, if I so desired." He tugged with more force than such a slender man should possess, hurting her arm and upsetting her balance. "It's much more pleasant to accept my coins."

Despite their similar heights, he was stronger, and Leila staggered, catching herself by slamming her free hand against the lace of his cravat. Even though she lacked her usual high heels and powdered curls, he surely ought to recognize her at this close range. He stank of ale and polluted lust, and she had to fight not to rub her twitching nose. Anger rising, she jerked her imprisoned arm. "Let me go, fool, or I'll have the magistrate after you."

"He's not here, is he, then? Damn, but you're a bawdy wench." Obviously still blind to anything but her gender and her clothes, Henry twisted his fingers in her unruly hair and pulled her toward him.

She'd been gently raised in the household of a marquess. No one had *ever* treated her in such a manner. Revulsion raised bile in her throat, but fury won out.

"Let me go, you jackanapes!" she cried loudly, stomping

his foot as hard as she could. But he wore boots and didn't notice. She kicked his shin, and he wrenched her hair harder. Leila screamed in stunned outrage, too furious to feel fear.

"Vermin generally wait until full dark," a deep voice intruded. "It's much too easy to put musket balls through tiny heads in daylight."

Dunstan. Leila scarcely had time to register his scent before Wickham released her. She stumbled backward, tripped in the soft soil, and fell on her rear, knocking the breath from her lungs. The tumble didn't disturb her enough to tear her gaze from the man who was strolling across the rough furrows, following her cat, Jehoshaphat.

Dunstan sauntered as lazily as the animal, as if he didn't have a care in the world. The tension in the powerful muscles of his shoulders gave the lie to his insouciance.

He didn't carry a weapon. Leila rather wished he did. Wickham's usually affable expression had turned ugly. Apparently he was better at recognizing men than women—but then, Dunstan's size and unfashionable black queue were unmistakable.

"Ives!" Wickham all but hissed in fury as the large man reached them. "They ought to have hanged you by now."

Dunstan rolled his big hands into fists that Leila admired longingly. If only she had fists like that...

"I have rich relatives to protect me. Who do you have?" he asked in mockery.

Recovering from the ignominy of her position, Leila brushed the dirt off her palms and remained seated. "No one," she replied for Wickham. "He is a leech who gambles his allowance and runs up debts in anticipation of his uncle's early demise."

Wickham gaped at her in disbelief. "Who do you think you are, a witch like yonder bitch on the hill?" He returned to Dunstan. "She is naught but a sharp-tongued vixen. It's none of your affair, unless you have taken to wallowing with pigs."

Leila removed her pruning knife from its sheath and contemplated how much of his boot she could carve before he noticed.

"Put the knife away." Dunstan's voice was cool and distant. "Wickham comes from a family of vultures and wouldn't recognize the superiority of pigs if it was explained to him."

She almost smiled at that. Sheathing her knife, she stayed sprawled where she was, admiring the silhouette of Dunstan's broad shoulders encased in white linen against the fading light of day. She remembered the rumors now—Dunstan was said to have killed Wickham's older brother in a duel over the feckless Celia. She ought to be afraid, but she was too interested in how Dunstan would handle the situation. She sensed it had become more his battle than hers.

She was beginning to understand why Dunstan hid behind a mask of brooding indifference. The likes of Wickham would crush a man who cared.

"You'll hang for what you did to George," Wickham snarled. "And then they'll boil you in oil for murdering your tramp of a wife."

"Run, fetch the magistrate and the rope," Dunstan offered, planting his fists on his hips and thrusting his square chin forward. "Or would you like to call me out? I prefer fisticuffs, but I can wield a sword if I must."

"I won't lower myself to dueling with peasants," Wickham sneered, retrieving his gloves from his coat pocket and pulling them on. "You will pay for my brother's death. I will see to it."

"Well, be about it, then, and leave the woman alone. It may come as a surprise to you, but sometimes when a woman says no, she means it."

Wickham laughed. "You believe that, do you? They all spread their—"

Dunstan's fist shot out so fast that he caught Wickham's tongue between his teeth. Leila winced as blood spurted and her would-be suitor staggered beneath the blow. Before she could scramble to her feet, Dunstan had casually lifted Wickham by the back of his coat and breeches and heaved him in the general direction of the house.

"I suggest you go back to your mother and tell her the nature of women," Dunstan called while his opponent scrambled up and rubbed his bleeding mouth with the back of his hand.

Rising, Leila stepped between them, shielding Dunstan with her back before the situation could deteriorate further. "Better yet, tell it to Lady Leila," she called gaily, enjoying her charade more than she'd enjoyed any London masquerade. "She has a whole family who might enjoy teaching you differently."

Dunstan's arm circled her waist, pulling her back against his solid chest to halt her taunts. Despite the violence of the encounter, he scarcely breathed hard. Rather than protest his audacity in pulling her close, Leila snuggled her posterior into his crotch and enjoyed the quickening of his breath and a more substantial part of his anatomy.

Cursing, Wickham disappeared into the darkness, but Dunstan didn't offer to release her.

"You have a wicked tongue," he murmured, his low voice in her ear shooting shivers down her spine.

His bold touch encouraged her more dangerous desires. Leaning into him, Leila scraped her fingernails lightly along the strong male hands clasping her waist. "Want to taste it?" she taunted.

His sharp intake of breath confirmed that he felt the same excitement she did. Her husband had never incited her to such a level of arousal, certainly never with all his clothes on and no other stimulation but an embrace. Inexperienced at wanting a man, she was half afraid of what would happen next, yet she trusted this Ives on a level beyond logic.

"You shouldn't be out here at this hour," he said. "Am I to expect trouble every time we cross paths?"

He didn't sound angry. His hand stroking her waist didn't *feel* angry. "Are we to cross paths often?" She dearly hoped so, if he would keep touching her like this. Why had *Maman* never told her a man's hand could feel so magical?

"Not if I can avoid it," he said dryly, stepping away. "Just so I might know who to avoid, do you have a name?"

The sudden coldness of his departure caused a rush of disappointment. She crossed her arms over her breasts and glared at the moonlit hill rather than look at him. He *still* didn't recognize her. Were all men blind?

A complex man was Dunstan Ives. In the interest of testing

her theory that he was a different man outside of the society to which he belonged, she answered, "Lily. And yours?"

"Is of no moment. Stay away from Wickham and his kind, Lily. They are not for the likes of us."

She heard him moving away, and she whirled around. "What kind is he, sir? The offspring of a younger son? A person of charm? And just what exactly are *we*? The morally upright of the world?"

He halted and turned to look at her over his shoulder. "Stay away from those who think they can take what they want. The likes of us cannot afford to lose what little we possess."

Could Wickham take her garden away? Could he take from her the best agronomist in the kingdom? Surely not. Nor could he rob Dunstan of his knowledge. With renewed confidence, she taunted, "I think we possess far more than you realize, and what we possess is far too difficult for worms like Wickham to take."

She couldn't read his expression in the dying light, but when he made no reply, she hastened to add what she had not said earlier. "I thank you for coming to my rescue."

"I did nothing but save the man a nasty knife wound. Be more careful in the future." He spun on his heel and strode across the newly plowed furrows.

"Wait a minute!" she cried.

He halted but didn't turn to face her.

"Why did you come here at this hour?"

This time he tilted his head and nodded at Jehoshaphat playing among the bushes. "I followed the cat."

He walked off, leaving Leila to stare after him. He followed her cat? Why? To see if it chased her rabbits? Because his was a protective nature that he concealed behind rudeness?

Twirling a curl thoughtfully, she wondered how long it would take to twist his head around and make him recognize Lily in Lady Leila. Would she have to strip off his surly mask before he could see behind hers? How best could she go about it?

And how furious would he be when he learned how she'd tricked him?

Seven

Saddling his horse, Dunstan plotted the route he would take that morning. He wanted to meet with one of the local farmers who had bought a new breed of sheep with wool much finer than that of the old-fashioned herd the estate kept. He and Drogo had had some success with sheep breeding at Ives.

Having no society but his own, he missed not having his brothers to consult. He told himself he would learn to live with it.

But no matter how he tried, he couldn't drive Lily's taunting words out of his mind. His whole body ached from last night's encounter. First Lady Leila, then her diametric opposite. He needed a woman. Soon.

Logic prevailed. He couldn't afford to support any progeny that might result from mindless rutting. He'd learned that lesson early in life. The parlor maid had seduced him the year that Drogo had inherited Ives. Bessie had been heavy with his child before he'd returned to school that year, and he and Drogo had been supporting her and his son ever since. Abstinence hadn't suited him, so he'd taken Drogo's advice and married soon after finishing school, but that hadn't worked any better. At least Bessie had enjoyed bed play. Celia had cost him far more and satisfied him far less.

Riding out of the stable, he reined in the old gelding to open the gate, then halted his mount at the sight of a shiny new carriage swaying down the lane. The roads here were too rough for city carriages. Leaning against his horse's neck, he amused himself watching the carriage wheels rub against brambles and lurch into ditches. A good highwayman ought to steal those pretty bays and make better use of them.

He raised his eyebrows as the contraption rolled to a halt in front of his gate.

A slight gentleman in a tricorne hat and silk frock coat stepped down. Even in London, his beribboned bagwig would look ridiculous on so small a man. In the country it was ludicrous. Dunstan bit back the urge to grin as high red heels stumbled in a rut, and the mud of the road splattered white stockings.

Dunstan's gelding nickered, and the fancy gentleman finally looked up—Leila's nephew, Viscount Staines.

With a sigh of aggravation, Dunstan swung down from the saddle. "May I help you?" He couldn't bring himself to say "my lord" or even "sir" to this fresh-faced boy.

"Ives," the young viscount said in what sounded like relief. "I must speak with you."

Well, he hadn't figured the boy meant to do anything else. Steeling himself against bad news, Dunstan tied his horse to the fence and led the viscount into the cottage. "You could have posted a letter."

"I hate writing." He sounded like a spoiled schoolboy refusing to do his lessons. "And my grandfather insisted I keep an eye on Leila. He doesn't trust her."

Probably with good reason, Dunstan thought, but held his tongue. Lady Leila was paying his salary. He owed her his loyalty, much as it irritated him to admit it. "The lady accepts my recommendations," he answered mildly, showing his guest into his chilly parlor. "Martha isn't here yet, so I can't offer you coffee."

The boy grimaced. "I hate coffee. Don't know how anyone drinks it. I don't suppose you can make hot chocolate?"

"I don't suppose I can." Impatiently, Dunstan gestured toward an ancient leather chair. "What can I do for you?"

Leila's nephew paced instead of sitting. "You've let my

aunt start building her gardens." He pulled two cigars out of his pocket and offered them both to Dunstan.

Dunstan accepted the gift. "She is my employer." Not commenting on the oddity of a boy handing him a cigar, he sniffed one.

Watching him from the corner of his eye, Staines waved fretfully. "My uncle wouldn't let her build gardens for good reason. This is prime hunting country, and my grandfather loves to hunt."

"Then your uncle shouldn't have settled the estate on her." Dunstan strolled to the window, idly poking the cigar with a lighting straw. When the straw encountered an obstacle, he turned his back on his guest, removed the childish device from the cigar, tossed it out the window, then lit the tobacco and drew deeply.

"My uncle was a besotted idiot, and Leila's father is a marquess with the greed of a loan shark. She was supposed to build a dower house on the hill and leave the fields open for a park." Outrage tinged the young viscount's voice. "If Uncle Theodore hadn't stuck his spoon in the wall before Grandfather, it would have been no problem, but now he's left me to deal with his wretched widow."

Dunstan stifled a snort of contempt at the whining boy. He had younger brothers who were more sensible than Staines. He took a long puff on the cigar until it smoked properly. Behind him, the viscount watched with barely concealed interest.

"If your father hadn't fallen from a parapet and got himself killed before your uncle died," Dunstan said carelessly, "the problem of Lady Leila would have been his instead of yours. I don't see that your grandfather can expect you to deal with a situation you inherited and over which you have no control. The estate is hers for as long as she remains unmarried. I should think you'd both best walk softly around her."

"My grandfather won't," the boy answered glumly. "He's old and set in his ways and expects everyone to jump when he bellows. He'll cut me out of his will if I don't do what he says. Lady Mary won't look twice at me then."

Dunstan figured he could go into his usual diatribe about

the pestilence of inheritance laws and shallow youths who expected wealth to be given instead of earned, but it wasn't his place. He wouldn't inquire about the greedy Lady Mary, either. If Staines was referring to Lord John's sister, she was cut from the same cloth as Celia and had been her closest friend. The boy was too young to be involved with avaricious females, but that was none of his concern.

Deliberately, Dunstan lit the second cigar with the fire from the first, turned, and held it out to the viscount. "Lady Leila will cut off your current income if you interfere," he warned. "This may not be a fashionable estate, but it will produce good income sufficient to keep you for a lifetime. Why gamble what you have in hand for what the future might bring? The earl will have you dancing on his strings until he dies if you give in now."

Staines gazed in trepidation from Dunstan's smoking cigar to the newly lit one held out to him. "Leila is likely to live as long as I do." Hesitantly, he accepted the roll of tobacco, inhaled, and coughed. "I'll never be in control of my own life. She has refused three offers of marriage that I know of. She's doing it to thwart me, I vow."

"That's possible, I suppose." Remembering the lady's repeated remonstrances, Dunstan added, "She may just want to make scents, though. Have you talked with her?"

The viscount's cigar crackled, then sputtered. He jerked it from his mouth and held it at arm's length with an expression of panic.

With deadpan interest, Dunstan leaned against the window frame, crossed his ankles, and, with one hand, casually opened the window wider.

Staines dashed past him and heaved the cigar onto the lawn. It shot a hunk of grass into the air with a satisfactory bang and a shower of sparks.

"*How did you do that?*" he shrieked, trembling a little as he turned back to eye Dunstan's peacefully smoldering tobacco. The boy shoved his hands under his armpits and visibly attempted to compose himself.

Dunstan shrugged, closed the casement, and leaning back, blew a smoke ring. "I believe you were in the same class as

Paul, one of my younger brothers. One of my more inventive brothers thought it vastly amusing to show Paul how to make cigars that exploded in the faces of bullies. I learned to dismantle them early on. You were saying?"

Irritated at the failure of his practical joke, the viscount answered petulantly. "Leila laughs at me and tells me the foxes may hide in her roses as much as they like. She hates hunting." He stiffened his shoulders and glared. "The gardens have to go. Grandfather will be here in September, ready to hunt grouse. If the gardens aren't gone by then, he will arrange for you to be."

Dunstan grunted. He'd expected that. He lived on the edge of desperation, and never had to look far to see the drop-off. "I'll see what I can do, but the lady is in the right of it. Marry her off, and she'll no doubt forget about her little diversion."

Marry her off, and he would no doubt lose his position. Six of one, half a dozen of the other.

"I'm not wasting my time out here all summer," Staines said. "I've better things to do. *You* tell her to marry. Pick someone out for her. Marry her yourself. I don't give a fart. Just get her out of my hair, and you'll have a position for life," Staines concluded, apparently pleased with his generosity.

"Not very tempting," Dunstan pointed out, deflating the boy once again. "I want land and freedom, not a landless ball and chain. Why should I be interested?"

He wished he had a choice, but his crop was planted. He couldn't leave, not until harvest. His gut twisted, but he refused to give the boy the power of that knowledge.

The viscount frowned as if he hadn't considered paying for what he wanted. Then a smile lit his beardless face. "If you marry her off, I'll give you this tenant farm."

"You'll deed it to me if she marries?" Dunstan could scarcely believe his ears. The boy had a few loose screws in his brainworks, but Dunstan wasn't one to argue the proposition. With a farm of his own as the prize, he would contemplate seeking a suitable mate for her—not that he had a chance of swaying a Malcolm one way or another.

He supposed he could speak with her cousin, Ninian,

on the off chance that there was someone Lady Leila might consider marrying.

Staines nodded eagerly. "The tenant farm isn't entailed. Get rid of her, and this house is yours. The acreage is small, but fertile."

Get rid of her, Dunstan thought dourly, lifting a skeptical eyebrow. The implication behind the command, given his reputation, did not sit well on his already grinding temper. "I'll see if I can persuade her to move the gardens, but I make no guarantee on the rest."

"I want her *and* the gardens gone." The boy all but stomped his foot. "She is living on *my* land, in *my* house. It isn't fair."

Life wasn't, but the boy must learn that lesson on his own. "I am not a magician. You might as well pray that your grandfather dies before September as to hope Lady Leila will be gone by then."

"I'd rather pay than pray. It's more effective. I learned one or two things in school." With the arrogance of youth, the viscount sauntered toward the door. "I leave her in your hands, Ives. We'll both be better off without her."

On that much he could agree. Dunstan remained propped against the window frame, smoking his cigar and contemplating a bloody hunting picture on the wall while the carriage rattled away outside.

Get rid of the flower gardens by September, or lose his experimental turnips.

Marry her off, and gain the land it would take him years to earn.

Impossible, yet tempting.

The brat was the devil's own. If the viscount had been one of his younger brothers, he'd have turned the boy over his knee and walloped some integrity into him.

In an ill temper, Dunstan stalked out, slapping his boots with his riding crop. He wished there were someone with a little more maturity and experience to help him argue this one out, but he knew Drogo would side with the damned Malcolms. That's what marriage did to a man, softened his brain. He was on his own now.

He avoided the flower garden for the rest of the day. He discussed sheep herds, field drainage, enclosures, and weather with men who respected land as something more than just another possession. He understood this life. He'd grown up with it.

He didn't understand the labyrinth of aristocratic society.

He didn't understand women either, but as the sun descended behind the hills, Dunstan's path wandered down the lane toward the mansion. He might slam women behind the barred door of his mind, but this particular woman was his employer, damn her. He needed to tell her what her conniving nephew was up to.

That excuse lasted only as long as it took to see the lady pacing the terrace that overlooked the unfinished gardens. Her silk skirts swept the cold stones while her guests laughed and chattered in the elegant parlor behind her. Swinging from the saddle, he wondered why she was out here alone.

Hair tightly curled, powdered, and ornamented with a lacy cap, wearing her closely corseted blacks, Lady Leila in no way resembled the free-spirited Lily, Dunstan noted with relief as he tethered his horse and strode toward her. He could resist a haughty aristocrat.

Still, the way she moved and the scent she exuded aroused him as swiftly as Lily did. The leather of his breeches threatened to cut off the flow of blood to a swelling part of his anatomy. Temptation dogged his every footstep these days.

The lady looked up at his approach, and a cautious smile warmed her features. She was his employer, and he wouldn't allow himself to be seduced by a bewitching female, he told himself. He didn't return her greeting.

Briefly, vulnerability was reflected in her features as her smile slipped away. He refused to let that affect him either.

She had a bevy of eager suitors in the house behind her. Could he encourage one of them? Hardly. If they were all the likes of Wickham, he couldn't blame her for refusing the twits.

He didn't know Wickham well, but if the man couldn't be trusted with a village wench like Lily, could he be trusted in the company of a lady? Her young nephew didn't seem concerned about the lady's best interests.

The thought stirred Dunstan's protective instincts, and he had to fight against them. Let her powerful family look after her.

Surrounded by society and meddling Malcolms, could Lady Leila really be as alone as she seemed? Impossible. Her femininity must be weakening his brain.

She turned her haughty gaze on the rosebushes sprouting new greenery. Her pride at the sight struck a responsive chord in him, and the possibility that they might share a common passion for living things unnerved him.

"They're still alive, I see," he murmured.

"I can't tell about the weak ones." She returned to pacing. "I suppose it's too soon. Do you think we might add a pergola on the far end for climbing roses and wisteria? It would make a nice transition to the next level, and I could add benches for resting out of the sun."

He'd had all day to think of Staines's threats and promises. He was an inventive man, and various arguments to dissuade the lady from her gardens had occurred to him. He simply didn't know how best to present them.

Perhaps if he pretended the regal Leila was as common as Lily, he could speak openly with her. If he ignored the height that brought the lady past his chin, he could almost imagine honest Lily beneath her powder and pride.

"This might not be the best place for a garden," he suggested cautiously.

She whipped around as if he'd slapped her. It was too dark to read her expression, but he could hear fear and wariness in her voice. "Why?"

"Apparently the earl runs his fox hunts through here. A pack of galloping hunters would destroy the roses."

She eyed him consideringly. "Or the thorns would destroy a few horses. The old man can find a new place to play. This is my land, to do with as I wish."

Dunstan shoved his hands into his pockets to keep them from straying elsewhere. She might be tall for a woman, but she was delicately formed, and he felt like an oaf next to her.

He had no need to impress anyone, but the worm inside his brain desperately wanted the lady to look at him with the same warmth and approval that Lily had.

"The viscount is determined to remain in his grandfather's good graces," Dunstan went on. "He is making extravagant promises to me in return for marrying you off. Isn't there somewhere else you could plant your gardens?"

"What extravagant promises?" she demanded.

His shoulders twitched uncomfortably inside his coat. "He promised to give me a tenant farm if I persuade you to marry."

"The ungrateful little monster," she muttered, returning to pacing. "I can see Lord John's fine hand in this. His sister is on the hunt for a husband, and Staines is easily malleable."

"Would that be Lady Mary?"

"Staines keeps poor company," she agreed, without answering directly. "If they twist him to their thinking, they'll likely try to murder me so he can have the estate."

Dunstan didn't think the adolescent viscount was that dangerous, but then, he hadn't thought himself dangerous either. Alarm filled him at the thought of jeopardizing another woman with his presence.

"The viscount and his grandfather have it within their power to destroy my crop as well as yours with a single ill-timed hunt," he said. He didn't think she understood how serious the consequences would be for him. "You had better be very certain gardens are what you want. If I lose my crop because of your disagreement, it would set agricultural advancement back a decade."

He watched her wrap her arms around her waist, as if she were holding herself together. Desire and a need to protect her surged through him again. For a brief, shattering moment, it only mattered that she was a woman, with all a woman's frailties. He ought to comfort and defend rather than berate her.

But he knew where that would get him—and he couldn't afford it.

He turned back to the garden. Work on the stone wall was proceeding nicely. It would fit in well with the stone terraces he would construct up the hill—if the lady didn't marry and lose the land.

"This conflict is not about turnips or roses," she finally answered. "It's about power and control. Those who have them always want more. People like the earl will never be satisfied until they have it all, because they think they're the only ones who are right."

She was a revolutionary, Dunstan realized. He lusted after a witch and a revolutionary. He cast his gaze skyward and wondered why the devil was tormenting him.

"You have more power and control than you need," he said, impatient with the dilemma. "If you move the gardens, the viscount might be persuaded to leave you alone. Why should I sacrifice my turnips for a passing fancy?"

"It is not a fancy. I'm very good at creating perfumes, and I wish to create bases of my own design. I need all these acres planted." She gestured toward the grassy lawn. "More bushes arrived today. Aside from the earl, I am the only family my nephew has. I would like to see him learn the proper care of his estate, but he cannot override my wishes so long as this land is mine."

Dunstan bit back the reminder that all she had to do was marry and the land would no longer be hers. She'd hired him to do a job, and he would do it. The temptation of finding a man to marry her so he could gain possession of the tenant farm nagged at the back of his mind, but he disliked the idea of being the one to end her dream, if that's what the garden represented. "I'll bring in more men to wall off the lower garden," he finally agreed. "Keep the bushes in water until we can plant them."

He started to turn away, but Leila placed a hand on his coat sleeve. He stiffened, fighting another wave of desire. She had a body to try a man's soul. He hungered to haul her by her slender waist into his arms and feel her against him as if she were Lily. How would her lips taste if he covered them with his? Would she yield readily to his tongue?

He simply had to remember that she was a lady and keep his hands to himself.

"Thank you for telling me," she murmured, interrupting his lustful ruminations. "Most men think women no better than beasts in the field, good only for rutting and fair game for a man's plots."

Disgruntled by her blunt honesty, Dunstan threw up his best defense. "On the whole, men have but the one thing on their minds and believe women think the same," he said harshly. "Women do not always discourage us in those beliefs."

"Well, in that case perhaps women *are* beasts," she said with amusement, smoothing his coat sleeve. "But even hens have the right to choose the best rooster. Give some of us a little credit for good taste."

"And credit some of you with fowl taste?"

She chuckled at his pun. "Some men are strutting cocks," she agreed. "I just don't think most women enjoy being held down by talons on their necks."

She sounded like Lily when she talked like that. Without thinking, Dunstan reached out and rubbed his thumb down the delicate line of her face. She didn't pull away. He couldn't believe he was doing it. He watched his hand as if it belonged to a stranger.

"Before the topic strays into breeding practices, I'd best bid you good night." He tried not to strangle on the words as her rigid posture softened under his caress. "This cock knows better than to dally with hens who expect him to pay the price of his sport."

She instantly shoved him away and almost spat her reply. "You have the brain of a peacock if you think I want payment for your *sport*."

That hadn't been what he'd meant, but if it got him out of there faster, he would let it be. He'd spent a long day resisting temptation, and he was sorely tried. Two damned women, and he wanted them both. May the heavens preserve him.

"Someone always pays," he retorted and strode off, wondering if it wouldn't be easier to find a good cave and become a hermit.

Eight

"HULLOOO, MR. IVES," A CHEERFUL FEMININE VOICE CAROLED as he stepped outside the cottage the next morning.

Dunstan blinked in astonishment at the array of colorful silks and golden curls bouncing up his walk. Fashionable females generally avoided him.

Catching his breath at the knifing pain of that reminder, he scowled at the intruders, recognizing Malcolms when he saw them. They must have been the guests the lady had entertained last night.

"We've brought you a housewarming gift," the elder cooed, batting her pretty lashes at him and handing him a beribboned basket.

He held the frivolous thing on the tip of one finger, wondering what to do with it. Did unmarried females usually carry gifts to widowers? Or to accused murderers?

"And we brought an invitation," the bespectacled younger female said shyly, handing him a card. "All the local ladies are curious to meet you, and we have promised that you will be there."

He scanned the neat penmanship requesting his presence at dinner at the manor house that evening. The widow had a whole company to keep her entertained. What could she want with him, other than the amusement of watching her guests laugh and whisper behind his back?

He handed the card back to them. "I have other obligations.

Give my regrets to—" He couldn't remember if these were sisters or cousins. There were too damned many of them, and they all looked alike. "—to Lady Leila."

They refused to take the proffered card. Two pairs of bright blue eyes stared soulfully at him from beneath bounteous blond curls. "Oh, you really cannot refuse," they said in chorus. The younger continued, "We have promised, and you would make liars of us. Ninian said you would be nice." The plea ended on a hiccuping lament.

They were but children, scarcely older than his son. Grimacing at the thought of the fourteen-year-old he'd left behind, Dunstan dug a hand into his hair. Ninian was an annoying pest, but she'd promised to keep an eye on Griffith for him. He owed her, and her family, however much he despised being obligated to anyone.

"I can't stay long," he warned.

"Oh, you will not regret it," the younger one exclaimed. "We will have so much fun! Leila has promised us dancing," she whispered in excitement, as if the idea were too delicious to say aloud.

Dunstan bit back a vivid curse. He felt old and jaded in the presence of such youth and innocence. With nothing better to say, he nodded curtly. The girls waved their farewells and wandered off, leaving him holding the gaily wrapped basket.

Carefully, he pulled back the gingham cover. The fragrance of new-mown grass under warm sunshine wafted upward. Frowning, he poked at the neatly wrapped packages within and finally peeled off the paper to uncover perfumed soap.

Snorting, he flung the basket into a chair and proceeded to the stable. Unlike the gentlemen of London, he preferred a good strong lye soap and a daily bath rather than covering odors with perfumes and lotions. Hell would freeze before he'd appear in public smelling of anything but himself.

❧

After spending a filthy day overseeing the drainage of the fens and avoiding the garden, where he might run into the too tempting Lady Leila, Dunstan dragged himself back to the cottage, hoping his housekeeper had left one of her savory stews on the stove for him.

To his disappointment, he smelled nothing cooking as he opened the kitchen door and discarded his muddy boots with the help of a boot hook. He was late today, but Martha usually left something simmering.

Flinging his coat and vest over a chair and padding across the stone floor in his stocking feet, he found Lady Leila's invitation to dinner propped against the saltcellar and cursed. He'd forgotten.

He glanced at the wall clock. He would have to hurry. With no time for a proper bath, he grabbed the soap at the kitchen sink, started to lather his hands, and caught the scent of new-mown grass. He'd always liked the scent of grass. Eyeing the fresh cake skeptically, he tossed it aside and reached for the sliver of strong soap. Martha must have found the basket and decided to freshen the kitchen with the scented stuff.

Dropping his mud-bedecked shirt on the floor, he poured some hot water from the stove into the sink, scrubbed his chest and shoulders, and shaved. He should be thankful he was no longer married. A wife would have hysterics seeing him walking half naked from kitchen to bedchamber. Bachelor life had its advantages.

Except in the matter of clothing. He had never wasted much time on London fashion. Poking through his wardrobe, he found that he'd not spilled anything on the frilled linen shirt he'd worn to Drogo's wedding. The fancified breeches still fit, but he'd ruined the silk stockings. Cotton would have to do. He didn't want to make a complete country dolt of himself, but he had no intention of competing with the beribboned beaus who were finding their way to the widow's door these days.

This summer should be a right jolly tickle while he waited to see if the lady accepted anyone's offer. Had he thought he had a chance, he ought to join the parade of suitors himself.

But he couldn't do that, not even to a Malcolm. Fear that deadliness might lurk in his heart chilled any desire to marry again.

Feeling like a fop in white lace jabot and black satin evening habit, wondering how the hell he would keep clean on horseback, Dunstan strode out the front door to discover a carriage waiting for him.

"There you are, sir. I was about to knock." The driver opened the door and bowed.

The widow wasn't taking any chances. Perhaps he ought to polish a few phrases of flattery so she'd be satisfied and leave him alone. *So lovely to be dragged out after an exhausting day to be entertained by fools and fops* didn't sound like a practical suggestion. Perhaps, *Madam is too kind to flaunt her charms in my face, knowing she can scream for help should I reach for them.*

Did he want to reach for the lady's charms?

Better he should find Lily. At least she was honest about her desires.

Crossing his arms and leaning back against the seat, Dunstan scowled as the carriage swept up a lane illuminated by torches and linkboys running about with lanterns. The scene was Celia's favorite fantasy—glittering jewels, gaily bedecked finery, and prancing fops to bow and flatter and flirt.

He had to stop thinking so cruelly of his late wife. She'd been young and infatuated with the idea of someday becoming a countess. Perhaps if he'd indulged her more, she might have matured enough to see the foolishness of society.

Then again, perhaps not. Lady Leila obviously hadn't.

Entering the chandelier-lit foyer and surrendering his hat to a severely garbed butler, Dunstan stalked into the mansion's immense formal parlor. Gilded furniture and mirrors reflecting elegant gowns bedazzled his eye.

Silence descended the instant he entered.

Devil take them all.

Clenching his jaw and straightening his shoulders, Dunstan strolled across the room as if he possessed it. Inwardly, his skin crawled. The widow's London suitors must have brought the gossip with them. Even the locals watched him with suspicion.

Narrowing his focus until the entire company disappeared, Dunstan cast his gaze across the immense handwoven carpet to where the Black Widow waited. He might not know how to deal with women, but he would learn how to manage this particular Malcolm, if only for self-preservation.

Lady Leila smiled beguilingly from beneath a coiffure of tight white curls adorned with diamond butterflies. Concealing most of her curves with a flowing *habit à la fran-çaise* of black crepe accented in white lace, she drew him like a bee to nectar. Her provocative touch and enticing perfume haunted his dreams. Fury simmered at his helpless attraction to her as much as at the idea that he'd been manipulated into this predicament.

To hell with Malcolm witches and their beguiling eyes. He captured hers from across the room.

The midnight blue of the lady's gaze sparkled in the candle-light, striking Dunstan with the force of a blow. Her eyes were the shape and color of Lily's eyes. What manner of witch was this, who could steal color from the eyes of another?

Don't panic, he told himself, forcing his nervousness down to his belly and striving to regain his senses. *Use logic*. Even Malcolms couldn't steal eyes. It had to be the strikingly thick black lashes fooling him. Malcolms were fair and should have light-colored lashes...

He lifted a suspicious glance to the lady's powdered curls. What color did the powder conceal? Was she even a Malcolm? He hadn't looked closely at the woman in London. Was this even the same person? She stood as tall as he remembered, taller than Lily. She wore the cosmetics required of society. She could have darkened her lashes. Perhaps the illusion was a trick of candlelight. He'd only seen Lily in the gloom of evening and thunderclouds.

He couldn't possibly believe the open, honest Lily could masquerade as a Malcolm, could he? To what purpose? It had to be the lady.

His discomfort subsiding beneath a seething fury, Dunstan strode forward.

⤜✦⤚

By the goddesses, he was magnificent.

Leila didn't need Christina's ability to read auras to know

that Dunstan Ives was toweringly, breathtakingly furious as he navigated the path between them.

He swaggered through her parlor as if born to a kingdom, his broad back straight and proud. Though he wore only black with a minimum of lace, he exuded authority—and glowering majesty. She almost expected her guests to bow before him.

The man who halted before her had a tremendous control she couldn't help admiring. A slight twitch of his jaw was the only outward manifestation of his discomfort. He made a gentlemanly bow, sweeping back his long evening coat.

Even though she could understand his intimidating effect, it amazed her that people could be so blind as to believe he had murdered his wife. A man like Dunstan Ives would not soil his hands or waste his time with the blood of an adulteress, although he might coldly cast her to the wolves and go about his business without a second thought.

That realization chilled her and should have been sufficient warning. It wasn't. Some imp of hell goaded her on. Or the dire need for this man's support against the wolves at her door.

"I am grateful that you have torn yourself from your work to visit my humble home." She smiled for their audience, but sarcasm dripped from her tongue.

The fury in his eyes could scorch. "And I am humbled that you have been so good as to invite me," he repeated, as if by rote.

"Oh, very good. Now tell me another." Returning to the coquetry that came to her as naturally as breathing, Leila drawled with artificial sweetness, "I particularly like the lies that begin by comparing my eyes to moonlit nights."

He straightened and stared down at her as if he were contemplating the matter. It took him so long to reply that Leila wondered if her coiled hair had come undone or if her beauty mark had gone askew.

Then she realized he was studying the way her corset molded her breasts above her bodice, and heat colored her skin. She considered swatting him with her fan, but she needed it to cool herself. She had wanted his attention, but this wasn't what she'd had in mind. She could have desire from any man. From Dunstan, she wanted a meeting of the minds.

The thought of their bodies meeting stimulated far more than her mind. She took a deep breath, and his gaze burned hotter. She might melt into a puddle and sauté her toes if he did not respond soon.

"I am an agronomist, not a poet," he finally answered. "Perhaps I should compare you to the fertile valleys between the Gloucester hills?" His words taunted despite his innocent tone.

"Comparing me to dirt—how unique." With a sharp crack, Leila snapped open her fan and gazed past him to her guests. "You are late. That may be fashionable, but it gives these fools time to talk. I need to speak with you about Staines, but not now."

She could see her nephew whispering to Lord John and Lady Mary in the far corner. What mischief did they stir now? She wished she had sufficient influence with the boy to divert him from those parasites, or that his grandfather would deign to teach him responsibility. She hated to be the one to stand in the old earl's stead, but if she was all Staines had, she would have to find some way to teach the boy his future role as the owner of vast properties.

Thank heavens Wickham had had the presence of mind to excuse himself and leave this morning before encountering Dunstan again. She didn't need fisticuffs in her parlor.

"Let us pretend there is naught on our minds but each other," she murmured to Dunstan. "It is time to go in to dinner. Give me your arm, and we will lead."

He stiffened. "As I told the young ladies, I have other obligations this evening. You must dine without me."

"What obligation could possibly prevent your taking an hour to eat?" she demanded, refusing to be denied. It was time they learned to deal with each other on an equal basis. With Dunstan's formidable aid, she could defeat her nephew's annoying plots and rid herself of the hordes of suitors he imposed upon her. She would like to rip through Dunstan's thorny emotional walls with a sharp sickle, but thought it best to try her feminine wiles first.

"I am your steward, not one of your suitors," he demurred with just the right tone of false politeness to prevent her from smacking him. "My presence is not required."

"Don't be ridiculous. You are the son of an earl, a noted agronomist, and this is a country gathering." She instructed him as if he were a child. Irritated by his continued determination to ignore her, she retaliated. "You *are* aware that every man in society desires my company, and that you should be honored by my request?"

"You will notice that I do not frequent society," he retorted.

Leila gritted her teeth. He did not desire her? Fustian. He'd certainly shown desire for her as Lily. He simply refused to admit she was one and the same.

Had she really expected him to? Had she thought she could throw out her snares and reel him in to do her bidding? How stupid of her. Ives were not men to be led about by their noses—or other body parts. And Dunstan Ives was a law unto himself.

Perhaps that was what society sensed and feared. Or—

Perhaps he feared society and all it represented—including her.

Perhaps they both preferred Lily, for different reasons.

Fascinated, Leila dug her fingers into Dunstan's arm and all but dragged him into the dining room. Did she sense anxiety beneath the stubborn anger? How could she find out?

Somewhere inside him was a man who protected maidens in distress, saved baby rabbits, and developed turnips for needy farmers, a man who possessed the integrity to warn her when her nephew schemed against her. She needed to reach that man, to free him from his self-imposed prison. Perhaps then he might see that she wanted the same thing he did—respect for their abilities.

If she could not entice him with her usual snares, or reason with him as an equal, or call upon his chivalry, how could she persuade him that she might have a useful gift related to her talent for scents?

Observing how Dunstan stonily ignored her guests in the same manner as they ignored the possible murderer in their midst, Leila hid a smile of triumph as the answer to her dilemma materialized.

All she had to do was discover who had killed Dunstan's wife.

With his name cleared, perhaps he would feel as free to speak with the Lady Leila as he did the village Lily. Of course, once he discovered how she had manipulated him, he would no doubt explode like some foreign volcano.

But even that thought excited her.

Stiffly, Dunstan seated Lady Leila at the head of the table. Her exotic scent filled his senses and made his head whirl. She might be too tall and grand to be Lily, but he desired her in the same way. It was insane, not to mention dangerous.

Her giggling young sisters followed them to the table, their gleaming golden locks reminding him with whom he was dealing. *Malcolms!* They would wrap him in invisible webs and squeeze what they wanted out of him.

What was it they wanted?

To his horror, he discovered that Lady Leila had seated him at her right, with one of her sisters on his far right and the other directly across the table. Desperately, he reached for his wineglass, then remembered that alcohol relaxed his control. He couldn't afford to lose his head in this company.

"You have the aura of a thundercloud," the older sister whispered. "Do you not like dinner parties?"

They were children. He couldn't yell at children. Dunstan scowled at Lady Leila on his left, but she was giving instructions to a footman.

"I do not have polite conversation," he replied. "Unless you wish to discuss the benefits of marl in poor soil, I cannot keep you entertained."

The younger one, Felicity, leaned forward. "We could discuss your late wife. That's what everyone else is doing. Did you really fight a duel with Mr. Wickham's brother over her?"

He had no intention of telling her what had happened that day.

Why the devil did she wear her gloves at the dinner table? Grumpily assessing this Malcolm eccentricity, Dunstan responded more curtly than he intended. "I'm a farmer. I don't fight duels." He glanced again at his hostess, who was chatting with the vicar on her left. Why the deuce had she placed him here? He tugged at his constricting neckcloth.

"I heard your wife died in some outlandish out-of-the-way place," Christina continued, "and that Mr. Wickham's brother was the only possible witness, and you killed him. But you do not have the aura of a killer."

Dunstan glared at Christina. She observed him in return with interest and not an iota of fear or ill will. He tried to look away and examine Lady Leila's midnight-blue eyes instead, but she was sipping from her wineglass with her lashes lowered. She had no doubt inflicted these bothersome girls on him for some nefarious purpose.

"You have probably slain more beaus with your wiles than I have slain with my fists," he told Christina through gritted teeth.

Across the table Felicity giggled. "I've never felt anyone vibrate a table before. You are a most intriguing man, Mr. Ives."

Dunstan sought Lady Leila's attention again, but she had now engaged the vicar in a debate over the merits of mulching roses. He longed to join the discussion, but the determined child on his right was analyzing his *aura* again. Dunstan slumped gloomily in his seat.

Surveying the laughing company, he caught the disdainful glance of Lady Mary, a feebleminded goose who had been Celia's best friend. Dunstan gulped his water as if it were ale, but that didn't prevent him from noticing Lady Mary's brother, Lord John, murmuring to the young viscount. When Staines glanced up at Dunstan with surprise, Dunstan figured his days on the estate were numbered. Discarding his water, he reached for the wine.

Focusing on the beautiful woman on his left, who was laughing merrily at something her sister had said, he fretted that the lady was the only obstacle between him and complete humiliation. How long before the forces of society battered her into submission?

As soon as the ladies departed from the table, he would escape this hell. If his employer wished to speak with him, she could do it on his terms, on his grounds.

❧

"Those dark Ives looks give me shivers." Wrapped in the linen folds of her nightdress, spectacles perched on the end of her nose, Felicity curled up in the middle of Leila's bed. "I think they eat Malcolms for midnight snacks."

Leila hid a smile at her sister's innocence. The child would learn of male appetites soon enough. "We need not have anything to do with Ives men," she reassured her.

Her *sisters* need not have anything to do with an Ives. *She* did. Drat the wretched man for escaping before they could talk after dinner.

"I'd much rather talk with Ives men," Christina said excitedly, putting down her hairbrush. "Perhaps we could discover who really did kill Celia."

"I scarcely think that's a wise idea unless we can tell truth from rumors," Leila replied, pacing her bedchamber. Her mother would berate her from now until doomsday if she involved her sisters in such an investigation. But how could she distract them when her own thoughts kept straying in that direction?

"They say Celia spent all Dunstan's money and ran away with the jewels he'd bought for her," Felicity offered.

"Rumor has it that Dunstan found Celia and her lover together," Christina added. "A passionate man might kill in the heat of the moment. But he seems far too cold for that."

Leila stared out the dark window to the lights of Dunstan's cottage. "I have watched him. He does not respond as other men when goaded. The more furious he becomes, the more discipline he displays."

Of course, he had almost broken Wickham's neck the other night when he'd heaved him across the field.

"Do we know where the murder took place?" Christina asked.

"At an inn in Baden-on-Lyme, not far from the Ives estate," Leila replied. The location gave Dunstan opportunity, in addition to motive, and was another reason why society condemned him. Who else could have followed Celia so easily, or would have wished her dead?

Even Felicity looked interested now. "I don't suppose Celia left a journal or anything I could touch?"

"Not that I know of," Leila said sharply. "And you're not to stop at the inn and ask."

While her sisters fell eagerly into discussing the murder, Leila watched wistfully from her window. She wished she could be the one to solve the murder, but all she knew how to do was produce perfume. She would need to enlist the help of Ninian, or perhaps her powerful aunt Stella, if she was to help clear Dunstan's name.

If her family saved his reputation, she could find a way to offer Dunstan a good life—one in which he didn't have to hide behind his mask of indifference.

Unless she was deceiving herself, and he had killed Celia, of course. *That* could be a problem.

Nine

Standing in the courtyard where a carriage waited to return her sisters to London, Leila hugged each in turn. "I will miss you. I'm sorry I won't be there for your come-outs. Have *Maman* or Aunt Stella send some of the younger ones to keep me entertained in your absence."

"You would overshadow us if you returned to London," Christina said, hugging her back. "Although that might not be a bad thing. Maybe Harry would fall in love with you, and I could be free to choose my own husband."

"That won't happen," Felicity said gloomily, returning her spectacles to her pocket. "Not unless you lie and say he has a muddy aura or some such."

"Then they might find me an old man, which would be worse." Christina picked up her cloak and tied her bonnet strings. "It's a pity the other Ives men have no titles or wealth. They're far more interesting than anyone else I've met."

"Dangerous, you mean. Only ninnyhammers prefer dangerous men," Felicity said, tucking her book into her basket. "You haven't been the same since you saw the lot of them at Ninian's wedding, all dark and glowering and blowing up the place with a cannon."

"It wasn't a cannon," Leila corrected. "It was an old musket. Now go on with the two of you. I've work to do, and you have a long way to travel." Stifling pangs of envy and loneliness, she bustled them into their carriage.

She sighed as the horses pulled away in a splatter of mud. She'd had family and society around her for as long as she could remember. Perhaps her place was with family, as the ungifted one guiding her sisters through their Seasons. Was she being arrogant and self-absorbed to assume that her perfumes might have some value?

Glancing up at the windows of the separate apartment her young nephew kept, she set her chin determinedly. Staines might as well realize that she had no intention of backing down. Her land would go for flowers.

As much as she would like to strangle her husband's nephew, she understood Staines's need to belong somewhere. His own father had died and left him nothing. The old earl took an interest in him only when the boy did something of which he disapproved. Leila didn't feel qualified to lecture him on the company he kept. He would have to learn for himself the difference between real friends and false.

Perhaps he simply needed a little more time to grow up—somewhere else, preferably—until he rid himself of sycophants like Lord John and Wickham.

She longed to oversee the progress of her garden and talk with Dunstan, but the sound of voices through the open windows of the breakfast room reminded her of her many obligations. What would it take to send the leeches away?

Could she persuade her suitors to pursue a more eligible marriage partner? Leila brightened as the advantages of this plan took root. Should Lord John find a wealthy wife, he needn't pass his sister off on her nephew, as seemed to be his current intention.

She could outfox Lord John in the blink of an eye. Hurrying into the house, Leila caught up a letter from her solicitor on her desk and folded it so her houseguests could not see the writing. With an innocent demeanor, she drifted into the breakfast room where the lazy louts gorged on her cook's hearty fare like the locusts they were. "Ah, there you are, Staines. I've just received a letter from my dear friend Lydia. She's in Bath and complaining of the lack of elegant society. I think I shall gather a company and relieve her boredom. The country grows tedious."

Her nephew shrugged and speared a bite of egg. Lord John looked up with interest. "Lydia Derwentwater?" he asked. "She just came into an inheritance, didn't she? Why is she in Bath?"

"To spend it," Leila replied. "You should enjoy meeting her. She owns some of the best hunting stock in the country."

That caught Staines's interest as well. Lady Mary's bland features flickered with a scowl, and Leila wickedly decided that sending her nephew to another woman might be a fine idea. "Besides, *Maman* and Aunt Stella are talking of sending the young ones to stay here until the Season ends. The place will be inundated with nannies and governesses."

The look of panic on all three faces was priceless. Content that she'd done her worst, Leila swept away in search of her gardening hat. She had an idea for a fountain and was eager to ask Dunstan about it.

If she could just reach some degree of understanding with her damned steward, they could discuss what to do with Staines over the longer term.

She found Dunstan riding through the garden, overlooking its progress. The clouds had departed, and he'd doffed both coat and vest in the warmth of the sun. He appeared as much a part of his animal as the horse's mane.

Leila breathed a sigh of relief at the sight of oxen pulling the sled while Dunstan rode his horse along the perimeter, surveying work on the wall. He hadn't turned against her after his conversation with Staines and last night's uncomfortable dinner party. Thank heavens.

She loved the idea of having a man who would stand up for her, even if she had to pay him to do it. If she correctly understood the reason behind his surliness, Dunstan Ives had probably been loyal to his adulterous wife while she lived and continued to hold his opinion of her to himself after she was dead. She should never have worried that a man who was so loyal and trustworthy would bow to Staines's wishes against her own.

Standing on the edge of the lawn, Leila surveyed the work done so far. A path that wound between lavender, roses, and delphiniums had begun to take shape, constructed with small pebbles taken from a nearby stream. As she studied the developing landscape, she watched Dunstan on horseback with fascination. It wasn't just his imposing size that held her interest, but his air of authority and command. If she was right about his high integrity, he was the kind of man she'd once dreamed of having for herself.

As Dunstan's gaze fell upon her, Leila's heart beat faster. Rather than let him see what must be clearly written on her face, she lifted her unwieldy skirts and paced the rows in search of the ideal place for her fountain.

He instantly urged his steed across the field and dismounted next to her. "The field is no place for a lady. It distracts the men and slows the work. You do want the garden completed sometime this summer?" he asked mockingly.

She tried not to gape at the sweat-soaked linen plastered to his broad chest. He'd obviously been working as hard as any laborer. She let her gaze dip down to the flat muscles of his abdomen beneath tight breeches. *Oh, my.*

He stiffened and reached for the vest he'd discarded across his saddle, but his gaze never left hers as he tugged on the long garment.

Skirts blowing about her ankles, Leila searched his face. She enjoyed his odor of responsibility, but lust tended to override all else. He didn't avoid her eyes this time. Did he see her? Really see her? She longed to talk with him as woman to man without any walls between them.

She had the power to *make* him see her for who she was, if she was brave enough.

Excitement beat in Leila's chest. "I wish to help. Where should I start?" she asked with a deliberately Lily-like toss of her head, even though her curls were bound tight and hidden beneath her wide hat brim.

She watched his gaze linger a moment too long on the powdered strand curling above her neckerchief, and she smiled in satisfaction.

He nodded curtly toward the far end of the row. "They've dumped a pile of manure over there," he taunted. "You could dig it into the bed."

So much for pleasantries. As if he'd forgotten her existence, Dunstan turned away from her, ordered the men back to work, then crisscrossed the field, stopping to haul away stones when necessary and guiding the oxen over difficult ground.

She realized she was standing outside the familiar world into which she'd been born, and uncertainty hampered her. Perhaps her instincts were wrong. Perhaps Dunstan *didn't* desire her. He certainly did an excellent job of ignoring her.

Leila strolled down the row of recovering roses, listening to the laborers curse the stones, the animals, and the heat. They never cursed Dunstan, but listened when he spoke, obviously fearing the man while respecting his knowledge.

As she studied her stubborn steward, the scent of him emerged inside her mind, a scent she yearned to replicate in her laboratory. Could one replicate power and authority? She would combine it with the carthy scents of grass and dirt, well doused in musk. The different aromas played notes in her head that aroused and excited her. She would make a fool of herself shortly if she did not concentrate on roses instead of Dunstan.

In the warmth of the sun, her heavy gown began to stick to her back as much as Dunstan's shirt clung to his, and she wished for Lily's simpler attire. She would become filthy and malodorous if she remained out in the sun and manure.

So would Dunstan.

Leila's thoughts flitted to the bathing place she had found on her first visit to this estate. She thought it might once have been a holy well where the goddesses dwelt. She had no difficulty mixing the pagan beliefs of her ancestors with civilized religion. In actuality, she'd never given religion much thought at all, but the bathing place was a world of its own, and she craved it now.

Could she profane such a place with an Ives?

It was a heathen idea borne of her heathen sensuality, but Malcolms had never bothered with the normal boundaries of civilization. Maybe her ancestry was finally calling to her. Instead of stifling her natural instincts, shouldn't she obey and see where they led?

Excitement coursed through Leila at the possibility. Stripped of all the refinements of her privileged position, she could revert to the pagan residing inside her. She could find her inner essence, and maybe, someday, it would lead to her Malcolm gift.

Then perhaps Dunstan would see her for who she really was—a woman like no other, and one who valued his opinion.

Energized by the thought of having a true helpmate in this project, she glanced sideways at Dunstan and discovered him looking back at her. Tension swelled between them as he studied the way she dabbed her handkerchief at the perspiration trickling down her throat to her breasts. He reined his horse onward, taking his gaze away, but Leila felt it like a living thing rippling across her skin. He did desire her, as Adam desired Eve.

He desired her whether she was Lily or Leila. That was a starting place.

She'd never given her body to a man other than her husband. Stooping to check another bush for buds, Leila let her imagination conjure images of Dunstan naked and aroused. She could imagine even further than that, and moisture pooled between her legs, making her tremble.

Desire, hot and thick, hampered her thoughts. When Dunstan ordered the men to take a dinner break, she sat on the wall of rocks and took deep breaths.

She needed the field plowed. Dunstan mustn't stop now.

But there was nothing to prevent them from visiting her cave once the work was done.

How would she get him there? Did she dare?

Would the experience open his eyes and persuade him to see Leila as Lily? Or would it just enrage him past caring?

Nothing ventured, nothing gained.

Deciding Dunstan was much more likely to follow Lily than Leila, she offered him a beaming smile that left him looking stunned, then skirts swaying, she left the field.

❧

Women plotted methods of driving men mad, Dunstan decided as the men dragged themselves out of the field at day's end. The image of Lady Leila watching him with Lily's eyes still seared his mind.

He'd wager the mystery of the lady's eyes could easily be solved if he applied his mind to it. Lady Leila had probably thrown him together with one of her family's by-blows for some design that was beyond his ability to comprehend. His family tree had sufficient illegitimate twigs on it for him to know the high probability of such occurrences. For all he knew, Lady Leila and Lily were plotting together to make him insane. They looked enough alike to think alike.

The wretched memory of last night's dinner clawed at his insides. Lady Leila was an older, more experienced version of Celia at her worst—with nothing better to do with her idle life than taunt and torment.

And yet midnight-blue eyes had haunted his sleep. Lily's eyes, he decided. Not the lady's.

Lady Leila smelled of roses and powder. Lily smelled of mud and fresh air. They couldn't be one and the same. He desired the free-spirited wench, not the corseted proper lady.

Even as he thought of her, Lily slipped into the field through a thicket of old hedge he'd not ripped out yet. While he watched, she stooped to examine a rosebush just as the lady had done earlier. Black curls tumbled down her back, lifting in the evening breeze.

Dunstan removed his sodden handkerchief from his pocket, wiped his brow, and wearily picked up the horse's reins, ignoring the tempting female whirling about in happy circles beneath the newly constructed arch at the garden entrance. With a concerted effort, he focused on admiring the loamy furrows of rich earth spreading around him and savored a sense of accomplishment.

Neat rows and new green leaves lined the landscape as far as the eye could see. The stone wall prevented the lambs from gamboling through the lavender beds. The first timbers of a pergola stood at the end of a curving garden path.

Trying not to think too hard of the havoc a bratling like Staines could wreak on these gardens and his crops, Dunstan grudgingly admired the woman who was expressing her delight with such exuberance. His respect for Lily was based on more than lust. Whoever or whatever she was, she'd ensnared him with her lightheartedness and quick wit as much as with the enticing blue of her eyes.

Unlike the lady's corseted gown, the bright blue linen of Lily's bodice clung to breasts as full and unfettered as ripe melons. Lily—his mind insisted. Lily of the valley, a wildflower free for the taking. Lily of the muddy fingers and tart tongue and refreshing honesty. Lily, who lacked proper respect for his authority.

Because she wasn't just Lily?

Groaning, Dunstan dismounted and tied his horse to a tree. He still had to lead the oxen back to their field.

He was a man, and men lusted after beguiling wenches like Lily. He could accept that. But he could never fall for a manipulative Malcolm. He simply couldn't conceive of it, didn't dare think of it. He preferred keeping the two women separate in his mind—the legitimate lady and her illegitimate cousin.

No fluttering fans or powdered hair or artificial beauty patches disguised the female who was currently playing hide-and-seek with her cat. Dunstan could almost feel the thrust of her breasts in his palms, so keenly did he want them. Once, he'd touched her with his crude hands, and she hadn't objected.

Sweat poured from his brow. He wiped it on his shirt-sleeve. He wanted to strip off his shirt, but he didn't dare—her presence prevented it. Another part of him wanted to don his coat and hide behind it, as if she were the lady he feared—

He was afraid of Lady Leila.

A cold shiver of shock shot down his spine. *Afraid of a woman?* Afraid of a lady—like Celia.

The door in his mind slammed open, ripped off its hinges.

Midnight-blue eyes lifted to watch him, and Dunstan couldn't swallow the lump of panic in his throat as their gazes met. Lily's fingers molded and patted the rich soil around a loose rose cane, and he could almost feel those fingers kneading his bare flesh.

Maybe Lady Leila was the phantom. Maybe Lily had stepped into her shoes. Maybe he was going mad.

Maybe he'd better run for his life, but his life would be worth nothing if he ran. What would happen if he stayed and acted on the tension building between them? What would his life be if she really were the lady whom all his instincts feared?

His mind refused to juxtapose the elegant, aloof lady with her delicate black gloves and jewels against the image of the accessible lass digging her dirty fingers into the raw soil. Where was the fair-haired, haughty Malcolm in this dark-haired, rebellious gypsy?

Would a real lady kneel in the dirt and look for rabbits? Celia wouldn't have.

Ladies didn't belong in fields. Ladies weren't supposed to perspire. Yet he'd forgotten the one important element in all of this—

Lady Leila was no ordinary lady. She was a Malcolm.

And he was looking at a Malcolm—irrevocably and irretrievably a confusing, conniving, surely illegitimate Malcolm, despite all appearances to the contrary.

He wanted two women, and both were Malcolms.

Ten

DUNSTAN TUGGED THE OXEN'S HARNESS, INTENDING TO LEAD them back to pasture, but Lily's magical voice halted him in his tracks. "I have something I'd like to show you."

She had a lot he'd like to see. Grimacing in exasperation as his unruly thoughts took a wrong turn before he'd even left the field, Dunstan glanced briefly in her direction.

She'd skipped across the furrows until she stood mere yards away from him. A rising breeze caught her black curls, lifting them off her shoulders to uncover curves molded by a V of perspiration. Firm and high, her breasts taunted him.

He liked the bright blue on her—so much happier than the widow's weeds Leila wore.

"I must take the oxen back," he answered curtly, leading the animals away. He didn't know what game she played, but he'd be better to stay out of it.

"We go through their pasture to reach the place I want to show you." She hurried across the remaining rows to join him. "You will like this place. I promise."

He was too tired to argue. Or too riddled with lust. He drove the oxen toward the gate, all too aware of the woman striding easily beside him. She carried herself as regally as a lady in her parlor. Beneath the aroma of manure, he detected the hint of rose perfume. How could he have missed that earlier?

Perhaps Lady Leila had given the perfume to her, as she'd given the soap to him. He tried to shut the door in his mind. He couldn't put all the pieces together—the blatant provocativeness, the easy laughter, and blunt honesty of Lily with the sultry flirtatiousness, conniving eccentricity, and regal elegance of Lady Leila.

A taunting voice in his head warned him that all women looked alike in the dark. All he had to do was close his eyes.

Except that he didn't dare close his eyes around a Malcolm.

Lily seemed preoccupied and tense, as if uncertain of her invitation now that she'd given it. Perhaps she would change her mind, and he could go home to soak in a tub of hot water.

He refused to look at her again. Until he could provide for his own livelihood, he had no right to look at any woman, aristocrat or otherwise. His private investigator had reported he'd made little progress in discovering Celia's killer. It could be a lengthy and expensive investigation. The real murderer might never be known. He might never comprehend the depth of his own depravity.

With the oxen safely in their enclosed pasture, Dunstan glanced at the setting sun. "A full moon tonight," he commented idly. "A good night for planting."

He sensed more than saw her startled look.

"Were you planning on planting anything?" she asked, striking out across the field without looking back to see if he followed.

"They're planting at the south farm today and tomorrow. That's why the oxen were free." Wondering where she could possibly be leading him, Dunstan took more interest in his surroundings. They'd circled the hill and come out on the other side, where weather had eroded the loose soil, exposing outcroppings of rock. Definitely not suitable for planting here. He could see why the late Lord Staines had chosen this site for the widow's dower house. That, and the trees on the hillside. Malcolms loved trees.

The two women, Leila and Lily, blended together in his head—haughty Lady Leila with her hints of vulnerability and brazen Lily with her lack of servility.

The thought that the two women could be one who had tricked him for a reason beyond his ken irritated the back of his mind. What the devil could she be up to—whoever she was?

"Do flowers fare better if they're planted in the full of the moon?" she inquired, scrambling over a large rock.

"Probably, although I've never planted flowers, so I can't say. Are we going rock climbing?" Dunstan reluctantly followed. He couldn't imagine Lady Leila climbing rocks.

When Lily attempted to climb onto a ledge that was almost as high as she was, he caught her waist and lifted her up. His palm brushed the softness of a full buttock, and he winced with a surge of reawakened desire. This woman could not be Lady Leila. Touching a lady with such familiarity would have resulted in having his head knocked off his neck.

Yet even Lily had swatted him the first day they met.

When his steps hesitated, she glanced back impatiently. "It's right here. We won't go far."

He swung his booted foot over the ledge and hauled himself up so he could stand beside her. In the twilight, he could just discern a darkened crevice between two slabs of upright boulders. "A cave? You want me to see a cave?"

"Not just any cave. A *special* cave. You'll see." She fumbled among the rocks until she produced a flint and taper.

He struck the flint for her, and she thrust the candlewick into the spark. The flame shone wanly in the daylight, but brightened as she slipped through the opening.

Dunstan had to squeeze through edgewise to follow, ducking to keep from knocking his head. Lily waited for him inside, her candle casting shadows over a high cavern that smelled of dampness and soil. She stood tall and proud as any lady, and he no longer fought to separate the two women. He simply knew he wanted this woman, couldn't have her, and that he'd tempt the devil to follow her anywhere.

"Fascinating," he said wryly, not seeing beyond her supple curves and a banner of silken hair.

"Isn't it?" she agreed in awe, not realizing where his thoughts had traveled. "You can feel the power here. The gods must have blessed this place." She moved forward, taking the light with her.

Crazy Malcolms. If he needed any more proof of her lineage, black hair or fair, talking of gods and power should do it. Unless all women were plagued with fantasies of things that remained unseen.

"There," she announced with satisfaction, coming to a halt before a grotto of rising steam.

Forgetting the conundrum of her identity, Dunstan blinked in disbelief. Bubbling water smelling of minerals foamed at the base of the moss-covered rocks he stood upon. Someone had carefully cultivated a garden of vines that climbed and clung to the walls, reaching for the sun that must shine through the hole above, where he could see stars now. Flowery perfume wafted beneath his nose, and he almost expected faerie lights to twinkle around them.

"What is this place?" He'd intended to sound curt, but a note of awe spoiled the effect. It had been a long, long time since he'd enjoyed a sight like this one.

Her laughter floated like harpsichord notes—not beside him, but below. Startled, he tore his gaze from the amazing greenery to examine the bubbling spring. He could see only a pool of blackness.

"It's wonderfully warm," she called. "Come, join me."

He damned well couldn't even *see* her. She'd been standing right there beside him, where the taper flickered from a notch upon the wall—where her filthy gown and petticoat now lay flung across an outcropping.

She was naked and bathing in the spring.

The breath caught in his lungs, and heat poured into a part of his anatomy that had led him into more trouble than he cared to remember. He mustn't succumb. Mustn't let her magic draw him deeper—to places he shouldn't go but that every male part of him demanded he explore.

Yet she could be in danger in that black pit, he told himself. It was enough to lead him to the brink of temptation.

He couldn't see her in this midnight blackness. Apprehensively, he sat on the edge of the pool and jerked off his boots and stockings. What if she bumped her head on the rocks and drowned herself? "Are you all right?"

"I'm fine. It's not deep."

Light from the taper leaped and played along the ebony surface beneath the starlit hole above, but below, the water's edge disappeared into deep shadows, frothing beneath him, yet invisible elsewhere. He still couldn't see her.

The steaming water beckoned. He could almost imagine the feel of it against the sticky sweat on his skin. But it wasn't the temptation of a heated bath that called to him.

This woman had trusted him with knowledge of this special place, expected him to enjoy it as she did. He knew how it felt to have a heart's desire treated as nothing. He couldn't wound her by disparaging her dreams any more than he could have harmed his younger brothers.

Dunstan hauled his linen shirt over his head. Steam from the pool caressed his bare chest. He stood and stripped off his breeches.

Logic screamed for him to grab his boots and run. Pride, lust, and darker emotions overruled the thought of ignominious retreat.

Velvet moss eased his entry into the steaming waters. Instant heat soaked through his weary flesh, drawing him deeper. The healing power of mineral water relaxed every taut muscle, and Dunstan groaned in relief. If the little witch thought to seduce him, she'd underestimated the effects of a hot bath.

Little witch.

Warning bells clamored, but heated languor slowed his brain, and a musical voice distracted.

"There should be soap on the ledge behind you."

Caught in the spell of the pool, he'd momentarily forgotten her. Steam rose around him, making it impossible to see his hand in front of his face. No longer wary, he groped along the ledge until he located the waxy oval. He'd never taken a mineral bath. He thought he could learn to enjoy the experience.

"Are you certain we should use this place?" he called into the darkness. The pool only reached his waist at the deepest point, so he lost his fear that she would drown in it.

"The gods own this place. Ask their permission."

Amusement laced her voice, combined with the rhythmic splashes of bathing.

The soap's scent reminded him of the bars Lady Leila had sent with her sisters. The aroma of new-mown grass blended with the earthy odor of the cave in a subtly pleasing combination.

Ducking his head beneath the water, scrubbing at the day's grime, Dunstan thought he'd never experienced such a thorough sense of well-being. She was right. He didn't know the how or why of it, but this was a special place. He should thank her for it.

Enough soaks in here, and he might scrub out all the tension and anguish of the past few years, even if he couldn't scrub away the memories. Perhaps he could bottle this water. He would send a vial to his brothers for further study. The minerals might have some beneficial effect, like those in Bath were said to possess. In fact, this might be a related spring.

He grasped for rationality rather than thinking of the woman splashing naked and free somewhere in the pool beside him. In here, she was a nameless, faceless female, with no confusing eyes or hair color to distract him. Her name no longer mattered.

Standing again, Dunstan raked his dripping hair back from his face. Refreshed and invigorated, he glanced around the mossy chamber with interest, feeling more in control.

Moonlight poured through the opening above. A silver glow illuminated the dangling greenery, and he thought he detected tiny white flowers like little stars peeking through the moss on the walls.

Dunstan searched the darkness for the sorceress who'd brought him here. "Lily?"

"I think I could live in here," she called softly, much closer than before.

A flash of white and green swung by, and he stepped backward in surprise.

Laughter trilled out of the darkness, and the ghostly form swept by again. This time, he recognized the apparatus, and his eyes widened, studying the dangling vines. Someone had hung a swing from the roof.

In the silvery light, he traced the vine-covered rope until it disappeared into the gloom over his head. It couldn't be safe. He transferred his gaze back to the specter in white flitting back and forth on the swing. Lily, of course. Brazen woman.

The wet gauze of her chemise trailed behind her as she swung. The breeze from her movement plastered it like a transparent skin to her body. Already drying, her black curls spilled in tendrils down her back and over the water when she leaned back to pump the swing higher.

Dunstan tumbled through some hole in time to his youth, where all things were possible and each day presented one miracle after another for his pleasure. He could smell the grass he'd rolled in, feel the potency of adolescence. Years of cynicism dropped away, leaving him buoyant as he waded through the pool to her ridiculous swing.

She laughed in delight when he caught the ropes and brought her to a halt. She didn't fear him as others did, and that alone lightened his burden. She trusted him.

She saw beyond his reputation and trusted what she saw. He could feel the realization cracking the rock-solid barrier he'd erected in self-defense against the cruelties of society. He'd never fully comprehended how much unswerving trust could mean.

Holding the rope, Dunstan looked down into eyes of dancing mischief almost hidden behind a curtain of thick black lashes. The steam had turned her cheeks rosy, and her full lips glistened temptingly. He only meant to thank her, to push her swing as one would play with a child.

Except she wasn't a child.

With the scent of burgeoning spring rising between them, Dunstan bent and cautiously placed his mouth across hers, prepared to retreat at the first sign of protest.

Lightning struck and fire scorched his bones at her passionate response. The heat rising through his bare limbs was no longer derived from water. Full lips melted to lush invitation, and Dunstan released the rope to clasp female curves perfectly fitted to his wide hands. His fingers reveled in the touch of heated silk.

She didn't shove him away.

Hundreds of lonely nights dissolved with the sigh of her desire. He could no more resist that sigh than the sun could resist rising in the morn.

She moaned beneath the insistent slant of his mouth and opened to the command of his tongue. He dived deeper, exploring the taste of honey, wrapped in the intoxicating scent of wine and roses. He could do this without losing control. They didn't have to go beyond kisses. He held her trapped and clinging to the ropes. He could stop at any time, he told himself, and no one the wiser. He just wanted one more little taste…

Boldly, he slid his hands up to capture the full globes of her breasts beneath wet linen, relishing feminine roundness yielding against his rough hands. Once there, he couldn't resist brushing his thumbs across the puckered crests.

Instead of breaking the kiss, she murmured against his mouth and rocked closer. With that unspoken permission, Dunstan stepped between her thighs so she could not mistake the extent of his arousal. The musky heat of her beckoned the animal part of him that had overtaken his thinking. The swing was a perfect height. Only a scrap of gauze barred the gateway to heaven.

"Please," she murmured urgently against his mouth.

He deepened the kiss and indulged in the sensual pleasure of stroking a woman's softness. Her equal excitement drew him on, one irresistible step after another.

Pulling away from her honeyed mouth, Dunstan dipped his head to sample the heady liquor of her breast through the veil of her chemise. She gasped and leaned back, still clinging to the rope but offering herself more fully and freely than any woman in his life had ever done.

The experience awoke in him a frightening urge to become part of her, to see where she could take him.

Despite the warnings clamoring in the back of his mind, he couldn't *not* step closer. Cupping her hips, Dunstan swung her into him, suckled deeper, and was rewarded with her shudders of pleasure. He could still escape. He could still walk off and end this madness. He was a man of formidable discipline, not one who must rut like a beast in the field. He would stop—as soon as he gave her pleasure in return for what she had given him.

He slid his hand across her bare thigh, pushed aside the fine linen, and stroked her moist curls, locating the center of her sex.

She almost slid off the swing at his caress. Hastily relinquishing temptation, Dunstan caught her waist to prevent her from falling away from him.

Standing naked so close between her thighs, his hands occupied in keeping her seated, there seemed a simple means of providing the pleasure she craved. If he pushed inside, just a little, he could ease the tension pumping through them. The mystery of who or what she was outside of here was no longer as important as who they were together, right now.

Pressing his fingers into the firm flesh of her waist and buttocks, Dunstan let the ecstasy of moist heat tempt him. Angling her hips and the swing, he rubbed cautiously against the nub that made her quiver.

He hadn't considered the danger of her long, shapely legs wrapping around his thighs, lifting her hips higher—until his short strokes combined with her strong pull drove him fully into her, and she cried out in delight.

Sweat poured off his brow, and his blood surged to the place where they were joined. He'd learned how to draw back before release. It was only release he feared. He couldn't afford to create any more babes. Holding perfectly still, he took her mouth and drank deeply.

She licked his lips, sucked his tongue with eagerness, and fell back on the rope swing until the seat almost swung away. Dunstan grabbed her hips and supporting her weight, swung her back. Pure, intoxicating pleasure gripped him as he filled her to the hilt again, and her muscles tightened around him. He could feel her contractions, knew she was close, knew he need only—

She flung her arms around his neck, held him with her thighs, and climaxed ecstatically, hips pumping, breasts crushing into his chest. With no more command than an adolescent youth, Dunstan lost control and filled her womb with the hot, intoxicating flood of his seed.

Eleven

LEILA SIGHED RAPTUROUSLY AS DUNSTAN'S BRAWNY ARMS lifted her from the swing and lowered her into the heated waters. Every particle of her being glowed. She drank deeply of the scent of sex, and it smelled of pleasure. She wanted to do it again.

"Thank you," she murmured, her knees still wobbly as she rested against his muscled chest. "I had no idea..."

"Women seldom do," he replied, reaching for the soap on the ledge. "If they'd just stop and think once in a while, half the world's problems would be solved."

Well, obviously the experience hadn't been as soul-shattering for him as it had been for her. What was happening inside his dangerous head now?

Warily, she glanced up at the tic in Dunstan's jaw, but warm water and scented soap bubbled around them, and she could sense nothing else beyond his expression. This man said what he meant without dissimulation.

With ecstasy, she forgot wariness to admire the wet mat of hair narrowing down his broad chest to an interesting region disguised by lapping water.

Ignoring her sigh of delight, he gently lathered the soap into the place he'd bruised with his lustiness, and she relaxed and let the pleasure return. "Beasts in the field we are," she agreed.

She sensed his sharp look and didn't care. Let him think she was whoever he wanted her to be.

"I behaved as such," he agreed. "Did I hurt you?"

He had, but only because it had been so long for her, and she was unused to a man of his size. She could learn to accommodate him, if he gave her the chance.

Her growing desire as his fingers caressed her certainly proved her animal nature. It was a pity they couldn't do it again. The scent of the soap washed around them, and she rocked provocatively against his hand. Whatever anyone said, Dunstan Ives was a gentle man. For all his gruffness, he was treating her with the tenderness and regard due a newly tried virgin.

Devil take it, but he still concealed the gentle, funny Dunstan behind the thorny walls of the joyless, unfeeling one.

Tentatively, she reached out to him, hoping he would let her—all of her—past his barriers now. "It's as if I can only be myself with you," she murmured, gifting him with a piece of her she had granted none other.

"Not all of us have a problem being ourselves." Abruptly, he lifted her from the water and set her on the mossy rocks.

The shock of the cooler air against her heated skin didn't numb Leila's desire. "You do," she argued, reaching for her petticoat. "You deliberately hide and deny your true feelings, shutting everyone out. Why can't you just enjoy what we've found here together?"

Standing in the water, Dunstan shrugged. "I am simply being rational. Once we start down this path, it is difficult to stop. It is better for all concerned if one of us practices restraint."

"I thought it was quite the best thing that's ever happened to me. I have no desire to stop." She tugged at the petticoat strings with irritation.

"Aye, and pleasure is your only thought," he mocked, climbing out after her. "Some of us have responsibilities to consider."

Leila's eyes widened at the silhouette he presented in the light of the rising moon. He was engorged and ready for her again. Her husband had *never* accomplished that.

But Dunstan Ives was in the full vigor of manhood. Not a skinny adolescent nor a flabby old man, but a firmly muscled male in the prime of life. She gulped when he turned his back on her, displaying the way those broad muscles worked. She wanted to make love again, in the full light of day. She hadn't even begun to appreciate the power of the male body.

He was pulling on his breeches. He intended to walk away. Every inch of her that was female cried out in protest.

But she wouldn't give him the gratification of knowing he'd brought her to such a state. "Why shouldn't pleasure be the only consideration?" she inquired. "We're neither of us married. We hurt no one."

He tugged his breeches flap closed and fastened it before turning. Leila thought she ought to be incinerated by the blast of fury from his eyes, but she was made of stern mettle and merely waited for his reply.

He visibly softened at the sight of her sitting nude upon the mossy bed, but his tone remained curt. "You might at least pay heed to the results of such sport."

The results? Beyond pleasure? She'd found none. She blinked and tried to gather her failing wits. It was difficult, with all that lovely naked chest looming over her. As if he understood her state, he grabbed his shirt and yanked it over his head.

"Children," he explained gruffly when his head emerged from the linen. "Every pleasure has its price."

Oh, children. Leila curled her lip and would have laughed, but she thought it would injure his Ives pride. Ives men never denied their reputation as prolific breeders, and gossip had it that they produced only sons—usually illegitimate ones, from what she heard.

"I was married for seven years and never produced a child," she said, knowing that most men assumed the woman was at fault in such cases. "And should a miracle occur, I would not make demands of you. You really think too much, you know."

She shouldn't have added that last, but she couldn't resist. She swallowed a giggle at the irritable way he shoved a hand through his hair and glared down at her, as if he had no idea what to make of her. Men seldom followed her advice, but at least this one listened. She supposed she ought to dress before he blamed her for tempting him again.

"I'm not a fool, madam," he said, recovering his place

in their argument. "I have made it a point to study human breeding practices as thoroughly as those of sheep. The risk is high if proper precautions aren't taken, which we did not, if you would take time to remember."

Well, she'd been warned that Ives were practical men. Pulling her petticoat over her wet chemise, she reached for her bodice. She heard his sharp intake of breath at the amount of flesh left revealed, and secretly gloating, she took an unnecessarily long time fastening the bodice hooks, starting with the bottom ones so he must watch her breasts until the very last minute. She noticed he didn't turn away when she pushed them higher.

She dearly adored this business of being admired by an angry Ives. To have a man whose intelligence she respected admire her for other than her display of wealth gave her a new and welcome sense of power.

Apparently physical intimacy made it easier to understand him. The thickheaded man saw Lady Leila in terms of the duplicitous Celia, so he preferred thinking of her as simply Lily—a woman he could control as easily as he did his horse.

"Nevertheless," she said, "I have no need of you or your support, so you may go about your business with a peaceful mind. I do not charge for the pleasure," she added wryly.

Grabbing her by the arm, Dunstan hauled her to her feet. "Sons need fathers." The words came out as almost a curse. "I already have one son I neglect by being here. I'd rather not have two to feel guilty about. If you do not care about yourself, care about the child you might breed."

Leila rolled her eyes and tugged her gown into place. Ives pride went too far. She began tying her skirt to her bodice. "Women take care of children. Men don't. It's a fact of life. You're simply angry because I made you lose your precious control."

That silenced him. Momentarily.

"I'll see you home." Stiffly, he stepped back to retrieve his boots.

The goddess in heaven, she railed inwardly, watching him through lowered lashes while she finished dressing. After today, they couldn't continue pretending she was two different people. Or that they meant nothing to each other.

Or perhaps *he* could. Men thought of sex as a simple act of survival, like eating.

Irritated at the thought of being no more than a receptacle for grunting male appetites, and exasperated by Dunstan's denial of who she really was, Leila swung around. He still had his broad back to her. With a final roll of her eyes, she put both hands against his back and shoved him into the pool.

"You're a churlish bigot, Dunstan Ives! Try seeing beyond your own damned self sometime."

While he shouted his protests, she stalked from the cave.

⌘

Dripping from head to toe, Dunstan rode his gelding after the wretched female, following her to the mansion's dairy door, where she slipped inside and out of sight without acknowledging his presence.

Her disappearance left a gaping hole in the night.

Damnation.

Leaning against the horse's neck, Dunstan stared up at the lights of the big house, watching as kitchen candles and fires died, downstairs lamps were doused, and new ones appeared in upper-story windows.

She'd said she could be herself only with him. Who the devil was she, then? The fair-haired witch who dominated society and ruled this household? Or the black-haired wench who cavorted in fields and pleaded for the lives of baby rabbits?

Or both?

A chill shivered through him that had nothing to do with his damp clothing. What had he just done?

Watching a familiar female silhouette glide past an upstairs window, he suffered the terrible conviction that she was right. He was a bigot. His prejudice against society had blinded him to the truth. He detested the aristocracy because of his father's neglect and the decadence of men like Wickham. He detested aristocratic women because of Celia's betrayal and her abominable friends.

He'd detested Lady Leila for all those reasons and because Malcolms were uncontrollable and unpredictable.

If the knowledgeable, courageous lady who had hired him was really the wench who had taught him the true meaning of pleasure, then he'd denied the truth out of prejudice.

The possibility that he could be so blind appalled him. He took pride in being a man of science—observant, open-minded, and aware of his surroundings.

The slender figure lighting a candle in the window above taunted him with his failure. It was past time he opened his eyes and learned the truth, even if the truth had the power to destroy him.

He turned his steed toward home. Once there, he hurriedly stripped off his sodden boots and changed into dry clothes.

Scientific observation required that all theories be confirmed from as many sources as were available. Before contemplating further action, Dunstan walked back to the mansion, stalked up the front steps, and asked for the viscount.

Staines seemed surprised by his appearance, but eager for companionship. He introduced Dunstan to the smoky male environs of the towering library and offered a brandy. "I'm leaving for Bath in the morning. Have you news for me?"

"We've planted the wheat," he announced, as if he reported to the brat every day.

Staines grimaced. "I'll take your word that improvements have been made."

"Wheat's the first course of my system. Next year, we'll plant turnips. Instead of selling off the lambs, we'll be able to keep them through the winter and feed them with the roots."

"What's the point of keeping the smelly creatures?" The viscount slumped in his seat. "I'd rather sell them and spend the money."

Patience was not one of Dunstan's virtues, but he held his tongue and tried to remember he had a son to support and an investigator to pay. And he needed verification from the stripling before he made an utter ass of himself. "You will earn more money by producing wool every year," he explained to the boy. "The object is to make every investment return more than you put in."

The viscount finally looked intrigued. "Turnips don't

cost much, lambs are free, and wool produces more income than mutton?"

"That's the substance of it." No point in going into the details of labor and expenses now. He needed to hook the lad's interest first. He needed the boy's support should the lady marry.

The idea of the lady marrying chilled him to the marrow— surely out of fear of losing the turnips, he told himself.

"Each year, I'll cultivate more fields," Dunstan continued. "The system feeds itself. Barring a natural disaster, it will provide a foolproof return on your investment."

"Barring a natural disaster or Leila's roses," the boy complained. "I wish you would rid me of them. My only income comes from the estate."

That was the opening he wanted. Relaxing in the sumptuous leather chair, Dunstan fingered the stem of the brandy glass and worded his question carefully. "Do you want me to rid you of Lily or the roses?"

"Lily?" Staines stared at him in disbelief. "She allows you to call her *Lily*? Only her sisters do that."

Dunstan drained his brandy glass, hoping for numbness as the alcohol burned through to his empty stomach. A red-hot haze of anger cloaked his brain in confusion. He'd been duped. He need only check the color of the hair of the woman in the room above to prove his own stupidity.

❧

Standing in the open, arched balcony window of her room, Leila watched the last lamplight flicker out on the floor below. Even the servants were retiring for the night. She'd heard Dunstan ride away an hour ago.

How enormous was the risk she had just taken? Did Dunstan finally see her as she really was? Or did he simply think her an easy wench, free for the asking?

If a man with the intelligence of Dunstan Ives couldn't see her as she was, who could? She longed for the acceptance and understanding even her family couldn't offer. She wasn't just "the black-haired Malcolm" or "ungifted Lily" or the "eligible Lady Leila." She was a woman with needs and desires—a woman who yearned to be held in a man's arms, to be listened to and respected. Was that so very impossible?

Or had she only made the man she wanted monstrously angry? Dunstan wouldn't walk out on her and abandon his turnips, would he? Would he continue pretending she was two people?

Would he come to her bed?

She was wide awake and hungering for what she couldn't have.

Spinning on her slippered heel, she paced the spacious room her husband had had decorated for her. She had just experienced more life in a mossy cave than she'd ever known between these gilded walls.

She longed to experience more—craved it.

Perhaps she could don her peasant clothes and entice Dunstan back to the cave again.

Perhaps she could slip into his house, tempt him with wine and perfume, and they wouldn't go any farther than his bed. She would set candles burning all around so she could see all of him.

She almost set out in search of a box of candles before she stopped herself. She wasn't thinking. She was behaving like a bitch in heat.

Dunstan Ives would not lightly take a Malcolm for a mistress. Yet why, by all that was holy, couldn't he be like every other man in society and just accept what she offered without considering the consequences?

How could she survive without taking his body into hers again? Cupping her breasts through the silk of her nightdress, she tried to arouse the sensations he had taught her, but she needed the fiery heat of his breath, the musky smell of his skin, the brush of his thick hair. She needed *him*.

"Once wasn't enough, my lady?" a masculine voice inquired from the window.

Gasping, Leila swung around.

Dunstan sat on her windowsill, arms crossed, booted legs sprawled in front of him. Bareheaded, with his silky hair drawn back in a dark ribbon, he could have been a highwayman off the road. But he carried an air of authority and power that no common thief could ever match.

She wouldn't waste her breath asking how he got there. He was an Ives. They were all in league with the devil. He probably snapped his fingers and flew.

She refused to fear him, but she hoped to placate him. She needed him too desperately, in too many ways, not to try.

"Odd, how prejudice can blind us to the obvious," she answered, then inwardly winced. Well, that certainly wouldn't smooth his ruffled feathers. Where were all her social skills when she needed them? Turning away, she picked up a brush and bent to pull it through her hair.

In the resulting silence, the tension between them rose to an unbearable degree.

When she looked up again, Dunstan's broad form filled her full-length mirror. She admired the quality of the lace on his jabot rather than wonder what he might do with his hands.

"Your hair is supposed to be blond like your sisters' and your cousins'." Without permission, he took the brush from her and began plying it to her tangled curls.

"I am the only black-haired Malcolm. Anyone in London could have told you that."

"You deceived me. Why?" His hands in her hair were gentle. His voice was not.

"It was not intentional, I assure you. I simply let you think as you pleased." Leila closed her eyes and luxuriated in the sensual pull of the brush in her hair. She could smell him so vividly that she could see him in the cave again in all his glory.

"I suppose I deserved that. I'll try not to be so blind next time," he said.

"It's about time you opened your eyes to many truths. I'm not any of the things you think me. Most of all, I'm not Celia. It's bigotry and prejudice to lump all women into the same shallow mold."

"You deny you manipulated me? Isn't that what women do best?" Dunstan threw the brush on her dresser, pulled her hair behind her, and ran his hand beneath the loose fabric of her neckline. Heat enveloped Leila's bare breast, desire pooled deep beneath her belly, and she almost moaned as he caressed her nipple into an aching peak.

He bent his head down to her, and she arched her neck to accept his kiss. His mouth seared hers, spreading liquid heat through her limbs, while her hand instinctively reached to comb through his hair. The demanding invasion of his tongue weakened her knees, and hope pounded in her heart. Perhaps he had forgiven—

He stepped back, leaving her cold.

She stood still, praying for his touch, yet fearing his words.

"You're an incredibly responsive woman," he said thoughtfully, watching her in the mirror. "Any man would pay well for what you offer so freely."

She wanted to slap him, but he let a handful of her hair slip through his fingers, and she stood frozen, fascinated, waiting to see what he would do next. "I've known only one man before you," she finally said. "Don't you think I deserve an opportunity to learn more?"

"Not at my expense and without my consent. You have no understanding of what you have done by involving me. I doubt that either of us can afford to act on our desires."

He stood behind her so she couldn't tell the extent of his arousal, though the passion between them was too potent to ignore. The scent of him filled her head, and she could *feel* him inside her in some primitive manner she couldn't define. Not physically, but the person he was: the lonely man, the arrogant intellect, the commanding presence.

She stepped backward, but he merely caught her arms in a powerful grip and forced her to look in the mirror. At them. They were both tall, black-haired creatures, she thought wildly. She had cultivated the expressionless features of vapid beauty. His chiseled face was an impenetrable mask by nature.

"I didn't hear you saying no earlier." Her voice shook, and she closed her eyes again so she didn't have to see what he was doing to her.

"You hear me saying no now," he replied softly. "I cannot afford to dally with Lady Leila any more than I can afford

Lily. What we did tonight was a mistake. You ask too much of me."

"You are being unreason—"

Relentlessly, his deep voice continued, murmuring against her ear. "I suggest that you decide which you most want planted, your roses or yourself. Leave me be, Leila."

He abruptly stepped away. Stumbling, she struggled to recover her equilibrium, but Dunstan had already crossed the room to the window.

If she had a temper, she'd fling everything within reach at the wretched man who was now lifting his booted foot over the sill.

Instead, she collapsed onto the carpet, wrapping her arms around her knees and rocking back and forth in an agony of unrequited desire while the wicked wretch disappeared into the night.

Twelve

ATTEMPTING TO WASH BEFORE DAWN THE NEXT MORNING, Dunstan inhaled the scent of sweet grass, felt his body tighten with longing, and flung the cake of soap across the room with a force that dented the wainscoting. The *witch*. Even the soap raised visions of last night's ecstasy—an ecstasy he dared not repeat. Denial was much harder now that he knew what he denied.

He breathed deeply, attempting to control his towering temper, but the lady had dug her claws into his soul, and he couldn't pry her loose.

Damnation, but she'd tasted of lavender and honey and fitted his rough hands as if she belonged there. Creamier and more tender than silk, her flesh had branded his palms so he could feel naught else. A *lady*. Not a common wench. A *Malcolm*. Not a laughing maidservant.

Why *him*? She may as well have made a pact with the devil.

He gripped the rough windowsill and watched a distant curl of smoke rise against the dawn sky. He hadn't slept a wink all night. He never should have kissed her. He was a condemned man.

Well, that wasn't anything new.

With that wry realization, he straightened. The witch might as well have his soul, since he was damned to hell already.

She would turn him to putty if he let her. He'd already compromised his turnips by helping her with the gardens when he should have been persuading her to give them up—or to marry.

Yet he couldn't ask her to do either.

His brothers might jeer at his superstition, but Dunstan fully accepted that Malcolms were witches. He had his hands in the earth every day and knew that the powers of nature were far beyond his comprehension. Call the Malcolms forces of nature instead of witches, perhaps, but he couldn't command a Malcolm female any more than he could direct the sun or the rain.

He would rather trust the devious lady than her addlepated young nephew. At least he and Leila had similar goals in mind, odd as that might be.

Stomping down the stairs to the kitchen, Dunstan vowed to avoid women from this day forth.

Grimacing, he stirred the banked fire in the stove and pumped water to fill a pot.

"I have a proposition for you."

The female voice emerged from the shadows.

Startled, Dunstan nearly dropped the kettle. He glanced around for the source of the voice and discovered Leila's black-and-white cat curled on the pillow of his cook's chair. Even witches couldn't make cats talk.

A waft of heavenly roses surrounded him. Leila.

She was inside his *head*.

No, he couldn't believe that. He was bigger and stronger and in control here. She was simply a calculating wisp of female.

Cautiously, he searched the dim corners of the lofty room.

A teacup rose to the pale ghost of her face against the backdrop of a still-dark windowpane. Clenching his teeth, Dunstan stepped deeper into the kitchen. He really needed to start carrying candles with him.

Sitting on the windowsill, she wore black gloves against the morning chill and a black velvet cloak that enveloped her in night. Her inky curls spilled down her back, unbound and unveiled. No longer denying what his senses told him, he fully recognized the lady as the wench.

"How long have you been here?" he demanded, finding

the teapot still warm. He poured a splash of tea into a cup and gulped the soothing liquid.

"Long enough to let the fire dwindle. I don't sleep much."

He heard the shrug in her voice, wanted to believe the lonely vulnerability behind it, but couldn't. "I assumed witches slept in the daylight."

"I'm not a witch."

This time, her sadness penetrated his defenses as surely as her perfume permeated the air. He tamped down his sympathy, reluctant to let her beneath his skin again. "Fine, you're not a witch. You're a woman. That's bad enough."

A wry laugh escaped her as she extended her cup for a refill. "Being a woman is terrible, I agree. How would you like being no more than a pet to be cuddled or cast aside on a whim? Treated as if you hadn't a thought in your head? It's a credit to our gender that we do not all rise up some frosty morn and slit the throats of the men around us."

Devil take it, she was doing it again, crawling inside his mind and making him like her. The woman was as dangerous as he'd feared. "What do you want?" he asked curtly, deciding it would be safer to remove her from his kitchen as swiftly as possible.

"As I said, I've come to offer you a proposition. I do not own my land outright, so I cannot deed you the acreage you need for your experiments. But if you will work with me, I can offer you something better."

Dunstan froze. He didn't think he wanted to hear her offer, but he didn't have much choice unless he bodily heaved her out. And if he touched her, he doubted he'd have the strength to let her go.

Taking his silence for permission to continue, Leila did so. "I can offer to clear your name."

He waited. What she offered was so far beyond the realm of possibility that he figured there must be more to it. Even *he* didn't know if he was innocent. His investigator had sent notes reporting little progress. He saw no point in telling her he was already doing all that could be done.

Impatient with his silence, she set down the cup. "If we

clear your name, you can take a position anywhere. You can
work with some of the best agricultural experts in the country,
earn a respectable reputation, buy your own land. Isn't that
what you want?"

More than life itself, but he wouldn't admit it. He had
pride and an aristocratic name, and he was supposed to be
above caring what the world thought. He refused to reveal the
weakness in him that craved respect and recognition, and the
driving need to make a difference in the world. He *knew* he
could improve living conditions for farmers, but he wouldn't
beg for the opportunity to do so.

"And what would I have to do so you would consent to
wave your magic wand and create miracles?" he asked.

"You needn't be sarcastic." She hopped down from the
window ledge and paced the tiled floor, her petticoats rustling.
"I need your cooperation with the gardens and with handling
my nephew. I cannot do it alone, and I don't want you siding
with Staines and his cohorts simply because they're men and
I'm not. I need your knowledge and experience and the
chance to develop new flower strains. All my life I've been
denied the opportunity to develop my talents, and I won't
wait any longer."

Dunstan closed his eyes and heard her words echoing his
own. He felt her hunger for knowledge as surely as he felt his.
Worse, he understood her unspoken need for recognition of
those talents. The lady wanted what he wanted.

"I can't help you," he said flatly, grinding out any foolish
desire to dream. Until he was sure he hadn't killed Celia, he
had to carry on alone. He had the blood of one man on his
hands. The thought of having Celia's—it was beyond bearing.
Nor would he risk endangering others.

Developing new flower varieties would take time he might
not have, should proof be found that he'd caused his wife's
death. In pursuing his investigation, Dunstan was acutely
aware that he might bring about his own doom.

Leila swung around, and even through the shadows he
could see the flare of ire in her eyes. "Can't accept my help,
or won't?" she demanded.

"Both." He rose and removed the boiling water from the stove, pouring it over the coffee he'd ground. "You'd fare far better if you went back to London where you belong."

"I could easily hate you," she whispered. "I despise ignorance and prejudice, and you are guilty of both if you think me powerless. I can clear your name."

"Even if I am guilty?" He didn't turn to see how she took that idea.

"You're not," she replied. "I'd know if you were."

If she only knew how much he needed to believe that... He shook his head in refusal.

"I know we think differently," she said with an edge of desperation. "But can we not respect those differences and join our talents to make us stronger?"

Differences? They were too blamed alike in some ways, or he'd not hear her loneliness echoing inside his head. He refused to harm her any more than he already had by his presence. What were the chances of making an interfering Malcolm understand that? "Try respecting *my* wishes and leave me be," he replied.

Pouring his coffee, Dunstan felt a fresh rush of air caused by the lady's angry departure. He raised his eyebrow at the purring cat she'd left behind. The feline merely licked its paws.

"I don't suppose you were a man before she cast a spell on you?" he inquired aloud, needing to hear the sound of a voice in the silence she left behind.

The cat yawned, stretched, and leaped from its perch to the windowsill, turning expectantly and swishing its tail.

～

"Leila—Lily—dear one, where are you?" a high-pitched soprano sang gaily. "I am here to help. Tell me all!"

Smiling at her mother's airy assumption that she could solve the problems of the world when she could barely keep her buttons fastened and her scarves about her, Leila rose from where she was planting seedlings. Hermione fluttered down the hillside, her hat askew and her skirts billowing. As a child, Leila had firmly believed her mother could trail dust in a rainstorm.

Now that her nephew and his companions had departed to chase heiresses in Bath, Leila felt safe enough to dress for comfort. Shaking out her worn gardening skirt, she strolled up the hill more sedately than her parent came down it.

She should have known one of her elders would arrive as soon as Christina and Felicity returned home. It had been weeks since they'd left—and since she'd last seen Dunstan anywhere except in the fields.

The dratted man was avoiding her. She knew he was out there doing his duty, for the staff of gardeners had multiplied and activity in the fields around her had increased daily. She feared that if she intervened, he would pack up and she would never see him again.

Leaving him alone was proving to be the most difficult thing she'd ever done in her life. She was accustomed to going after what she wanted, and she wanted Dunstan Ives. She needed to hear his voice, needed the reassurance of his presence, needed much more than was good for her.

Her feelings for him terrified her far more than she could ever admit. How did people live with these rampaging emotions beating against the walls of their hearts?

"*Maman*, how are you?"

"Harried, dear girl, absolutely harried!" Her mother hugged her. "I don't know why one of you couldn't have a talent for dressmaking. It's all so confusing. I'm sure I don't know which gowns to choose, and the modistes insist we need them all—even the bilious green one."

"The bilious green modiste?" Leila asked with laughter.

Ignoring her daughter, Hermione glanced at the flower garden. "Very pretty, dear, but there's not enough, is there?"

Catching her mother's shoulders, Leila steered her toward the house. She loved her careless, scatterbrained parent. Hermione had a generous heart and a gentle soul. She simply didn't have a lot of brains. Or normally functioning ones, anyway.

"I have to start somewhere, *Maman*. How are the girls? I take it they are arguing over the modiste's recommendations?"

"Christina is quite impossible!" Hermione wailed. "She says it's an extravagant waste of time and money to clothe her since she's already betrothed. Instead, she's been frequenting gambling hells and coffee shops. I vow, I almost had failure of the heart when that Ives boy brought her home wearing breeches."

"I certainly hope the boy was wearing breeches, *Maman*." Leila tried not to hear what her mother was saying. It could very well be the prelude to a plea for her to come home, and that she was determined not to do, despite her homesickness.

"Do not be difficult, dear. You know what I mean. Christina was wearing breeches, and the Ives boy had to drag her home where she belonged."

"Which Ives boy, *Maman*? There are so many."

Hermione waved a frail hand. "I don't know. One of the curly-haired ones, the bastards. Very polite-spoken, I must say. Ninian is having an influence. But that's not what I'm here for. Where is that other wretch, the big, fearsome one? I want a word with him."

Oh, dear, she was in for it now. She couldn't let her mother loose on Dunstan. It was a pure miracle that the marchioness was so thoroughly distracted by her younger daughters' Seasons that she hadn't noticed Leila's flush at the mere mention of Dunstan's name. Malcolms always sensed sexual involvement, or imagined it around every corner.

"If you mean Dunstan, I daresay he's draining a fen or moving a pond or building a fence somewhere," Leila declared. "Shall we have some tea while you tell me everything that is happening in town?"

"No, no, I haven't time, dear." For a small woman, Hermione was strong—and determined. She strode directly toward the carriage waiting in the drive. "Take me to him."

"*Maman*, I don't know where he is," she protested. "He is a busy man. Come in and visit, and we can send someone to look for him."

Hermione tugged a flying scarf into place and fixed Leila with her sharp blue gaze. "I know you would not willingly attach scandal to our name and ruin your sisters' Seasons, but I cannot trust an Ives. If you insist upon associating with a suspected murderer, I must know he's truly innocent."

"Aunt Stella has a hand in this, does she not?" Leila asked

with resignation. Her duchess aunt had a way of knowing about matters in which she had no right to interfere. There would be no arguing with her mother once Aunt Stella became involved.

Leila glanced down at her dirty blue skirt and couldn't help imagining Dunstan's expression when she showed up dressed like this with her mother in tow. She rather thought her flighty mother terrified logical Ives men as much as the reverse.

Hermione clambered into the carriage with the aid of her footman and waited for Leila to enter before answering. "We're concerned, dear, that's all. The girls stopped to visit Ninian, and you know how that is."

Leila did. Ninian mothered everyone, even though she was younger than half her cousins. Leila might resent everything about her angelic married cousin, except it would be like resenting the sun or the moon. They merely beamed down anyway.

"*Maman*, I don't suppose I could talk you out of this, could I? I've already offered Dunstan Ives our help in clearing his name, and he's refused it."

Hermione rapped on the driver's door, and the carriage lurched down the drive. "I don't doubt he did, but you can never know what an Ives is thinking. They're positively inscrutable."

Dunstan was not. He was as obvious as a blizzard on a sunny day. He wanted her, and he hated her for it. Simple. In a billow of skirts and petticoats, Leila flopped down on the seat cushion. "We could ask his maidservant if she knows where he has gone, I suppose."

"That's what I thought," Hermione replied, tugging at an unfastened glove loop.

Leila rolled her eyes as her mother's ancient carriage rumbled down the drive.

Dunstan had warned *her* to stay away, but he hadn't said anything about her mother.

Thirteen

Riding behind a tenant who was returning the oxen to their field, Dunstan noticed a movement on the rocky hillside harboring Leila's cave. His heart lurched and his palms perspired in expectation until he urged his mount past the animals and realized the activity on the hill in no way involved Leila.

He cursed his foolish disappointment even as he identified the climber as a young lad. When another figure pushed up from a prone position near the cave vent, Dunstan's disappointment turned to rage. If some wretch had discovered Leila's bathing place and spied on her—

Slamming that thought to a halt, he pondered the idiocy of caring and scarcely heeded the man who stood on the crest of the hill—until he realized that the Herculean figure silhouetted against the sky was watching him. *Adonis.* Or whatever in hell his name was.

Adonis had first appeared out of nowhere at the marriage of Drogo and Ninian. He'd been appearing and disappearing ever since. He was more Ives than any Ives—with a more prominent nose, a browner complexion, and thicker, blacker hair than any of them. But he hung on no known branch of the family tree.

Unable to ignore the Ives talent for breeding sons—in and out of wedlock—the family had accepted Adonis's appearances with wariness and his departures with relief. Adonis never seemed to care one way or another.

A youthful shout from the side of the hill returned Dunstan's attention to the forgotten climber, and his heart nearly stopped beating. His son, Griffith, hung on a rocky shelf, attempting to pull himself over. What the *devil* was he about? He would kill the boy, if the boy did not kill himself first.

With a lazy stride, the big man on top of the hill sauntered down a path nearest the lad, leaned over, and apparently spoke a few words of encouragement. Heart in mouth, letting the oxen driver go on without him, Dunstan halted his horse at the foot of the rocks to watch his one and only son clinging to his precarious perch. He didn't dare shout at him from down here. One quick move, and the boy could plunge to the rocks below. It wasn't a long fall, just a cruel one. Images of his son's broken, crumpled body obliterated all other thought.

Grasping the last shred of his control, Dunstan dismounted just as Griffith found a handhold and began hauling himself upward. Dunstan gulped a lungful of air and swore that if he didn't keel over in terror first, he would heave the pair off the top when he reached them. Why, by all the planets, had the boy's mother let him loose in the company of the lunatic Adonis?

With careless disregard to his coat and stockings, Dunstan took the shortest route to the top, pulling himself up by tree trunks and through brambles. By the time he reached the crest, Griffith lay gasping for breath in the grass while Adonis looked on with amusement.

"Well met, my friend," he called. "I believe this one belongs to you."

Griffith shot up like a jack-in-the-box. Still gangly and loose-limbed at fourteen, his ragged dark hair falling across his bronzed brow, he scowled at Dunstan with an easily recognizable Ives expression. The boy had been sullen earlier this spring when Dunstan had left him behind with his mother. He had apparently graduated from sullen to rebellious in a few short months.

"Does your mother know where you are?" Dunstan all but shouted. He never knew what to say to his son. He and Bessie lived in different worlds, and he'd long ago come to accept that a child belonged with his mother. Yet he wasn't so certain how much longer Griffith could be called a child.

The boy crossed his arms and glared. Dunstan raised a questioning eyebrow to the man who looked on—the man who always looked on, observing and never participating.

"I found him tramping the road to London." Adonis answered the unspoken inquiry with a shrug of his wide shoulders. "Thought maybe you'd want him more than the rogues he accompanied needed him."

"They were my friends," the boy muttered. "I was fine. You didn't have to interfere."

The big man gently cuffed the back of the boy's head. "They were rogues who could have sold you to the press gangs or employed you as a thief, among other things."

Trying not to let his terror of what might have happened explode into rage, Dunstan focused on the one argument that was capable of making an immediate impression on his rebellious child. "Or they could have been rogues who would terrify me and your mother by holding you for ransom," he added. He knew his son was devoted to his mother.

"What would *you* care?" Griffith retorted, though he had the grace to look guilty.

"You're my son. What do you think?"

The boy narrowed his eyes. "I think you wish I'd disappear, that I'd never been born. That's what I think."

Dunstan crossed his arms and glared back. "I think you wish *I'd* disappear and never been born, and then you wouldn't have to deal with anyone but your mother."

"That's stupid," the boy retaliated. "If you hadn't been born, then I wouldn't be here either. Everyone knows that."

Dunstan lifted his gaze to Adonis, who was grinning openly. "See, he's an Ives. Not stupid, just pigheaded."

"So I've been told, though I've yet to discern the difference." Adonis nodded at a carriage rumbling down the road below. "Why is it that whenever a tempest brews, a Malcolm appears?"

"I might ask that of you," Dunstan replied grimly, glancing in the direction indicated but not recognizing the vehicle. How could Adonis know who was in it?

Ignoring the gibe, Adonis chortled and tugged the boy's collar. "If the Malcolms get you in their clutches, you'll be fortunate if you aren't transported home on a broom."

Griffith looked as if that possibility would be far preferable to reaping his father's wrath. He glanced toward the road with interest.

"I'll leave the two of you to the ladies." In threadbare shirtsleeves, his coat flung over his shoulder, Adonis eased toward the far side of the hill. "I'll catch up with you later."

"Wait!" Dunstan called after him. He despised being in debt to any man, and he owed this one a far greater debt than he could ever repay. To lose his son would have killed him—a sudden insight that hit him with the impact of a runaway carriage. "I owe you. Come to the house, and we'll talk."

Adonis eyed him skeptically. "There's naught we can say to each other."

Dunstan grasped his son's shoulders with both hands and let a tide of gratitude relieve him of the hostility and suspicion he'd harbored for the interfering stranger. "He's all I have," Dunstan said simply, squeezing Griffith's shoulders and telling himself it was the sun causing the moisture in his eyes now that he had the boy in his hands again. "Come for dinner."

Adonis glanced at the approaching carriage, then back to the wide-eyed boy who was soaking up the exchange. "Later, then."

Although he strolled away as if he had all the time in the world, he was well out of sight before the carriage reached the foot of the hill.

"He's peculiar," Griffith muttered.

"You're in a cauldron of trouble," Dunstan retorted, releasing him.

Dunstan had been only seventeen when he'd fathered the lad, eighteen the day Griffith was born. He'd held him as a babe once or twice when he'd been home from school, watched him grow from a distance, but Celia's death had separated them as surely as his marriage had. He abhorred the thought of hurting his child, yet he didn't seem capable of doing anything else.

The role of father did not come naturally to him. Dunstan's own father had barely acknowledged his existence, so he had no good example to follow.

If, as Leila had accused him, he'd been blinded to her nature by his prejudice against society, was it possible that his feelings of resentment toward his father had spilled over into his relationship with Griffith? Just how narrow-minded had he been all these years?

And how the hell could he fix it?

With younger brothers aplenty, he knew how to play the role of older sibling. Perhaps that would suffice for now. "Come along. I imagine you're a mite peckish after that climb. What were you trying to do?"

"Adonis said this is a faerie hill, and I was trying to find a way in." Griffith scrambled down the path. "I'm so hungry, I could eat a cow."

Dunstan lingered a moment longer, watching the ancient carriage rattle and jolt below, and wondered again—how the devil had Adonis known who was in it?

Leila stepped from the coach and eyed the bleak stone front of Dunstan's cottage. "He's not here," she told her mother as the footman assisted her down.

"How do you know that, dear?" Hermione asked placidly, catching her floating scarf and knotting it over her bodice. With a vague gesture, she sent the footman to knock.

Leila always knew when Dunstan was near, but she didn't try to explain that to her mother.

She removed her lace cap from her pocket and tied it in a demure bow beneath her ear so she did not look quite so disheveled in her dusty gardening clothes. She watched as Dunstan's maid appeared in the doorway, then threw them a glance over the footman's shoulder and shook her head.

The footman returned with the message that the master was with the men in the south field and was not expected back until dinner.

"Perhaps we could go to the south field," Hermione suggested.

Catching the scent of new-mown grass carried by a sudden breeze, Leila shook her curls. "He's on his way, *Maman*. Let's go in and have some tea." She strolled up the stone walk. "My mother has traveled a distance," she said to the maid still standing in the entrance. "Might we rest and have some refreshment?"

Minutes later, they were comfortably ensconced in Dunstan's front parlor when the front door sprang open and a dirty young man flew across the threshold, followed by Dunstan in a rumpled and dusty frock coat.

Leila hid a smile at her host's disheveled state. She shouldn't have worried that she wasn't elegant enough for him.

From beneath lowered lashes, she watched Dunstan's surprise and what she hoped was a brief flash of appreciation at her appearance. Then he concealed his expression and collared the lad to perform the necessary courtesies. His son! She'd known Ives boasted of bastards, knew of Dunstan's illegitimate brothers, she'd just never thought to come face-to-face with his son, especially one nearly full grown.

The boy grimaced and looked longingly toward the kitchen. The dark coloring, large bones, and stubborn jaw proclaimed him Ives well enough, but his nose lacked the usual prominence. Leila knew nothing of boys and could not ease the awkward silence that fell after introductions were completed.

"Martha will feed you. Don't go any farther than the kitchen until I come for you." Dunstan sent the boy away and glanced down at his own dirty attire. "I apologize, ladies. I did not expect company. Will you give me a moment?"

"We shouldn't have come, *Maman*," Leila whispered as Dunstan disappeared upstairs.

"Nonsense." Hermione bit delicately into a watercress sandwich and glanced about her. "After years of raising girls, I find these Ives men fascinating. Even the young ones are exceedingly… masculine."

Grumpily, Leila snapped a ginger biscuit and savored the flavor. "You have two full-grown stepsons, *Maman*. And Father isn't exactly lacking in masculinity."

Hermione tut-tutted and sipped her tea. "You know

perfectly well that they have their lives, and we have ours. It is all very polite and not at all the hurly-burly of Ninian's household, where men are underfoot at all hours. The poor dear. With her sensibilities, I cannot imagine how she suffers the chaos of all those big men hurling passions about as if they were javelins."

Sometimes, her ladylike, gentle mother was entirely too perceptive. Contemplating Dunstan and hurling javelins, Leila did not dare reply.

"Martha, I thought I told you to get rid of this soap." An irritable male voice floated down the stairs and through the partially closed parlor doors. "I'll not go about smelling of perfume!"

Leila lifted her gaze to watch a spider spinning a web in a corner of the ceiling.

Martha's murmured reply could not be discerned, but a deep growl carried easily. "Then who put the blamed thing in here? I threw it out this morning."

Hermione raised her eyebrows over the brim of her teacup. "You're making soap on your own now, are you, dear?"

"I must practice on something." Leila wanted to get up and walk out, but that would only raise her mother's foolish suspicions. The marchioness dearly wanted to believe her eldest daughter had inherited her gifts, but Leila had never made a person happy or content or even moderately satisfied with her fragrances, as her mother did. Although, if Dunstan's shouts were any indication, she'd certainly succeeded in eliciting his anger.

"Practicing on an Ives is a trifle untraditional, is it not?" Hermione suggested softly as heavy footsteps clattered down the stairs. "I did warn you about them, did I not?"

Thankfully, Dunstan burst in before Hermione could voice her disapproval of what must be written all over Leila's face. Her family meant well, but they interfered at the most embarrassing moments. She sipped her tea to hide her flush.

"I apologize for making you wait, my ladies. How may I help you?"

Dunstan had smoothed back his thick dark hair, secured it with a ribbon, and donned a frayed frock coat of midnight blue trimmed in the barest hint of silver to match his gray vest. Leila liked that he'd dressed for her, but he could just as well have worn rags. She saw the man inside the clothes, and she quivered at the hungry look he bestowed on her. Physical awareness heated the small parlor far better than any fire.

Hermione cast a disapproving look at Leila and shook her head—whether in dismay or acceptance of the inevitable, Leila couldn't tell.

"It's how we may help you that counts," she murmured, setting down her cup. With her clear, unwrinkled skin, the marchioness looked as wide-eyed and innocent as a newborn babe. "Do sit, dear, and have a sip of tea. Did you know Ninian sometimes speaks with ghosts?"

Leila bit back a grin as Dunstan all but rolled his eyes and gingerly perched on a chair, clearly unaware that her mother had discerned the tension between them and already reached a conclusion.

"And my brother sees stars that are not there," he added, humoring an old lady while taking the cup Leila offered. "We all have our eccentricities."

"Be that as it may," Hermione continued, "we are here to help. My daughters tell me your name has been wrongfully maligned, and we must correct that."

Dunstan's expression reflected his impatience. "I trust you did not travel all this way on a fool's errand, my lady. I have told your daughter I have no interest in what other people think."

Hermione's limpid blue gaze regarded him sorrowfully. "And do you take no thought to others who might be affected? Would you have your son grow up to believe notoriety is acceptable? Would you never visit with your brothers or nephew for fear of tainting them with the gossip? And your mother—your dear, sainted mother! How could you let her suffer beneath this dark cloud?"

"*Maman!*" Leila thought Dunstan might explode if her mother did not cease at once. He gave off a heat so strong that she could feel it welling up, threatening to blast them. The sensation of being drawn into those emotions both frightened and excited her. "*Maman*, you go too far."

"My lady is all that is kind," he said coldly. "But the matter is not easily resolved and is none of her concern. I regret that I've caused anyone to believe otherwise."

"Oh, don't be so damned polite, Dunstan." Tired of the posturing and frustration, Leila slammed down her teacup and surged to her feet. "You've already made it plain that you don't care a wink about others, so pardon us if we don't care what you think. Come along, *Maman*. Let the man burn in a hell of his own making."

He stood when they rose, but she knew he was as furious as he'd been the night he'd invaded her bedchamber.

Good. Maybe he would try it again. This time, she'd be ready for him.

Fourteen

"Have a way with the ladies, do you?"

Still steaming from the encounter with Leila, Dunstan resisted the urge to plow his fist into a jaw that was too much like his own. Adonis sat sprawled on a settee before the kitchen fire, looking very much at home while working a metal puzzle between his nimble fingers.

"I was polite," Dunstan retorted. Noting the remains of bread and cheese on his son's plate, Dunstan dug in the pantry for the same, despite Martha's complaint that dinner would be ready soon enough.

"They're right, you know." Apparently not the least bit embarrassed to reveal he'd been eavesdropping, Adonis stretched his shabby boots across the floor. "You hurt your family by not clearing your name."

Dunstan shot him a warning look and jerked his head toward his son. "There's a time and place for everything."

"Tell your father why you ran away." Adonis lifted his lengthy frame from the bench and dropped the tangled wire puzzle on the table in front of Griffith. The tangle instantly separated into three unbroken hoops. After setting a fresh loaf of bread on the table, Martha glanced over Griffith's shoulder with interest, then returned to her cooking.

"How did you do that?" In awe, the boy poked at the pieces.

Gritting his teeth, not wanting to have this conversation, Dunstan dropped down on the bench across from his son.

Grabbing the hoops, he snapped them into a tangle again. "Why did you run away?" he asked Griffith, repeating his guest's question.

Griffith wriggled uncomfortably. "Just 'cause."

"You will haul all the water for this house for a week as punishment for worrying your mother." Dunstan chewed a chunk of bread and cheese while he planned his words. "She must be frantic. We'll have to send a messenger immediately to let her know where you are."

"I'm staying?" Griffith eyed his father warily.

"That depends. Will you write your apologies to your mother?" Dunstan demanded, knowing how Bessie doted on the boy.

Griffith grimaced and returned to playing with the puzzle. "I left her a note." At Dunstan's silence, he shrugged but didn't look up. "I'll apologize."

"Then you may stay. But you must still carry water for a week."

"*All* the water?" the boy objected. "Do we have to take baths?"

"One every night if you do not tell me what made you run away."

Griffith sighed, rolled his eyes, fiddled with the puzzle, and finally muttered, "The other boys made fun of me."

"That's what boys do. You must taunt them back." Outwardly unsympathetic, Dunstan sliced more cheese, but inside, his gut twisted. Children were cruel. The tormentors of his youth had given up when he'd grown larger than they. Griffith was large for his age, too, so his foes probably weren't just the boys in his school.

"Ma said to ignore them." Griffith stuffed a huge piece of bread in his mouth and chewed angrily.

Adonis snorted from his corner. "Your mother obviously isn't a Malcolm."

"Shut up, or I'll label *you* a Malcolm," Dunstan said without ire. His gaze didn't waver from his son. "Fighting someone your size might quiet one or two bullies, but there's always one more. I trust you're not ashamed of your birth? Your mother explained why we could not marry?"

Griffith scowled. "I'm not a simpleton. Earls' sons don't marry maids. Ma says I should hold my head up and be proud that you acknowledge me, because many wouldn't."

But better men than he would have brought the boy into their home and schooled him to a better life. He'd still been a boy in school himself when Griffith was young, and he'd had no house to bring him to. Later, after he'd left school and married, Celia had had hysterics when he'd suggested it. Life never offered simple choices.

"We were too young to marry," Dunstan corrected the boy's assessment, softening some of the stark reality. "Your mother is a fine woman, or I'd never have left you with her. So what is it you are fighting about?"

Even as he asked the question, he suspected he knew the answer. The argument with Leila had already warned him.

He'd thought that by removing himself from his family's village, people would forget the tragedy of Celia's death and life would go on.

He realized now that he'd been licking his wounds instead of thinking.

"They say you murdered your wife," Griffith muttered at the table. "And I called them filthy liars."

Dunstan knew the boy wanted to hear that his father was not a murderer. He wished he could offer that reassurance. To his shame and humiliation, he could not. He didn't believe himself capable of so heinous a crime, but he had no proof that he didn't murder Celia, and plenty to show that he might have. "Martha, would you excuse us for a minute?"

"I'll be setting the table. Don't you be filling up on bread!"

In the silence that followed the old woman's departure, Dunstan placed his broad hand over his son's slender one, absorbing the warmth and life vibrating there. He couldn't lie, but he couldn't hurt the boy either.

"If I did not kill Celia when she took a lover, do you think I'd kill her after she'd been out of my life for over a year?"

The boy shook his shaggy head. "I called them all rotten liars," he repeated vehemently, "but even the women whisper, and I cannot shut them up."

"The Malcolms have the right of it," Adonis said from his bench. "You must clear your name, not hide here. You're an earl's son. Make society work for you; use what fate has given you for the good of all."

Dunstan shot him a hostile glare. "If I had any chance of proving who killed Celia, don't you think I would use it?" Stubbornly, he resisted telling Adonis that he saved every penny he earned to pay someone to do what he could not.

"Malcolms see and hear things no one else can. Have you asked for their help?" Adonis asked.

"We are talking about women who talk to trees and let birds loose in churches," Dunstan protested.

"It's daunting to deal with the inexplicable," Adonis acknowledged, working another tangled wire puzzle he'd produced from somewhere about his person. "Celia lived in London. Malcolms live in London. They have more opportunity than you to investigate."

"Let them meddle on their own. I don't fit in their gilded parlors. I'm a farmer."

"You're an earl's son," Griffith protested.

"I'm an earl's son who's more comfortable with a herd of sheep than with those bewigged buffoons in London," Dunstan insisted. "At least I can take a stick to a sheep's hindquarters and poke it out of my way."

"With all that wool on their heads and in their eyes, the London gentlemen resemble sheep. Carry a stout stick and treat them accordingly," Adonis advised.

Dunstan swallowed a smile at the image. "I don't think Malcolms would appreciate my poking the ladies."

Accompanied by their guest's shout of laughter, Martha returned to hear this last. "Sir, I cannot think that's a thing to be saying in front of the lad."

The lad was grinning hugely. Relieved to see the boy could smile, Dunstan rose and hugged his cook's shoulders. "How say you, madam? Can a sheepherder shear the woolly sheep of London?"

"Only if he learns to dance, sir," the old woman said with a smile. "I hear the sheep of London are most fond of dancing."

Adonis unfolded his long frame from the settee and performed an elaborate bow before Martha. "My lady sheep, might I pull the wool over your eyes?"

His son's giggles inspired Dunstan to fall in with the insanity. Lifting his cook's hand in the first stand of the minuet, Dunstan made a courtly bow, caught her stout waist, and spun her around.

Griffith howled, and Adonis caught the flustered cook to promenade her down the kitchen floor, singing, "To London we will go, to London we will go, heigh-ho, the merry-o, to London we will go!"

Joining in his son's laughter, Dunstan knew he should be protesting loudly that they would not be going to London soon, but he hadn't laughed in so long, his jaws ached from disuse. It felt as if a thundercloud had temporarily lifted from his shoulders, and he didn't wish to hasten its return.

He'd forgotten how much he enjoyed the camaraderie of his brothers. He'd spent too damn much of his life alone.

If only he could clear his name, he could have his family back again.

But he'd promised Leila his aid here, and he wasn't a man who broke promises.

❧

"It's all very well to laugh and dance and dream, but I can't go to London immediately," Dunstan told Adonis the next day, watching an approaching storm drive leaves into the hedgerows outside his doorstep. "Unlike you, I have a son to support and responsibilities to live up to. I must make arrangements."

Adonis shrugged. "Then make them quickly, or your noble brother's wife will wander off in the company of her fair-haired cousins to investigate what you have not."

"I'll talk to Lady Leila." Frowning and swatting his boot with his crop, Dunstan watched the clouds building on the horizon. "Perhaps she can call off Ninian and the others until I have time to get there."

Talk to Lady Leila. As if the two of them could exchange sensible words without setting off small explosions in the atmosphere. Her appearance here with her mother, looking like Lily and behaving as Leila, had completely unsettled him. He was having difficulty accepting that a lady could be as approachable as the wench in the field.

Laughter rumbled from Adonis's deep chest. "If you believe a stern word from you will call off the ladies, you know nothing of Malcolms. I can't decide whether I'm more amazed that Ives and Malcolms have survived all these years without each other, or that you haven't killed each other already. I wish you well."

The big man strode off into the gloom without a word of farewell. One of his boot soles flapped as he walked, and Dunstan made a mental note to write Drogo and have boots made for the braying jackass. He didn't know how they would deliver the boots, since Adonis disappeared and reappeared at will, but he owed the man.

He owed the man far more than a pair of boots.

He turned and caught Griffith standing warily behind him, watching Adonis depart. "You know you need to finish school," Dunstan said.

With his hair slicked off his face and wearing one of Dunstan's old coats, the lad looked more man than child, until he grimaced. "I've learned all they can teach me."

He'd learned all the village school could teach him because his father hadn't sent him off for a better education. Another faulty decision, Dunstan supposed, and one not easily corrected now. He didn't have the funds to send his son away to school, but he knew an idle mind didn't benefit the boy. Perhaps if he called off his investigator and went to London on his own, he could use those funds for Griffith's schooling. But what would he do with Griffith while he was off to London?

"We'll speak of school later." Deciding he had time to ponder the matter, he sought some means of communicating with his son now that Adonis had left them alone in each other's company. "In the meantime, you can help me work the field. I assume your mother hasn't mollycoddled you into believing you're too good for hoeing."

Had Griffith meant to protest the assignment, he shut up about it after the implied insult. Dunstan had learned one or two things by dealing with his younger brothers. "I've been writing a pamphlet on turnip production. It's on my desk. Go over that for me, reading it for information, then editing for errors and clarification. When you're done, I'll show you what needs doing outside."

The boy nodded. "You're not sending me away?"

"You're my son," Dunstan affirmed, understanding the source of the boy's continuing uncertainty, "and I'll do what I can to be a father. Don't expect a great deal of me. I believe I saw my own father once a year at best, so I have no example to draw on."

The boy's stiff stance relaxed, though the wariness didn't leave his eyes.

Had he done this to his son? Dunstan wondered. Shut him out as he'd shut out all society? If so, Leila had been right to call him narrow-minded. What else had he turned his back on while immersing himself in work?

Guilt from the deaths of Celia and her lover was burden enough to bow his shoulders. Repeating his father's mistakes with Griffith would guarantee him a place in hell. But he knew nothing about how to correct the situation.

He'd have to learn.

Satisfied that his son was adequately occupied for the moment, Dunstan strode out the door. He had an insane urge to discuss his lack of assurance about fatherhood with Leila. He needed a perspective he didn't possess. He wasn't a mathematical genius like Drogo or an inventor like their younger brother, Ewen. He lacked the ability to analyze anything except what grew in the field. Leila was the one who understood people.

But how could he tell Leila he had to go to London?

Fifteen

Upon the heels of Hermione's departure, Staines returned from Bath with a party of his friends. The lot of them galloped and hallooed up the drive, pulling their mounts up short until they reared in protest, laughing when one of the more drunken riders fell backward into the hedges.

Boys! Leila swung from the window in a swirl of skirts. Staines was barely nineteen. She shouldn't expect him to behave with the dignity of his late uncle. But 'twas a pity he didn't find more reserved company.

She'd thought that giving her nephew the freedom of the estate would ease some of his resentment of her and teach him responsibility, but she could see the boy was not so easily appeased.

He might grow into his position in a few years, but she didn't have the patience to endure even a few days of these surprise parties. He had no right bringing a horde of men here without her permission.

Loneliness and frustration assailed her, and she retreated to the converted dairy for solace. Perhaps she ought to give up and return to London, where she knew and understood the rules and could break them with impunity. She knew nothing of growing things, after all. It had been boredom and arrogance to think she could develop new strains of flowers.

If she couldn't create fragrances, she had no reason for existing.

Leila slammed a beaker down on her laboratory table

and reached for a vial, doing her best to divert her morose thoughts. She wanted a distillery of her own. Her talents were limited by using the distillations of others. Men who knew nothing of the correct phases of the moon for picking petals diluted the strength and power of the blossoms.

She wrinkled her nose at the scent rising from the open vial. The grower who had produced this oil had mixed his roses. It wasn't pure. It reminded her of that pest Lord John, whom she'd seen arriving with the rest of Staines's friends.

A tight smile formed as she grabbed an infusion of lilac to blend with the rose oil. Scanning the shelves, she found a tincture of myrrh, and with even more wicked humor, a decoction of camphor. They all reminded her of Lord John, and each scent had a purpose. Lilac for memory, myrrh for purification, camphor for psychic strength. Lord John was about to have his very own perfume.

If he and her nephew hoped to steal her land and her future, they sorely underestimated the will of a Malcolm.

"Leila, I have brought you company!"

Staines's shouts echoed the length of the tiled corridor from house to dairy, but Leila didn't bother removing her apron or checking her cap for escaped curls. For the sake of respectability, while in the house, she wore her wild nest of hair pinned close to her head, but she had no wish to encourage her nephew's illusions by pretending she cared about suitors.

Outside, a cloud obliterated the sunshine, perfectly reflecting her mood.

When her nephew entered the dairy with Lord John, Leila was doubly glad she hadn't bothered with her appearance. Narrowing her eyes, she glared at the pair of them. "You could have given me some warning that you were bringing guests, Staines. It's extremely rude to burden the servants without preparation."

"Build a dower house if you don't like it," he answered with the petulance of a schoolboy. "I thought you'd be glad to have company. How you can endure no society but that of sheepherders is beyond me."

"Sheepherders are polite," she answered shortly, adding the contents of her mortar to the beaker of scent.

"Don't blame Staines for my eagerness," Lord John intervened. "I could not wait longer to see you again."

Leila clenched her teeth. They both must be drunk to irritate her this way. "Staines, you might at least consider my wishes in your choice of company."

"You might at least consider that this is my house and I don't wish to be told what to do!" he shouted. "Come along, John, we needn't stay here to be insulted."

The boy slammed out through the low dairy door, into the rising wind. His lordship didn't follow.

"Your servant's garments become you," he murmured from much too close.

"And I thought you were interested only in my wealth," she answered coldly.

"Who told you that?"

"What does it matter who told me if it's true?"

Rubbing her nose in irritation, Leila decided he smelled of rotting wood and fungus. Perhaps she ought to add dried toadstools to the perfume she was creating for him, to complement his natural scent. Her skin crawled as he hovered closer. She'd never been quite so aware of his shallow character before.

As she opened a box of the toadstools, a wave of dizziness caught her by surprise. Swaying, she closed her eyes to halt the gyrating of her surroundings and grabbed her workbench for support.

Before the swaying steadied, a wavy vision formed behind her eyelids. She sensed a dank woodland, still dripping with rain and smelling of rotting timber and toadstools, but the image forming against that background held her spellbound with dread. A heavily pregnant young woman garbed in the rags of an ill-used serving maid knelt on the forest floor, weeping.

Over her stood a cold young man—Lord John. As the maid wept her heart out, holding her burdensome belly, the young man tossed her a few coins and walked away.

"I'm not some gazetted fortune hunter," Lord John shouted in the real world.

In the world behind her eyelids, the maid's anguished cries rose above the shout.

Nauseous, Leila swallowed hard and willed the painful scene away, but the image in the vision and the man in the room with her blended into one. Clinging to her workbench, she still heard the woman crying even as the scene faded and Lord John's voice intruded.

"Rich or poor, I treat all women with the respect they deserve."

Thunder rolled outside as Leila opened her eyes to see her suitor's open, handsome face. Lord John's blond good looks might normally have diverted this conversation, but the odd vision caused her nerves to crawl. What was wrong with her? Had she just seen this young fool with another woman? That wasn't possible. Perhaps the toadstools were infected with some noxious element. She'd heard of such. But what had she seen?

Shaken by what she'd experienced, Leila felt a scrap of the impending storm take root within her. Inexperienced at handling tempests in any form, she let the storm's tension speak for her. "And what respect is that? The same respect with which you treat maids foolish enough to get caught with your child?"

Shocked, Lord John grabbed her wrist. "Who told you that?" His abrupt jerk on her arm shook the beaker she held, splashing several drops of liquid across his silk coat.

Lightning struck in the distance, thunder crackled, and the musty aroma of a forest after a storm permeated the air. His lordship shrieked, pulling his arm back as if he'd been burned.

"You witch! You've ruined my coat. Have you no idea what it costs to keep up appearances?"

Stunned by his sudden transformation from charming gentleman to ranting madman, Leila could only stare. The appalling fragrance so matched the scent she associated with Lord John that he did not seem as aware of it as he was of the spots on his silk coat.

"Appearances require a great deal of acting, do they not?" she taunted. Speaking her thoughts was so freeing, she gleefully sought another insult. "Does Staines know you and your sister would most likely starve if you couldn't live off his largesse?"

"What do you know about surviving on a meager allowance?" he shouted, then looked startled to realize he'd said such a thing.

"I'd know better than to gamble away my only income," she retorted. "And counting on appearances to win you wealth is as much a form of gambling as playing cards."

Lord John paled as her suspicion apparently hit a nerve. "You bitch! Had you accepted me as your husband, I would have taught you better manners."

Without further warning, Lord John swung his aromatic arm across her worktable, smashing the contents to the tiled floor. Glass shattered and vials spilled until the air reeked of conflicting odors. With a triumphant smirk, he met her gaze. "Do not underestimate my influence on your nephew, my dear. One way or another, I will be master here. You'd best learn proper deference."

Outside, the wind howled, shivering the roof timbers.

Inside, the tempest railing at Leila's restraint finally exploded. Grabbing a broom, she swung with all her might at Lord John's frock-coated shoulders, connecting soundly. "Out, you wicked toad of a man!" she screamed. "Out, and don't come back! I curse the day you were born and every day that you live hereafter. Out, heathen, before you defile this place once more."

Dodging the painful whacks of her broom, Lord John ran before her tirade, covering his head with his hands to protect it from her blows. "You'll regret this," he called, but the rest of his incoherent curses were drowned as he dashed outside, into the sudden downpour.

Standing in the doorway, watching the villain escape into the fog of the storm, Leila took a deep breath of fresh air to clear her head.

Had she just had a fit of madness? Shouldn't a sane person be terrified of what had just happened?

Leila turned her perceptions inward but experienced only a dawning sense of wonder and curiosity.

She'd had a vision. She'd seen Lord John as he truly was. Or at least that's what she thought she'd seen, before she'd gone mad and lashed out without regard to caution or propriety.

It had felt wonderful.

Leila sniffed the vial of toadstools in her hand and tried to summon the vision again, but it was gone. If only she could duplicate the circumstances…

The perfume had so wonderfully mimicked Lord John's character. Perhaps she should attempt to reproduce another perfume for someone else…

Perhaps she ought to find a less explosive personality on which to experiment.

༄༅

Riding out after the storm passed over, Dunstan realized he'd turned his horse in the direction of Leila's mansion when he met up with a local squire going the other way. The man's horse limped, and the squire threw Dunstan a rueful look as he halted in the lane. "Damned mare pulled a shoe. You're late; you'll miss the fun."

"What fun?" It was afternoon, too early for evening festivities and too wet for outdoor ones.

The squire grinned. "Didn't get an invite? The new viscount is a chip off the old earl's block. Hunting mad, he is."

"Hunting?" An ominous premonition formed in Dunstan's midsection.

"Rabbit hunting," the squire exclaimed in jolly tones. "Great fun, if you don't mind the trampling of fields this time of year."

"The viscount is hunting rabbits?" One man alone might avoid turning a newly tilled field into a quagmire. Dunstan couldn't imagine the citified young viscount hunting alone.

"He brought a party of young bucks down with him from Bath, all eager for sport. Better hurry if you want to catch up with them."

Fear and fury welled equally as Dunstan touched his hat in farewell and kicked his horse into a gallop. The damned fool Staines could turn a month's hard work into a wasteland of trampled plants and mud.

Dunstan heard the horn and shouts of the hunt as he raced around the bend. Kneeing his mount, he sailed over the hedgerow into the oxen field, hoping to cut them off. If they stayed to the pastures, all might be well.

His heart sank at the sight of drunken riders galloping around the hill, yelling and whooping, in pursuit of a pack of hounds. He would need a squadron of cavalry to stop that lot. No sane man raced his horse through wet grass in such a manner. They'd all break their necks before they trampled any fields.

They were headed straight for the new flower gardens.

If they destroyed the budding roses or the first shoots of lavender, it would break Leila's heart. The heedlessness of the brats shot fury straight to his brain, and Dunstan kneed his horse into a gallop that would cross the hunt's path at the diagonal. His clod-footed farm animal didn't have the speed of their fine Arabians, but it had the sureness of foot to navigate the slippery ground.

The dogs howled past his horses' hooves, chasing a hare straight through the arched garden gate into the thorny thicket of roses. The recently turned earth glistened with moisture from the storm. The light hare led the dogs away from her young and deeper into the garden. The hounds slopped mud as they ran, trampling the primrose border. Dunstan gritted his teeth at this desecration of weeks of hard work and turned to concentrate on the larger danger.

Intercepting the path of the riders before they could leap the hedges into the rose beds, Dunstan raised his crop to the hindquarters of the lead horse. At his whack, the animal whinnied and reared in panic. The horses racing up from behind split and poured around the first one while its rider cursed and tried to rein in his angry mount. Dunstan didn't linger to help but raced alongside the pack heading for the hedge, herding them as he would sheep, with blows and shouts.

He couldn't steer thousands of pounds of horseflesh all by himself.

He forgot the drunken riders the instant he realized Leila was standing in the center of the muddy rose bed, musket in hand, black curls streaming behind her in the wind.

Alarm struck his gut with the force of an iron fist.

❦

At the first howl of the hounds, Leila had known what Staines and Lord John were up to. Without thought, she'd grabbed the hard pellets of bath scent she'd just finished making and picked up the old musket the gardeners used to scare crows away from her seedlings.

She'd raced to the garden, adding the flower-scented beads to the gunpowder as she ran. Furious, she'd raised the weapon toward the oncoming marauders.

She'd found the first red rosebuds opening just this morning. In a few short days, they would fill the air with rich perfume. Her heart's desire was so close…

Musket lifted, she sighted along the barrel and aimed. This time, she would allow no man to stop her.

Dunstan's furious flight across the pasture stilled Leila's hand. Mad though she might be, she couldn't harm the one man in the whole countryside who had the courage to waylay the drunken lordlings. Even in his unfashionable brown wool, Dunstan was a formidable sight, whipping his brawny arm right and left, lashing the young fools into order. The ribbon of his queue had come undone, and his raven hair streamed behind him.

The hounds rushed howling through the arched gateway, sweeping past Leila's bedraggled skirts. Her hair had fallen down her back in her haste to reach the roses. Could the vandals read her expression, they'd run for their damned lives. She waved her arms and shouted curses, wishing she could turn them all into toads. She imagined magic leaping from her fingertips.

Except she had no magic.

It was Dunstan who deflected first one rider, then another. Had the danger to her garden not paralyzed her thoughts, she would have admired his skill and bravery.

Taking courage from him, she raised the musket over the party's heads, and pulled the trigger. The unorthodox ammunition hailed in stinging bites over hounds, horses, and hunters, fouling the air with a stench of burned bath powder.

If the pellets hit Dunstan, she would apologize later.

Horses screamed in fright. Hounds scampered for the hills. Perfumed smoke curled and choked the air as Dunstan used his crop on another rider who couldn't control his mount, setting the animal off in a different direction. Several of the more drunken hunters fell, landing on the muddy ground with grunts and curses. Leila noted with satisfaction that her nephew was among them.

Her satisfaction lasted only long enough to see a black stallion bearing down on her in complete disregard of the mud or the tender rose canes he trampled. Unlike the other members of the hunting party, this rider appeared to be in complete control of his mount.

Lord John.

Leila's concern had been entirely for her infant plants rather than herself until she registered the young lordling's icy eyes. Trapped in a thicket of thorns, she could not run. Her musket, now empty of ammunition, was useless as anything but a cudgel. Heart pounding in sudden fear, she raised the barrel and prayed she could beat off a ton of galloping horseflesh.

She didn't have to.

Dunstan streaked across the trampled bed to intercept horse and rider. Leila shut her eyes tight in anticipation of the imminent collision. A horse shrieked, a man shouted, and she was abruptly airborne.

Clutching the solid arm wrapped about her waist, she opened her eyes to see the grass flying by beneath her. She was out of the briars. At Dunstan's grim expression as he reined in his mount, she thought perhaps she was in the soup instead.

Leila clung to his coat sleeve, refusing to be let down until Dunstan slid off the horse with her. She didn't want to release him. She'd not thought herself frail until he held her so effortlessly, and now she didn't want to be parted from his strength. She would have been crushed by all that horseflesh if Lord John had had his way.

She glanced at the garden and trembled in rage and grief.

Her rosebuds! Falling to her knees on the edge of a bed of new reddish-green leaves, she hastily checked the canes.

With a cry of hope, she located first one unfurling flower, then another. She scanned the beds that Dunstan had planted in meticulous circles, the arching rose stems that would cover the garden in heavy fragrance and glorious color in less than a month. They were still almost entirely intact.

She gulped back sobs, yet tears of relief rolled down her cheeks. "You saved my roses!" Weak with gratitude, Leila flung her arm around the powerful leg of the man standing protectively over her.

He reached down to help her up. Fighting tears and steadying her shaking knees, she fell into Dunstan's comforting embrace. Absorbing his surprising tenderness, Leila was slow to realize his attention had strayed to the shouting, cursing men who were picking themselves up out of the mud.

She dug her fingers into his solid arm and dared a glance back at her once beautiful garden. The vandals had uprooted tender seedlings, trampled neatly tilled furrows, and wrecked the pergola and paths. But Dunstan's reckless action had saved the roses.

When she looked across the field, her heart froze as she realized that the cost of her stupidity was far higher than a few flowers.

Staines, Wickham, Lord John, and several stragglers were coming toward them, their furious gazes fixed on Dunstan. She knew she didn't possess the physical strength or the authority to save Dunstan as he'd saved her.

He knew it too. He stiffened, but no expression reached his eyes.

"He's a murderer, Leila!" her nephew shouted. "This is what comes of harboring a murderer. We could all have been killed."

Leila could feel Dunstan's explosive tension beneath her fingers, but he didn't strike out as another man might have. He was twice her nephew's size and could have broken him in two. Right now, her fury was such that she wished Dunstan *would* break the brat. But he didn't lift a hand to defend himself.

"I want you off my land," Staines ranted. "You have twenty-four hours to pack and leave."

"I work for the lady," Dunstan answered coldly. "You are not in a position to tell me what to do."

"He's in a position to have you charged with assault and locked up until assizes are called," Wickham shouted. "I can bring charges, if I wish. Everyone knows you killed my brother."

"George was stealing my horses," Dunstan said. "No court of law will condemn me for giving him the chance to defend himself."

George Wickham had also stolen Dunstan's wife, but neither man mentioned that fact, Leila noted as she watched the scene unfold. Nor did they mention that Lord John could have maimed her in his malicious dash across the garden. Staines, possibly at the behest of his grandfather, meant to drive her away, regardless of the consequences.

Driving Dunstan away would accomplish that.

"You killed George and you killed your wife," Wickham shouted, as if Dunstan had said nothing. "And now you have nearly injured Staines. They should lock you away for the safety of society."

While Wickham spoke, Lord John smugly studied Leila in her torn gown, loose hair, and muddied face. Then, with a triumphant smile, he swung on his heel and walked away, satisfied that he'd had his revenge.

Leila watched Dunstan's fingers clenching in helpless fists as he stood there, defenseless against their foolish threats. He'd ridden into battle to defend her like a knight in shining armor, but the guilt festering inside him stripped away the bright armor, leaving a man wounded to the depth of his being.

Somehow, she had to free this valiant knight from his demons.

Turning on her nephew, Leila waved her musket at him. "You are no longer welcome in my home," she shouted, pleased to see him flinch at the reminder that the house and grounds still belonged to her. "You and your wretched friends may play your games elsewhere. I'll have the servants pack your bags and heave them into the drive. Should you ever show your faces here again, I'll call the magistrate and hire men to cast you bodily into the street."

"*He's* the cause of this!" Staines shouted back, pointing at

Dunstan. "Wickham told me what he did to his wife. You can't consort with criminals, Leila! My grandfather will order him arrested."

"Your grandfather isn't here. Leave, before I call in the magistrate."

Furious, the young viscount stomped after Lord John and Wickham.

"My turnips are already planted," Dunstan said flatly as the young lordlings sought their animals. "I cannot leave."

Leila punched the powerful arm that had supported her. "You'd better worry about your head instead of your damned turnips. His grandfather is an earl who can influence the magistrate with just a letter."

She could save his turnips. But she wasn't a witch or a miracle worker. He had to save himself.

The odor of Dunstan's fury was fresh and bracing and far stronger than Wickham's bitterness or Lord John's cruelty. She knew that by working together, they could resolve this crisis.

And she also knew that working with Dunstan Ives could be a danger to her heart and soul.

Remembering his courageous action when no one else had come to her aid, Leila was willing to take that risk.

Sixteen

TAKING LEILA UP ON THE BACK OF HIS OLD GELDING, DUNSTAN wrapped her in his arms as if she belonged there. He wanted the right to shelter this spirited woman forever, protecting her from the world's iniquities.

And he wanted to console himself in the process, he acknowledged.

Not understanding why he felt compelled to protect a woman who possessed far more power than he ever would, he was silenced by confusion.

In his arms she felt slender and defenseless.

She was a Malcolm, he reminded himself, and anything but defenseless. She tilted her chin defiantly, as if she were prepared to take on an army. Dunstan relied on her good sense not to plot anything foolish. The idea of what a Malcolm might do in retaliation gave him cold shivers.

She didn't protest when he delivered her to her door. "I need to speak with you tonight, after I remove these leeches," she told him with her accustomed authority, although her wording revealed a hint of vulnerability.

He hesitated. For the good of all, he needed to pack his bags and leave.

As if understanding his intention, Leila continued before he could reject her plea. "I learned something important today. I'll wear sackcloth and ashes if I must. I promise not to manipulate, seduce, or whatever else you expect of me, but I must talk with you."

He didn't tell her that he wanted to see her so much that he feared himself and not her. Speaking to the butler who appeared behind her, reassuring himself that her loyal staff would take care of her and follow her orders to bar the gentlemen, Dunstan turned to find Leila watching him with eyes shimmering with hope and trust.

She trusted him—a man whom all London despised.

He couldn't disappoint the one woman who believed in him.

Dunstan set his jaw, nodded curtly, and departed. He had the sinking feeling he'd just committed his fate to forces beyond his control.

At home, he ignored Griffith's questions, changed from his muddy clothes, silently shared the supper Martha had left, and cogitated on the enormity of his problem.

He could lose his crop as easily as Leila had almost lost hers.

He didn't waste time questioning the injustice that gave power to spoiled brats. Instead, he applied his formidable thought processes to the dilemma of saving both his experimental plants and his hide, while also protecting Leila's interests.

Dunstan remained confident of his ability to turn the lady's estate into a viable, profitable farm that would feed and clothe an entire village while keeping her nephew in silk coats. But he'd been arrogant in thinking that he could ignore society. Pride came before a fall, and there was his stumbling block.

He couldn't ignore the society he despised, and that despised and feared him in return. They would crucify him. Leila was part of that society. Because of him, they might crucify her as well.

He forced aside a rising panic and proceeded logically, one fact at a time.

A man was only as good as his reputation. It wasn't enough to have a gift for growing things. Stoically, he faced that sorry fact as he had not done before. He'd counted on men recognizing his abilities, but how many would see beyond scandal to his unfashionable achievements? In the eyes of the world, he was a man who had murdered his wife and nothing else.

Had he any true urge to kill, he would certainly have done so today when that nasty bit of venom had threatened Leila.

No matter how hard he tried, he couldn't imagine killing Celia, despite her treachery. He was a grower and a nurturer, not a murderer. He didn't even own a sword, much less a pistol.

But the world had no reason to believe him if he couldn't believe in himself.

While seeing Griffith into bed, banking the fires, and trimming the candlewicks, Dunstan followed the logical progression of that realization. It led directly to Lady Leila.

He couldn't reject her summons this time. He had to tell her his reasons for leaving.

It took no more thought than that to lead him into the warm evening air where insects hummed, night birds called, and his horse nickered in anticipation.

All his senses quickening, he fed the horse a handful of oats, bridled him, and in too much haste for a saddle, mounted and rode to the manor.

He tied his reins to a low tree branch and, not wanting to disturb the household or taint the lady's reputation, took a pathway behind the house to just below Leila's balcony. A candle burned somewhere deep within the room.

Testing a thick rope of ivy, Dunstan pulled himself upward, finding footholds in the uneven stone to support his weight.

No draperies concealed the view through the balcony door as he swung his leg over the railing. A candle flickering on a bedside table illuminated Leila curled upon the turned-back covers, her hair spread across the pillows as if she'd fallen asleep waiting for him. Trying the French door and finding it unlocked, Dunstan watched her turn on her back as he entered. Her blue velvet dressing robe fell open to reveal the gossamer glimmer of her nightshift.

Thinking that she had awakened, he approached the tester bed, but Leila tossed restlessly. He wondered if she dreamed of him as he often did of her.

More arrogance for him to think so.

Tension coiled as he debated leaving without speaking to her.

Uncertain whether he could resist the tentative strands binding them, he hated to wake her.

He rubbed his hand over his face in frustration and caught

a glimpse of bare leg in the flickering light. The lady had beautiful limbs, and curves a man would die to touch.

As a young man, he'd been infatuated with Celia's beauty, but what he felt now was far beyond such a small thing as infatuation. Crossing his arms and leaning against the bedpost, Dunstan gazed upon a woman who had courageously held off a tribe of drunken lordlings, a woman who believed in herself enough to dare hire a man with his black reputation, a woman wise enough to believe in him without question.

A woman who had offered her body and herself without expecting anything in return—not wealth or title or even a declaration of affection.

Leila stirred again, one leg pushing at the covers, and he couldn't tear his gaze away from the sight. Her robe formed a velvet backdrop to rich curves revealed by the sheer gown. Even a saint wouldn't have been able to resist, and Dunstan knew he was no saint.

He sat on the bed's edge and inched her gown higher, caressing a shapely calf to wake her. She merely shifted position so that her toes crept across his knees.

He'd had years of practice in self-control, but this woman defied his ability to maintain it.

Lifting her bare foot, Dunstan kissed her toes, touching them with his tongue. Even the bottoms of her feet smelled of roses, and he gave in to the temptation to suck on a pink delicacy. She moaned and arched her hips.

Enthralled, Dunstan tasted her ankles, ran his fingers up her calf, and slid her gown higher to see if he could elicit further response. The idea that a lady as sophisticated and beautiful as this one might succumb to a rustic like him appealed to his baser instincts far more than he cared to examine.

To his utter delight, she moaned again, muttering something in her sleep. Her hands lifted and dropped helplessly against the covers.

He wanted her to dream of him.

No longer hesitating, Dunstan slid her gown upward, uncovering the perfect curve of ivory hips, flat stomach, and rich midnight curls begging for his caress. The tightening in his groin warned of the danger of this game he played, but after she'd won the round in the cave, he deserved this sweet revenge.

He touched her where she was moist and ready and paused to see if he'd woken her yet. Her eyelids remained closed and still, but her breasts rose and fell at an increased pace.

With a smile of satisfaction, Dunstan dipped his head to taste the honey. He would wake her now.

⚜

Dreaming of rippling water and velvet air caressing her breasts, Leila dug her fingers into the sheets and shivered with arousal. The scent of fresh grass and hot sex returned her to the grotto, where she flew wild and free over the water, knowing Dunstan lurked in the shadows. She could feel the cool, moist air, the heat of desire, and she wanted him desperately—

Heated lips tugged between her parted legs, and she cried out as her body bucked in anticipation.

The dream of the cave receding, Leila awakened with a cry of protest at the unknown invader, but the fire heating her blood urged mindless surrender. The devil had a firm grip, and his tempting tongue had already led her body to the precipice. She quaked and shuddered as he pressed deeper, demanding total capitulation. Without her will, her hips arched to accept it.

The heat dissipated, leaving her hungry for completion. The loss awoke her enough to associate the scent of new-mown grass with the dastardly man lifting his dark eyes to meet hers. The sight of his rugged cheekbones and thick black hair aroused her even more. Bending over and bracing himself on one elbow, Dunstan suckled her breast, sapping any token protest. Before she could recover, his knowing fingers sought and stroked, then opened and invaded, driving all thought from her mind.

Choking back moans, Leila surrendered to waves of pleasure. Her hips drove upward, demanding more, and when he obliged, using mouth as well as fingers, she shattered into a thousand multicolored pieces. He'd overpowered her will, her body, her senses, possessed her in some manner she couldn't comprehend, without losing a particle of himself in the process. He was still fully dressed.

She had no strength left with which to fight when he finally lay down beside her, a possessive hand cupping her breast.

"I'll be leaving for London as soon as I can find help to oversee your gardens," he announced.

"Even if he is the heir, Staines is no longer welcome on this land, so long as I live," she murmured in protest. "I've had their baggage thrown out and ordered the servants to bar the doors against them." Her body still ached, and this disturbing man beside her was responsible. He couldn't leave now that she'd cleared the way for him to stay.

"That isn't the solution. They'll throw slanderous charges at me, and he and his grandfather will find ways to punish you."

Surely he couldn't be as calm as he sounded. Leila reached for the broad expanse of shirt looming over her, undid the ties, and reveled in the sharp intake of his breath. So, he wasn't as entirely in command as he pretended.

"They tried to destroy me." Her voice cracked slightly. "They tore up my laboratory, damaged my flower beds, and would have done worse had you not arrived. I could not let them go unpunished."

"Your laboratory?"

Soothingly, Dunstan kissed her forehead and smoothed back her hair, and Leila fought back tears at his tenderness. She wanted to be angry, to fight and throw things, but she was new to these emotions, and his concern weakened her. Defiantly, she slid her hands beneath the shirt she'd opened, shoved it from his shoulders, and rubbed the hard swells of his bronzed chest, basking in his shudder of desire.

She didn't want to think about the months of work lying on her laboratory floor or of the seedlings trampled into mud. She definitely didn't want to think about how she had failed as a Malcolm, failed her family and herself.

"Why would Staines destroy your laboratory?" he demanded when she rearranged her position to brush his stockinged leg with her bare toes.

"Staines didn't do it," she murmured against his shoulder,

disappointed that he didn't accept her invitation. "He's merely
a child who thought all would go his way because he wished
it so. He wants me to marry Wickham or Lord John and leave
him alone to play in his sandbox."

At the mention of that hated name, Dunstan tensed. "Did
Wickham hurt you?"

Leila's ebony curls brushed his chin as she shook her head.
"Lord John. That's what I wanted to tell you. We were in
the laboratory, and I had an extraordinary vision of him as
a spoiled young man casting aside a pregnant maidservant.
It caught me by surprise, and I spilled a few drops of scent
on him. We exchanged words, and he struck out wildly,
destroying my things. I chased him off easily enough. But I
need to see if I was hallucinating or if I can make the vision
come again."

Steeling himself against his baser urges, Dunstan brushed
kisses across Leila's head, soothing her confusion and unhappiness, while seeking that place in his mind where logic rather than
impulse dwelled. She didn't need his anger at a time like this.

"What kind of scent?" he asked when she curled against
his shoulder.

She chuckled, and Dunstan relaxed his guard. If she wasn't
weeping, he could handle this talking business. He couldn't
remember ever carrying on a conversation with a nearly naked
woman while lying in bed, but he could come to enjoy it.

"I created a wicked scent just for him. I used camphor and
myrrh, and he didn't even notice that he reeked of toadstools."

In the back of Dunstan's mind, a warning bell clamored.
This was no ordinary female he held. This was a sophisticated,
knowledgeable woman of unusual insight whose family could
topple governments with the sheer weight of their wealth and
power. If they chose to use their unnatural gifts as well, who
knew what they could accomplish?

"You created the scent just for Lord John?"

Leila kissed a sensitive place behind his ear, and it took
every ounce of Dunstan's strength to stay with the conversation. She licked his ear, shooting a prickly path of desire clear
to his groin.

So much for her promise not to seduce, although to be fair, he'd started this game. How could one carry on a rational discussion with a woman draped in velvet and little more?

"That's what I do, create scents," she answered matter-of-factly. "It's the reason I want a garden. I have a nose for fragrances that suit people."

More likely, she has a nose for trouble. Dunstan's hand strayed to caress the globe of her breast, but the warning bells clamored louder, and he focused upon her words. "Suit people?" he asked.

Her laughter was low and warm. "Like the one you're wearing. It smells of all the good things of the earth, sun and green grass and heat. I made it just for you."

The soap he couldn't throw away. Firmly, Dunstan lifted her from his side, far enough away to let his lust-riddled brain concentrate. "You bewitch your perfumes?"

"I don't bewitch anything," she answered impatiently. "I have no gifts like the rest of my family. I'm a useless, powerless bit of fluff."

The pain reflected in her assertion caught him by surprise. He couldn't think of any woman less like fluff than this one. "I've never heard of a Malcolm who doesn't have some weird power," he said gruffly, before he could reconsider.

She smacked his arm. Definitely not the right thing to say, he guessed.

"I have an excellent nose for scent. That's my talent, and it's not weird. French perfumers are much sought after for that ability." She propped herself on her elbow, black curls falling over her bare shoulders and breasts. She ran her fingers up and down his shirt, dismissing the subject with deliberate seduction.

He might rouse to the seduction, but his mind had gripped an anomaly and clung to it like a dog to a bone.

"You created a scent for Lord John and saw a vision of what lies behind his genial expression," Dunstan pointed out with inexorable certainty. "Your soap follows me around like a pet puppy. What truth did it reveal to you?"

Her fingers stilled, and she stared at him in the candlelight. Her eyes weren't the fair blue of her sisters' but a deep blue that appeared nearly black in this light. Velvet lashes ringed them, and he had the wild notion that she should always dress in velvet. It suited her, rich and sensuous, crushable and lovely.

"My soap makes you smell desirable?" she asked mockingly.

"Maybe its scent duplicates my fear and prejudice." He answered his own question, following the path of his logic. "I was afraid I'd killed Celia, afraid all the world rejected me, and I hated society for it."

"*My* soap exposed your fears and prejudices?" she scoffed. "And that's why you came here tonight? Because you no longer fear you killed Celia? My, my, that soap must be tremendously good to convince a mighty Ives he's not a fool."

Dunstan laughed aloud at her backhanded insult, but he heard her self-doubt, and the vulnerability behind it. Since his own doubts ran rampant, he had no experience in how to reassure her. "I think more experimentation may be called for," he answered, attempting to think while she wreaked havoc with her manicured fingers. "But it is entirely out of character for Lord John to lose his temper with a woman he wishes to court."

Releasing him from torment, Leila fell back against the pillow and stared at the canopy. "Men do stupid things. Just look at you. I'm lying here at your disposal, and all you do is talk."

He chuckled and leaned over and kissed her jawline, relishing her quiver of desire.

She responded by tugging his shirt out of his breeches and running her hands beneath it. He must either roll out of bed now, or give in to the lady's demands.

Respect their differences, she had asked of him that morning after they'd made love, and he'd told her to go away. Her suggestion didn't sound so foolish now. Plants required both sun and rain to grow. It took both man and woman to make joyous love. Perhaps it took an agronomist and a witch to find Celia's murderer or to discover the source of her Malcolm power. Two sides of the coin to make one whole.

She was courageous and strong and independent. She believed in him. He need only believe in himself, and she was his for the taking.

With a woman like this to encourage him, he could do no less.

Heart rising to his throat, self-doubt threatening to engulf him, Dunstan quit fighting the magnetic pull between them.

"Tell me," he whispered, nibbling her ear. "Does the seed we planted grow yet? Shall we expect a harvest after Christmastide?" He placed a hand low on her abdomen to tell her he wasn't talking about gardens.

Dunstan's arousal pressed against Leila's hip, his kisses whispered promises she willingly accepted. Why did he not simply take her instead of asking questions for which she had no answers?

Impatiently, she ran her fingers over the firm muscles of his chest, but a small stirring of panic lodged in her heart as she counted the days. She couldn't be pregnant, not in one try, not after all the years of failure. But he was an Ives and she was a Malcolm…

Defiantly, she ran her hands down his abdomen and lower, pressing her fingers to the thick shaft straining at his buttons. She smiled at his muttered curses. "I prefer to tend that field myself," she answered sweetly. And she wanted it plowed. Now. She squeezed and elicited another curse.

"It only matters in how I take you," he muttered. "I would not risk getting you with child if we escaped the first time."

The flutter of panic spread deeper, but she wouldn't give in to it. She might be a poor excuse for a Malcolm, but she could deal with whatever this Ives chose to give her. Her fingers pried at his breeches buttons, and this time he didn't halt her. He groaned when she finally gripped his heavy flesh, and a thrill of triumph excited her. She might be a failure at many things, but not in seduction.

"I'll take the risk," she murmured, pushing his shirt up to kiss the broad, lightly furred chest looming over her.

"I'll not." He rolled off, leaving a cold draft where he'd warmed her just seconds before.

She would have gone for his jugular except she could see he was tugging off his shirt and sitting on the bed's edge, yanking off his boots. Her insides clenched in anticipation. Powerful muscles rippled across Dunstan's back as he stood to remove his breeches, and she wished she had more candles when he faced her. She'd known he was a large man, but her breath caught in her throat at his impressive size.

She wanted to cry in protest when he slipped a sheath over all that potent flesh, but it would have been a foolish objection. Instead, she reached up and tied the silken strings. He had Griffith and didn't need children of her, just the pleasure she offered. She could accept that.

His kiss, when it came, removed any regret.

"You're the most fascinating woman I've ever met," he murmured against her lips, pushing the velvet robe from her shoulders. "You should wear blue more often. It suits you as well as red." He possessed her mouth with his tongue, forestalling any protest.

Leila couldn't have spoken had she wanted to. She drank in the soul-satisfying nourishment of his kiss while his talented fingers cupped and tantalized and caressed until she nearly burst with anticipation. She dug her fingers into his strong upper arms, but Dunstan merely positioned his weight over her and continued to leisurely explore her mouth, filling her lungs with his breath while his hands mastered her in other ways.

Pushing her bodice aside, he deepened his kiss. With his fingers plying the aching peaks of her breasts, Leila moaned in submission. She traced her hands over his chest, sought to return the pleasure, but he was well beyond her command. He parted her legs with his knees, and she could not have stopped him had she tried. She didn't try.

"I don't think I can share you with another man as I did Celia," he murmured, releasing her mouth and trailing feathery kisses across her cheek. "Tell me I'm the only man you need."

It frightened her to think in such terms, of being possessed solely by one man again. She was her own woman now. He had no right—

"Tell me and mean it." He bent and licked her nipple, and she arched upward. She could feel the brush of his arousal where she needed him, but he merely slid back and forth, searing but not satisfying.

She ignored his demands and wrapped her legs around his waist. He was stronger and held back, poised at the brink but no closer. "Leila," he warned, "say it now, or we'll both lose. I know you're not Celia, but I cannot share you."

The thin edge of control in his voice shattered her will. To be desired so intensely by this man was well worth whatever she gave up. That he needed only her promise to trust her said more than she dared hope. She knew he would not ask had he not decided to stay with her and help her. Joy and relief added to the intensity of her desire. "I could never want another," she agreed, with terrifying honesty. "Please."

"Ah, Leila…" He kissed her and whispered, "Thank you," so quietly that Leila wasn't at all certain she'd heard him.

Without warning, Dunstan lifted her so he could remove the gown tangled around her waist. Taking a rosy nipple in his mouth, he positioned himself between her legs. She whimpered, but not in protest. The refined lady arched her hips in womanly demand, and he was lost in the warm cream of soft curves and her scent of roses and cinnamon.

Her musical cry pleased his ears as he gripped her thighs and sheathed himself in the passage moistened by his earlier love-making. He nearly passed out from the rush of blood as her inner muscles tightened around him. Clinging to his restraint, he deepened his invasion until she bucked and writhed and wept beneath him. He knew that by taking possession of her like this, he bent her to his will. Power was a dangerous thing. They would both be better off recognizing their limits now.

"You had best not use your spells on me," he murmured, pressing a kiss into the curve of her jaw and throat.

"They're not spells," she protested breathlessly.

His thumb rubbed the place where they were joined, and she protested no more.

Unable to hold back as her muscles gripped him, he withdrew slightly and plunged again. Her shuddering cry of pleasure was his undoing. With a few short strokes, he drove her to screams of joy. As she quaked beneath him, Dunstan released all the hunger and need in a prolonged explosion of ecstasy.

It was simple, really, Dunstan decided as he collapsed into Leila's welcoming embrace. He was in control so long as he did what she wanted.

Seventeen

"I AM NOT A FREE MAN, LILY," DUNSTAN REPEATED, FASTENING his shirt in the feeble light of a candle lit from the guttering flame of the last one. "I have a son who deserves my attention, and you have a reputation to uphold. I cannot stay with you."

Sitting up against her pillows, Leila pulled a sheet over her breasts as if that gesture could hide the stabbing pain of his departure. Tears threatened to spill from her eyes as she watched him prepare to leave her. She'd thought he *understood*. How could he abandon her like this? The bed was already turning cold where he'd lain beside her. Hadn't what they'd just done and said meant anything to him? She hid a tear by lifting the pillow still containing his heady scent and burying her face in it.

"You called me Lily," she murmured, focusing on the one thing she might settle between them. "Does that mean you prefer to think of me that way and not as a viscountess?"

Dunstan unexpectedly placed one knee on the bed, cupped her jaw with his big brown hand, and stroked her cheek as gently as if she were a child. As she peered from her pillow, he offered a wry, self-deprecating smile that charmed her. "Lady Lily," he corrected, "both lady and beautiful flower. But I need to think of you as my employer now, if I'm to do this right."

"Do what right?" she whispered in confusion. How could he act as if she mattered to him and yet still leave her alone?

He pressed a kiss to her forehead and stood up again, returning to dressing, speaking as if he were her estate agent, and she were behind her desk. "I'll give orders to have your garden repaired and reassure your tenants that you, not Staines, are in charge, but I must leave for London as soon as possible."

"You would go without me?" she asked incredulously, finally grasping what was happening.

Dunstan drew on his breeches and tucked in his shirt. "You may go or stay, as you wish. I have no say in the matter. I'm just telling you I'll be going to London, and I must take Griffith with me. I'll no longer neglect him."

Leila flung off the sheet in a rage as she fully understood why the infuriating man meant to abandon her. *Now* the damned man had decided to clear his name! Why the devil hadn't he said so? Or asked for her help?

Heaven forbid an Ives should ask a Malcolm for anything. How the *devil* did people get through each day while driven up and down by these insane currents of emotion?

"What do you intend to do," she asked in impatience, "parade through ballrooms demanding to know who killed your wife? Hold them at bay with explosives until someone admits his guilt?"

She hunted for her robe amid the covers, noting with satisfaction that Dunstan's hands had halted over his buttons. Defiantly, she swung her naked posterior practically in his face.

"I have no idea what I'll do," he admitted. "I'll just do what needs to be done."

"Ha! You can't hide the smell of fear, Dunstan Ives. The idea of London terrifies you. You'll be lost without me."

She pulled on her robe and tied it closed before turning around at Dunstan's unusual silence. He stared at her, his breeches still partially unfastened. "What?" she demanded. "Do I have feathers in my hair? It's not as if I rise from bed in perfect elegance, you know."

"The smell of fear?" he asked with a degree of care.

She gestured impatiently and sought her brush on the vanity table. "It's nothing to be ashamed of. Yours is merely a fear of ignorance. Now Lord John…" She shuddered as she attempted to restore order to her curls. "The man simply reeks of hostility when he's upset."

"What else do you smell on me?" Dunstan asked, returning to fastening his breeches.

Leila smiled at his reflection in the mirror. "Do you seek compliments, sir? What do I get in return? Will you tell me my eyes are as dark as midnight?"

"Leila," he answered, coming up behind her and removing the brush from her fingers, "don't tease. I've not the patience for it. Tell me what you smell on me, good or bad."

She frowned at his tone but shrugged. "You smell of the same scents as the soap I created for you. You smell of the earth, and sunshine, of confidence and power. And of desire," she added wickedly. "Your desire is more powerful than that of most men. Now, you must return the favor. What am I?"

"A witch," he said deliberately, holding a strand of hair in one hand and gently tugging the brush through it with the other. "You terrify me. All I can see are your striking looks. I sense your arrogance and some instinct I cannot define or understand, but I can't smell fear, Leila."

"That's because I'm not afraid." She took the brush back and pulled it more rapidly through her hair.

"People can't smell fear, Leila," he said softly, gripping her shoulders, forcing her to look up at their reflections. "I can't *smell* desire, even if I know you feel it."

"Don't be foolish." She glared at the reflection of his shirt, wishing he were a shorter man so she could see his expression in the mirror. "How would you know when I feel lust unless you smell it?" Something in the way he gripped her shoulders warned her that this conversation was important to him. She stiffened and turned to read his face. Surprise and something less identifiable floated in the air between them.

He'd tied his hair back in its queue, emphasizing the squareness of his beard-stubbled jaw. His open shirt revealed a strong brown throat and an enticing mat of dark curls that her fingers itched to touch. Rather than looking piratical, he looked fascinated—by her.

Dunstan's lips curled up at one corner. His whole demeanor

changed when he smiled, creating a bone-melting charm. Her heart lurched beneath that look, and she wished they could tear off their clothes and return to bed. He wished it too. She could smell it. She eyed him suspiciously.

"I know you feel desire," he said, "because I see it in your eyes and in the way your lips grow wet and inviting and in other ways I can't specify. But I can't *smell* desire any more than I can smell fear."

"Well, I always knew Ives were peculiar creatures." She turned back to the mirror, but the brush lay limp in her hand. Whatever the scent that he gave off now, it made her uneasy.

He chuckled and ran his hands up and down the velvet arms of her robe. "Not as peculiar as Malcolms, my dear. Tell your mother sometime that you smell fear and desire; see what she says."

Her family accepted eccentricity without a second thought. Caught up in their London whirl, they took Leila's social graces for granted and paid little heed to the subtleties of character and emotion she discerned. Only Dunstan had done that.

People truly didn't smell fear? She simply couldn't conceive of it. She'd known the scent from a very early age. She'd learned to recognize scents from her mother's pomanders, hadn't she? The candle recipe that stimulated desire was one of her mother's most popular scents. Surely people smelled the lust in it.

"You're being ridiculous." Her uneasiness didn't disappear, but Leila fought it. "If you don't want me to go to London with you, just say so. Don't make fun of me."

"I daresay I'll poke fun at you as often as you do me, but this isn't one of those times. I'm quite serious, Lily. Other people don't smell fear or lust, or earth or sunshine. If we hold soil to our noses, we smell dirt, but I don't think that's what you meant, was it?"

"No, of course not." Growing irritable, she slapped the brush back on the table. "Dirt smells like dirt. Some smells good, some smells musty, or whatever, but it's dirt. Smelling of earth isn't the same. It's… it's…" She struggled to define exactly what she meant by earth. It represented all the good, solid things of this world, life and fertility and… the language lacked the right words.

"It's something you smell that others do not." Dunstan leaned over and placed a blood-tingling kiss on her cheek. "Let us respect our differences, as you said, and learn from each other."

"We disagree on everything," she reminded him. "How will we do that?"

"I have no idea, but it certainly won't be boring," he answered, caressing her cheek. "Believe in what your nose tells you, Leila. Your family can do what others cannot because they *believe* in things others call foolish. Trust your instincts."

He released her to finish dressing. Leila clung to the warmth left by his hands as long as she could. Desire seeped through her veins, and in its wake came a powerful need to explore.

Trust her instincts.

Instinct said she belonged with Dunstan Ives, that he could teach her far more than she would ever learn on her own.

Yet as a child, she'd been taught to distrust Ives men, that they had nothing to offer Malcolm women.

Trust instinct? Trust an Ives?

Eighteen

UNCERTAINLY, LEILA FACED THE BOY OPENING THE DOOR OF Dunstan's cottage later that morning. He was nearly as tall as she, with a shaggy head of dark hair and striking black eyes just like his father's. It was one thing to take a man as lover. It was quite another to face the reminder that he had a family and a life beyond the one they shared in their private moments.

Was she selfish in coming here to ask that he delay the trip to London just a little longer? She needed more time to experiment. He needed more time to learn how to behave in the city. She wanted him to take her with him, but she didn't know how to suggest it.

She'd never had to share her actions and decisions with anyone, or ask them to share theirs. Even when married, she had made her own choices. Uncertainty made her nervous.

Wrapped in her own concerns, she'd done her very best not to think about Dunstan's family, but something told her she'd better confront that reality now.

"Lady Leila?" the boy asked with the same uncertainty that was unsettling her.

"And you are Griffith." He reeked of rebelliousness, but his age offered a better excuse for it than that of her grown nephew. "You are the perfect image of your father. Is he here?"

"Yes, m–my lady," he stuttered, glancing back into the house.

"Griffith, who is it?" Dunstan called from the interior.

Pleasure shivered down Leila's spine at the sound of his

voice. When he appeared in the room behind Griffith, her skin tingled with remembered joy. The loneliness inside her opened up and welcomed the man walking toward her with such masculine assurance. It was rather an intimidating experience not to restrain her feelings as she was accustomed to doing, yet she smiled in trust and relief at his approach, and a pleasurable warmth enveloped her at the appreciative look he offered in return.

"Let the lady in," he ordered. Still in stockinged feet, he shrugged on his vest and dug at his disordered hair to straighten it, as if he'd just arisen from bed—as he probably had, given their late hours the night past.

Griffith stepped aside, and Leila brushed by him, unable to take her gaze from the man who had taught her so much already, the man from whom she could learn so much more. Anticipation spilled through her like that of a child at Christmas. "I have been thinking."

A wry smile curled Dunstan's handsome mouth. "Always a dangerous proposition. Griffith, you had best run outside before the lady explodes."

The boy looked from one to the other of them and didn't budge.

"I don't think warning him of an impending explosion is the correct incentive to send him away," said Leila. Such silliness, yet she couldn't help tweaking his Ives nature. "Tell him nothing will explode, and he'll wander away in boredom."

Griffith bit back a grin and edged toward the kitchen. His father chuckled and relaxed. "All right, so we know each other too well. It's probably not wise to teach him Malcolm tricks either, so perhaps we should go outside."

"I'll hoe the turnips," Griffith offered, skipping backward, still watching Leila. "You're prettier than Aunt Ninian," he blurted.

"Out!" Dunstan roared, not turning to watch his son. "Or you'll haul water the rest of your born days."

Reddening, the boy turned and ran.

"Shame on you," Leila chided, sweeping past him to examine the sparse furniture of the parlor, suddenly nervous at being left alone with a man who knew her better than she knew herself. "He's a charming boy. You must teach him to speak properly, not bellow at him as if he were a beast in the field."

"That's what we beasts do—bellow. You shouldn't come here unescorted. It doesn't take long for tongues to flap."

She waved a dismissive hand. "Let them flap. There are things of far greater importance on my mind."

He stood behind her but didn't touch her. She wished he would. She knew why he could not. The trust between them was still too fragile.

She stood here, in his house, knowing they could never share it. She shivered and crossed her arms to cup her elbows.

"I'm listening," he informed her gravely.

"Thank you for that." She lifted her chin and stared at the wall. "Before you go to London, you must teach me…" She hesitated, uncertain how to ask for what she wanted. "I wish to learn if there is any truth about what you said last night. About my ability to smell emotions."

His fingers brushed her shoulder, briefly, reassuringly. "That might be easier done in London. You need people on whom to experiment."

She took a deep breath of relief. He understood. She swung around and dared face him. She didn't read censure or disbelief or amusement in his eyes. He truly believed she had a gift, and he respected it. She could not describe the heady delight bubbling up inside her. Impulsively, she stroked his newly shaven jaw.

"I lived in London all my life and knew nothing of my gift. Perhaps I need to be isolated to fully realize it. Help me."

"How can I possibly help you when merely being associated with me could ruin your reputation?" he asked. "I cannot stay here. I must take Griffith back to Drogo and do what I can to clear my name."

"If you go to London, you will bellow and frighten people, then become angry and wring necks to achieve what you want," she predicted. "And nothing will be resolved."

He scowled and looked ferocious. "I know how to behave."

"You crushed a cigar on Lord Townsend's foot," she reminded him. "You lurked in the conservatory and steamed.

What are the chances that you'll discover anything worthwhile talking to plants?"

He rubbed the back of his neck and stared at her with a look of growing incredulity. "I'll never hide from you, will I?"

"Did I read you correctly?" Leila asked in delight. "Am I right?"

"You want me to tell you yes and unleash another demon into my life?" he asked.

She beamed. "Teach me to experiment, and I shall teach you to behave."

"You'll what?" he roared.

"Teach you to behave." Demurely, she lifted her skirts and moved toward the door. "We can go to my laboratory. Perhaps you can teach me how to duplicate my vision. Ninian is arriving shortly. It would be rude of you to run away before she arrives. I've arranged a small dinner in her honor. You can come and learn social manners. We'll share our differences. It will work."

"You've cast your wits to the wind!" he shouted after her. "I'd rather become a monk and take a vow of silence than be forced to sit through another of your dinners!"

She heard his irresolution through the bluster. He wanted to work with her but simply couldn't admit it. She threw him a dazzling smile over her shoulder and slipped out the cottage door. Maybe she would manipulate, just a wee bit.

The stubborn ass needed it occasionally.

❧

"Lily, Lily, we're here, Lily!" Gay, childish voices called down the stone corridor leading to the dairy where Leila was experimenting with a scent for her maid. "Mama says you may have us until eternity or the end of summer, whichever comes first. What's eternity, Lily?"

Leila smiled at the question from her youngest cousin, then let the smile fade as she sensed another presence.

Setting her latest perfume on a shelf, she unfastened her apron strings and waited for the onslaught of laughing waifs racing toward her.

She lifted and hugged the little ones, crouched down and

kissed the older ones, inhaled deeply of innocence and imagination and the fearlessness of inexperience. They chattered
of horses and coaches and the puppies they'd seen at the inn,
and Leila listened to them all while conscious of the woman
waiting patiently in the doorway, her young son in her arms.

Ninian.

Short and fair as a Malcolm should be, Ninian had been
raised in the far north of England, too far distant from the rest
of the clan to ever be one of them.

Leila blinked at that realization, and glanced up at the
serene young woman. She had always been envious of her
younger cousin, but she saw their similarities now. Despite
her powerful gifts, Ninian still stood outside the family circle,
as alone as Leila felt.

Ninian raised a questioning eyebrow as Leila came forward.
Apparently she had communicated her feelings in some
manner that only Ninian could read. Lifting Ninian's young
son into her arms, Leila gestured for the lot of them to precede
her. "Tea and tarts for everyone," she cried. "Off with you,
ladies. Wash your hands, and tell Nurse to wipe the dirt from
your faces."

Chattering children raced ahead, leaving Ninian and Leila
to saunter behind them. In Leila's arms, Ninian's one-year-old
sucked his thumb and looked about with typical Ives curiosity.

"You should have children of your own," Ninian said.

Remembering her panic of last night when Dunstan had
forced her to think of such things, Leila attempted to stay
calm. No one knew exactly how accurately Ninian could read
emotions because she was usually discreet, but Leila would
rather not take any chances. "Should, or will?" she asked,
hiding her anxiety.

"It's much too early to tell of a certainty," Ninian replied
without any sign that Leila's question was unusual. "Grandmother
was very vague about when babes have souls. Until they do,
there is little to detect but their physical presence."

"How soon did you know?" Leila tried not to hold her
breath. It had been not quite a month since that first magical
night in the faerie cave. Her courses were late.

"I passed through a faerie grove and felt Alan's soul enter me." A smile teased the corner of Ninian's lips. "I think Grandmother sent me an Ives soul on purpose."

"Then it probably entered kicking and screaming," Leila replied, her mouth drying as she considered all the ramifications of an Ives growing inside her.

They'd reached the front foyer, where she must let Ninian go to her chamber and freshen up, but she couldn't bear to dismiss the subject yet. She needed to know if she could possibly be carrying a child after all these years of barrenness.

She rather thought that was why Ninian was here.

Ninian offered one of the dreamy smiles that made her Ives husband swear she departed from her head and visited other planets. Reaching for her son, she beamed benevolently at Leila. "The kicking and screaming will come for you when your big bad Ives learns he's sired a girl."

She ascended the stairs, tickling the child in her arms, leaving Leila hanging on to the newel post with both hands.

Nineteen

AT DAY'S END, AFTER ASSIGNING THE RESPONSIBILITY OF temporary stewardship to one of Leila's more promising tenants and reassuring the workers that all would continue as usual, Dunstan returned to the cottage with the intention of checking on his experimental crop. He hungered to return to Leila's bed tonight, but the risk of discovery was high now that Ninian had arrived. He was too damned tired to keep climbing vines. Besides, finding protectives out here wasn't easy. And no matter how Leila protested, he didn't dare risk a child while a hangman's noose hung over his head.

He needed the peace of growing things to settle his confusion.

Hurrying around the cottage, he stopped cold at the sight of Griffith sitting in the middle of his field, a pile of turnip tops in his fists.

Rage and panic roared in Dunstan's ears. *How many of the plants had the boy pulled up?*

He'd worked a lifetime developing that seed! The plants were irreplaceable.

Dunstan bit his tongue, stiffened his back, and marched into the field to investigate.

"Problem?" he asked without expression.

Griffith raised a blank countenance. "I'm weeding, as you told me to do."

"I trusted you to know the difference between weeds and

crop." The boy wasn't dumb. Had he pulled up the plants in anger?

"And if I don't? Will you send me away?" Griffith demanded.

Dunstan had been planning to send him to Drogo when he left for London. Now he took a deep breath, capped his anger and impatience, and sat down in the middle of the field with his son. "I told you, I'm no good at being a father. You have to spell out what's bothering you in simple terms I can understand. You're my son. That doesn't change if you pull up a whole field of turnips. What's wrong?"

"You're planning on going to London without me. I heard you."

"I'm planning on leaving you somewhere safe while I look for a murderer," Dunstan explained.

"You never wanted me;" Griffith interrupted with a cry of protest. "I'm just an expense to you."

Dunstan didn't welcome this irrationality when he already had more problems on his plate than he could handle. Children had damned bad timing. Dunstan propped his head in his hands and stared at the dirt. "*Celia* didn't want you. You know that. It's hard for women. And your mother didn't want to give you up. I tried to do what was best."

Inexplicably, an image rose in Dunstan's memory, one of Griffith as a toddler falling down in his haste to greet him during one of his infrequent visits. Dunstan bit back a curse of regret. At the time he'd wanted to lift the boy and hug him, but he had felt too awkward to try. And now the boy was too big to hug and too old to give his trust easily.

He'd missed out on the simple love of those early years. He needed to find some way of making up for it now. "I was young and stupid, but I wanted you. I just didn't think I deserved you."

"You wanted *her* more than me," Griffith interpreted. "Just like you want these turnips more than anything else. And they'll die, just like your wife did."

Out of the mouths of babes.

Reaching over, Dunstan grabbed his son's hair and tugged him closer. Griffith struggled, but that only served to hurt him. Dunstan waited until the boy quit resisting and leaned closer. "Crops aren't people. They're important, but not as important as you. And from now on, you come first. Is that what's bothering you?" Dunstan released the boy's hair, stood up, and pulled Griffith up with him.

"Lady Leila will come first," his son answered flatly. "You'll send me off to school so you can have her."

Ah, one more reason he needed to stay home and not see Leila. *Devil take it.*

"I'll send you off to school, but not because of the lady." He needed a drink. He needed food. He needed his son to believe in him. Dropping his arm around Griffith's shoulders, Dunstan steered him toward the house. "I hereby give you permission to punch my arm if I ignore you, all right? But sending you to school is for your own good; it's not ignoring you."

"I'm a bastard. They'll laugh at me."

"You're an Ives bastard. The school is well accustomed to us. Besides, I can't afford to send you just yet. You'll have to hoe turnips until I can. So, tell me why you pulled up the turnips."

"They have grubs. I read that Michaelmas daisies prevent grubs." Griffith still sounded wary, but he didn't move from Dunstan's loose embrace.

"Michaelmas daisies?" Dunstan imagined a healthy field of turnip greens surrounded by scented flowers come fall, and despite his exhaustion, he grinned. "I'll tell the lady you're on her side. Maybe she'll hire you instead of me. The two of you can plant rhododendrons in the wheat and lavender in the potatoes."

"You don't believe me." Sullenly, Griffith tried to jerk away.

Dunstan wrapped his arm around his son's neck and knuckled his hard head. "Did I say that? We'll grow great blooming bouquets out there if we must. Those turnips are our future, and I'm trusting you to help me with them."

Griffith turned to him with a reluctant light in his eyes. "Me? You'll listen to me?"

"Why not? You're my son, aren't you? Who else would be smart enough?" With a smile, he shoved the boy toward the house and the tantalizing aroma of roasting beef.

The boy whooped and ran for the door.

The boy's excitement eased some of Dunstan's hurts, enough to keep him searching for the right thing for his son.

It would be a hell of a lot easier if someone would present a scholarly pamphlet on what the right thing was.

❦

Following Griffith through the kitchen door, Dunstan let the boy run ahead as he halted to investigate the scented letter waiting on the washstand. Opening it, he scowled at the lavishly scripted invitation to tomorrow night's dinner. Leila might as well offer temptation on a silver platter. An entire evening watching her breasts pushed up for viewing but not touching—the damned woman knew how to drive a man to his knees. A week ago he would have resisted without a qualm. Now...

He threw the invitation down to follow the sound of voices. To Dunstan's surprise, Ewen, his younger brother, sat sprawled on the settle before the fire, the gears of the kitchen clock spread about his feet while Griffith watched him with absorption.

"What the devil are you doing?" Dunstan demanded, pouring a mug of ale before Martha could fetch one for him.

"Showing Griffith how to fix clocks." Ewen cleaned a gear with an oily rag and, with intense focus, sharpened a prong.

"You rode all the way out here to show him how to fix clocks? Have the lot of you decided I can't survive on my own?"

Surprised, Ewen looked up from his task. "Why would we do that? You're more adept at surviving than all of us put together."

Mollified, Dunstan threw his leg over a bench and sat down. "Damn right. So now tell me again why you're here."

"To learn more about canal locks. I needed to see if the one in Northumberland could use the same kind of gears they use here, or if we need to design a new system." Ewen handed Griffith a knife and let the boy screw one part to another. "I've invented a better method of opening the locks, but the gears I've found aren't strong enough."

Since the nearest canal was fifty miles from here, Dunstan figured Drogo was behind the side trip, but he wouldn't argue the point. Ewen lived in a future world of his own imagining, when he wasn't charming women into bed, but he had a level head when he applied it. "Can't help you there. I can provide you with turnips and perfumes, but not gears."

"Perfumes?" Ewen lifted a handsome black eyebrow, then a wicked grin spread across his face. "There's a girl at home who would enjoy perfume."

"*Malcolm* perfume," Dunstan warned. "And Leila would have to meet your lady friend before she could create one for her. She's experimenting and would consider it a favor if you asked for one for yourself."

Ewen's eyes immediately narrowed. "Malcolm? I thought you were planting turnips, not consorting with the lady."

Pretending he was busy working on the clock and not listening, Griffith earnestly applied his knife to the screw. Dunstan wasn't fooled. He tilted his head to indicate his son and didn't take up the argument. "You'd probably be better at helping her than I am. She's setting up a distillery to use once I have the gardens in place."

"A distillery!" Ewen's eyes lit with interest. "For perfumes?"

"For scents. I think the perfumes are mixed later." So, he wasn't being entirely truthful. He wasn't lying either. He just wanted Leila to have an opportunity to experiment on Ewen. His brother always appeared cheerful and carefree, but there was far more to Ewen than met the eye. Would Leila be able to discern that?

Did he really want to know? The idea of a woman who could uncover one's deepest, darkest secrets was altogether frightening.

"I could spare another day," Ewen agreed. "Do you think the lady would let me take a look at her distillery? Perhaps I could make a few suggestions."

Smack into the trap he fell. Trying not to show his satisfaction, Dunstan nodded. "I'll send a note. We'll see."

To make Leila happy, he could wait one more day.

Leila smiled in pleasure as the three Ives males strode into her parlor. It was pure fate that had led Ewen here just in time for her dinner party. She desperately needed to speak with Dunstan, but she realized he might not have come without Ewen.

She'd hesitated about inviting Griffith, but this was a rural gathering. His social education shouldn't be neglected as his father's had been.

Heads swiveled as the men entered. Several of her male guests gravitated in her direction, some in her defense, others out of self-protection, she suspected. Looking over the company from his imposing height, Dunstan scowled at their antics, then offered a polite nod to Ninian. So, he wasn't totally hopeless. He only despised idiots.

Smiling at that realization, Leila turned her attention to the other two late arrivals. Ewen surprised her by beaming with good cheer at her appraisal. She rather thought a charming Ives a contradiction in terms.

The boy stood near his father's side, and Leila admired the way Dunstan squeezed his son's shoulder reassuringly. The obstinate man was as terrified in this setting as Griffith, but he refused to show it.

If she actually carried a child, it was comforting to know its father was a good man.

Taking the responsibility of social arbiter firmly in hand, she advanced on her new guests as if they were royalty. "How marvelous that you could come," she trilled. "I've heard so much about you." She offered her hand to Ewen and batted her lashes at Dunstan. "You must introduce me, sir. I've been all that's impatient to meet the brother who captures lightning."

Dunstan scowled at her foolery, but he performed the introductions with the expertise he must have been taught at his mother's knee. The man wasn't untrained, just contrary, Leila reflected, offering him her best smile. She felt a heartbeat of triumph at his startled but softening demeanor.

"I must introduce this charming young man to a friend of mine." With skill, she separated Griffith from his all-male family. Divide and conquer was a tried-and-true tactic.

She introduced him to one of her younger neighbors and

left the two young people in easy conversation amid the adult whispers flying about their heads.

Turning back to the doorway, she noted Dunstan had already appropriated a glass of brandy from her butler, and Ewen had gravitated to the prettiest young woman in the room. Good, keep the one occupied while she took care of the other. Dunstan Ives was easily the most fascinating man here, and despite their wariness, not one of her female guests had failed to notice his impressive physique.

Although she preferred to pull him aside and keep him to herself, she had promised to train him in better social manners. All he really needed was to relax.

"He's shy," she whispered into the ear of a baronet's sister, who was nearly gawking. "Talk to him about your horses."

"I couldn't," the girl whispered back, horrified. "He's terrifying."

"He's *terrified*," Leila corrected. "If you know anything at all of turnips, he would be forever grateful." Firmly, she steered the girl in Dunstan's direction.

"Turnips?"

Leila didn't give her a chance to question more. "Miss Trimble, the Honorable Mr. Dunstan Ives. Miss Trimble has one of the finest stables in the area, sir. She knows all about horse breeding." All right, so mentioning anything so indecent as breeding was inappropriate, but she couldn't help it. The man needed to be jolted out of his self-centeredness. The young lady's gasp of horror ought to bring out the protective Dunstan.

It did. He immediately looked sympathetic. "My brother is interested in developing his stable," he said smoothly, giving Leila one final glare before turning his attention to the crimson-faced girl. "Perhaps you could give me some pointers."

She'd known she could rely on him. The man had "responsibility" engraved on his forehead. Now, to other matters.

"He's a murderer," Sir Bryan Trimble hissed as Leila drifted to his side. "You place us all in grave danger by dealing with the likes of him."

On her scale of importance, the young baronet did not register higher than an ant, but he might make a good test subject. Fair hair thinning, jowls already forming, he had the air of a man who considered himself to be the height of rural society. He would be looking for a wife to add to his consequence. Leila smiled and patted his arm. "You are so kind to think of our welfare. With men like yourself about, I feel quite safe. I've been testing new scents from my flower garden. Would you care to try one?"

Eagerness replaced his disapproval. "Of course, my lady, anything to please you."

The man she would really like to try her perfume on was Ewen Ives, but he was much more complex than the man on her arm. Start simply, she decided.

She escorted the baronet to her laboratory, and he watched in perplexity while she mixed scents and chatted. If he'd thought she'd brought him here for a bit of wooing, he was sadly disappointed, but he had the courtesy not to show it.

Perhaps she ought to teach Dunstan such manners.

Then again, she rather liked the surly Ives just the way he was. Smiling at that thought, Leila added a hint of rosemary to her concoction, then tested the fragrance. Raw, but she didn't have time to let it age.

She offered her guest the bottle into which she'd poured the fragrance. "Would you care to test it?"

Before the baronet agreed or disagreed, a shadow dimmed the candlelight, and Dunstan loomed in the doorway. No scowl hinted at his thoughts as he propped his big shoulder against the wall, crossed his legs at the ankle, and lifted a brandy glass to his lips. "You should invite the rest of your guests for the evening's entertainment," he advised.

Everything that was feminine inside her went pitty-pat and melted at the smoldering look he turned in her direction.

"I cannot offer every guest a perfume of his or her own," she said sweetly. "And Bryan is a special friend. Perhaps, if you're very nice, I'll prepare a scent for you," she teased.

Not liking the loss of her attention, the baronet grabbed the bottle and tilted a puddle of fragrance into his palm, then slapped it to his sagging jowls. Unwittingly, he riveted both Leila's and Dunstan's attention with that gesture.

"A stable!" he cried in fascination. "It smells like my favorite London stable."

Leila sniffed the fragrant aroma. "Manure is an honest smell, sir," she asserted cautiously. The scent seared her nostrils, and to her astonishment, she recognized the familiar sensation of the room spinning. Excitement and fear assailed her as she grasped the worktable to steady herself.

The laboratory faded into a stable, an expensive one. High ceilings, a carriage with prancing horses... A woman's laugh. Familiar, hauntingly so. Fury welled, strangled by helplessness and humiliation—not the woman's emotion, but that of the man she mocked...

"Leila, are you all right?" Strong hands gripped her arm, gently retrieving her from emotional torment.

She blinked and glanced around. No stable. No woman. She leaned into Dunstan, letting his heat and strength ease her confusion. The baronet merely looked puzzled.

"Did you know Celia Ives?" she demanded of the young man, having no idea why she asked.

Behind her, Dunstan stiffened, but the laughter still echoed inside her head—tauntingly familiar laughter. Celia had been a vain, shallow creature who enjoyed flaunting her beauty and humiliating those she thought unworthy of her. A rural baronet would be an object of ridicule to her, however suited to her country origins he might be.

"I may have met her in London," the baronet answered warily.

"In a stable?" Leila replied, then mentally slapped herself. She was too new at this. Had she really felt this young man's anger and humiliation? Or did her perfumes just give her headaches and strange notions?

The baronet's obvious discomfort answered her question, even when he refused to do so. Bowing, he made ready to depart. "If you will excuse me, my lady, I'd rather not discuss the dead."

Before Leila could throttle the fool, Dunstan intruded. "Poorly done, sir. The lady gave you a gift. The least you can do is offer honesty in return."

The baronet looked startled, rubbed frantically at the smell on his face, and appeared ready to bolt.

"I'd offer you my soap," Dunstan said in an effort to sound sympathetic, "but the lady believes I smell like dirt."

Leila almost giggled at the baronet's distress. He glanced at her, then at Dunstan, and without another word, raced from the room.

"That was unkind," she chided. "I do not think you smell like dirt any more than I think Sir Bryan smells like a stable."

Dunstan slanted a glance down at her. "What was that about Celia?"

"I don't know." Leila tried to recall the moment, but it was already fading now that the scent of straw and manure had departed. "I don't understand what is happening to me. I thought I heard her laughing, and it felt as if Sir Bryan was the one she laughed at."

Dunstan snorted. "Undoubtedly so. He's just the sort she would humiliate. If you heard Celia, then you must be a witch."

In wonder, Leila tried on the appellation like a much-desired cloak. A witch.

Maybe she was.

She didn't understand the how or why of it, but joy infused her as an immense world of opportunity opened before her.

She could hear and see people who weren't there.

Her mother would be so proud.

Twenty

DUNSTAN WATCHED LEILA'S PROGRESS THROUGH THE PARLOR in the aftermath of her interminable dinner. He'd sat on the edge of his chair throughout the meal, fretting over her decision to include him among her party, while her damned guests ignored him and chattered about her perfume experiments as if they were some new parlor game.

He had to admire Leila's determination in going after what she wanted, even as he worried every single minute she spent experimenting on other men. What if others reacted like Lord John? What if she stumbled onto some deep, dark secret in the same way she'd stumbled onto the baronet's memory of a stable?

Dunstan had attempted to pin down Sir Bryan and question him about Celia, but the man had given his excuses and fled. Did he dare trust Leila's strange perception and harass the man for more answers?

He couldn't imagine Celia spending time with a mere baronet—a rural one at that, admittedly, though, she'd had a fancy for fine horseflesh.

The vicar gazed at him as if awaiting an answer to a question, and Dunstan stumbled back into the conversation, muttering something inane as Leila led Ewen away. His heart thudded off-kilter at the picture of Leila and Ewen together.

"I'm of the opinion that plants have male and female parts as animals do," Dunstan said, intruding on the vicar's monologue against the "unnatural" practices of scientific sheep breeding. "Plants breed just as indiscriminately as cats if left untended. Excuse me, I must speak with my brother."

Leaving the vicar speechless, Dunstan attempted to veer behind a gaggle of ladies and escape the room. With a rustle of silks and satins, the ladies swung en masse to surround him.

"Is it true, sir," one of the bolder matrons demanded, "that bagwigs have gone out of fashion in London? I cannot persuade my Harvey to part with his."

One of the younger women tittered and hid behind her fan. The older ones watched him expectantly.

Feeling like an insect pinned to cloth and framed behind glass, Dunstan grimaced, rolled his fingers into fists, and said the first thing that came to mind. "Wigs attract roaches, madam. If you'll excuse me…"

He escaped amid gasps and flapping fans. No doubt he'd said the wrong thing again. Why did the fool women ask such questions if they didn't want his opinion?

Stretching his shoulders against the constraint of his coat, Dunstan eluded the rest of Leila's guests and escaped in the direction of her laboratory. He should ask her to create a magic potion to make him comatose if he was to parade around London seeking Celia's killer. He wasn't cut out to be courtly.

He burst through the dairy door in time to catch Ewen and Leila laughing intimately, and the ugly serpent of jealousy coiled and spat in his chest. He wanted to wrap a possessive arm around the lady's slender waist, kiss her lovely nape, and defiantly mark his claim.

He had no right to do any such thing.

A subtle scent of fire and smoke and things he couldn't name wrapped around him as both dark heads turned in his direction, still laughing. "I take it Ewen's scent is that of a clown?" Dunstan asked.

"Your brother has a very charismatic soul," Leila said playfully, appropriating Dunstan's arm and leaning against him as if she belonged there. Her powdered hair brushed his jaw, and her swaying skirts wrapped around his leg, enfolding him in their exotic scent.

Dunstan watched Ewen's reaction to their familiarity. His younger brother—charismatic soul that he was—had a way with women. He'd been born flirting with the midwife.

Ewen merely grinned and winked at Dunstan. "I think she means I'm damned to hell and is too polite to say it."

The subject of hell was much too uncomfortable for a man accused of wife murder. Dunstan shrugged and tried to pretend he didn't have a ravishing Malcolm's breast pressing into his arm. "Have you examined the distillery?"

"He says he can improve upon the design," Leila answered for Ewen. "By this time next year, I could have my own rose distillations," she said with a sigh of ecstasy.

"I'll sketch something for you," Ewen promised. "May I have this fragrance? I rather like it."

"It smells of wizardry," Leila acknowledged. "Fitting for a mechanical genius."

"Wizardry does not have a smell," Dunstan reminded her.

"I think she means I smell like grease," Ewen said cheerfully, taking the stoppered bottle she offered. "But I like the smell. I'll test its appeal on the ladies."

He slipped the vial into his coat pocket and strode off whistling before Dunstan had the presence of mind to object. He didn't know if he wanted to object, not with Leila hanging on his arm.

"Will you stay tonight?" she whispered, studying him from beneath thick lashes. When he did not answer, she released his arm and gravitated toward the table.

Dunstan felt large and oafish in her slender presence, but he knew it was her elegant silk and powdered curls that distanced him. He told himself he needed that distance; otherwise he was a doomed man.

"I don't think it's wise of me to stay," he said carefully.

Moving vials into order, not looking at him, Leila nodded. "Could we not... have a *special* place? Somewhere where we could just be us?"

Dunstan groaned at the temptation she dangled before him. Knowing she felt as he did would bring him to his knees faster than tears or promises. He could resist histrionics, but he had no experience with wistful desire. "It will only make matters worse," he admitted, praying that she understood without an explanation.

"I thought men... I thought it was easier for you." She lit a candlewick, and an odor of vanilla wafted on a breeze. Tense, she studied him, her dark eyes wary. "Do men not take mistresses and discard them with abandon?"

"Not this man," he snapped, his resistance fraying.

She looked unhappy, as if he'd confirmed what she already knew. "It doesn't seem quite fair," she murmured. "Half the population of London flits from bed to bed without a care. Lovemaking is a mere entertainment for them."

"And London is where you think I belong?" he asked dryly.

She shook her head in a flurry of powder and curls. "No. I'm just confused. I know you desire me. And I desire you, as I have never desired another man. It's a new and frightening experience for me. I cannot understand why it is wrong to act on our desires."

Dunstan rubbed his hand over his face and wondered if he was an even bigger fool than he thought. He could have the lady in his bed. Why deny himself the pleasure?

But he was beyond the point of being satisfied just to have her in his bed. He needed far more of her than that, far more than he could ask of her, given his circumstances.

The knowledge that he wanted more than a brief affair clawed his insides raw.

"I'm an accused murderer with no prospects for the future, Leila. All I can offer you is a fine romp in bed and a bastard in your belly. I'll be leaving for London shortly. I suggest you think hard about what you're asking of both of us."

"I *have* thought hard." She leaned against the table and hugged her elbows as if she held herself back. "I suggest *you* rethink if you believe you can leave for London without me."

The idea of tarnishing her reputation with his appalled him. He couldn't take her to London with him.

But succumbing to the desire to possess her one more time, Dunstan bent to kiss her defiant lips. The taste of Leila's eager tongue soothed his battered patience, stripped away his cold restraint, and nearly undid him.

Before he could capitulate to his baser nature right here in her laboratory, with all her guests outside, Dunstan reluctantly stepped away, leaving her gripping the table behind her and looking stunned.

"We have no future," he reminded her, "and you can't go to London with me."

She merely stared, waiting, her kiss-stung lips moist and beckoning, her breasts rising and falling with the passion he'd provoked.

He could no more resist her temptation than turnips could resist rising to the sun. "Tonight, in the grotto," he agreed, then swung on his heel to go in search of a stiff drink.

Leaving Leila contemplating the empty place where he'd stood, her heart pounding, her head spinning.

She was on the brink of discovery. A precious, valuable gift was hers to explore.

A child could be growing inside her, a child that both terrified and thrilled her.

She had everything she'd ever wanted at her fingertips. Why, then, was it not enough? Why must she seek out an Ives who made it evident he merely desired her body and no more?

She wanted to discuss her discoveries with the man who had valued the talent she'd ignored because it came too easily. She wanted days and weeks to design a garden she could share with the man who could best appreciate it.

All her gifts were meaningless without that someone to share them.

Looking at the empty beaker she held, Leila abruptly set it aside and hastened back to the gathering in her parlor to see if Dunstan had left.

The parlor was full of people yet empty of Ives.

And she realized that loneliness was far worse when she was denied the presence of the one person in the entire world who could understand the secrets of her heart.

❧

Having left Ewen taking apart Leila's distillery and Griffith perusing her library, Dunstan sat on an overturned wooden

pail in the midst of the leathery green leaves of his turnip bed
to clear his muddled mind from an overdose of socializing.
With his evening vest and coat unfastened, his fancy dress
shoes caked in mud, he lifted a mug of malt to his mouth and
drank deeply.

Lily waited for him in a magical grotto where she would
ease his aching desire.

Leila wanted him to take her to London.

He couldn't bear harming another woman. He couldn't let
a woman come between him and his son again. Need warred
with responsibility.

Dunstan wiped his mouth on his coat sleeve and glanced
around at his green companions. "You'll make some young
sheep a good fodder," he told them. "Better fodder than I am,"
he continued stoically. "Sam Johnson must have been talking
about me when he said, 'If a man don't cry when his father
dies, 'tis proof he'd rather have a turnip than his father.'"

He raised his mug to the splinter of new moon. "I don't
want my son to prefer turnips to me," he told it. He wasn't
drunk, he knew, but who cared if he made an ass of himself
out here? His little green friends didn't. A man could think
straighter with a mug of whiskey and silence, and for once in
his misbegotten life, he intended to think before he stepped
off the deep end.

"Of all the men she knows, why would she want me?" The
one man she couldn't have, he knew. "'Woman's at best a
contradiction still,'" he quoted, but the turnips didn't respond
to his erudition. He sprawled his long legs out in front of him
and contemplated the real reason he sat in this field when a
beautiful woman awaited him.

"I don't need witchy Malcolms telling me things I don't
want to know." He sipped more carefully, waiting for his
green friends to argue that one. They didn't.

"She'll make me as daft as she is," he agreed with the
night breeze. "Manure! She smelled manure and heard ghosts
laughing." He scowled and drained the mug. She'd heard
Celia laughing. Could he live with that? What else might she
see or hear?

"Problem is…" He let the statement dangle. "Problem is, I don't think I can leave without her."

The moon didn't howl in disbelief. His green friends didn't turn their backs on him, although he thought they shuddered a little. He shuddered with them. Or maybe his head spun. Leila had that effect on him. He could control turnips and steer his own path, but he couldn't control Leila any more than he could steer the stars.

"She only wants me to share her bed," he told the breeze in confidence. He wanted the breeze to tell him to go ahead and seduce her. Instead, it spoke with Drogo's voice, reminding him of what he could not forget. "She can't have babes, she says. Anyway, it's not as if I'd have to support one," he argued. "She could afford to wrap it in silk batting and hire it the best teachers. But she's barren."

His green friends laughed at him. Malcolms were never barren.

Rising to stand legs akimbo in the middle of the field he'd thought would be his future, Dunstan propped his hands on his hips and shouted at the moon, "Am I supposed to stew in my own damned juices?"

The moon didn't reply.

London and the search for Celia's killer loomed before him. He had to clear his name, if only for his son's sake.

And to protect Leila.

Leila. She waited for him, a beautiful woman offering answers he wasn't prepared to accept.

He could no more leave her waiting than the moon could stop from setting. He didn't think he could prevent Leila from going to London with him either, not when it was what they both wanted, even if it wasn't wise.

Perhaps he could publish his own quote: "Wisdom goes out the door when women walk through it."

Twenty-one

FLOATING NAKED ON THE QUIETLY BUBBLING WATER OF THE grotto's pool, watching the waning moon through the opening above, Leila was thankful for the peace of this private place.

Her hair drifted like seaweed on the clear water. The night breeze carried the country fragrances of hay and someone's chimney smoke. The smoke reminded her of a cozy winter's night. Relaxing, giving in to her senses, Leila let the vision of a crackling kitchen fire rise behind her closed eyes. Instantly, she smelled roasting chestnuts and heard her mother laughing merrily with Cook while discussing the newest babe's first mashed potatoes. Filled with comforting sights and sounds, her vision enticed her to embrace the changes ahead—a baby of her own to love and hold. Contentment erased some of the turmoil the evening had stirred.

The vision popped as another scent intruded, and her heart beat faster. She wasn't surprised when a shadow appeared on the mossy bank above her.

"Join me," she invited, not caring how Dunstan took the invitation. She needed his strength tonight.

He didn't hesitate for long. She watched him drop his coat and vest upon the rocks, then sit to remove his boots. Dunstan Ives was probably the most challenging man she'd ever met. She respected his intelligence far too much to manipulate him now, but given his earlier words and action, she had a strong notion he would react negatively to her news.

A little voice said she had no reason to tell him. She didn't know anything of a certainty. Ninian could be wrong.

She knew what would happen if she didn't speak. The desire between them was like a palpable flame drawing them together as Dunstan slipped into the water. Her nipples already stood at attention, and her womanly parts tightened in expectation.

The same womanly parts that could be harboring a tiny Ives seed, growing with every passing minute.

For all her experience and sophistication, she was as frightened as any young maiden at the changes that might be happening within her.

She heard his splashing as he approached, curled her arms around his brawny neck when he caught her waist. Weightless, she lifted her head for his kiss, and he obliged.

She could feel Dunstan inside her with no more touching than his tongue to hers. His arms tightened, his big hands caressed her wet skin, their lips melded, and their tongues twined. The faeries that dwelt here sang in harmony.

A shadow passed between them, and somewhere deep within her womb an old soul found safe harbor and a new life quickened.

She carried Dunstan's child. Leila knew it with the instincts of her ancestors.

Dunstan gently carried her from the warm water to the mossy bank. Steam rose around them, yet she shivered as his broad frame covered her. Naked and inches apart, they could no more stop what would happen next than a nightingale could change its song.

"You're bewitching me again, aren't you?" he murmured, pressing kisses down her cheek.

"Am I? I didn't mean to—" Fascinated by such a notion, Leila decided that if bewitching Dunstan was her one and only gift, it might actually be enough.

"I didn't mean to do this again, not until my name is clear." His mouth located the sensitive place behind her ear.

She sighed at the luxury of this ache he created. The moss beneath her was softer than feathers. She smoothed her fingers over his muscled chest and slid them downward. She didn't want to stop now. What she had to tell him could wait. "I've thought about it, Dunstan, just as you asked. If there's no future for us, let us have the present."

To her joy, he didn't argue. He touched his forehead to hers in a gesture of surrender. "I'm trusting you to know your own mind. You have no idea what a leap of faith that is for me."

Leila dug her fingers into his silken hair, absorbing the strength of his heartbeat where he leaned against her. "We're neither of us children any longer. There's no harm in what we do here."

"There can be if we bring a child into the world," he said in reply, slipping downward to address her breasts.

Leila gasped as Dunstan tugged delicately with his mouth, and a river of desire ran into her womb. She tried to part her legs, but his knees held them firmly together. Terrified that he would deny her again, she responded without thinking. "It doesn't matter." She clutched the solid flesh of his upper arms, her fingers not quite circling them while she tried to think and talk and melt all at the same time.

He took one last tug and reluctantly halted, gazing down at her with wary eyes. "It doesn't matter?"

He knew. He was too much a part of the earth not to know. Knowing wasn't the hardest part, though. Leila tugged at his arms, trying to force his mouth upward, to hers. "Talk later," she protested. "I need you inside me right now."

Accepting the inevitable with masculine fortitude, he didn't argue. With lingering kisses and slow caresses, he opened her, explored what was his to claim, and entered her with all the care she needed right now, with a care that had her weeping helplessly even as she cried out in rapture.

With the fatalism of the doomed, Dunstan closed his eyes and poured his life's fluids deep inside the woman he'd made his in some primal manner he had yet to understand. Briefly, the pleasure of his release overrode all else. Emptying his mind with his seed, he collapsed against Leila's generous curves, kissed her throat, and rolling onto the mossy bed, pulled her on top so he needn't suffer the torment of separation just yet.

Letting pleasure wash through him, he absorbed the sensation of molding his hands to Leila's soft buttocks. He nipped her shoulders with kisses, trying to cling to mindlessness. The press of her fertile belly against his abdomen tortured him into awareness.

The possibility of having a woman like Leila in his bed every night exceeded any dream he'd ever allowed himself, trespassing on the realm of the impossible. He was a practical man not inclined to fantasy. He tried not to think about what she hadn't said, but the little green worms gnawed deeper. He had to know.

"Tell me now," he demanded.

"Ninian says it's a girl," she whispered. "You needn't worry about raising a son. Malcolms can take care of girls."

Dunstan wanted to laugh out loud at the outrageousness of her declaration. He wasn't a simpleton. He knew it was bloody well too soon to know if she carried a child for certain. He knew children were easily lost in these first months. To actually declare the sex of the child while it was no more than a sprouting seed bordered on the insane, not to mention the illogical.

But because it was Leila, he didn't laugh. He didn't try to imagine a faerie girl-child in a household of brutish male Ives either. One giant leap at a time.

Eyes closed, he let the silken glide of her skin flow over him. "I don't suppose Ninian knows if our daughter will be as beautiful as you?"

He'd startled her, he could tell. Opening one eyelid and peering out, Dunstan caught the laughter welling up and curving Leila's lovely lips. A rare treasure, indeed, was this black-haired Malcolm. Now, if he only knew what to do with her.

She sprawled across his chest, dug her fingers into his hair, and covered his stubbled jaw with kisses. "You're a lunatic. I have found the only Ives in existence who is insane enough to understand a Malcolm. How did this happen?"

Dunstan leaned his head back and opened his eyes fully to stare at the sliver of moon above her coal-black curls. A trick of the light sparkled starlight in her hair, and for the moment he believed in faeries.

She felt so real against him, so soft and hot and perfectly formed to ease his needs. If they never left the cave, he would be content.

"Fact of life?" he guessed. "Fluke of nature?" He tried telling himself that Ives men didn't have daughters, but that didn't work any better. The woman in his arms might misunderstand or confuse things, but she wouldn't lie.

The woman in question nibbled his beak of a nose. "You're avoiding thinking about the child, aren't you? You're very good at shutting out what you don't want to know."

"I figure you and Ninian and the rest of your witchy family will think about it for me. A man has few choices once the seed is planted." He realized he'd spent a great deal of time feeling helpless and out of control since Leila had entered his life. One more event over which he had no say seemed a natural state of existence. In a way, lack of control had a liberating effect.

She bit a little harder, and Dunstan avoided her sharp teeth by sitting up and positioning her on his lap, although he wasn't completely ready to take her yet. The thought of an Ives girl child had shaken him. He couldn't remember an Ives ever having a girl.

She watched him through worried eyes. "Are you taking this seriously, or just humoring me?"

Dunstan narrowed his eyes so he could see only the shadows of the cave and not the full globes of the breasts pressed into him. That didn't help his concentration any. "Which would you prefer?" he asked, playing for time.

"You believe me, don't you?"

"I believe it's too soon to know, that it's impossible to tell, and that Ninian is an addlepated lackwit who ought to mind her own business."

She pinched him beneath the arm, and Dunstan swatted her hand away.

He opened his eyes fully and drank in the beautiful wanton pleasuring his lap, and terror took root alongside joy in his heart. "I have nothing but a bog and my name to offer you," he said simply. "How can I rob you of everything for which you've worked so hard? As Adonis would say, it's a wee bit difficult to do the right thing when you cannot ken what it is."

She wrapped her arms around his neck and leaned her head against his shoulder. Dunstan held her there, reveling in her slender curves, wishing she were his to wake up next to every morn.

With Celia's ghost haunting him, how could he ever trust himself with another woman? What if he lost his temper and hurt Leila or the babe? And how could he ask her to give up her garden for him?

They were so wrong for each other that even the gods in heaven must be shaking their heads in dismay. He had nothing to offer but guilt and disgrace, and she would sacrifice everything if she took his name.

He'd known terror a time or two in his life, but nothing to compare with what faced him now. He knew what duty and responsibility as defined by society called him to do. And he knew that way lay disaster.

No matter what he did, he would hurt her or their child.

"We can wait," she whispered. "It's too soon, as you say. Ninian could be wrong."

He grunted in disbelief. "Aside from the fact that the blasted she-devil is never wrong, and that we knew full well we planted the seed beneath a full moon, how do you see it?"

"I've never had a child," she murmured into his shoulder. "I've rocked my little sisters and cousins, felt their milky breath against my cheek, listened to their baby cries and laughter, and never even thought to have a child. I planned on being the elderly aunt to my sisters' children, admiring and admonishing from afar. I'm rather taken with that role."

A new fear yawned deep in his gut, and Dunstan clenched her tighter. He didn't doubt that Malcolms had the power to make an unborn child go away if they wished. He wouldn't believe it of them, but he knew they could. He quit breathing, afraid to answer her.

"I'm terrified," she whispered. "Women die in childbirth,

and I'm not ready to die. I don't want to grow huge as a mountain so I can't bend over my laboratory table."

Dunstan sought words of reassurance, but before he could find a way to convince her that she wanted his bastard, she spoke again.

"But it's not too soon for me to know that your child's heart beats within me, and as terrifying as it sounds, I desperately want to keep her. Will you let me?"

The breath practically exploded from him, and he hugged her harder in relief. "A child belongs with its mother—and its father." One more reason he must clear his name.

"I will never deny you your fatherly rights," Leila said with a seductive smile, then distracted him by burying a kiss at the base of his throat and wriggling her bottom where he needed her.

That was the least of their problems, Dunstan figured, before lust claimed his brain and all rational thought fled.

❧

"Li-li-li-lyyyy!" a childish voice sang through several octaves as Dunstan escorted Leila across her front portal a little later that evening.

She smiled at the half dozen little girls in long, frilly night-dresses who spilled down the stairs as if they'd been watching for her. The youngest one stubbed her toe and fell down. The eldest matter-of-factly picked her up and set her on her feet. The lot of them gazed up in awe at Dunstan—who stood frozen, panicked as a hunted stag.

"You promised us a bedtime story," one of the girls cried. "We want the one about Cinderella."

The toddler stuck her thumb in her mouth, assessed Dunstan with gravity, then wrapped her free arm around his leg and sleepily pressed her cheek into his knee.

He turned to Leila with dark eyes filled with horror, and she bit back a grin.

"What do I do now?" he whispered.

"Pick her up and carry her to bed," she advised. "It's much too late for any of the little imps to be up."

She could see him working her words through the churning gears of his mighty brain. Little girls—nurseries—golden curls—

"I'll have one like these?"

Panic tinged his voice, but Leila recognized pride and wonder as well. Amused, she watched as Dunstan very carefully crouched to pick up the toddler. For a large man, he was tender and graceful, gathering the sleepy child in the same way he would lift one of his lambs.

"She might have dark hair," she warned. "Most Malcolms don't, but I've always been the exception."

He still looked fairly stunned, but heat warmed his gaze. "Very definitely exceptional," he murmured.

The memory of their earlier lovemaking rose between them, and Leila blushed and turned away just as Ninian came down the staircase. The dark-haired boy in her arms had taken apart a large wooden soldier and was industriously putting it back together again, oblivious of the circle of golden-haired females around him.

"There you are," Ninian called. "I told them they might stay up until you returned." Glancing from Dunstan to Leila, she smiled knowingly. "I suppose I should be glad you returned at all. If you have things to talk about, I'll settle the girls into bed for you."

They hadn't even begun to discuss London, much less their future. Fearful that Dunstan would panic and run, Leila started to suggest they go to their sitting room. Dunstan surprised her by overriding Ninian's suggestion.

"The girls need their bedtime story, and I need to pry Griffith out of the library. We have to pack. We'll be leaving for London in the morning."

Leila thought she'd like to capture the moment of frozen silence that followed this announcement and pin it in a picture book for safekeeping. He'd even caught omniscient Ninian by surprise, but the young man standing in the doorway farther down the hall held Leila's attention most forcefully. Griffith looked in turn startled, proud, and delighted.

She had no idea how *she* felt.

"I can mind Griffith," Ninian offered. "He is no trouble at all. You and Leila—"

Dunstan handed his sleepy burden to Leila, then gestured for his son. "He needs to learn how to go about in company. I'm not much of an example, but I'm all he has." Casually, he dropped his hand on Griffith's shoulder when the boy came to stand beside him. His son practically beamed with delight at his father's recognition.

Leila searched Dunstan's rugged face, but though she understood his character, she could not read his mind. "What of your turnips?" she asked.

"The turnips will grow without me. And the gardeners know what to do with your flowers. There are more important things than turnips and roses. I cannot have a future unless I clear my name, and I have more need to do so now than before." He searched her face, waiting for her response.

"It's the height of the Season," she said slowly, watching his eyes. The stubbornness and determination that made up much of his character overpowered all the other scents she'd thought to find, leaving her at a loss.

He met her eyes with a steady gaze. Leila understood he was doing this for her and for their child, but he wouldn't force her to come with him. He sought to protect her reputation and understood the importance of her gardens and her research here. He placed her desires over his own.

Joy welled up from deep within her heart and spilled out to curve her lips upward. He did not demand that she marry him and hand over all her wealth for the child's sake. He did not ask that she help him steer through society's dangerous shoals. She could stay here and meddle with roses and perfumes to her heart's content, and he would not say her nay. He offered her the freedom of her own decision.

In appreciation, she offered him the same freedom of choice.

"May I accompany you?" she asked softly, for his ears alone.

"And all these?" His gaze fell upon the little girls waiting impatiently for the adults.

"They shall go with us, as far as the Ives estate. Ninian dislikes London." She watched him accept the inevitability of traveling in coaches filled with little girls. He was a big man, in more ways than the obvious.

With a look of understanding, Ninian gathered the children and bustled them up the stairs with promises of an exciting new bedtime story.

A little shakily, Leila turned to Griffith. If Dunstan could learn to deal with little Malcolms, she supposed she must learn to deal with young Ives. It seemed her future would be inextricably entwined with his. The thought both frightened and delighted her. If all Ives males were as challenging as Dunstan, she would never have a dull moment. She would certainly never lack company or need society for amusement.

The boy watched her with curiosity. She didn't think an Ives existed who didn't possess an avid curiosity.

Her daughter would be an Ives.

"And you, Griffith?" she asked the boy. "Will you mind my borrowing your father upon occasion? In return, I promise to find entertainments you'll enjoy in the city."

The boy's eyes gleamed in anticipation. "If you would, please? My father hates the city and will growl and bark the whole time."

Dunstan growled and caught the boy by the nape. "I will not," he barked.

Not in the least terrorized, Griffith nodded, winked at Leila, and slipped out the front door, leaving Dunstan and Leila alone.

"Everyone who is anyone will be in London now," she warned him.

"Which should make my task simpler," he agreed. "Everyone who knew Celia in the last days of her life will be there. Finding a murderer involves an easier logic than solving the problem of what we will do after that."

"We will go on as we have," she declared. "Once your name is cleared, no one can threaten us again."

He snorted in disbelief, but she knew his was a cynical nature that must be convinced. She would show him. They could do this. He could raise turnips and his son, and she could raise roses and their daughter. She was very good at managing things.

But the next days and weeks promised to be a whirlwind, spinning the peaceful life she'd planned out of control.

Actually, she rather looked forward to it.

Twenty-two

"YOUR SISTERS AND I EXPLORED THE INN WHERE CELIA DIED," Ninian told Dunstan and Leila over the rattle of the coach headed for London. The children were traveling in a separate carriage with the nursemaids, giving the grown-ups peace in which to talk. "It is a very old inn, with too many ghosts and vibrations to easily tell one from the other."

Dunstan crossed his arms and glowered at his sister-in-law. She had maneuvered her way into Leila's coach when he'd hoped to have Leila to himself. He'd brought his gelding. He should have ridden outside—would have, if he'd known he would have to endure this prattle of ghosts. Two days of traveling in Ninian's company might test any doubts he possessed about his self-control.

"If Celia's ghost existed, she'd no doubt name me murderer just to give me grief," he said in contempt. He didn't need damned interfering Malcolms cluttering up his investigation. Did none of them know how to mind their own business?

Leila tittered, caught his glare, and covered her laughter by looking out the window.

Dunstan fought back a twitch at the corner of his mouth. He didn't know if she was laughing at him or at Ninian's fancies. He just liked that she was laughing. That still didn't ease his righteous anger at being chaperoned by his sister-in-law when he wanted Leila alone.

He had a sneaking suspicion that Malcolms exaggerated

their peculiarities for their own purposes. Women were still women, no matter what unorthodox talents they harbored.

He glanced surreptitiously at Leila. Beneath her gray cloak, she wore a glimmer of blue. She wore colors for him, instead of the widow's weeds in which she appeased society. He let the pleasure of that thought relax him as he sat awkwardly on the narrow carriage seat.

No other woman had cared to please him. He would do whatever was necessary to return the favor—such as trusting her strange abilities.

But that didn't mean he had to do the same for her cousin. He glared defiantly at Ninian, waiting for her to utter another asinine observation.

"Felicity says the desk Celia sat at gave off vibrations that brought to mind a green stone. Did Celia have any green jewels?" Ninian asked.

"I gave her jewels in every color of the rainbow," he admitted. "She would coo and bat her lashes and wish for red ones, and I'd give her them. And then she'd buy a green gown and pout until she had something to match. The woman was insatiable."

Celia had never worn blue for him. He would cling to that thought and believe that Leila and her family meant to help, not harm, no matter how witless their talk of ghosts and vibrations sounded or how irritating their meddling.

"Perhaps she was robbed?" Leila asked from her corner of the carriage.

I should think she'd have pawned or sold most of the jewels to keep her London creditors at bay," Dunstan argued. "I did not pay her bills."

"Tracking her gems is where we should start, then," Leila decided. "Make a list of where you bought them and what they looked like."

The task gave him something to do besides mentally stripping off Leila's clothes and looking for signs that she was increasing with his child, not to mention the other things he might do once he had her naked.

"Drogo is in London," Ninian warned, apropos of nothing.

"I shall take the girls with me to Ives so they won't be underfoot. Drogo will be happy to have you and Griffith for company in town, Dunstan."

He shot her a look from beneath lowered lids. Damned woman was reading his mind again. She was telling him that to see Leila naked, he'd have to slip her past his eagle-eyed brother. The alternative was to find some way around Leila's scatty mother to the upper stories of her father's town house.

He would have to watch Leila laugh and flirt and not be able to touch her.

In her corner, Leila wrapped her cloak more tightly around herself and shifted in her seat. "Dunstan..." she warned in low tones.

"Dammit, I'll ride outside with Griffith." How the devil would he live with a woman who could *smell* his need for her? He gave the roof a great whacking thump and threw open the carriage door before the coach could barely grind to a halt.

"They can't help themselves," Ninian said reassuringly as the door slammed shut and the coach lurched into motion again. "Sex is always uppermost in their minds. One must simply dig past it to their brains."

Leila thought she would like to imitate Dunstan's glower, except her cousin wouldn't heed her any more than she heeded Dunstan. "I cannot imagine how we will find one murderer in all London," Leila said, changing the subject. "This is an impossible mission."

"Perhaps so," Ninian said tranquilly, "but our search will give Dunstan time to become accustomed to having a family. He's been alone far too long and fights our assistance every step of the way. You will be good for him."

"Only if we keep *Maman* and Aunt Stella away from him," Leila answered. "They will pry his head off his shoulders once they know he does not intend to marry me."

"Doesn't he?" asked Ninian, opening a book she'd brought with her. "Perhaps you ought to mix another perfume for him if you believe that."

Leila entwined her fingers and squeezed. Marrying Dunstan would cost her the land and freedom she'd waited years to gain.

He didn't always agree with her, but he hadn't insisted that she marry him. She would trust that they were in agreement on the subject.

But that didn't mean anyone else in their respective families would honor their decision.

∾

Dunstan thought he might explode and save everyone the quandary of what to do with him.

Pacing the worn planks of the hall outside the rooms they'd taken at an inn on the road to London, he tried to appear to be a civilized gentleman and not a crazed beast, trapped by fear and anxiety.

Girlish giggles and the murmured remonstrations of an assortment of nannies and nursemaids seeped through the walls of the rooms to his right. On his left, the rise and fall of feminine voices, light steps, and laughter identified Leila and Ninian and their maids. He was surrounded by females and about to lose every iota of control he'd ever possessed.

Leila had looked green by the time they'd reached the inn. Nervousness ate at his stomach. He knew nothing about women who were breeding. He could vaguely remember Bessie flinging ribbons and hay at his head when she'd discovered her condition. She'd burst into hysterical tears every time he looked at her for some months after, and he'd looked often because she'd grown a splendid bosom. Then he'd gone off to school and knew no more about the episode until he'd returned to a squalling red-faced baby boy.

He'd been pretty well terrified then, too, but he had been little more than a child himself, and no one had expected him to be responsible. Or even reasonable.

A door creaked open, and Dunstan glanced up hopefully. He needed to talk with Leila. She could settle some of his panic simply by telling him she was feeling fine.

He breathed a sigh of relief at the sight of her slipping through the doorway at the end of the hall. He waited for her to look in her direction, praying she had some notion of where they could go to be alone. He shared his room with Griffith.

She hurried toward him, her light slippers tapping against the floorboards, her blue skirts swaying. "Thunderclouds will form in here any minute now if you don't stop your pacing," she scolded. "I've never known a man who could boil air as you do."

"How am I to rest when you looked as green as my turnips?"

Pleased surprise lit her expression. "Are you worried about me? I'm sorry. I did not know. I'm quite fine. Ninian tells me travel sometimes exacerbates the sickness of these early months. If that's all that has upset you, you may rest easy now."

"Rest? Do you think I'll ever rest again? I've been wanting to do this ever since you flounced down the steps this morning."

He pressed his mouth to hers and reveled in the answering passion he found there. This wasn't a woman who played games. He tasted the sweet wine of desire on her tongue, and her nipples became hard beneath his groping fingers. She sighed into his mouth, and Dunstan thought he would like to lift her skirts and take her right there.

The giggles behind the door prevented that action.

"I'll go mad," he muttered, bending to press a kiss behind her ear and absorb the flowery scent of her skin.

Deliberately, she slid her fingers to the buttons of his breeches. "It would require but a minute—"

Dunstan caught her hand and moved it to safer ground. "It would take far longer than a minute, longer than a night or a week or a month. And it will have to wait until we've returned to the privacy of the country. I'll not have both our families looking over our shoulders while we rut like animals."

She stood on her toes to nip his earlobe, then retreated to a safer distance. "You are looking for an argument to distract you from what lies ahead, and I'll not give it to you. I've been thinking of what you said about not giving Celia an allowance to live on in London."

He stiffened. There was a subject guaranteed to take the heat out of his desire. "I couldn't afford two households and didn't see any reason to encourage her misbehavior," he explained.

She dismissed his excuses with the wave of a hand. "So what was it she *did* live on? Or who? Think about it."

She swung on her heel and stalked away, leaving Dunstan to groan in an agony of frustration.

❧

"Tell me I'm beautiful," Leila said to Dunstan, twisting her gloved hands in her lap as the coach lumbered through the fading light of a London evening after they'd left Ninian and the girls at the Ives country estate in Surrey. Griffith had elected to ride on the driver's seat outside the coach to better observe the exciting city he'd never seen.

"Why tell you what you already know?" Dunstan inquired curtly.

Leila thought he'd thrown his nervousness out the window miles ago after enduring two days of feminine upheavals. This day alone, the youngest babe had been nearly trampled by the horses, the eldest had insisted on riding astride with Griffith, and Leila had cast up her accounts twice—and Dunstan had seemed to accept all of it with remarkable aplomb.

When Ninian had insisted they all stop and say farewell to her son in the nursery, and the one-year-old had lofted a ball straight into the air for longer than the laws of gravity allowed, Dunstan had exchanged looks with Leila but hadn't said a word. So what was bothering the damned man now?

"It would make more sense to reassure you that you're far more intelligent and gifted than Ninian," he continued, but even his unexpected flattery sounded brusque.

The closer they came to London, the more distance he set between them. She had tried chattering about friends and family. He withdrew further into brooding silence.

Leila leaned her head back against the seat, closed her eyes, and tried to read his scent, but she knew how he smelled far too well by now and found no surprises. "Ninian can heal people," she answered with a sigh of frustration. "I can only make odd perfumes and smell things."

"Leila, you haven't any idea what you can do," he said angrily. "You've only just figured out that perfumes or smells give you odd insights. Ninian had her grandmother to teach her from childhood what she could do. It's all a matter of education."

Well, at least she'd elicited some response from him.

"You needn't shout." She glared out the coach window. "And you needn't speak to me of education. If it's your worry over how to go on in society that has you growling, then you're no better than I am. You need only a little experience, and you'll have the silly sheep fawning all over you."

"I don't give a damn about sheep," he muttered.

"Then tell me what you do give a damn about!" she shouted, her own nervousness nearly equaling his as they drew closer to their destination.

"Hanging," he said bluntly. "Leaving you and Griffith and our child alone with my black reputation to ruin you."

"You didn't kill Celia. Surely you know that."

"That doesn't mean I can prove it." He leaned back against the seat and crossed his arms defiantly.

Giving up on improving his mood, Leila leaned forward. "Then tell me what happened that day. Maybe there is something in the tale that can help us."

"You think Drogo hasn't already thought of that?" Shadows cast his face in darkness, but an errant light from the window caught the worry marring his wide brow.

Leila reached across the space between them to touch his knee and remind him that he had her now. He didn't have to face the investigation alone. "Drogo isn't me. If we're to work together, then I must know everything you know."

His queue fell over his shoulder as he turned away from her to glare out the window. "If I knew anything, don't you think I would have done something sooner?"

"Tell me," she demanded, refusing to take "no" for an answer. "Start with George Wickham."

Closing his eyes and rubbing his forehead, Dunstan spoke as if the devil tortured the words from him.

❧

Surrey, 1751

"What the deuce do you think you're doing?" Dunstan demanded.

Climbing over the stile to reach the horse pasture, he glared in disbelief at the drunken fop who was attempting to round up two skit-tish carriage horses. One of the tenants had alerted him to the theft, but he hadn't believed any thief could be stupid enough to operate in broad daylight.

The young robber's chin lifted defiantly from the folds of his disheveled neckcloth as he grabbed one horse's harness. "I've come to retrieve Celia's horses."

Dunstan remained on top of the wall and crossed his arms to hide the pain at the mention of his adulterous wife's name. Which one of her many lovers was this? Judging from the richness of the silk coat, he'd say one of the wealthy, aristocratic ones. Celia liked titles. "They're not Celia's. They belong to the earl."

The young man shrugged. "The lady says they're hers. My pair went lame, and she offered these."

"The lady lies." Dunstan tried not to bellow and frighten the high-strung animals. "If the horses are hers, why does she not come to the door and ask for them?"

The mare flung her head, and Celia's drunken victim nearly fell over his feet to maintain his hold. Recovering, he grimaced. "The lady is afraid of her husband."

Fury flooded Dunstan's reason. The fool lordling didn't even know who he was.

He didn't know whether his anger was directed at himself for the lack of sophistication that failed to distinguish him from his tenants, or at Celia for her treachery. It scarcely mattered since the result was the same.

"Apparently Celia isn't afraid that her husband will hang you for a horse thief," he answered cynically.

Stepping down the other side of the stile, Dunstan began crossing the pasture, debating whether to collar the fool and heave him into a steaming pile of horse shit or kick him all the way back to Baden and Celia.

To his annoyance, the young man produced a pistol from his coat pocket. "Don't come near me! I'll report you to the authorities."

This close, Dunstan recognized the shivering idiot as one of the fast set Celia used to invite to Ives—George Wickham, heir to an earldom.

At the same time that Dunstan remembered him, Georgie Boy saw past Dunstan's rough clothes and flushed with recognition. "Ives! I should think even an ignorant hayseed would have sense enough to keep his distance when his wife asks for what's rightfully hers."

Ignorant hayseed! Dunstan's temper soared. Stalking across the remaining distance, he rolled his fingers into fists.

Panicking, Wickham dropped the horse's reins and gripped the pistol with both hands. "For my lady's honor, I challenge you to meet me."

Honor. As if Celia possessed a shred of it. Eyeing the shaking pistol with disdain, Dunstan calculated his chances of disarming the drunken rake to be fairly good, but he wasn't much interested in contracting lead poisoning if he could avoid it. His fingers itched to remove Wickham's empty head from his noble shoulders, but his rage was directed more at Celia than her latest victim. "Go back to Celia and tell her to buy her own damned horses."

"I'm challenging you to a duel!" the lad screamed. "You cannot treat a lady as you have and not expect to die for it."

Impatiently, Dunstan approached the armed thief. No one deserved to die over Celia, but he would send the nodcock back to her smelling like the horses he would steal.

"I'm warning you, Ives! You cannot beat me as you do her. Produce your weapon, sir." Wickham retreated another step.

Beat her! Dunstan snorted at the ridiculousness of the lie. "If I'd beat the damned woman, she'd not be alive to torment either of us now."

Rather than argue further, Dunstan lunged for the lunatic. Wickham dodged, and Dunstan's fist grazed his weak jaw. Caught off balance by the blow, Wickham lurched backward. Heel sliding in a pile of fresh manure, he shrieked as he slipped and tumbled over—falling on his gun arm.

The weapon discharged, smoke filled the air, and to Dunstan's horror, the Honorable George Wickham lay sprawled in a pile of horse shit, his life's blood seeping from a gaping wound in his side.

❧

"'Out, damn spot!'" Dunstan muttered as he sat on the marble steps outside his brother's rural mansion, staring at the damning iron-red spot crusted on his boot.

Dipping his handkerchief into the tankard of ale beside him, he attempted to rub the offending blot from the muddy leather. "Macbeth," he grunted. "I'm not an ignorant hayseed." Wickham's insult still rankled, but his adversary was no longer alive to hear his argument. The horror of that pool of blood formed a blank wall of denial beyond which Dunstan couldn't see.

"Sir?" the sheriff's assistant inquired uneasily while the sexton and a field hand loaded the body of the once Honorable George onto a cart.

Dunstan raised his glower from his boot to the young man, who was shaking in his. Dunstan had no weapon except his fists, but that was all he needed to frighten the boy.

Why the hell had Celia sent George Wickham to steal Drogo's horses? Dunstan couldn't send the frightened assistant into the devil's den to ask.

He closed his eyes and let the deputy off the hook. "'It hath been often said that it is not death, but dying, which is terrible.' I always liked Fielding's satire." Boot cleaned, he drained the tankard of ale, rose from the stone stoop, and glared at the sheet-covered body in the cart.

"'The grave's a fine and private place, but none, I think, do there embrace.'" But quoting poets wouldn't answer the question at hand, he knew. "Guess I'd better find the bitch, tell her she's not embracing the Honorable George anymore." He dreaded the confrontation. An entire barrel of ale wouldn't numb him sufficiently to make it bearable.

The sheriff's deputy looked mildly alarmed. "Sir, I know it was a matter of self-defense, and your brother is the magistrate, but perhaps you should let someone else speak with the lady…"

Dunstan watched the cart carrying the body rumble down the lane, away from the estate, and shook his head. "'Affection is enamour'd of thy parts, And thou are wedded to calamity.' Calamity, she should have been called."

Celia could drive a man to murder.

When a footman arrived with a silver tray, tankards, and a pitcher of ale, Dunstan poured a fresh cup of fortification. "Liquid courage, it is."

The deputy glared at the footman. "He should be taken to his chambers. A man just died here. This is a serious matter."

The footman shrugged. "He don't quote poetry 'cept when he's cup-shot. Ain't seen him like this"—the liveried lad wrinkled his nose in thought—"since the mistress left him back a year or so ago."

Dunstan glowered at the loquacious footman, set the empty tankard on the tray, and stalked toward the stable muttering, "'Of comfort no man speak: Let's talk of graves, of worms, and epitaphs.'"

Not being one to stick his head in a noose, the deputy dismissed any further attempt to stop him the moment Dunstan ripped the stout oak bar from the stable and flung it halfway across the yard.

༄

Dunstan didn't remember much of how he'd reached the inn in Baden, but once there, the landlord confirmed what Dunstan had already known. His adulterous wife was waiting upstairs for the return of her lover. No amount of ale could erase that damnable tiding.

"Celia!" Dunstan bellowed as he pounded the wooden door of her chamber. "I need to talk with you."

She laughed, the light, tinkling laugh that had once caused his gut to clench with desire. She always laughed at his bellows. Or yelled back. That last time, she'd run away.

Mind reeling, Dunstan rubbed his aching forehead and steadied himself. He was a big man who could handle his liquor. He'd never passed out from drink before. Of course, he'd never watched a man die either. Maybe he had drunk a wee bit more than usual, but he was thinking straight enough to know it wasn't seemly to shout his news about George from the hall.

Contemplating the stout door standing between himself and his faithless wife, Dunstan allowed his rage to build, replacing the guilt and shame of watching a weak young man bleed to death for no good reason at all.

Celia had told George Wickham that Dunstan beat her. She'd sent him to steal horses she'd known weren't hers. She knew Wickham carried a pistol. She knew Dunstan didn't even own one.

The callousness of her behavior filled Dunstan with such rage that he ripped the chamber door from its leather hinges with one good pull.

"You meant for George to kill me!" Dunstan flung the door down the stairs and strode into the room.

Beautiful, sophisticated Celia stood in the room's center, laughing, undismayed at his crude entrance. "Of course, dear, but I figured you had even odds. George isn't very smart. How is he?"

In a moment of crystal clarity, Dunstan comprehended the enormity *of his wife's duplicity. She'd drained him of every penny he possessed, run up debts in his name far higher than he could pay in a lifetime, and knowing she no longer possessed the power to twist him to her wishes, she must have decided he was expendable. She had hoped Wickham would kill him and free her to marry another.*

That poor pitiful creature back there had paid the price of her scheming. Without wondering why she was willing to sacrifice her lover, Dunstan let his last flickering ember of affection for her die into ashes. "George is dead, may you rot in purgatory," he declared.

He reached for her, staggered, and blacked out.

⤞⥿

"And that's the last I remember."

Sick to his stomach, Dunstan watched out the carriage window rather than look at the lovely woman seated across from him. He held his breath in fear of her scorn.

"You passed out," she said without a shred of doubt.

His breath expelled in relief. He didn't understand why or how, but she believed what he could not. "I didn't drink enough to pass out. They found Celia dead and me sleeping in the hall outside. I must have staggered there somehow."

"Then we must discover who entered Celia's room after you left."

"No one," he asserted now that they were on familiar territory. "The sheriff and Drogo and my hired investigator have all inquired about the inn's occupants. It was the usual assortment of farmers and shopkeepers she never would have acknowledged. None of them stirred themselves to go upstairs to her rescue while I bellowed at her. They only discovered us when one of them stumbled over me in the dark later."

"Someone she knew was there," Leila replied firmly. "Who would have benefited from her death? Or yours?"

Dunstan blinked. "My death?"

"Of course. Letting you take the blame for Celia's murder would certainly remove you from society and, with luck, see you incarcerated and hanged. For all we know, someone may have encouraged Celia to want you dead."

"I have nothing anyone could gain, dead or alive," he protested. "Celia was the only one who would benefit."

"We're almost there." She glanced out the window at the Ives town house.

"I ought to see you home first," he argued upon discovering their route.

"No, it is better if my family does not see us together tonight. They are all in residence this time of year."

Guilt swamped him again as he realized she could not be seen with him in front of her family.

"If your mother suspects about the child," he said cautiously, "you may tell her I stand ready to do the proper thing whenever you ask it of me." Swallowing a lump of apprehension so large that it threatened to choke him, Dunstan offered all that he owned, his very tarnished name.

Leila cast him a sidelong look. "I thought you said we couldn't marry."

Setting aside his towering uneasiness for Leila's sake, he reassured her as best he could. He'd done nothing else but think of these things for the last hours. "We can do whatever we choose to do. You are the one who would sacrifice the most, and I refuse to ask it of you. But if your family forces the issue, and you would feel better for it, I'll gladly offer my name."

She nodded, but he couldn't read her expression in the heavy gloom. Until recently, he had thought he might suffocate did he ever say the word "marriage" to another woman, but he seemed in rather good condition now, all things considered. He took a deep breath and found that everything functioned fine.

"You are right," she agreed, to his relief. "I'd lose my land, and you would not be happy living in town on my money. I have no wish to marry again. We must be circumspect until we return to the country."

Dunstan didn't think it would be as easy as all that, but he would let her fool herself for a while longer. She hadn't laughed at his offer, but treated it logically, as he did. He liked the way her mind mirrored his. "Once we're back at your estate, I'll be but a stone's throw away," he said. "You will have your land and your roses, and I'll take measures so Staines cannot threaten either of us."

The viscount had promised him the tenant farm if he married her, but Dunstan didn't think Leila would appreciate living in a cottage or losing her gardens. Her wishes came first. Besides, he didn't trust Leila's spoiled nephew to keep his word, especially if he remained in the decadent company of men like Henry Wickham and Lord John Albemarle. Leeches like that would part the lad from his money in one manner or another soon enough.

The coach rolled to a halt in front of the aging Ives town house.

Leila leaned across the seat and pressed a kiss to Dunstan's cheek. He caught her chin between his fingers and placed a more lingering kiss on her lips. Brushing a stray tendril of hair from her forehead, he released her. "I'm not a man of fancy words, Leila, but you have only to send for me, night or day, and I'll come. I wish I could promise more."

"That is all the promise I need," she murmured. She patted his cheek and straightened her shoulders. "I am my own woman now. I make my own decisions. Give my regards to Drogo."

Dunstan shook his head but didn't argue as he climbed out. He knew their future would be far more complicated than she anticipated.

And first, before he could do anything about Leila and the child she carried, he must find a killer.

Twenty-three

THE WITCHES ARRIVED THE NEXT AFTERNOON, SOONER THAN Dunstan had thought they would.

Arms crossed, leaning against the upstairs window overlooking the narrow street below, he impassively watched the scurrying of footmen and passersby as the Duchess of Mainwaring and the Marchioness of Hampton, Leila's aunt and mother, respectively, stepped from their carriage to the cobblestones.

He'd given Leila's family a whole day to amass weapons and outrage. He'd known Leila couldn't keep the child a secret from her unnaturally perceptive family.

In most worlds, two middle-aged ladies would not constitute a military force, but in his world, they had the power of an arsenal, two battalions of soldiers, and untold cavalry. Even the bystanders stood back and watched as the women ordered parasols and shawls retrieved from the interior, berated a young boy for not aiding his mother with her packages, called for their driver to check the lead horse's leg, and handed what appeared to be silk sachets and a lecture to a bedraggled young woman clinging to a toddler.

Leila's absence was ominous.

Well, at least the battle would be fought on home ground and with two of his brothers present.

Not bothering to check the knot of his cravat or brush back the hair escaping his queue—although he was tempted to check for gray strands—Dunstan sauntered into the upper hall and listened to the low conversation of his brothers below.

Since Ninian had married Drogo, she had made some impression on the decrepit mansion and all-male household simply by hiring capable servants and ordering the chaos of male accouterments confined to a limited number of rooms. A little paint, some feminine wallpaper in a parlor or two, and a few pieces of furniture that didn't rattle or collapse when sat upon constituted the remainder of her achievements. The floors still creaked, the walls still bent at odd angles—and sound still carried from the foyer to the upper levels.

"We don't have to open the door," his twenty-two-year-old half brother, Joseph, was suggesting to the elderly butler. "Or you can tell the footman we're not at home. Isn't that what Ninian does when she's busy?"

"Open the door, Jarvis." A voice of authority easily recognizable as the earl's rumbled up from the hall Dunstan couldn't see. "I doubt they paraded out here to visit Ninian. The Duchess of Mainwaring knows precisely where everyone is at any given time." Without a break in his tone or any indication that he could see up the stairs, Drogo continued, "Dunstan, you might as well come down now. They'll only hunt you throughout the house if you don't."

"Give me time to stick some hay in my hair," he replied, stomping down the creaking stairs two at a time. "Perhaps it will remind them I am but a lowly farmer."

"I shouldn't think they've forgotten," Drogo answered wryly, studying Dunstan through knowing eyes. "They're Ninian's aunts, and they've been more than helpful to us, so try to behave."

Eyes wide behind his spectacles, Joseph watched Dunstan as if he were a condemned man on the way to the gallows. "You didn't ask them to find Celia's killer, did you?" he asked in disbelief.

No Ives in known history had ever *willingly* requested Malcolm aid. They may have been forced to accept it upon occasion, but to ask for the meddling women to interfere, with some hope of controlling the outcome? No chance. One didn't tamper with forces of nature.

And yet Dunstan had done exactly that.

"Ninian and Leila have already put their heads together, so that's out of my control," he admitted, catching a glimpse through the open door of the ladies consulting each other while the footman took their cards. Perhaps if he went outside and met them, he could keep his brothers from interfering.

"Joseph, I suggest you stop gawking and return to whatever it is you're supposed to be doing," Drogo said in a tone that brooked no argument.

Joseph shrugged and gave Dunstan a look of sympathy before removing a polished stone from his pocket and handing it over. "Here. Felicity said this stone has powerful vibrations of good fortune. You'll need it more than I."

"Right." Dunstan shoved the pebble into his pocket. He'd stuff birds there if he thought it would allow him to survive this confrontation with his skin intact.

Dunstan didn't have time to formulate an answer to the query in Drogo's lifted eyebrow. While Joseph scampered out of sight, the ladies ascended the outside steps and appeared in the doorway like avenging angels.

"Dunstan Ives!" the duchess thundered, shoving her open parasol through the narrow opening and clacking it against the tiled floor. "We're here to speak with you."

Tall and as stately as Juno, she cut through the waters of turmoil like a battleship in full sail. In elegant blue-striped taffeta, she squeezed through a doorway designed for men and not women, momentarily crushing her panniers. "Ives! It's good you're here. Let us repair to the salon. Come along, Hermione." The wiring beneath her skirt sprang to life again as she gestured to her shorter, stouter sister and led the way.

"I think hanging might be easier," Dunstan muttered, catching one of the marchioness's drifting scarves as he and Drogo fell in behind the ladies.

"I'll stand behind you in whatever you choose to do," Drogo murmured in return. "I'll not see you suffer another disastrous marriage."

Relieved that his brother supported him without question, Dunstan squared his shoulders and entered the salon with determination.

"Call for tea, sir," the duchess commanded, immediately reducing the earl to a lackey. "Ninian has done a poor job of teaching you manners."

"It isn't Ninian's job to teach me anything," Drogo returned, signaling Jarvis to do as he'd been told before closing the salon door.

While his brother took up a position leaning against the mantel, Dunstan paced in front of the ladies. "I trust Leila has explained why we've returned to London, and you have come to offer assistance." Always take the strongest position first, he'd learned long ago.

Leila's mother gasped and waved her shawl in front of her face as if she were in need of air. The duchess merely sat with spine rigid, hands on the knob of her parasol, glaring.

"Do not take that officious tone with me, young man," the duchess commanded. "Leila has told us how you have helped her learn of her gift. We are grateful."

Almost falling over his feet at this unexpected acknowledgment, Dunstan halted his march across the floor and stared at the old witch. Too caught up in his fears, he hadn't noticed the subtle fragrances of the two ladies, but he should have. Leila had packed all her vials of perfume bases when she'd left the country. The first thing she would have done upon arrival would have been to tell her mother what she'd learned of her gift, then experiment on the family.

He admired Leila's cleverness. He had the overwhelming urge to grin hugely, but he didn't want to give himself away.

"I have nothing to do with Leila's gifts and talents," he answered, pacing once again. "She simply needed to be left alone long enough to develop them." He wondered what artifices the perfume had revealed in these women, or if it was only his imagination that the perfume had any effect at all.

"It has always been our policy to let our children explore their gifts at their own pace," Hermione said. "I tried to encourage Leila," she continued almost apologetically, "but she is so opposite of everything I am that—"

The duchess interrupted. "Leila has always been headstrong and determined and has known precisely where she was going and what she had to do to get there. She has manipulated all of us since she was small, but not once did we think of how she managed it. We were simply glad that she could go on without much help from us."

"And no one thought it odd that she smelled fear or cowardice?" Dunstan inquired.

Hermione gesticulated helplessly. "We're all so odd, dear, how could one notice the difference? Of course, it was unusual, but so is her black hair. And I smell love and happiness and conflict when I create my fragrances, so I thought nothing of it. I'd hoped she would build upon her talent for scents, but I simply didn't..." She gestured again, unable to explain.

"Listen to us," Stella exclaimed. "We are simpering like ninnies instead of telling you just exactly what we think of you." She glared at Drogo. "I want to demand that your brother marry my niece, but I cannot help but admit my admiration instead. It's quite the outside of enough. You shall have to do it for me."

Perplexed, Drogo looked to Dunstan for an explanation.

Dunstan wrapped his fingers around Felicity's stone in his pocket and sought the diplomatic words he needed—as if he had ever in his life practiced diplomacy. "Leila has the ability to see the true nature of people through her sense of smell," he explained. "In a way that we can't explain, we think it may relate to the unique perfumes she creates. She's not had time to experiment, so we don't know the extent of her gift."

His logical, scientific brother crossed his arms and nodded, waiting for further revelations.

Dunstan tried to think of a polite way to explain the ladies' current dilemma. "I think what the duchess is trying to say is that she cannot bluster and threaten me when what she really feels is gratitude because I have helped Leila understand her gift and made her happy."

"Threaten?" Drogo asked calmly, turning his gaze to the ladies.

The marchioness fluttered her hands again. "I know Leila is very headstrong, and it must be my fault, but surely, my lord, you cannot approve of her bearing your niece out of wedlock. I know it is done, and that she has her reasons, but really, sir..."

The duchess raised her expressive eyebrows, and silence froze the room while Drogo absorbed the implications of this outburst.

Dunstan winced as the earl grasped the gist of the problem and shot him a questioning look.

"They say the child is a girl," he offered, as if that explained it all. "Leila thinks she will have no difficulty raising a girl on her own. I have promised to be at hand to help as I can. It is her choice," he continued. "She will lose her home and land and the gardens if we marry."

The Duchess of Mainwaring rose in a rustle of taffeta. "I will not allow a breath of scandal to harm my daughters or my nieces," she lectured. "You will find the foul villain who has besmirched your name, then you will marry Leila."

Dipping her powdered curls so that the absurd flowers on her cap bounced, she motioned for her sister to rise. "Come along, Hermione. I am certain that Ives men know their duty."

Straightening her rumpled skirt, searching for her misplaced parasol, and pulling her neckscarf askew in the process, Hermione turned a firm gaze in Dunstan's direction. "Felicity's come-out ball is tomorrow. You will be there."

Dunstan bowed gallantly and waited for Jarvis to escort the ladies out. Then, collapsing on the sofa, he buried his head in his hands and moaned.

"Lady Leila has enjoyed commanding society these few years past," Drogo said from his position at the mantel behind Dunstan. "And you despise that society."

"She is everything that Celia wanted to be," Dunstan agreed, "and everything Celia could never have been."

"I see." Drogo dropped into a chair opposite and crossed his foot over his knee. "No, I take that back. I do not see. The two of you could not have created a child together if you had nothing in common."

Agony ground through Dunstan's gut at the dilemma of having to explain what he and Leila had done. It was inexplicable. He'd had no right to look at another woman. Leila must have been insane to hire him in the first place. None of what had happened made logical sense.

He would rather eat glass than expose his feelings. Ninian

could probably explain them better than he could. Or Leila. Maybe he should send for Leila. How did he explain that they did not want to marry but desired each other's company? It didn't make sense even to him.

"Leila wants me to develop new strains of flowers for her," he said. "She needs to create new scents that now she only smells in her head." He understood that much, at least. "The scents somehow give her insights into the people around her, or they reveal their true personalities in some manner because of the perfume.

"To develop her power will take a great deal of land, labor, and time. She is willing to sacrifice her position in society if that's what it takes." Dunstan rubbed his fingers into his hair, willing himself to believe that last.

Drogo tapped his boot with his fingernails. "'Sacrifice' being the key word here? She enjoys London and society and all the fripperies of her sort?"

Dunstan nodded against his palms. "I believe so. She's had parties of people coming and going ever since she retired out there."

"So it isn't just your lack of land or wealth that is the problem," Drogo observed.

"No," Dunstan agreed. "She does not wish to marry again. She doesn't want to give up her estate or control of her life, and I should imagine she will not wish to give up London either, once she has what she wants."

"And if she marries you, she loses her estate."

Dunstan nodded again. "I am the worst thing that could happen to her."

"Yes, I can see that," Drogo said thoughtfully, still tapping his foot.

He rose, and Dunstan could see his own reflection in his brother's boots. He didn't look up to read Drogo's expression. He didn't need a lecture right now.

"I have confidence that you'll do what's best for all concerned," Drogo said. "You won't need me tomorrow evening, will you? Venus will be in conjunction with Mars, and Tom Wright and a few others have invited me to an observatory."

Drawing down his eyebrows in confusion, Dunstan glanced up. "That is it? No lectures on doing the responsible thing? On honor? On supporting my offspring?"

Drogo tapped his fingers impatiently against his thigh. "Both of you are of an age to know what you want. I've enough to do with the younger ones. I will support you in whatever decision you make. You know you're welcome to return to Ives or to take charge of the Wystan estate in Northumberland, should you wish. I have no doubts about your competence. An Ives female!" The earl rolled his eyes heavenward and stalked out, leaving Dunstan to stare at the yellow-silk walls.

Free to do anything he liked…

But he could do nothing at all until he cleared his name—as the duchess had so bluntly pointed out.

With that goal firmly in mind, Dunstan shouted for Joseph, who would no doubt be hiding in the walls and have heard everything already.

Griffith appeared in company with his curly-haired uncle. Joseph and Griffith were eight years apart in age, miles apart in experience. For a moment, Dunstan hesitated. He didn't want to involve his son in this investigation. He didn't want Griffith exploring dangerous city streets. He wanted to keep him sheltered—yet he could not.

Dunstan pointed at the door. "The two of you, find David and Paul." His youngest half brothers were never in school where they belonged. "If Ewen is in town, call him in as well. We're about to search all the pawnshops in London."

"How can Griffith help?" Joseph demanded. "He knows nothing of London."

"Teach him," Dunstan ordered. Joseph and his two younger brothers had a fairly strong grasp of what it took to keep a lively Ives mind occupied. He could trust them with his son. "The two of you can visit the better shops. He might recognize Celia's jewels faster than any of you can."

The pride he saw in Griffith's expression nearly broke his heart. He should have included his son long before now. He prayed that he had many years left to spend with him.

Joseph broke into a grin. "Finally decided you didn't murder the twit, did you? Good. Now we'll get somewhere."

Slapping Dunstan's back in satisfaction, Joseph dashed out with Griffith hot on his heels.

When the hell had his shy baby half brother grown into a confident man-about-town?

Dunstan sighed at the impossibility of dealing with London and fatherhood and murderers and matters he knew nothing about.

Remembering the command of Leila's aunt and mother, he added a trip to the tailor to the list of impossible things he had to do. He mustn't shame Leila at Felicity's come-out.

He would rather wrestle crazed killers than attend a frippery ball.

Twenty-four

"You've had time enough to interview half of London," Dunstan declared, pacing the parlor and jerking back the velvet curtains to discover the current source of the racket out on the street.

Viscount Handel, his personable investigator, merely crossed his leg over his knee and smiled. "And so I have. Your late wife had a large and varied circle of friends."

"All male," Dunstan said with derision.

"Mostly," Handel agreed. "Men prefer to dally with married ladies. Less consequence, particularly if the husband is disinterested."

Forced to confront the idea that he must have seemed a disinterested husband to Celia's paramours, Dunstan winced at the guilt inflicted by Handel's observation. He turned away from the sight of a carriage driver shouting curses at a pedestrian in the street below and sank into a chair.

Was his guilt even greater because somewhere in his soul he was glad Celia was dead? Rubbing his forehead, Dunstan tried not to think that. It was almost worse than believing he might have killed her in a drunken fit. Whatever Celia had been, she hadn't deserved to die.

"Did any of Celia's lovers happen to be in the vicinity of Baden the night she died?" Dunstan asked.

Handel shrugged. "Not that they'll admit. I've been investigating alibis as best I'm able. The height of the Season had not begun, so the entertainments here in London were few. Lady Willoughby held a soiree, and many of Celia's friends attended that night. They can attest for each other."

"How many does that leave unaccounted for?" Dunstan demanded with impatience.

"That depends on who would have a motive to kill her. There doesn't seem to be any. George Wickham was head over heels in love with her. Lord John Albemarle was seen with her upon more than one occasion, but he's unmarried and seeking a wealthy wife, so that's of no account. There's a Sir Barton Townsend who frequents that crowd, but no more so than half a dozen others. Even Lady Leila's young nephew, Lord Staines, was known to have gambled in her company when he was down from school. I'm exploring Celia's favorite gaming houses, hoping to uncover someone who might have owed her a large sum. That's my only theory at the moment. That, or she knew something she shouldn't."

Could the laughing, lovely girl child he'd married be guilty of blackmail? It didn't seem likely, but she must have supported her lifestyle somehow. "See if Sir Bryan Trimble was in London then. He's a baronet from near Bath. Apparently Celia humiliated him."

Even as he made the suggestion, Dunstan couldn't believe he was using information gained from a Malcolm vision to search for a murderer.

Then again, since Leila was the Malcolm in question, perhaps it wasn't so odd—no more so than his belief that she could smell emotion.

"My brothers do not go about much in society, but if there's any way they can help, they're willing," Dunstan continued. "Give us a list of people and questions, and we'll start on it. There's some chance Celia may have been robbed, so we're trying to locate her jewels." He didn't care to explain that a Malcolm child thought Celia had had at least one of her jewels with her in Baden, and it had disappeared along with all the rest.

Handel's brows drew together in thought. "Excellent idea. I had assumed that you—or the earl—gave her an allowance, but was there some chance she pawned them?"

"I gave her no allowance." Dunstan peered glumly out the window again.

"I should have asked." The viscount thrummed his fingers on his crossed knee. "Tracing her income could be significant. She rented a small flat, but it was located in an expensive area. Someone was paying."

"Perhaps she paid with the jewels I bought her, since they were never found."

"George Wickham had an allowance, but he wasn't wealthy." Handel rose from the chair, apparently eager to follow this new lead. "Neither is Lord John. Perhaps Sir Barton Townsend. He wasn't seen with her much, but they flirted publicly. They might have had an arrangement. I'll inquire more deeply."

"I need to pay you for your efforts so far." Dunstan retreated toward the desk. "You must have expenses."

Handel shook his head. "This investigation gives me a good excuse to spend my evenings in gaming houses and bad company. I assure you, it's no more than I would have spent on my own. I'll charge you handsomely for my bad habits when I solve the crime."

Dunstan had the uneasy feeling that Drogo was paying the man, but he couldn't argue. He would repay his brother when his crop came in. "Keep me apprised of all suspects. The more eyes and ears we have, the faster we'll learn."

Handel nodded. "I'm glad of your help. See you at Lady Felicity's come-out this evening?"

"I'll be there."

⁂

"You're not wearing black," Leila exclaimed, hurrying across the empty dance floor toward the man towering at the top of the grand entrance staircase leading into the ballroom. That he'd chosen to dress fashionably rather than appear as a brooding menace to society warmed a piece of her frozen heart. "The green is absolutely perfect on you."

Dunstan frowned at his elegant frock coat and gold-and-white-striped silk vest, then shrugged and fastened his dark gaze on her. "The tailor said this color is all the fashion. Looks like parrot feathers to me. He said I couldn't wear popular styles but this one would suit. I'm not certain but what I've been insulted."

His lack of vanity melted Leila's heart a little more. "He means you are much too broad and manly to be encased in padding and frippery. He's chosen an excellent cut for you instead. You will set the fashion this season."

Apparently mollified, he stomped down one side of the split semicircular staircase leading to the lowered floor of the ballroom. Located on the third floor of the marquess's London residence, the ballroom was designed for impressive entrances. He glanced with curiosity at the glittering candles and festive ropes of flowers on the high ceiling. "Why did you ask me here early?"

"I thought you might be more comfortable if you were already ensconced in the gaming room when the crowds arrived. Besides, I wanted to see you before I'm lost to family duties." Leila smoothed his cravat, not because it needed it, but because she wished to touch him.

He quirked a supercilious eyebrow. "Did you wish to see if I would shame you by wearing boots and moth-eaten wool?"

She batted her fan against his nose. "I wished for you to kiss me, but now I do not. Go sulk in the conservatory, but try not to throw anyone over the balconies this evening. It's Felicity's first ball, and she's terrified."

A dark gleam lit his eye, and in the second before she realized she'd thrown down a gauntlet, Dunstan clasped her waist, crushed her panniers, and hauled her into his arms. She had time only to grab his shoulders for balance before he bent her backward and took her mouth with the soul-stirring kiss that she had spent nights dreaming of.

"Leila," a panicked girlish voice called from the landing of the private floor below the ballroom. "Where are you? I cannot wear these gloves!"

Dunstan lowered her slowly to the floor again, not completely releasing her. Gasping, Leila raised a hand to her heated cheek. She'd never had a suitor accept her challenge and act on it. She'd best learn not to tease men like Dunstan.

She didn't think another man like Dunstan existed. In his presence, all others paled to foppish caricatures. By the goddesses, what was he doing to her? She ought to be more in command of herself.

"Give me some task so I do not lose my mind these next hours," he demanded, returning her to her senses.

"What did your investigator say?" Leila asked. "Did he give you names of suspects? Perhaps we can question them together."

"I don't like involving you any more than I already have. My brothers are helping me." Before she could argue, Dunstan eyed her stack of inky curls. "It's not fashionable."

"Anything I do is fashionable." She slapped his arm with her fan, irritated by his refusal of her aid but softened by his look of approval. "Do you like it?"

"I like that you did it for me." Appreciation rumbled through his tone and gleamed in his eye.

The man didn't know a word of polite flattery, but his blunt honesty had her hot and flustered and wondering how the evening might end. "Go hide where you will, and I'll find you later," she ordered.

He looked amused but stepped away so she might flee to her sister.

By the time the first guests arrived and the family had formed a receiving line to greet them, Dunstan was nowhere to be seen. Leila kept an anxious eye on the ballroom, but she couldn't expect him to be loitering there, admiring the decorations.

The first indication that all was not as it should be came with a scent Leila could only describe as buoyant. She'd never before attempted to identify scents or connect them with character traits. "Buoyancy" didn't seem to be a quality other people noticed.

Nervously, she glanced over the rapidly filling ballroom. The musicians had taken their places in their balcony and had begun tuning their instruments. Her mother had added the fragrances of pleasure and happiness to all the candles, so the crowd murmured contentedly.

Identifying smells didn't seem to be a very exciting gift, but if it was somehow related to her visions...

Leila glanced uneasily toward the fountain room—in the direction of the conservatory and the apparent source of the whispering disruption below. What could the scent of buoyancy mean?

Leila leaned over to whisper in Felicity's ear. "Did you invite more than one Ives?"

Still holding out her gloved hand to the next guest, Felicity cast her a sidelong glance. "I invited all of them. Should I not have?"

"Depends on how much you wish your guests to talk about your first entertainment. I think, perhaps, I ought to leave you in *Maman's* capable hands while I investigate."

Felicity's eyes widened, but she said nothing as Leila flirted with the next gentleman in line, caught up her skirts, and took his arm to descend to the ballroom as if she'd planned it all along.

Once on the main floor, she escaped in the direction of the fountain room. Before she reached it, an iridescent bubble bumped her nose and popped. Another bubble caught in the lace of her elbow-length sleeves, and a few more sparkled like diamonds against her long gloves. Around her, shimmering clouds of tiny bubbles rose on the breezes of the two-story ballroom, reflected in the mirrored walls, and drifted upward on air heated by hundreds of candles.

Their guests murmured in wonder and delight as the more observant among them elbowed their way toward the source of this new entertainment. Leila didn't have to wonder. She knew.

She bit back laughter and maneuvered her way through the crowd. She was quite certain she had not smelled the buoyancy of bubbles. They smelled distinctly of soap. She had no notion whatsoever what the dratted man was about, but she knew precisely what she would find when she reached him.

Sweeping into the small antechamber with its bubbling fountain of water circled by velvet sofas, Leila fixed her sights on the broad green-clad shoulders and dark hair rising above a crowd of bewigged gentlemen. Two more men with dark queues had joined him, although how they'd entered without her notice, Leila had no notion.

The fountain frothed with bubbles, and the spray lifted thousands more into the warm air, where a breeze from the open conservatory door blew them toward the ballroom. It was quite the most fascinating sight—except that everywhere she looked, the bubbles popped against silk and left tiny iridescent water stains.

So far, no one had noticed.

She tapped her closed fan against a familiar broad back and almost dissolved beneath the brilliance of Dunstan's grin when he turned to her. "This is your idea of behaving?" she asked pertly.

"Mine," one of the younger, curly-haired Ives said proudly. "I thought Felicity would enjoy it."

"Joseph, is it not?" Leila eyed him cautiously. "You're the architect who designed my uncle's folly? I thought Ewen was the inventive one."

Politely, Dunstan didn't touch her, but she felt as if he had. He stood close, wrapping her with his awareness—and his buoyancy.

He was actually enjoying himself! The real Dunstan Ives had emerged from his brooding shell. For her? She thrilled to the idea.

"They threw Ewen out of school for this trick," Dunstan answered for his half brother. "Joseph and David merely improved upon his concept." Dunstan nodded to the second Ives standing beyond Joseph. "They made certain the fountain wouldn't overflow and flood the ballroom as Ewen's did."

Taller than Joseph, giving signs that he had inherited the same broad shoulders as Dunstan, David colored but made a proper bow. "We have been trying to determine if there was some way of pumping the waters in accompaniment with the music."

"In accompaniment with the music—of course." Leila refrained from rolling her eyes and took Dunstan's arm instead. "I shall be certain Felicity thanks you appropriately when she is available. Might I borrow your brother for a moment?"

Before following her, Dunstan caught his brothers' attention. "Remember what I said earlier. Keep your eyes and ears open. David, don't leave Joseph's sight. Don't flash that gaudy thing too much, just make certain the right people see it."

For the first time, Leila noticed the emerald pinned to the boy's cravat. He reddened at her look, but nodded at Dunstan's orders.

"What are you up to?" she whispered as Dunstan led her toward the conservatory. His size allowed him to saunter through the crowd with ease. Men fell away as they passed. Whispers followed in their wake, but he seemed supremely unaware of them.

He shrugged at her question. "Stirring trouble?"

"That certainly ought to let all society know you're back," she said wryly as they reached the open glass doors.

"I don't intend to hide. I must either go about as if I've done no wrong, or hang myself from the chandelier to achieve public approbation," he said, swinging her through the open double doors and into the humidity of the indoor jungle.

"Did that emerald belong to Celia?"

"One like it. That one's glass." Dunstan caught a coil of her hair around his finger and drew her toward him. "I don't feel like a monkey in a suit when you're around. All I think about is you."

She drank in his words, knowing from the tense muscle jumping over his cheekbones that he did not say them lightly. Perhaps he was feeling as light-headed and confused as she was. "Will you dance with me later?" she whispered.

His mouth relaxed into a smile when she did not laugh at his declaration. "I will, if you make it a country dance," he agreed. "I can manage that without crushing too many feet. Did you know that your nephew frequented the same crowds as Celia?"

"No, but I should have if she dallied with the likes of Wickham and Lord John. They've been invited tonight. Who else is on your list?"

"Townsend, and I imagine anyone else in that crowd. But there is no motive that we can discern. Could she have been blackmailing someone?"

"I shall speak disparagingly of Celia and see what happens,"

Leila promised. "It's one thing to know I can smell fear, and quite another to figure out how to use that knowledge. Watch closely and listen in, if you can."

Dunstan eyed her low-cut bodice and growled. "I'll watch closely, no doubt, but not for Celia's sake. Do not smile too brightly at the louts, or I'll be hard-pressed not to tell the world you're mine alone."

His possessiveness tugged at Leila's heart, and she would have gasped at the surprise of it had she not perceived the same startlement in Dunstan as the words emerged from his mouth.

"I think you know my smiles at any other man mean nothing," she muttered.

"That's not been my experience with women, so don't test me on it," he warned. "I know I have no right to place my claim on you, but I'm not strong in logic at the moment."

She understood. Primitive feelings warred in her breast as well, feelings that neither of them dared act upon, as he had warned. "Did you love Celia?" she whispered, entirely against her will.

Dunstan froze for a moment, then leaned against a table. An orchid trailed across his forehead, and he brushed it away. "I doubt I know the meaning of love," he answered carefully. "Celia was lovely, enchanting. She was like a beautiful butterfly that couldn't be pinned down. I had some odd notion that if I set her free, she would see the world for what it was and come back to me."

Leila heard the self-disgust in his voice. "You loved her," she said with conviction, having seen him with his son and understanding his enormous capacity for that emotion. "You loved her, you gave up your son for her, and she betrayed you. But those who love and respect you will never betray you as she did. Trust us." Nervous at revealing far more than she'd intended, Leila straightened a pin in her hair and adjusted the silver butterfly adorning it. "They're preparing for the first dance. Behave, and I'll find you later."

Dazed, Dunstan let her escape, standing at the conservatory entrance as he watched Leila's ebony hair soar past all the commonplace whites and grays around her. Even the brilliance of her midnight-blue gown seemed to outshine the pallid pinks and greens of the other guests, and something deep within his chest stirred and woke. He had very little comprehension of society's idea of female perfection, but amazingly, Leila satisfied his every definition. Pride that she had chosen him above all others suffused him with confidence.

Swallowing a large lump in his throat as he considered Leila's parting words, Dunstan stared at the brilliant chandeliers smoking with pleasant aromas in the next room. Could his guilt over letting Celia die actually be the guilt of having lost one he once loved?

He would have to be soft inside to have loved Celia, even for a short time, yet he had perceived his feelings as love. And he wasn't a soft man, was he? Leila was daft to suggest it.

No, she wasn't. Leila could see right through him, painful as that was to admit.

Joseph and David crept back to see if he'd survived his encounter with Leila unscathed, and Dunstan offered them a wry shrug. "Still have the skin on my back. Go fight over Felicity. I'll be fine."

His illegitimate half brothers had grown up in London, and possessed the town polish of their sophisticated mother but not the advantage of marriage lines to give them names. Dunstan was grateful for the Malcolm eccentricity that had allowed them to be here. He supposed he ought to show his gratitude in other ways.

Refraining from dropping cigars on the feet of pompous asses would be a start. He was torn between wanting to stay out of sight so as not to taint the ball with the stigma of his black reputation and wanting to parade about the ballroom to show he had nothing to fear. The latter had the advantage of allowing him to keep an eye on Leila.

His concern for the lady won the battle.

Marching back to the fountain room, Dunstan silenced a whispering twit by glowering down at him from his lofty height, sauntered past a gaggle of Leila's suitors with a hauteur that had them stepping out of his way, and stalked into the spinning glitter of dancers in the main room.

Leila had taught him that he had nothing to be ashamed of if he preferred pigs and sheep to society's entertainment. He was a farmer, and if society didn't like what they saw, that was their loss and none of his. Seeing the glittering company as individuals instead of objects to be despised had a freeing effect on him.

He shrugged off any lingering anxiety and waded into the crowd. Music poured around him in accompaniment with the swirl of skirts and laughter. The heavy perfumes of hundreds of people pressed into the same warm room thickened as he proceeded deeper into the crush. Powdered and bewigged men whispered behind his back. Ladies in enormous swaying panniers tittered behind their fans and followed his progress with their gazes. Towering over most of them, Dunstan would once have felt awkward. Tonight, he had only one thought—his height allowed him to find Leila in the crowd.

A slow smile curved his mouth as he located her stack of dark curls in the center of the dancing. Measuring Leila's exotic features against the classic perfection of other women, he supposed she was more striking than beautiful, but her glowing character lit her from within.

Dunstan stuck his hand in his pocket and leaned one shoulder against a fluted pillar. He smiled for Leila's sake when she flung him a laughing glance.

He had no reason to believe she wore her hair unpowdered just for him, no more than he had reason to believe she laughed more gaily or glittered more brilliantly for his benefit. But the way her gaze sought him out gave him the confidence to believe she did.

Keeping her in sight, he relaxed and turned his powers of observation on the rest of the crowd. He noted the entrance of Lord John Albemarle and the young Viscount Staines before Leila was aware of it. They escorted a woman Dunstan recognized as Lord John's sister, Lady Mary. Behind them followed Henry Wickham, looking disdainful.

Dunstan watched his elegant enemy whisper into the ear of another gentleman, observed with interest the way murmurs rippled through the crowd wherever the foursome walked—knew when he gradually became the focus of every gaze within their vicinity.

Dunstan had no quarrel with the Malcolms, and he sincerely liked shy Felicity. He didn't want to disturb the child's first ball. But hell would freeze over before he let maggots like those four malign his family and tarnish his reputation with their lies.

Grimly, he shoved away from the post and plowed straight through the crowd in the direction of the troublemakers.

No more hiding out, licking his wounds. He might not care about himself, but he was prepared to fight for those he loved.

Twenty-five

LEILA'S NOSE FOR TROUBLE TWITCHED, BUT SHE COULDN'T BREAK away from the dancing without causing concern and disruption.

Trying not to panic, searching for Dunstan through the swirl of dancers, she survived the final steps of the dance, curtsied to her partner, and instantly swung toward the entrance.

Her breath caught at the sight of Dunstan offering his arm to the insipid Lady Mary.

She'd never suffered a moment's jealousy in her life, but flaming arrows of fury shot through her breast now. At the same time, the scent of calamity rose from across the ballroom. Glancing around, she realized she wasn't the only one who sensed danger.

Aunt Stella appeared in the doorway leading to the gaming rooms. The duchess always knew what was happening and who was involved.

Leila's mother fluttered nervously toward Felicity, shooing her in the direction of the supper room.

With a sigh of resignation, Leila noted that both Joseph and David Ives had miraculously appeared from wherever they'd been hiding. Violence simmered in the air.

As Dunstan descended the stairs with Lady Mary, Wickham stared daggers after them. Lord John appeared on the verge of apoplexy, and Staines seemed slightly bewildered.

If Leila could have been certain the ballroom wouldn't burst into flames from the mounting tension, she would have watched the coming confrontation almost with anticipation.

But flames seemed the most likely result. Gathering her skirts, she sailed toward Dunstan and his companions, cursing the musicians who struck up a country dance just before she reached them. She would kick the obstinate Ives for fomenting rebellion, but the music carried him away from her. In retaliation, she caught Wickham's arm.

"You're late," she reprimanded him. "I saved this dance for you."

Looking startled and just enough off balance for Leila to lead him into the dance, Wickham glanced from Lady Mary to Dunstan and back to Leila. He smiled slowly. "My pleasure, my lady."

The steps of the dance did not leave her in his company for long. She landed in the arms of young Joseph Ives for a lengthy swing. "Keep Felicity occupied," she hissed at him as they circled together. "I'll deal with your brother."

"You'll be the first one who could deal with him, then," Joseph warned. "Rampaging bulls have more restraint than Dunstan when his temper rises."

"It's not aroused yet," she assured him, before swirling away to her next partner.

She linked arms with Dunstan in the allemande—just long enough to catch a strong whiff of his jealousy. She shot him a warning look, which he ignored with a smirk.

The man was *jealous*. Over her? Simply because she danced with Wickham as he danced with Lady Mary?

She'd stirred an Ives to an irrational emotion! Dunstan's proprietary attitude made her feel—desired? Powerful? And deuced annoyed that he still thought her no better than Celia.

The music brought her back to Wickham before she could think of any magic spells with which to cast all men to Hades.

"Perhaps we should retreat to the balcony for fresh air after this invigorating dance?" Wickham inquired as the musicians plucked the last note.

She could better smell his intentions in the open air. Or drive Dunstan from mischievous to dangerous in a matter of seconds.

"No, thank you," she answered, trying not to glance around

too obviously. Where *was* the damned man? She still sniffed danger. "I must see to our other guests."

With a gesture of dismissal, she turned away, only to bump directly into Lord John. Foreboding permeated the air around him. "I did not expect you to show your face, sir," she said coldly, sweeping her skirts away from him.

"I am the innocent here, my lady," he protested. "You are the one who invites murderers to accost my sister."

Damn Dunstan. Just what was he up to? And where?

Raising her chin so she must look down on the arrogant young lord, Leila regarded him with hauteur. "If there is a murderer here, sir, I wish you would point him out to me. I've seen no evidence of one." Lifting her heavy silk, she nodded regally at a lady beyond his shoulder. "Now, if you will excuse me, I have other guests."

Lord John grabbed her elbow and whispered in her ear before she could escape. "I'd suggest you strive to find my company more to your liking, my lady. Your nephew may soon become part of my family, and I can make both your lives exceedingly unpleasant if you do not act with a tad less condescension."

She gifted the puppy with a look of scorn. "I believe you mistake me for Celia Ives," she said, startling even herself with the comparison. "I suggest you find someone who is more your kind to terrorize. I'll not let you blackmail the boy into marrying just so you might live off him like the leech you are."

Now that Staines had been brought to her attention, Leila searched the room for him. Instead, she discovered Dunstan bearing down on them with menace written across his taut jaw. She almost laughed at the odor of cowardice emanating from the young lord, who abruptly released her elbow.

Dunstan halted in front of them before Lord John could escape. Although he clasped his big fists behind his elegantly garbed back, the set of his jaw alone was menacing. "Her grace commands your presence, my lady," he intoned without inflection. His gaze fixed challengingly upon Lord John even as he spoke to Leila.

"I daresay if she did, she also commanded yours," Leila

replied wryly. "So which battle do you wish to commence first, hers or yours?"

With a wicked gleam, Dunstan offered his arm. "Malcolm women frighten me far more than this insect." He didn't even glance back at Lord John as he added, "We'll meet another time, sir. Your sister awaits you on the balcony."

Covering her hand with his own, Dunstan dragged Leila through the crowd of curious onlookers and toward the anteroom where her aunt waited.

Dunstan's large stature provided an easy target for slanderous tongues, but he shielded her from them as he escorted her through the throng. Leila had no doubt that he would defend her with his last breath, should it come to that.

She patted his arm. "You are a very admirable man, Dunstan Ives. I do not have your courage and fortitude, but I shall attempt to learn them. I'm certain those qualities would benefit our daughter."

Unwilling to admit any more than that, Leila sailed forward to greet her aunt, leaving Dunstan stunned. He couldn't dismiss the pride she'd instilled in him with her words. He'd always had some inkling of his own worth, but Celia had called him cold, and his mother had recommended humility.

Lady Leila apparently wished to imitate him.

He didn't think that a wise resolve. Rather than ponder her meaning, he concentrated on the ladies' argument.

"You endanger yourself and all around you with this investigation, Leila," Stella admonished her niece. "Take your Ives and his ways back to the country where they belong, and let us find the villain on our own."

"Lord John has some hold over Staines. I could smell it on him," Leila argued. "I can't leave now. They're all part of the crowd Celia frequented. One of them could have killed her, and they could harm Staines as well."

"Nonsense. Your nephew is busy preening and playing the gallant. He's perfectly safe. Go back to your gardens."

"Until we clear Dunstan's name, I will go nowhere."

While admiring Leila's willingness to stand up to her powerful aunt, Dunstan preferred she didn't go so far in his defense. Gently catching her elbow, he steered her out of the path of her aunt's ire. He did not fully understand the duchess's Malcolm power, but he did not trust any Malcolm in a temper. Sometimes they did not know the full extent of their own abilities and came to grief for it. He'd not have anyone harmed because of him.

"You owe me a dance, my lady, but nothing more," he said. "My brothers and I will conduct our own search without endangering others."

"Your brothers!" Leila whirled around, not heeding his warning. "Find them at once. I need them to watch Wickham and Lord John."

Dunstan groaned as the duchess ruffled her regal feathers and looked prepared to bite. She would turn them all into peacocks in a moment.

"Your grace, I'll take care of this," he assured the older woman. "I believe the lady is my responsibility now."

He thought the duchess looked approving as he directed Leila out of the room. Unfortunately, the termagant on his arm wasn't quite so understanding.

"I am *not* your responsibility," she insisted, even as she followed him. "If anything, we are equals in this. I can certainly deal with my aunt far better than you."

"No, you can't. The two of you will soon be fighting like cocks over who's in charge of the henhouse. Take a lesson from Ninian, and let the duchess believe she is."

She eyed him with disfavor. "An astute observation from a man who talks to plants."

"At least the plants have the sense not to talk back. There's Joseph. Where are Wickham and Lord John now?"

She halted, forcing him to do the same. Patiently, Dunstan waited while she glanced around, although he suspected she wasn't looking so much as smelling what the air carried. The back of his neck prickled at that realization. He was involved with a woman who could smell a thief at a hundred yards. Maybe farther. He would have to test the theory.

"Wickham and Lord John have not left. I daresay they're in one of the anterooms, fomenting trouble. I do not at all understand what they're about—"

"I've talked to Lady Mary," Dunstan interrupted. "She and her brother will hold their gossiping tongues from here on out." Looking elegant and unconcerned, Dunstan shoved his hand in his pocket and scanned the crowd in search of his brothers.

"*You've* talked to Lady Mary?" Leila could almost summon a vision of the scene from his scent of satisfaction. "What did you do, threaten to tar and feather her?"

"I simply reminded her that I have not called in her gaming debts to Celia."

"What gaming debts?" Leila asked in astonishment, then understanding the depth of his scent of satisfaction, she cried, "You didn't *know* she had gaming debts! You bluffed."

"That crowd gambles," he said with a shrug, focusing on the approach of an unpowdered dark head. "Celia always cheated. It was a reasonable assumption."

Before Leila could respond, Joseph arrived, dragging a terrified Viscount Staines with him. "Tell him what you told me," Joseph demanded, shaking the lordling's arm.

"I... It's W-Wickham," the young viscount stuttered. "And Lord John. They have a witness."

Dunstan fought a surge of panic by crossing his arms and waiting, staring the boy down with what he hoped was a formidable glare.

Staines shot a pleading gaze at Leila. "I only wanted you to marry so I could have my estate back," he muttered. "And Henry Wickham is a good sort. He would make you a far better husband than this murderer." He shot Dunstan a bitter look.

"Wickham is a nasty toad, and you'll get warts just breathing the air around him," Leila retorted. "And if you marry Lord John's witch of a sister, she'll bake you in her oven and turn you into a gingerbread boy."

Beneath his powdered wig, the young viscount paled, but tearing his arm from Joseph's grip, he straightened his spine and glared back. "At least I do not consort with known killers. Wickham has located a witness to Celia's murder, just as he said he would. He and Lord John are to meet him at the inn in Baden-on-Lyme in the morning. They mean to see Dunstan hang."

Dunstan fought to keep his hands to himself rather than wring the truth from the boy. "If this is another of your practical jokes, Staines, I'll dangle you from the Tower wall."

"It's not a joke." The viscount looked terrified again, and his gaze darted about, searching for his friends. Then, confident no one could overhear, he continued. "I'm to go with them. Wickham says that your brother is the magistrate there, and he will never arrest you, so I am to act as witness and come back here to have you arrested."

Although music flowed and the voices of a hundred people filled the air, Dunstan heard the tolling bells of doom. For Leila's sake, he blocked them out. "Use your wits, Staines. Until you do, Wickham will use *you*. If you'll excuse me, I mean to find out what they're up to for myself."

Nodding at his stunned audience, Dunstan swung around and stalked toward the door.

Twenty-six

LEILA DIDN'T KNOW WHERE THE DAMNED MAN THOUGHT HE was going, but she didn't intend for him to go alone. She would never believe Wickham's witness over Dunstan's innocence.

But before she could run after him, she had to clean up the mess he'd left behind. "Joseph, notify Drogo at once. Have your brother follow Wickham and Lord John. Staines, unless you wish to be leg-shackled to a witch far worse than me, you'd best hie yourself back to Bath and stay out of this. For once in your life, listen to your elders, will you?"

Satisfied she'd terrified her nephew enough to make him listen and that Joseph already hastened to do as he'd been told, Leila sailed after the wretched Dunstan.

"You don't really believe that any witness Wickham has found is legitimate, do you?" she called down the stairs from the hall outside the ballroom.

Having already reached the second-floor landing, Dunstan merely glanced over his shoulder. "I intend to find out." He continued taking the stairs down to the street two at a time.

"They're plotting something, Dunstan," she shouted, lifting her skirts and racing after him. "Don't fall into it." When he did not halt, Leila flung her fan at his broad back. "Unless you wish to see me tumble down these stairs, you'd better slow down!"

That brought him to a halt. He turned and planted his massive arms on either side of the stairs to prevent her passing.

"Go back to your family," he ordered. "I want you to have no part in this."

"I *am* part of it!" Ducking beneath his elbow, she hurried out of hearing of any bystanders. "You're the father of this child I carry," she whispered in seething anger. "Don't tell me I'm not part of you."

"I'll not have you harmed by their trickery. I'll get to the bottom of it." He clattered past her, blocking any fall she might take as they raced down the last stairs.

Halting in the shadows of the foyer, whispering so the waiting footmen couldn't hear, Leila smacked a fist of frustration against his broad chest. "Don't *do* this, Dunstan. Let us work together and find the truth."

The man reeked of self-doubt and anger and a scent that she longed to believe but couldn't. Every bone in her body ached to take him in her arms and tell him how much she loved him. But if even *she* was terrified by these newly discovered emotions, what might revealing them do to this man, who seemed so bent on self-destruction?

"I will do nothing dangerous," Dunstan promised. "I mean only to find this witness and hear his story. If I killed Celia in a drunken rage, I need to know it."

"You would never do such a thing," she told him. "If you truly believed in my abilities, you would trust me in this."

He hesitated, and Leila held her breath, hoping, praying that he would have confidence in her. Despair whipped through her when he shook his head.

"We may both be sensing only what we want to believe. I cannot take the risk. I need time to figure out what to do if the witness is right."

Fury swept through her with the force of a wildfire. Drawing back from him, Leila all but spat in his face. "What if one of them is Celia's killer? What if they lie in wait to kill *you*?"

He froze and regarded her with wariness. "Did you smell something on them that you have not told me? Have you had another vision?"

He believed in her.

"The circumstances must be right for me to see anything. I do not know how to make it happen. But I know you didn't kill her. It only seems reasonable to conclude that one of her friends must have."

"Or a common thief who broke in to steal her jewels. Stay with your family where you are safe. I'll look after myself." His hands formed fists, and his voice was harsh, but his gaze upon her was infinitely sad.

She wanted his trust, not his regret, and he wasn't giving it to her. Furious, she backed away from him. "Go, then. But do not expect me to do as you wish, either. If we cannot act together, then I am free to act alone."

"Leila, I'm counting on you not to do anything foolish. Your family needs you."

"Your family will need me, too, if you insist on playing the part of braying donkey. Don't concern yourself over your son," she added scornfully. "Griffith will only be devastated if you insist on sacrificing yourself on the altar of self-pity. I'll see that my family gives him a little more guidance than yours has."

She watched Dunstan's big body jerk as if she'd truly pierced him, but he wasn't a man to bow to a woman's words. His long, dark queue fell over his shoulder as he bent his head and brushed his hand against her cheek. She prayed he didn't find the tear streaking toward her chin.

"Thank you."

Without another word of warning or explanation, he strode past the footman at the door and into the street.

Desperate to follow him but knowing she mustn't do so without aid, she turned back to glance up the stairs and discovered her whole blue-eyed, blond-haired family hovering on the landing above.

Interfering, manipulative witches they might be, but she loved the way they banded together in times of need.

With joy, she understood that they banded together for *her*, because they accepted and loved her just the way she was. Flying up the stairs and into her mother's arms, she poured out the problem while the music of Felicity's ball soared above them.

❦

"Staines and Lord John left with Lady Mary," Christina reported, rushing into the family parlor where everyone waited.

Crashing past a footman who was attempting to prevent his entrance into the parlor, Joseph Ives shoved his way into the family conclave. "I can't find Viscount Handel or Henry Wickham," he announced, "but David is following Lord John."

Behind him sauntered Joseph's older half brother, Ewen, accompanied by Dunstan's son. Leila wished she could reach out and reassure the worried boy, but Griffith's expression was as closed as Dunstan's at his worst.

Even Ewen's normally charming mien looked grim as he took in the gathering of Malcolms in one glance. "Drogo isn't home. No one knows where he is."

Leila uttered a foul curse under her breath. As magistrate over Baden, the Earl of Ives was Dunstan's best hope of staying out of prison. "Find him," she ordered.

"He'll find us," Ewen countered. "Griffith and I are riding out to Baden tonight." He turned to meet Leila's gaze. "Is there any message you wish me to carry?"

"That I'll have Dunstan's head on a platter for shutting me out," she answered with mocking sweetness. "Wickham and his dastardly tricks do not alarm me, but tell your noble brother I'll personally rip all his turnips out of the ground if he thinks to desert me."

"Please, Mr. Ives."

To Leila's surprise, Felicity interrupted them. Even Ewen looked startled as he turned his full attention on her younger sister.

"I'm certain the secret lies in Celia's jewels." Felicity twisted her gloved hands together and regarded him with an earnest expression. "If you could find the green jewel, it would help tremendously."

Her offer produced a genuine look of concern from the normally careless Ives. "We're making every effort, Lady Felicity. And I almost forgot, I brought you a gift in honor of your come-out." From the capacious pocket of his coat, Ewen produced a miniature mechanical toy and held it out for her.

Leila held her breath as her sensitive sister gazed on the tiny bouquet of enameled roses with longing. With one gentle finger, Felicity reached out to caress the toy. Then, smiling rapturously, she accepted the gift, touching off a pin that produced a tinkling cascade of music.

"Oh, my!" she exclaimed, holding the roses in the palm of her hand. "It's marvelous. Thank you so very much. How does it play?"

Watching the roses dance on her glove with fascination, Ewen shrugged and tore his gaze away. "Bits of metal turning around. I need to work on the gears some more. But the flowers last longer than real ones."

Leila doubted if the heedless Ives had any idea how unusual is was for her sister to accept objects from virtual strangers. She would ponder the oddity another time. Dunstan occupied her thoughts too fully now.

Admiring her unusual gift, Felicity looked dazed, but Ewen merely nodded at Leila, bowed his farewell to her mother, and strode out, accompanied by his brothers.

Leila frowned as Christina slipped out with the Ives men, but the younger ones apparently knew each other well. She glanced apologetically to Felicity. "I'm sorry, dear, but I have to leave you on your own. I can't lose to stupidity the best, most boneheaded agronomist who ever lived!"

The duchess managed to look both imperious and uncertain. "There is no chance that he is truly a wife murderer?" she demanded.

"None, Aunt Stella. You have my word and Ninian's. Both of us cannot be wrong."

"Then we must go on as if nothing has happened." Stella tugged her sister's lace neckerchief back into place. "Come along, Hermione, Felicity, we will be missed." Frowning, she glanced about. "Where is Christina? Lord Harry will be looking for her."

"Lord Harry left earlier," Felicity whispered, throwing Leila a glance, then following her aunt toward the door. "Perhaps Christina has gone to find him."

Leila sighed in relief as her shy sister diverted the attention of their mother and aunt, and they returned to the safety of the ballroom.

Sweeping past the footman at the door, seeing no sign of either Ives or Christina in the hall, she fled to her chamber to change from her ball gown into traveling clothes.

◈

Leila slipped down the back hall, away from the laughing, chattering guests departing at the front. She'd donned her blacks again, to better hide in shadows.

She couldn't wait until the ball ended, not if Dunstan and the others were already on the road to Baden.

She knew that this so-called witness must be part of an evil plot. She simply could not imagine how the villains planned to perpetrate it, or why. Or even who the villains *were*. Wickham might have become deranged with grief over the loss of his brother, but he'd had no reason to murder Celia.

Leila gasped as a shadow darted out of a gateway and fell into step beside her. She would have thought it another young Ives were it not for the scent. "Christina! What on earth are you wearing?"

"Breeches," her sister replied. "It is the safest way to travel. You really ought to try it. The freedom is wonderful."

"I do not have the time or presence of mind to reprimand you and explain why you're mad to go about like that. Go home, where you belong." Reaching the side street, Leila gathered her skirts and hastened toward the waiting carriage.

"I'll ride beside the driver. Moonlight isn't enough for him, but I can see even better at night. Lots of things have auras."

"Only living things have auras," Leila argued, but her sister was already stopping to talk with a gentleman who was opening the carriage door. She squinted in the darkness to discern the man's identity. "Lord Handel?" she asked in surprise.

He bowed. "Lady Leila. I tried to catch Dunstan before he departed, but he was too far ahead of me. Would you know how I might get a message to him tonight?"

The man's heady perfume covered a scent of anxiety and concern. She was learning to sort scents and pay more attention. Biting her lip against her fear, Leila nodded. "I am following him to Baden. What may I tell him?"

Handel studied her, then apparently concluded she meant well. "Sir Barton Townsend argued with young David Ives over a rather large gem he wore in his cravat this evening. The baron then spoke with Henry Wickham and Lord John. I could hear only part of the conversation, but it seems the stone greatly resembles one that Celia Ives flaunted frequently. Sir Barton seemed to be accusing the other two of lying to him, but I could not catch more than that."

"And what has this to do with Dunstan?" she asked.

"I cannot say for certain, but I followed Wickham to a pawnshop not far from here. The shopkeeper would not let me in after Wickham left, so I could not question him. I'll do so in the morning. If you would just relay the message?"

"I shall."

If, that is, she caught up with the wretched Ives before he got himself killed.

❧

Still in his fashionable evening clothes, Dunstan arrived in Baden-on-Lyme just before dawn. Cursing the haste that prevented him from changing into more suitable attire, he swung down off the horse he'd borrowed from Drogo's stable and handed the reins over to a sleepy groom.

The hairs on the back of his neck prickled as he stared up at the aging inn where Celia had been found with her neck snapped. Once upon a time he had come here regularly to drown his sorrows in the tavern. They knew him here. The innkeeper's livelihood depended on Drogo and the Ives estate. That alone should keep them silent.

But did their silence hide an ugly truth?

Striding up the stairs into the inn, he prepared to face the consequences of whatever had occurred the night of Celia's death.

He found the lobby empty and unlit. Taking a bench in the tavern that most suited his breadth, he found a hollow in the wall that fit his shoulders, sprawled his legs across the wooden bench to a chair beyond, and closed his eyes.

He woke to a slash of sunlight across his eyelids, a cock crowing, and the unsettling sensation of people staring at him. A crick in his neck told him he wasn't in his bed, and the nervous twisting of his stomach reminded him of the night past. Setting his jaw, Dunstan donned his most stubborn expression and opened his eyes.

He recognized the local constable first. Gray-haired and portly, the man twisted his hat between his fingers.

Dunstan swallowed a lump of fear at the memory of waking up this same way the morning after Celia's death. At least this time he did not wake with an aching head.

Twisting his stiff neck slightly to the left, Dunstan registered Henry Wickham's sneer. No surprise there. Beyond Wickham stood a third man—a simpleton who did odd jobs around the village. Dunstan had given the boy a coin or two upon occasion to watch his horse. The lad was harmless enough, and not smart enough to lie, but he might be susceptible to suggestion.

Shoving away from the wall, Dunstan stood, towering over all of them. He experienced a twinge of satisfaction when the effete Wickham backed off. Attempting to look nonchalant, Dunstan glanced down at his fancy evening coat, brushed off some of the travel dirt, then raised an inquiring eyebrow at the constable. "You have something you wish to say?"

"I'm sorry, sir. There's an inquiry 'as been made. I'm to ask if you know to whom this here button belongs." The constable held out a glittering gold button with the Ives coat of arms embossed upon it.

Only one person in the world had been foolish enough to revive that ancient insignia. Celia. She'd discovered it with a childish cry of delight and immediately ordered it attached to every piece of paraphernalia her imagination could dictate— including the buttons of her mantle.

Dunstan experienced a burning sensation in the back of his eyes as he remembered Celia flashing her gold buttons in the sunlight, laughing with pleasure.

They'd carried her body home in that mantle the day she died. Dunstan clenched his fists and met the constable's eyes squarely. "My late wife had buttons similar to that. Where did you find it?"

Outside, horses clattered and wheels squeaked, signaling the arrival of a carriage in the yard. Feminine cries distracted his audience. They turned as one to look out the wavy panes of the bow window.

Apparently too impatient to wait for a footman to pull down the steps of the coach, a lady in black threw open the door and leaped down.

A lady in black. Dunstan swore a silent curse as the renewed pain of Celia's death mixed with humiliation and shame. If the worst happened and they proved he'd killed Celia, he wanted to remember Leila laughing and dancing and flashing him a taunting smile in a fancy ballroom. He didn't want her here.

"Where did you get the button?" Dunstan repeated harshly, forcing the others to tear their gazes from the window.

He heard Leila enter the foyer, heard the imperious command of her voice to the innkeeper, and wished himself to the devil. More male voices joined the argument. He thought he recognized Lord John's, but not the others.

He scowled at the constable, who gulped and hurried to speak.

"Paulie 'ere says as you gave it to 'im the night the lady died. Paulie isn't much of one for lyin'." The constable watched him hopefully, waiting for an explanation.

Paulie had a button wrenched from Celia's mantle. Before the day of Celia's death, Dunstan hadn't been near his wife or her clothing in months. *But he'd given the button to Paulie.*

He'd been beyond furious that night. He'd had a man's blood on his hands because of her. She had laughed. Could he have reached for her? Ripped the button off?

Dunstan took a deep breath as he sensed Leila's entrance. For her sake, and that of his children, he couldn't believe himself capable of violence. "I was drunk when I saw her last, as I've told you," he replied coldly. "She could have thrown the thing at me for all I remember." He didn't remember her throwing anything, but then he didn't remember her dying not twenty feet away from him either.

"You give it to me when you woke up," Paulie said excitedly. "It was in your hand, 'member?"

"There was buttons tore off the lady's cloak," the constable confirmed. "P'raps they came off and you found 'em at 'ome?"

"I would have left them at home if so." Celia hadn't been home to lose them there. Dunstan struggled to remain calm in the face of the evidence against him. Celia hadn't been wearing a cloak when he'd seen her, had she?

The constable watched Dunstan, his brow crumpled in worry. "She was wearin' the cloak when we found her dead, sir."

Crushed between guilt and doubt on one side and fear for Leila on the other, Dunstan sought a way to end this humiliating scene, but he wasn't an imaginative man and couldn't think like a murderer. "Celia wasn't wearing a cloak when I saw her," he replied.

From the doorway, the stout innkeeper stepped forward, twisting his thick fingers in his apron. "She were wearin' it when we looked up to see why a door come flyin' down the stairs, milord. She stood there in the doorway, laughin' her head off."

Still refusing to look at the woman in the entrance, Dunstan bit back a hasty retort and worded his reply carefully. "She couldn't have been. I was in her way."

"Warn't no sign of you, milord, although we'd heard you bellerin' earlier, the ways you do."

"Then I must have already left." But he couldn't remember leaving. And he'd been found in the hall just outside her door. Surely someone would have seen him leave?

"She was talkin' to you when she turned around and went back in the room." The innkeeper wouldn't look Dunstan in the eye. "She was wearin' a big green necklace when I seed her last. She warn't wearin' it when we found her dead."

"He murdered her in a violent fit of jealousy, Constable," Wickham said with satisfaction. "He killed my brother, and now we have proof he killed his wife as well. I should imagine if you search his house, you'll find Celia's necklace there."

Dunstan's empty stomach clenched at this new information. Celia always wore gaudy jewelry. He never noticed such things, but in all likelihood she'd been wearing the gems when he'd seen her. Could robbery have been the motive? How the hell would he find out?

"Wickham is a coward and a liar!" Leila cried from the doorway. "Dunstan would never harm a soul."

He didn't want her involved in this. He'd ruined her reputation enough as it was. If she tried defending him now or using her witchy talents to hunt for murderers, she would only endanger herself and the child.

Dunstan finally allowed himself a glance at the woman who had given him something so beautiful he could place no name upon it. "Leila, go back to your family and stay out of it." Her eyes flashed blue fire, but he knew she was listening. "Let me handle this my way."

"You don't know what evil they've plotted," she protested.

"It's not your concern," he answered, willing her to heave things at him and leave in a huff. But his Leila was above Celia's histrionics. When she merely looked stubborn, he turned back to the constable.

"Lady Leila is an excellent judge of character. You would do well to listen to her and not to a man who wears hatred like a cross. Look after her, and I will do whatever you request."

"I'll send for the earl," the constable said anxiously. "He'll know what's best to do." Throwing Leila a worried look, the burly man caught Dunstan's elbow and led him past her to the door.

"We're sending for a London magistrate," Wickham cried. "The earl cannot judge his own brother."

"Go home, Leila," Dunstan whispered as she lifted terrified eyes to his. "I will do nothing until you leave."

Ignoring the grief and hurt in her expression, he strode out without a backward look.

Twenty-seven

RAGE WARRED WITH TERROR IN HER BREAST, BUT LEILA WOULD not give Wickham the satisfaction of seeing either. Facing his knowing smirk, she drew herself up haughtily. "You are a vile coward, sir. If you have some grievance with Dunstan, you should call him out in a fair fight. Hiding behind the words of a simpleton is the mark of a villain."

"Ives doesn't know the meaning of a fair fight." The voice came from behind her.

Leila swung around as Lord John entered the tavern, followed by Sir Barton. Remembering that Dunstan's brothers had promised to follow them, she glanced beyond the door. Joseph Ives was there, lounging in a chair in the hall. He looked tired, dusty, and disgusted. He'd apparently heard more than enough. She judged from his balled-up fists that he was feeling as frustrated as she was.

In her pocket lay the vial of perfume she'd made for Lord John. She fingered the small glass tube, wishing she could think how to make use of it.

She wanted to order Joseph to stay with Dunstan, but the smell of triumph and wickedness distracted her. She could not apply the scents to the facts she knew. She could smell guilt, but no doubt these men were guilty of many things.

"How would you know if Dunstan fights fair?" she demanded of the handsome man who had once courted her. "Were you there the day George pointed a pistol at

Dunstan? He never carries a weapon, so do not tell me that was fair."

Lord John's smug look only heightened her fury. She had to escape this room. Bile rose in her throat at the stenches emanating from these roaches her nephew called friends. She couldn't remember ever being so physically attacked by smell like this. Her head spun, and she couldn't think.

"Staines was supposed to be here, not you. What did you do to delay his arrival?" Wickham asked, distracting her before she could push past Sir Barton and leave the room.

"I spoke to him in a foreign language called the truth," she replied, maintaining her composure. If they expected her nephew to act as witness to this farce so he might run for a London judge, Leila was relieved he'd stayed away. But what would happen now? The constable had said he would notify the magistrate, but no one knew where Drogo was.

"Staines is a fool to listen to women." Wickham shrugged and appropriated a bench by the fire, calling for an ale and some breakfast. "Come speak softly to me, and I'll see if I can persuade your nephew to leave your pretty flowers alone."

Without Dunstan to stop him, Staines could run amok through her fields if he chose. The servants would not stand in the way of the man-child who controlled the estate's future.

She'd been a fool to place her land first, over a man who was worth far more.

That error she could correct, if the arrogant Ives would let her.

"May you spend your nights in a bed of thorns," she replied sweetly, before pivoting on her heel and marching out of the tavern. Joseph Ives had disappeared from the hall, she noted. She prayed he had gone to Dunstan.

Loud voices raised in argument in the stable yard drew her attention. If she did not mistake, one voice belonged to Christina in a temper.

"I will not listen to a man whose aura changes color with every passing moment," Christina was shouting as Leila stepped outside. "It's like making sense of a rainbow."

"A woman in breeches is an open invitation to scandal,"

Ewen shouted back. "We don't have time to watch over both you and Dunstan. Go back where you belong."

Standing aside, mouth agape, Dunstan's son listened to the senseless argument. At Leila's arrival, Griffith looked relieved and darted a worried glance toward the stable.

"Stop it, both of you!" Leila stepped between them. "I have enough to worry about without the two of you scrapping like children. Dunstan needs all of us. If you can't work together, go home."

"Lord John's aura is murky, but Wickham's is decidedly black," Christina declared with urgency. "I watched him through the window."

"You said Dunstan's aura was black, too," Leila replied wearily. "It is of no moment."

Looking smug, Ewen started to speak, but Christina shot him a glare, silencing him. "Dunstan's aura is mostly gray and blue right now. He is worried and depressed, but he's trying to do the right thing."

Ewen raised an eyebrow in an expression that was remarkably similar to Dunstan's, and the pain of that reminder tore at Leila's heart. Behind him, Griffith slipped away.

"And I suppose the simpleton with the gold button glows with rosy innocence?" Ewen asked in a scathing tone.

Christina shrugged. "He does, but that button could have come off anywhere. Or someone could have dropped it where Dunstan might find it."

"Have you found Drogo yet?" Leila asked. "As magistrate here, he can see justice done." She kept an eye on Griffith's progress across the yard. She could let nothing happen to Dunstan's son, no more than she could harm the child she carried. She was torn in so many different directions, she didn't know which way to turn.

"Drogo is observing some conjunction of moon and stars or whatever," Ewen answered. "Ninian is sending for him. I'll not let Dunstan rot in a stable until he's found." With that angry dismissal, Ewen stalked off after Griffith.

"Arrogant Ives pig," Christina muttered.

"Bankrupt, titleless, arrogant Ives pig," Leila reminded her, as her mind conjured the horror of Dunstan locked in a stable. "He is not for you."

Christina blinked in startlement at this observation, but Leila was staring across the yard while her stomach roiled. They'd locked Dunstan in a stable! The proud man who strode across acres of farmland in sunshine, treated plants as tenderly as children, and carried children about like lambs had no business being imprisoned in a windowless stable because of a lying worm like Wickham.

Or because he thought to protect her, the damned insufferable man.

Her heart ached with the desire to go to him, but she could not talk through a door with his brother and son about. She had only one meager hope left.

With all the guilt stinking the scene of the crime, surely one of the inn's occupants had to be Celia's real killer. It was up to her to find out which one.

❧

Sitting in the straw and leaning against the rough wooden wall, Dunstan contemplated closing his eyes and getting the sleep he'd missed, but if these were to be his last few days of life, he would prefer to spend them awake.

Passing his time cataloging all the mistakes he'd made seemed to be the only direction his thoughts followed. He avoided thinking about the mistake of Celia, because he still couldn't believe in his guilt. He stared at his big fists and couldn't imagine them circling Celia's pretty neck.

He wrenched his thoughts from his late wife and back to other failures. He knew it had been a mistake allowing others to usurp his duties to Griffith. If Wickham won, Dunstan would never have a chance to know the boy, to teach him how to get on in the world, to instill in him pride for who he was, so that he could march forth into life with full confidence in himself. A boy needed a father for that. Stupid of him to realize it only now.

Letting Celia live in London without him had been the act of a fool, too. Had he been there, perhaps he could have steered her away from soulless devils like the Wickham brothers and their friends. If he got out of here alive, perhaps he could guide Leila's nephew away from those dangerous shoals, though he hadn't done it for Celia.

He would do anything for Leila, even put up with her spoiled nephew so she could have her flowers. What he felt for Leila surpassed any meager infatuation he might ever have felt for Celia.

He wanted to grow old sitting beside the fire with her, watching their children romp and play, hearing her intelligent opinions of his fine ideas, and listening to the results of her latest experiments. Agony twisted his heart at the thought of never knowing to what extent she could develop her fascinating gifts.

He'd thought marriage a mere acquisition of possessions and had had no understanding of its true meaning until now—when it might be too late.

Dunstan buried his face in his hands at his mental list of rank negligence.

He'd fathered a babe out of lust and not love, conceiving another child that he might never watch grow.

Leila had said she admired him, and he'd brushed it off. She had been telling him something, and as usual, he'd shut his mind and hadn't listened.

It was much easier to be scornful and judgmental than to take the time to understand. Perhaps she ought to stay out of his reach, as silk should be kept from mud.

Yet she'd stood there in that doorway, listened to an honest man give certain proof of his guilt, and still she miraculously believed in him.

His guilt and doubt could destroy a woman he admired and loved beyond all others.

He loved her.

Rocking his head back to slam against the thick plank behind him, Dunstan stared at a glimmer of light coming from between the boards of the door to his prison. If he truly loved Leila, he ought to trust and believe in her. She'd said he was innocent. If he believed in her as she did in him, then he couldn't be guilty, despite the evidence stacked against him.

A murderer still ran loose. Somewhere in his mind, he'd known that, but it had taken this dark moment to acknowledge it.

Apprehension clenched Dunstan's stomach as he saw past himself and his guilt to the truth. He was locked behind barred doors, and Leila was out there while a cold-blooded killer roamed free.

Rage shoved panic aside even before he heard the hiss of a whisper behind his head.

"Dad, are you there?"

Griffith. What was the damned boy doing here with a killer loose? Dunstan slammed his fist into the wall until it shook. "Where are your uncles? Tell them to get me out of here! There's a murderer out there."

Silence. Then Ewen's voice intruded. "How did you know that? Your investigator just got here."

Oh damn, oh double damn, he had to get out of here. Dunstan scanned the walls, panicking at the knowledge in Ewen's voice. "Where is Leila? Lock her up somewhere. *Get me out of here.*" He ran his hands over the solid planks, searching for a rotted one, a weakness, anything. Taking a deep breath, he tried to think. "What did Handel find out?"

"He followed Wickham last night," Ewen answered.

Dunstan quit pounding on the planks and listened. "Wickham? Where did the bastard go?"

"To a pawnshop." Ewen hesitated, as if checking to be certain no one heard. "The proprietor wouldn't let Handel in after Wickham left, so he had to wait until this morning."

"What did he learn?" Dunstan continued running his hands over the planks, searching for a rotten board.

"Wickham retrieved some jewels last night. Handel just brought us a description. Griffith thinks they sound like Celia's."

"Wickham?" Dunstan couldn't conceive of it. That effete mouse dropping? Why would he know where to find Celia's jewels? Lord John was the dangerous one, wasn't he? The one who had destroyed Leila's lab?

"One of you, keep an eye on Leila before she does

something dangerous," Dunstan shouted. "Then get me out of this damned barn, so I can wring Wickham's neck and pull the truth out of him."

"I just sent Griffith over to the inn." Ewen kept his voice low. "Joseph's already there. But neither of them will persuade the fool woman to listen. You're the only one she'll heed. Can't you rip off the stall door?"

"Don't you think I would have if I could?" Dunstan bellowed in frustration. "The gems, they're evidence, aren't they? Can't you make the constable ask Wickham about Celia's jewelry?"

"Wickham passed the jewels to someone else last night," Ewen finally admitted. "We think he's hired someone to conceal them among your belongings."

Hellfire and damnation. Of course he had. Wickham might as well have said it aloud when he suggested it to the constable.

"Staines," Dunstan muttered. "He'll send them with Staines and hide them in the tenant house."

Wickham had known where to find Celia's jewels. Mealymouthed, smarmy Henry Wickham knew far more about Celia than he ought. George Wickham had had a passion for her, and Henry was trying to frame Dunstan. Where was the connection?

At least Leila's intuition had been vindicated. Another suspect existed besides himself. Fine lot that meant if he hanged and left Leila in the world with a murderer and his son without a father.

With a roar, Dunstan rammed his shoulder against the stable door.

Twenty-eight

BLACK SKIRT SWEEPING THE CARPET OF THE PARLOR SHE'D requisitioned, Leila rubbed her forehead. She'd been awake far too long.

She would never sleep again.

She didn't bother looking up as young Joseph entered. She hoped Ewen was keeping an eye on Griffith. She might as well learn to accept the presence of Ives men in her life. At some other time, she might even enjoy their support.

"What are they doing now?" she demanded.

"Wickham's gloating," Joseph reported, having just returned from the tavern. "He and Lord John and Sir Barton are playing cards, and Wickham's losing. I don't know where he's come into money from. He's a lousy gambler."

"So is Staines," Leila said. It didn't take a witch to add two and two and see these rogues gaining her nephew's wealth over a gaming table, pressuring him to marry Lady Mary in exchange for his debts. She simply didn't understand what that had to do with Dunstan or Celia. How did one go about finding a killer?

The vial of perfume in her pocket grew warm between her fingers.

"Where *is* the little lordling?" Joseph asked. "I thought he was supposed to be here."

"If he has any sense at all, he'll be halfway back to Bath by now," Christina answered. "Leila left him with a flea in his ear."

Not that it mattered much. Ewen had told them about Wickham and the jewels. Had Staines left for the country before or after Wickham had retrieved Celia's gems?

"Wickham has talked the constable into sending for a London magistrate," Joseph informed them gloomily. "They're waiting for his arrival."

Leila fought back a wave of nausea. Fingering the vial, she decided it was now or never. She had to believe she could use her gift to save Dunstan. She simply didn't know how to make it work.

Lifting her skirts, she hurried across the room before anyone could stand in her way. "I refuse to let those wicked devils gloat while a good man suffers."

"Leila, don't be foolish!" Christina called after her.

"Either I have power, or I don't," Leila shouted, sidestepping the young Ives who blocked her way. "I'll not wait any longer to find out."

Wickham, Lord John, and Sir Barton looked up in surprise as Leila swept into the room, trailed by her sister in breeches and Joseph with a scowl on his face. "To what do we owe this honor?" Wickham asked, lifting his mug and sipping in appreciation.

"To me," Leila answered with fury. "Without me, you would all be nothing. For my nephew's sake, I recognized you. And now, I think I'll have all London banish you."

Belatedly remembering their manners, the three young men staggered to their feet in bewilderment.

Wickham shrugged. "You're the one who decided Ives was more interesting. I'm the one who will inherit a title, not him. You made a poor choice, if you ask me."

"Leave her be, Henry," Sir Barton warned. "She's a Malcolm and not to be trusted."

"I am but a woman, sir." She swept closer, cautiously sniffing her surroundings. "And you did not offer to help me grow roses."

"Roses," Lord John scoffed. "Most women want jewels. Who could know you wanted foolish flowers?"

She needed to catch more subtle aromas. Or use the

perfume in her pocket. With a distracting sway of her skirts, she strode toward a window not far from their table. "Perhaps next time you will think to ask."

Behind her, she could hear Christina admonishing Joseph to hold his tongue. He was no doubt ready to tear her to shreds for even speaking with the men who had locked his brother in a stable.

She let the rage build within her and waited for the right moment.

"It's too late now to curry our favor," Lord John replied with scorn. "Your nephew owes me a debt greater than he can pay. Once he marries my sister, his house in London as well as the one in Bath will be open to me anytime."

"How very charming." Leila decided she would set fire to both house and gardens before she allowed that to happen. Curling her fingers around the vial concealed in her pocket, she loosened the lid. "Staines needs a man to look after him. He does not heed my counsel."

"He'll heed ours," Wickham snarled, reaching for his ale.

"No, he won't. He'll heed Dunstan's or none at all. I have proof of Dunstan's innocence. He'll be free shortly." She still couldn't ascertain guilt or innocence through their scents, and they would return to their gaming if she did not act now.

Before any of the men could suspect her intention, Leila whipped the vial from her pocket and raised her hand to fling it.

Lord John leaped toward her and smacked her arm away, dashing the vial—and her hopes—against the wall. The odor billowed on the air currents instead of soaking her adversaries. In despair, she knew she'd never wring a confession from them now.

Behind her, Leila heard Joseph's shout of anger at Lord John's hasty action, but before they could come to fisticuffs, Wickham intervened. Gripping Leila's wrist, he jerked her toward him. "Drenching us in your foul potions won't stop Dunstan from hanging," he warned.

Caught by surprise and off balance, Leila stumbled into his narrow chest. She was still devastated by her inability to save Dunstan and didn't feel fear for herself—until Wickham swung her around and wrapped his arm about her neck, playfully raising her chin… and the scent of murder exploded inside her head.

A vision of Celia rose through the darkness, and Leila screamed.

❧

Glancing down at the startled, drunken faces below her, Celia laughed. Then, turning back into the room, she fastened her mantle and nudged the big man on the floor with her toe. "I trust you killed him."

The man retrieving his cocked hat from the wardrobe shrugged and brushed at the felt. "He killed George. One way or another, he's a dead man."

Startled by his cold tone, Celia stopped laughing. She smiled again as he caressed her neck, lifting the heavy necklace fastened there. "Then we can be married," she purred in satisfaction. "Let it be soon, so the child has a name."

"But you were the one who sent George to his death," he murmured, running his thumb up and down her throat. "Bitch."

❧

"Dammit, Ewen, where's your inventiveness when I need it? Get me out of here!" Dunstan shouted as he pounded his shoulder against a door that would not budge no matter how much force he applied.

He heard his brother scrambling around outside the stable. He didn't ask what Ewen had done with the constable or the men who should be guarding him. He didn't care. He needed to reach Leila before she did something rash.

Despair raged through him as he nearly dislocated his shoulder slamming into the oak-hard door yet again. "Acid, can you not use acid?" he yelled. "Boil some water, put your infernal steam machine to use. Gunpowder! There's bound to be gunpowder."

"I've found it," Griffith shouted from the outside wall.

"Griffith? Ewen, why the devil isn't he at the inn?"

"Because he listens as well as you do," Ewen said in disgust. "Stand back. The brat has a solution."

"What? Lightning? Pulleys?" Dunstan let his thoughts roll

over the multitude of insane creations Ewen had perpetrated upon the world. Surely one of them had a use.

"An ax."

The wall behind him splintered beneath the force of a blade.

Dunstan would have laughed at so mundane a solution had the situation not been so dire. If no one had killed his guards, then they would be on him within minutes. He wanted to swing the ax himself. He possessed more brute strength than Griffith or his dandified brother.

"My son is an Ives, through and through," Dunstan said with pride as the hole opened. "Give it to me. Where are the guards?"

Griffith slid the ax handle through, as Ewen answered. "I just checked. Staines is entertaining them with cigars. You should hear them shortly."

"The devil he is! What's he doing here? Stand back." Swinging the ax, Dunstan tore through the splintered planks, widening the opening in a single blow.

"Staines has decided his bread is best buttered on the side of the Malcolms, from what I can tell. He just arrived in a tearing hurry, and I set him to distracting the guards."

After slashing through the remaining planks, Dunstan shoved loosened boards aside and stepped through the hole into freedom. He hugged his worried son, hoping to dispel some of the fear on his face, and demanded, "Where's Leila?"

Ewen nodded in the direction of the inn.

Small explosions coming from the front of the stable warned them that Staines's "cigars" had taken their toll. Dunstan shoved Griffith into Ewen's arms and sprinted across the muck of the stable yard toward the inn.

He heard Leila's scream before he reached the front door. Panic gave wings to his feet.

He burst into a tavern reeking of the perfume she'd concocted for Lord John. At the appalling sight inside, Dunstan slammed both his arms up to halt the man and boy who arrived fast on his heels.

Wickham held Leila's neck in the crook of his arm in such a position that it would take only one sharp move to crack it. Dunstan froze, assessing the situation.

Leila didn't seem to notice his arrival. Her captor glanced in bewilderment from her limp form to Dunstan and began to back away, dragging Leila with him. Wickham's drinking companions stared in astonishment, their mugs frozen in midair.

Without a word said, Dunstan understood—this was how Wickham had killed Celia. This was how he would kill Leila if no one stopped him.

"Drop her, you bastard," Dunstan ordered, cold calm replacing insane terror now that he had Leila in sight. He understood instantly that Leila's safety demanded his restraint. He didn't like the blank expression on her face. She wasn't seeing this room. What, then, was she seeing in that strange mind of hers?

"She fainted," Wickham said in puzzlement. "What lies have you told her?"

Dunstan was vaguely aware of his brothers and Leila's sister gathering behind him, but he remained focused on the man holding his life in his hands. "Let her go." He took a step forward.

Wickham stepped back. "Don't come closer! I won't let you kill me as you did George."

Appearing confused, Leila awoke enough to wrap her hands around Wickham's entrapping arm, preventing any imminent danger of snapping her neck.

Dunstan had to use every ounce of restraint he'd ever practiced to keep from dashing across the room to rip the bastard's head off. "Leila? Can you hear me?" he asked softly, then winced as Wickham jerked her head back farther.

Leila blinked, gasped, then instinctively stood on the tips of her toes. Apparently returning to consciousness, she gripped Wickham's arm tighter so she could breathe and speak easier. "Dunstan." She smiled faintly before her gaze swept the anxious faces filling the room and the seriousness of the situation showed on her face.

"Wickham, she is ill. Let her sit down," Dunstan said calmly, although his heart beat hard enough to pound through his chest.

Sir Barton eased toward the pair, but Wickham jerked

Leila's chin up higher. "Stay away! All of you, get out. This is between me and Ives."

Leila caught his eye, willing him to do something, but he wasn't a Malcolm and couldn't read her signal. He hesitated. What did she want of him? The room reeked of spilled perfume, and he swore he could almost smell fear.

"Christina, leave, please," Leila whispered.

The girl looked rebellious and didn't move. Dunstan grabbed Christina's collar and Joseph's coat and shoved them both toward Ewen in the doorway. "Out of here, all of you." He nodded at Griffith to indicate he should leave as well.

As the younger ones reluctantly departed, Dunstan lifted an eyebrow in the direction of Sir Barton and Lord John. Leila nodded slightly. Immediately, he caught their arms and shoved them toward the exit. "Out, all of you." He might lack understanding, but he still possessed brute strength.

And Leila's trust.

The gentlemen resisted, glancing anxiously at their drinking companion, but Wickham's furious gaze was focused solely on Dunstan. Silently, they followed the others.

With the room cleared of all but the three of them, Dunstan clenched his fists. "Now, let her go, you bastard."

"I'll break her neck if you take one more step," Wickham warned. "You have a bad habit of picking sharp-tongued vixens, don't you?"

Before Dunstan could adjust to this unexpected topic, Leila interrupted in a soothing voice. "Celia lied to you, didn't she, Wickham? You didn't really mean to harm her."

"She claimed she was with child," Wickham spat with disgust. "She told George she would marry him if he could only dispose of her country farmer husband. She was inordinately fond of titles, and George was in line for my uncle's."

Dunstan didn't wince at this portrayal of his treacherous, adulterous wife, or remark upon Wickham's willingness to admit it. He didn't fully understand the spell Leila was spinning but steeled himself to wait for some opportunity to intervene.

The possibility of losing his stubborn witch in a heartbeat shrieked obscenities through Dunstan's mind. Violent emotions boiled and threatened to explode, but he stood still, fists tight, waiting, trusting her.

"Then it was Celia's fault that George died," Leila said sympathetically. "She sent him to his death." She darted Dunstan a glance, warning him not to move.

What did she see that he could not?

"George was a drunken idiot," Wickham declared. "He would do anything Celia told him to do. He spent his inheritance on the brainless chit." He appeared startled that he'd admitted such a thing and shot a warning glance at Dunstan.

"As Dunstan did," Leila continued consolingly, heedless of her captor's grip. "Those buttons she wore were quite costly. How did Dunstan come to have one in his hand?"

A malevolent gleam lit Wickham's eye. "I put it there when I shoved him into the hall. Brilliant of me, wasn't it? Kill Celia and let her husband take the blame." Wickham laughed as if this was the funniest joke he'd heard, then looked startled again.

Dunstan swallowed a lump of fear. What would Wickham do if he realized Leila was somehow manipulating his revelations? She must have had another vision to know the right questions to ask.

He watched with his heart in his mouth as Leila reached behind her to pat Wickham's face, sending Dunstan a look that had him rolling his weight to the balls of his feet in preparation.

"Celia had no care for any man. It was *your* child she carried, wasn't it?" she asked of her captor.

"How did you know that?" Wickham demanded in astonishment. "After she sent George to his death, I had no choice but to kill her. She wanted *me* to marry her."

Dunstan could barely grasp the full extent of what Leila was doing, but he knew she used whatever provocative force existed inside her to pry this confession from Wickham. He had to admire the way she combined the knowledge gained from her vision with her instinct to reveal what others would conceal.

He—of all people—should have glimpsed the terrifying extent of her abilities.

Leila didn't need roses. She didn't need perfume to access her gift. She possessed a power far greater than the feeble ones of her aunt and mother.

And she would die because of him if he didn't do something soon.

Catching sight of Ewen positioning himself outside the open window behind Leila, Dunstan steeled himself to act before Wickham grew tired of answering questions.

Taking a deep breath and saying a prayer, Dunstan stepped forward. Wickham stepped backward—toward the window.

Leila fixed her gaze on Dunstan, forcing him to wait. "Of course you had no choice," she told her captor. "And George had already spent his inheritance on her, so there was nothing left except Celia's jewels. I begin to understand your predicament."

Wickham relaxed an infinitesimal amount. "I had to get George's money back," he agreed. "Her jewels were worth a fortune, and she refused to give them up."

Dunstan took another step forward. Wickham glared at him, but retreated to within reach of the window.

"She owed you?" Leila asked, holding tight to Wickham's arm and standing on her toes.

She prayed Dunstan would heed her look. Her heart pounded fiercely in anticipation. Did he understand? She could tell by the way his fists clenched that he wanted nothing more than to strangle Wickham, but he was restraining all that violent emotion—simply because she asked it of him.

He had the strength to heave Wickham through the window, had every incentive to do so, but Dunstan's intelligent gaze watched her with determination, waiting for her signal, trusting in her ability.

Trusting her ability—completely and without question. That was the only gift she needed.

Exhilaration blossomed inside her the instant Wickham's grip relaxed enough for her to make her move. She caught Dunstan's gaze, nodded briefly, and he exploded into action.

Before Wickham could react, Dunstan crossed the distance in a single step. Leila gasped in relief as he caught her waist and lifted her from the floor with his left arm. With his right hand, he snatched the arm entrapping her from around her neck with such force that she could hear the bones of Wickham's wrist snap.

As Wickham howled in pain, Dunstan lowered Leila's feet to the floor and twisted her captor's arm behind his back in a move that was so crippling, Wickham doubled up in agony.

Finally registering the shouts coming from outside the window, Leila moved back against the wall. With the ease of a man pitching dung from a stable, Dunstan hurled Wickham toward the open window, into the waiting hands of his brother.

Free at last, Leila flung her arms around Dunstan, letting him cradle her against his chest.

With her face buried in a broad shoulder, Leila felt Dunstan's grunt of satisfaction as Ewen climbed over the windowsill and throttled Wickham's windpipe in the same painful manner as he'd held hers—effectively preventing his escape and cutting off his howls of rage.

She was safe. Her heart beat with Dunstan's, her hair brushed his unshaven jaw, and his breath blew against her neck.

"Do you know what you just did?" Dunstan shouted in her ear.

"Made you angry?" she whispered, wrapping her arms around his neck and twisting his hair between her fingers. "You don't smell angry."

"Damn it, Leila, you could have gotten yourself killed," he roared in frustration. "Do I have to hang about all the time to keep you and your nose out of trouble?"

She peered at him from beneath fluttering lashes. "Would you?"

A familiar dry voice silenced all the shouting except Wickham's choked curses. "Am I to see all of you locked in gaol or just the one being strangled?"

Dunstan's brothers and son, and even Leila's nephew, held their tongues and turned expectantly to Dunstan.

Slipping past the men gathering in the doorway, even Christina looked to Dunstan to reply to the toweringly furious Earl of Ives. Drogo had commanded his herd of unruly brothers for so long that he'd taken on the authority of both judge and jury.

Leila smiled as Dunstan studied her face for reassurance, and she swelled with pride at his confident manner when he faced his imperious brother.

"I have matters under control," Dunstan replied. "You can go back and study the stars a while longer."

"I don't suppose anyone cares to explain what has happened here?" Drogo asked, his glance roaming from Ewen holding Wickham in front of the tavern window to Lord John and Sir Barton hurrying out the front door of the inn.

"Ask the witch in breeches," Ewen answered. "Then send her home where she belongs."

"Leave Christina out of this," Joseph shouted in her defense. "I have to stop those scoundrels heading for the stable. They might have evidence they can give." He shoved past Drogo to race after Wickham's friends.

Whoops of delight erupted from Griffith and the young viscount, both of whom dashed out in Joseph's wake.

Leila settled back into Dunstan's arms and all but purred. "I'm beginning to recognize the sounds of an Ives harmony. Do you think they can carry on without us?"

Being a man of few words, Dunstan elbowed his way past his bemused brother. While members of their families cornered Barton and Lord John in the stable, Dunstan flung open the door of the carriage that was still standing in the yard.

"I have nowhere to take you," he muttered in frustration as he deposited her inside.

Leila noticed in satisfaction that he didn't allow that little problem to stop him from jumping in and ordering the driver away.

Twenty-nine

"YOU COULD HAVE BEEN KILLED!" DUNSTAN RANTED AS THE carriage jerked forward. "What the devil did you think you were doing back there?"

"Trusting my instincts," Leila murmured, snuggling close until he wrapped his arm around her, "just as you told me to do."

"I'm telling you to forget instincts and stay in London and never smell another scent again," he roared senselessly. "I'd sooner rip my own heart out than see you take such risks."

Leila patted his rumpled cravat and pulled it loose. "Did anyone ever tell you how handsome you are when you're angry?" She chuckled at his outraged expression.

Dunstan caught her hand to prevent her marauding fingers from wandering farther. "If I don't have you soon, I'll go mad, but the only bed I own is two days away," he complained as the driver blew his horn and the carriage swung into the open road. He lifted Leila into his lap so the jolts of the swaying carriage wouldn't jar her.

She snuggled deeper into his reassuring embrace, felt the press of his rising ardor, and smiled in contentment. Dunstan might gripe, but he held her as if she were a precious jewel—or turnip, she thought with a smile. She would listen to his complaints for a lifetime in exchange for the security of his brawny arms. She would create a new perfume for him. He smelled of confidence and uncertainty at the same time.

"What about the bog you own? Isn't that near here?" She pressed her cheek into his rumpled coat, more interested in this discussion than what had happened back at the inn. "Does it have a roof and four walls?"

"A crumbling hunting box," he grumbled. "That is no place to take you. You need silk sheets and a maid to wait upon you. I need to take you home, where you belong."

"I need *you*," she stated firmly, kissing the strong column of his throat above his unfastened cravat. Men carried impossible ideals in their heads, she'd discovered. It was time she disabused him of a few of his. "I do not wish to hear your litany of denials until after you've held me long enough to blot out these last hours."

"Hold you is all I *can* do in that bog." His big hands slipped her hairpins loose, freeing her curls to fall about her shoulders. "I have things I need to say that require a romantic bower, but both our families would hunt us down should I take you back to the grotto now."

Leila's hopes took wing, although she had no reason to believe the obstinate man was ready to see things her way. He'd told her to rely on her instincts, and henceforth she would. "I want to see your bog," she demanded. "I want to hold you like this, with no one making demands of us for a while."

Raising an eyebrow at her insistence, Dunstan leaned over and hit the driver's door, gave him instructions, then settled her more comfortably in his lap.

He sat back and tilted her chin so their eyes met. "Now tell me what you saw back there."

She smiled in quiet pride. "I saw Celia."

She gave him a moment to bluster and complain. Instead, he blanched slightly beneath his weather-beaten complexion but nodded in acceptance and waited for her to continue.

Carefully, she explained what she'd seen and how she'd interpreted it.

"Henry looks enough like his brother George that no one thought to notice him when he left later," she added at the end of her story. "At the time, the innkeeper didn't know

George was dead, so I imagine he wouldn't have thought twice if he saw Henry leave."

Leila smoothed Dunstan's stubbled cheek with her hand as he closed his eyes against the pain of Celia's abrupt end. "You sacrificed everything for her—your son, your earnings, your future. You could not have done more."

He nodded wordlessly, and they rode in silence while he buried his grief for the wife he'd never truly known.

As the carriage carried them in the direction he'd chosen, Dunstan tightened his arms around her. "You're too dangerous to be allowed in public."

"I won't be your possession to hide away," she reminded him. Keep him off balance, she decided, and she might survive the sweet torture of his experienced fingers sliding across her bare skin as he sought the fastening of her gown. "I understand how you felt about Celia, but you know full well I'm not Celia. You'll have to trust me, because I'll not deny who I am for anyone ever again."

Dunstan nibbled her ear, and releasing the hooks at her back, slid his hand around to caress her breasts above her corset. "Not wanting to share you doesn't mean I expect you to fit some imaginary mold as society does. I want you to be all that you can be. I would have particularly admired your performance earlier if it had not nearly given me failure of the heart."

"You understood as no other man would have," she murmured in satisfaction. "You did not act the part of raging bull, but waited and trusted my instincts. That's why I love you."

At her declaration of love, Dunstan stilled, studying her through discerning dark eyes while his fingers rubbed across the aching tip of her breast.

He said nothing, and Leila would have beat him with her fist if she had not understood his dilemma. In some ways, they were in perfect agreement. In others, they were miles apart.

She stroked his scratchy jaw and smiled. "You told me to follow my instincts. Well, instinct says I should no longer hide what I feel."

Dunstan tugged at her corset strings so he might explore

her unfettered breasts. He'd much rather act on *his* instincts than talk about hers, but they'd done that before and ended up with nothing settled. "You probably know how I feel better than I do," he admitted. "That doesn't change our positions."

She grabbed fistfuls of his hair and drew his head up so he must meet her eyes. He kissed her lips before she could unleash her tongue.

Gratified by the small moans he elicited, he caressed her breasts and debated the wisdom of taking her in the rattling carriage. Remembering the child she carried, he resisted. But if he meant to continue resisting, he'd have to quit kissing. With a sigh of regret, he released her mouth, stole one more look at the fair swells he wished to claim, and pulled her bodice closed. "You want the words?" he demanded. "You want proof of what kind of besotted idiot I am?"

"Yes, please," she answered, with a coy flutter of lashes. "How will I know if my instincts are correct unless someone verifies them?"

Gads, she tugged at his heartstrings. Dunstan caressed her cheek and steeled himself. "I love you," he declared stoutly.

The words weren't as difficult to say as he'd imagined, and he repeated them with a sense of wonder. "I love you. I don't wish to share you with any other man." He blinked in amazement that he did not incinerate into a heap of ashes at the admission.

"I want to be able to talk with you anytime I wish." The words kept tumbling out, unrestrained. "I want the freedom of your bed every night of the week, and in between, if I can. I want to be with you when you discover more about your abilities, and I want to be with you when your experiments go wrong. Is that enough, or shall I rip my heart out and hand it to you?"

Perhaps he sounded a little too gruff. He'd scared Celia often enough with his crude outbursts. Leila, though, as she'd reminded him, was not Celia. She smiled in such genuine delight at his rough declaration that his heart ached even more at what could never be. His name might be cleared, but he couldn't take away her land and gardens and all her glorious hopes for the future by marrying her.

"Your heart is already in the right place," she replied, snuggling against his chest and burning a kiss where she'd opened his shirt. "It's your head that needs examining. I want all that you want, and more. You are far more important to me than land or roses or perfume. You are not a man who is happy with an empty bed, and I am not a woman who would enjoy seeing you share it with another. And our families have made it obvious they will not be happy if we have this child without the conventions being met."

Dunstan sank his hand into her hair and held her against his chest where he could not fall into her bewitching eyes and believe what he wanted to hear. "They want marriage," he said hoarsely. "But you will lose everything if we marry."

"I will lose everything if we do not."

To her, "everything" must mean him, though he could scarce credit it.

The carriage lurched, tilted, and righted itself, in accompaniment with his nervous insides. Its progress was growing noticeably slower. Dunstan glanced out the far window and prayed as he'd never prayed before that Leila could see beyond the immediate. "In a moment, you will see what madness you speak."

He held her tightly, knowing he would have to release her once her madness ran its course and her formidable intelligence returned. He ought to run to Scotland with her right now, while opportunity beckoned, but he could not lock her into a marriage she would regret. They'd both done that before.

Gently, he began refastening the hooks he'd undone. The carriage came to an abrupt halt. Leila looked at him questioningly but began righting her hair.

"We did not go far," she said.

Dunstan jerked his cravat in place to cover his opened shirt. "My maternal grandfather was squire here. I grew up in the countryside around Baden and Ives. Most of my grandfather's land passed to my mother's brother, but he knew my heart was with the soil, and he left me what he could." He set her on the seat as the driver climbed down to unlatch the carriage door. "I'd hoped one day to have sufficient money to drain this acreage and make it arable, but it's impossible to do that and support a family as well."

Dunstan stepped out of the carriage and looked around while Leila finished tying her ribbons. He breathed deeply of the moist air, smelled the dirt of home, and drew it into his starving soul before forcing himself to look at the hovel that would no doubt send Leila screaming back to London.

It hadn't improved with age. Made of stone, covered in ivy, thatched roof rotting and falling in, it looked as abandoned as it was. Sheep had harvested the worst of the weeds, and wildflowers bloomed heedlessly in protected corners, but it was still a hovel. He might long to restore this land, but even he wouldn't live here.

He turned and reluctantly held out his arms to swing Leila down. He might as well dash all their happy dreams now.

"Be careful of your shoes," he murmured, holding her in his arms for one brief moment before lowering her to the grass. He hadn't realized how much he'd longed for the right to hold her like this, to bring her to his home, to believe she would stand by his side through thick and thin.

No matter what the future held, Leila would reside inside him forever. She might as well know that.

Dunstan turned her to face the ramshackle dwelling and wrapped his arms around her waist from behind. He might have to show her, but he didn't have to watch her expression of horror as he did.

She stayed silent for so long that despair took root in his heart. "Once my name is officially clear, I am free to earn a living anywhere," he reminded her. "If you would not mind living with Ninian, I could return to Ives. We have choices," he tried to tell her, although he couldn't believe what he was saying.

"Those are roses blooming in that weed patch," she said with what sounded like fascination. "Can we look?"

Shaking his head at the vagaries of the female mind, Dunstan held out his arm and helped her climb over the weeds and briars and brambles. "Half of England is covered in roses," he reminded her. "If I drained the bog, you might have enough acreage to develop the garden you planned, but we would have to eat rose petals or starve. I have two children to consider first." That thought caused him both pride and pain. He wanted Griffith and his unborn daughter to grow up in a happy home with roses in their garden and a loving mother who would balance out his faults.

Leila crouched down to examine a burst of pink blooms buried in long grass.

"They smell of love," she exclaimed. "I've not seen this variety anywhere."

To Dunstan's utter shock, she leaped up and flung her arms around him. "I want a garden!" she cried. "I thought I could give it up, but I can't. I want a garden. I want *this* garden." She lifted magnificent blue eyes up to his and pleaded. "I can smell it here. It's perfect. I know it will take work, but it's here. I know it is. I can see it!"

Totally flummoxed and bewildered, Dunstan held her at the waist, and trapped by her bewitching eyes, he attempted to find logic in the insanity of her declaration. "What is perfect? The rotting thatch? The verdant weeds?"

"The land." She sighed in delight, snuggling into him. "It's not rocky like mine. It has lots of the moisture flowers need. It will grow wonderful roses, ones that smell of love. Can you imagine what I can do with a perfume that smells like love?"

"Other people don't smell love," he reminded her, although he could scarcely think clearly with her breasts pressed into him and her arms around his neck. "And you can't live here. It's not fit for a sty."

She waved a careless hand, released him, and darted off to examine another flower. "Lavender," she called in satisfaction. "It's an old garden. There could be treasures all over, old ones that are hard to find. I can grow the flowers that I need here. Here, I'll learn how to control my visions."

He followed cautiously in her path while seeking a way to make her idea work. He hated to remind her of the expense involved in draining this land when she seemed so delighted with it. She'd lifted his spirits, for no logical reason whatsoever, considering he was in imminent danger of losing his turnips if they married and Staines claimed her estate.

"I suppose I could work for Drogo and live in his steward's house again," he mused aloud. "None of my brothers seems eager to take up the position."

Crushing lavender to her bosom, Leila bussed his cheek. "That would be wonderful, thank you. You can help me develop new plants, and Ninian, who can grow things with her eyes shut, can help with the garden. And I'm sure Drogo will be relieved to have your wisdom again."

She watched him expectantly. Still confused and stunned that she might even consider living in a house other than her own, Dunstan said the only words that entered his paralyzed mind. "Will you marry me, then?"

He wanted to grab the words back as soon as he said them, but as always, she caught him by surprise.

"I thought you'd never ask." Holding the lavender, Leila flung her arms around his neck and kissed him with fervor.

Dunstan shook his head in awe of how easily she plucked his feelings from him. He didn't care if none of this made sense, if the earth trembled and the walls shook. He'd placed his future in her hands, and joy raced through him. Now was a time for acting and not thinking.

Lifting Leila by the waist, Dunstan carried her around the side of the house, out of sight of the carriage and driver. Setting her down in a patch of daisies, he reached for the nearest evergreen branch and snapped it off. While she rhapsodized over the colors and fragrances of the weeds, Dunstan snapped off every branch in sight, then spread her cloak over the lot of them.

Catching her by the waist again, he gently lowered her to the springy bed he'd made and fell down beside her. Warm air caressed his cheek as softly as Leila's fingers did when he bent over her.

"My wife should have silks and diamonds," he murmured, plundering her mouth before she could laugh.

Leila's tongue wrapped her sweetness around his, drawing

him nearer to heaven. When neither of them could breathe, he spread his kisses across her cheek.

"Your wife would prefer roses and lavender." She breathed a sigh of delight as he found a particularly sensitive place. "And this is the loveliest bed she has ever known."

Something primitive and joyous stirred in him when she called herself his wife. In gratitude at her acceptance, Dunstan unfastened her bodice again and spread open the front of her unhooked corset. Seeking the tender morsels buried beneath the frippery, he suckled deep and long until she could no longer speak but merely cried out in need.

"I will give you roses in winter," he vowed. "You will never lack for precious scents if you will have me."

"Give me *your* scent," she demanded, dragging his shirt-tail from his breeches and rubbing her hands over his chest beneath it.

That was one request he could grant without difficulty. Sprawling his great bulk between her legs, Dunstan propped his weight on his elbows and bent to press his kiss upon her eager lips. He wanted her promises in simple terms that even he could understand. "This seals our vows before God, Leila," he warned. "Be certain this is what you wish, because no matter what the future brings, you will not be rid of me once you're mine."

She yanked the loose ribbon from his queue and spread his hair over his bare shoulders. Dunstan felt himself falling into the depths of her eyes, but he hung on, willing himself not to move until he saw her answer in the loving smile on her lips.

"I vow to love, honor, and take thee in equality for so long as both of us shall live," she whispered solemnly.

In equality. Dunstan remembered Drogo's panic at that Malcolm vow, but he'd had time to understand it better than his noble brother. He'd never known such joy. He might be a man who couldn't live without a woman, but only *this* woman would do. "I vow to take thee as my wife, to love, honor, and respect thee in equality, for so long as both of us shall live, and beyond," he promised without hesitation.

Her eyes widened in delight at that, but he had exhausted

his supply of patience. Feeling like a pirate claiming a precious treasure, he joined his flesh with hers, celebrating the promises of their hearts with the pleasures of physical possession.

He'd conquered the lady's heart only after he had submitted his own heart to the power of her love, the only witchcraft needed for building a future.

Thirty

"I'D RATHER CHEW OFF MY OWN ARM THAN WEAR—" DUNSTAN snapped his mouth shut as his bride-to-be lifted amused eyes to his. Standing across the room, Leila wore a shimmery powdery-blue confection that matched the sparkles in her eyes, and every time he looked at her, he couldn't remember what he was complaining about.

Wearing a simple silver-blue gown adorned with blue ribbons, Ninian fastened a bunch of leaves and flowers to his lapel and patted it with satisfaction. "This is bay for love and honor and success, and a spray of jasmine for prosperity."

"A spray of bank drafts would work better," Dunstan grumbled, but he tugged to be certain the flowers were secure. He needed all the prosperity he could accumulate to support a wife as well as a son and daughter.

"I told you to keep Celia's jewels," Drogo said absently from where he leaned against the mantel, head bent over a book. "It was considerate of Wickham to save us the trouble of retrieving them from that pawnshop. The green one adequately repaid Handel, with some left over, and I never considered the money I gave you as a loan needing repayment."

"It was far and above our agreed-upon percentage for my work." Holding his chin high so Ninian could straighten his cravat, Dunstan stared over her head to the foyer of the Ives London town house. Beyond the foyer waited the formal salon, where Leila's female relations flitted about, decorating for the upcoming nuptials. He refused to be nervous about the eccentric rituals that lay ahead, but his gaze kept drifting to Leila for reassurance. The love he found in her eyes soothed his ruffled hackles every time.

"You don't like being paid to play in the dirt," his soon-to-be wife scoffed. "I see I shall have to negotiate your wages for you."

Dunstan grinned and dodged Ninian's interfering hands to cross the room. "Do you intend to douse Drogo in perfume and discover my true worth in his eyes?" He grabbed the lacy veil and circle of twigs with which her sister had just covered Leila's curls and tossed them in the direction of the fireplace.

While Christina rescued them from the flames, Leila boldly met his gaze. "Your lofty brother has no clue what you're worth."

"And you do?"

Before Leila could reply, her mother and aunt hurried across the foyer with a rustle of skirts and squawks of outrage to join them in the family parlor. "That impossible man is here," the duchess cried, at the same time that Hermione wailed, "Someone hung"—she spluttered and turned pink— "those *things* on the rowan tree!"

So that was where his extra supply of protectives had disappeared to, Dunstan realized. His brothers no doubt thought he wouldn't need them anymore. Why they had chosen to tie them to a rowan tree wasn't a question Dunstan cared to pursue. He chose to answer the duchess's complaint instead. "I invited the impossible man," he warned, stopping the duchess in her tracks. "Griffith requested it."

"Adonis?" Leila whispered beside him, having been told of the invitation.

Dunstan nodded while continuing to stare down the huffy duchess.

"Well!" Stella turned her attention to Leila's bare head. "Where's your circlet of rowan?" she demanded, sweeping across the room to snatch it from Christina. "And his?" She shot Dunstan a demanding look.

"Wear it," Leila ordered in an undertone as Dunstan

started to protest. "For me," she finished with a smile that smote his heart.

Dunstan bit back his grumble and let Christina stand on a chair to lower a circle of dried twigs and purple and white flowers onto his head. "I feel like one of your damned rose-bushes," he complained when Christina jumped down and eased out of his way. "Next you'll be sticking my feet in mud and telling me to grow."

Leila's muffled chuckle was music to his ears, so he didn't protest too loudly when Hermione fluttered about him with the silly cape they'd forced Drogo to wear at his wedding.

"It's Leila who will grow, dear," his mother-in-law-to-be corrected. She turned to Leila to adjust the cape Christina had placed over her shoulders. "You will need to leave for our home in Northumberland by fall so you do not risk having the child while traveling in winter."

Dunstan's life had been rearranged so completely these past weeks, he'd become accustomed to it, but he didn't have to let the interfering witches think they had the upper hand. He wouldn't question their belief that Malcolm babies must be delivered in Wystan, their ancestral home, but he could argue all else, with vigor. "We'll leave when I have my land drained, and not an instant before," he warned. "I promised Leila a garden, and she'll have one."

"Leila's dowry will pay for that drainage," Drogo reminded him, setting his book on the mantel. "You might give some consideration to her mother's concerns."

"It's Dunstan's land," Leila defended him. "Between us, it is a joint endeavor. We will use the sale of his crop and turnip seeds to pay for my flowers, so I will be in his debt, not the other way around. I will trust his judgment on when we should leave for Wystan."

"You are the one who twisted Staines's arm and forced him to give me the tenant farm, as promised," Dunstan reminded her, "or I wouldn't have turnips to sell. Let us not refine too much upon who owes what to whom."

Leila shot him a brilliant smile. "Staines was so grateful that he wouldn't have to marry Lady Mary that he would have

given us the entire estate as a wedding gift if he could have.
Do you think you might train one of your brothers to manage
his lands as well as you did? Bath is so far, I don't think you
can manage it and Ives, too."

Dunstan would have laughed at the impossibility of any
of his brothers dealing with the spoiled viscount, but he was
still off balance from the reminder that Leila would bear his
child in less than seven months' time. "My brothers might
explore our cave, could they find it, or dig for bones or
explode holes in the hillside, so I think I'd best find another
steward for your nephew. I owe him that much for deeding
the grotto to you, even if his grandfather will not let him
keep your gardens."

"We'll take what flowers we can to Wystan," Leila replied
serenely, tucking her hand into his. "Over the winter, we
can use the conservatory there, and you can show me how to
develop new varieties so we will be prepared when we return
to Ives."

Dunstan liked the sound of that, but a noise in the doorway
distracted him. He smiled at the sight of his son standing
there, the impossible Adonis at his side. The sudden look of
uncertainty in Griffith's eyes reminded him that in the flurry
of wedding preparations, he hadn't offered the boy the necessary reassurances. He still needed to hone his fathering skills.

"Lady Leila has a rather valuable stable that will need
tending when she brings it to Ives," Dunstan told the boy,
ignoring the chaos of activity around them. "I thought you
might help me with that this summer and come with us to
Wystan this fall, unless you prefer to attend Eton."

Griffith's eyes widened, but still hesitant of his place in
these grand surroundings, he hung back. "You would take
me with you?"

Leila tore her hand from Dunstan's grip and strode across
the room to reassure him. "I've talked with your mother. She
agrees that it is time for you to be with your father now. He'll
need your company when we go north. I've been told Ives
men don't fare well with only women around."

Griffith glanced dubiously over his shoulder to the parlor,

where loud male laughter mixed with feminine giggles. "He has a lot of brothers…"

"Who have no appreciation for the land from which they sprang," Adonis replied from the door. "They'll not venture out in the dead of winter, far from the distractions of city life, in the interest of keeping family company."

Dunstan would have disagreed, but Leila's fascinated gaze on this man whom no one could name or place irked his more proprietary tendencies. Crossing the room to join her, he rubbed his hand over Griffith's head. "Next year, Eton for you, boy, but this year is mine," he whispered, before wrapping an arm around his bride's slim waist. "A pox on you, Nameless," he said to Adonis. "What do you know of family life?"

Adonis's shaggy head swung slowly from Leila's admiring gaze to confront Dunstan's dangerous one. "I had a mother," he retorted. "I did not spring from under a cabbage leaf."

Dunstan dropped a kiss on Leila's curls, released her, rolled his shoulders beneath the tight fit of the coat to loosen them, and raised his fists. "If you had a mother, then you have a name. What is it?" He might not have any grasp of the feminine niceties strewn about him, but he knew how to stake his territory. It began by identifying the stranger's proper place in his universe.

Wide shoulders encased in a shabby blue coat, long legs in shiny new boots crossed in a relaxed stance as he leaned against the door, Adonis regarded his host's fighting stance. "You're planning to fight me for my name on your wedding day?"

"I figure I'm the largest one here and the most apt to win," Dunstan agreed, ignoring Drogo's polite cough.

Adonis turned back to Leila with a questioning lift of his dark brow. "You're prepared to nurse him back to health after I pound him through the floor?"

Leila flashed her most flirtatious grin, the one guaranteed to drive Dunstan's ire through the roof. "That's Ninian's talent. I'll just watch, thank you."

Dunstan laughed out loud in great, tumbling peals of joy. She'd just given him permission to do as he pleased, and encouraged him to do so with that smile. Gad, he loved the vixen.

First, though, he would have to settle this family matter, for there was no doubt in his mind that the ugly-beaked giant ornamenting the doorway had to be an Ives. No one else in all the kingdom could sport the dark looks and prominent proboscis better than his family.

"Leila understands character," Dunstan said offhandedly, not expecting his guest to grasp the significance of that. He would have to ask her later what she'd seen in Adonis that had led her to believe they wouldn't kill each other.

Adonis considered that a moment before saying, "Aodhagán."

"Aid-ah-what?" Materializing beside Dunstan, Drogo attempted to repeat the word.

Dunstan simply stared in puzzlement, wondering if the man spoke in tongues.

"Aodhagán," Adonis repeated. "That's my name."

"Gaelic," Hermione murmured, straightening the golden cape around Dunstan's shoulders. "Aid-ah-GAN, little fire. A very, very old name. I'm surprised your mother used it. We tend to use saints' names these days, not the old names."

Dunstan thought Adonis might strangle while processing this information from Leila's bird-witted mother. "*Malcolms* tend to use saints' names," Dunstan clarified.

"Well, our branch does," Hermione corrected, "but we are very forward-looking. That's not to say he's a Malcolm, dear," she added in a flutter of alarm at Dunstan's jerk of surprise at the suggestion that there were *more* branches on the Malcolm tree. "It *is* a very old name, after all. Anyone might use it."

Leila patted her mother's arm and steered her away from Dunstan, but her fascinated gaze remained on the man in the doorway. "I take it no one can pronounce your name, which is why you call yourself Adonis," she concluded.

"Among other reasons," the stranger answered with wary amusement.

"And would you care to enlighten us on the family name?" Dunstan persisted. He hadn't wanted to like the man, but he understood his humor. The god Adonis was said to be very handsome, and this giant looked like an Ives. Ives males had many reputations, but handsomeness wasn't the one that stood out.

Dunstan didn't flinch beneath the dark, considering look the larger man gave him. He had no particular desire to create a brawl on his wedding day, but he wouldn't avoid one either if the man insisted he wasn't part of the family. With all these women fluttering about, brawling seemed a reasonable alternative.

"Dougal," Adonis finally replied, in a curt, clipped tone.

"Dougal." Stella repeated the name thoughtfully while straightening Leila's veil. "Hermione, didn't we have a great-aunt who married a Dougal?"

"If you say so, dear. I believe the vicar just arrived. Shouldn't we be taking our seats? I don't know how much longer Felicity can keep the young ones behaving."

All around him, women flitted and fluttered and clucked. Dunstan merely took shelter by drawing Leila to him. She was his already, vowed beneath the heavens. The ceremony ahead was merely a formality. He had responsibilities now, and he meant to assume them. Drogo had his business in Parliament and couldn't be expected to handle every situation their rowdy family engendered.

And the big man standing before him was part of the family, regardless of the name he gave them.

"Aidan." Dunstan decided on the shorter name with satisfaction. "I'll be damned if I call you Adonis any longer. Griffith is to stand up with me, but I'd appreciate it if you would take the row with my brothers—if it's not an imposition," he amended, feeling Leila's tug on his sleeve.

Looking trapped, Aidan glanced from Dunstan's determined expression to Drogo's interested one, to the women, who did not appear to consider this request at all remarkable. His jaw muscle ticked, then set as he shrugged. "If you wish. But do not think you can hold me afterward."

"Of course not," Leila answered. "Though you'll want to stay for some of *Maman*'s punch, I imagine. And Ninian has ordered the most delicious little tarts. I believe Griffith has learned some trick with a puzzle that he wished to show you, but I'm sure you can do that anytime."

Hugging his magical wife, Dunstan kissed her ear. "Don't tease, Leila. You may tame only one Ives at a time, and that one is me." He gave his newfound friend a sympathetic glance. "Drogo has asked us to stay at Ives for the summer while I oversee the estate and drain my bog. You are welcome to join us when you can. The place is a monstrosity large enough to house two tribes."

"I think I prefer your bog," Aidan said dryly. "I'll fix the thatch in return."

"Would you?" Leila asked eagerly. "We're planning on that becoming my distillery, but it will be some time before I have flowers to distill."

Satisfied that he'd finally found a way to repay their odd relation for returning Griffith to him, Dunstan returned his attention to the matter at hand—surviving this public ceremony so he had the right to sweep Leila off to the house Drogo had given him at Ives, and the bed he now called his own.

"I think it is high time we suffer through the charade so we can go on to more important matters," he whispered in Leila's ear, planting a possessive palm over the place where his daughter grew. He was rather looking forward to the challenge of raising the only known Ives female.

"If you were not such a wonderful agronomist, I'd think you should take up the position of diplomat, my dear," Leila taunted.

Howling with laughter at the insult, Dunstan dragged her toward their waiting audience.

He might never take to society's ways, but he knew he could count on his wife to correct his faults and foibles. It just might take a lifetime to cure him.

He could live with that.

Read on for an excerpt from the next book in the Magic series

The Trouble with Magic

Coming August 2012
From Sourcebooks Casablanca

Spring 1754

"I *saw* him. Percy was there when his mother died, no matter what anyone claims," Felicity muttered fiercely, clinging to the rail of the family yacht as the ship lurched and slid into a trough between rough waves. Swaddled in a cloak, a scarf, and thick gloves, Lady Felicity stared into the April squall. She'd never seen the sea before. The salt spray stung her cheeks, and cautiously she licked her lips to taste the droplets gathering there. It even tasted of salt.

She ought to be afraid of the wild waves and the crack of lightning, but those were things she couldn't touch, so they had no power over her. Or she over them. At any other time she would have exulted in this new experience. Instead, dread of things she had set in motion churned her stomach. Beneath the dread shimmered a sliver of hope that her efforts would not be in vain.

The incident with Sir Percy had been her breaking point. Even her father had agreed that a relaxing journey to visit her sister in Northumberland might settle her nerves. Leila and her husband were staying at his family's estate in Wystan. As much as she wanted to see them and the new baby, it was the proximity to Scotland that drew her on. Felicity prayed she could find some way to escape her family's solicitude and reach Edinburgh and the one frail hope of ever having a normal life.

She *must* reach Edinburgh. A lifetime of pain and loneliness, denied even the simplest of human pleasures, would be unbearable. *Was* unbearable. She had broken her Papa's heart when she'd refused Sir Percy's proposal of marriage. And terrified herself.

"Quit saying that you saw Percy," Christina said. "If he really did murder his mother, he might murder you, too. How do you know he doesn't have spies following us?"

Exhausted by the constant tension and turmoil of touching strangers these past few days, Felicity still managed to cast her sister a look of incredulity. "Spies? Why in the name of the goddess would he do that? Nobody believes me. His servants swear his mother's death was an accident, that he wasn't at home the day she died. His steward swears they were together in London that day. I'm just an hysteric afraid of marriage."

"Well, you did become hysterical, and you *are* afraid of marriage," Christina said with equanimity. "That doesn't mean you aren't right, and if you are, you have made him very nervous."

"I have made *everyone* very nervous." Wrapping her mantle tighter, Felicity watched a seagull scream across the leaden sky.

"Come inside, Felicity," Christina urged. "The wind is increasing and will blow you off your feet."

Her sister was scarcely two years her elder, yet ages older in terms of experience and courage. Christina sheltered Felicity from life's buffets much as the rest of their family did, but Christina did it with impatience. With a shrug acknowledging her sister's concern, Felicity returned her spectacles to her nose and descended the companionway into the cabin below.

"The captain does not think we'll reach Northumberland today," Felicity said. Entering their private cubbyhole, she picked up her much-beloved and slightly bedraggled doll from the bunk, and gingerly occupied the bed's edge. Her doll exuded the joy of a long-ago Christmas and the memory of all the happy hours of play in the hands of her innocent sisters. It provided a balance against the cabin's dismal vibrations. "Leila and Dunstan will be worried if we're late."

"Perhaps Dunstan will tire of waiting for us in port and go home."

Christina said this with such glee that Felicity couldn't prevent a smile. "He's an Ives. He's more likely to set the Navy searching for us. I think Ives have gained the reputation of causing Malcolm disasters simply because they are such interfering creatures. They cannot leave well enough alone."

Christina laughed. "If *anyone* knew what we intend, they'd interfere." Sitting cross-legged on the bunk in an unladylike billow of skirts and panniers, she propped her shoulders against the wall. "This will be great fun, once we find some means of escaping interfering relations. I've never been to Edinburgh."

"I cannot see how we will go now," Felicity replied. Her dread roiled higher at the thought of such a reckless escapade. She was not an adventurer by nature. Only desperation drove her to this scheme.

"It will be marvelous fun," Christina reassured her. "We will see the sights and meet new people. It's a pity we cannot find you a husband while we're at it, one more to your liking than the stuffy ones Father prefers. Sir Percy would never have suited."

Felicity had thought bookish Sir Percy the ideal suitor— until she had seen murder in his touch. Half the reason for this journey was to hide her until her father could investigate her tale. She suspected the other half was his fear that this time her mind had taken leave of her senses, and a good long rest from the exigencies of London's social whirl was needed. Sir Percy was not at all the sort to make people think he could murder his mother.

"Well, Ewen Ives is still unmarried," Felicity said in wry jest, offering the worst possible example of a suitor she could summon, as far from wealthy, respectable Sir Percy as could be imagined.

Christina laughed at the notion of Felicity with one of the men in their brother-in-law's tumultuous family. "You'd spend the rest of your life chasing after the lot of them, attempting to prevent them from wreaking the havoc and ruin you'd discover on every object they touched."

"Well, it wouldn't be *boring*." But boring was what she

wanted—needed. Safe and boring, no unpleasant surprises, no jolts of pain or anguish or visions of death and destruction.

"Besides, Ewen possesses nothing for which Father could trade your dowry, and Father lives for haggling with suitors." Christina giggled at the thought. "Although, you must admit, Ewen is the most handsome of the Ives. And charming, when he chooses to be. He would dangle you with all his other conquests like a watch fob on a chain."

Felicity sighed. One of her favorite objects was a mechanical bouquet of porcelain roses that twirled to tinkling music. Ewen Ives had given it to her for her come-out last year. It held only his fascination with the motor without any deep, dark secrets attached. But handsome, charming men were not for dowdy, invisible girls like her. She had only briefly seen Ewen at a family gathering or two since then. Besides, her father would have a spasm of the heart if he knew she dreamed of an Ives. She loved her father and wished him to be happy with her choice.

The only way that would happen is if she found *A Malcolm Journal of Infusions*, which she needed to rid herself of this wretched gift—if it would do as promised.

First she must find the Lord Nesbitt in Edinburgh who had last owned the book—a century ago.

"More's the pity," Felicity said, "but it's best if we avoid interfering Ives if we can, although how we can avoid Dunstan when we are supposed to be staying with him and Leila is beyond my comprehension."

"We simply must convince Leila that we are grown-up enough to visit Edinburgh on our own," Christina declared.

Since Leila had married Dunstan Ives last year, she had become so engrossed in her studies of perfumes and scents that she'd scarcely traveled to London. Felicity couldn't predict how Leila would react to her younger sisters' dangerous mission.

"Perhaps she will be so busy dandling her new baby on her knee that she will not notice if we don't arrive at all," Christina suggested.

"She will more likely be pacing the dock with Dunstan. It's not as if I leave London with any frequency. Mama will have written her with lists and lists of instructions." Felicity clenched her fingers anxiously. "It's a wonder Mama did not lock me in my room for my own safety or that Father did not banish me to the Outer Hebrides after I swooned at Sir Percy's feet."

"*Percy*," Christina muttered with disgust. "A milksop like that could not so much as murder a bank ledger. I think your gift has gone awry."

Felicity hunched over her doll, hugging its familiar vibrations of love for comfort. "If I cannot be rid of this wretched gift, I shall never marry. I will grow old living in Papa's library."

Christina bent forward to brush Felicity's hair out of her face in a gesture of sympathy. "I'm sorry. It's just so very hard to believe that a fop like Percy could be dangerous. But you're right. If you're forever seeing a suitor's mistress in his snuffbox or reading his lascivious ambitions in his touch, you'll never marry. Don't worry. We'll find your book."

That was the ray of hope to which Felicity clung. She'd received too many unanticipated shocks upon touching seemingly innocent objects to ever be as courageous and trusting as Christina, but she was willing to brave more than stormy seas if at the end of the journey she could find the journal.

She knew her mother would be horrified if she was aware that Felicity was seeking the recipe that would rid her of her unwanted gift, but this latest incident had convinced her that she had no other choice if she wished to be normal and marry happily, as her family desired.

"I wish our great-grandfather had not been so spiteful as to sell off the Malcolm library," Felicity said, mourning the loss of so much knowledge. "There could be all manner of wisdom in those books, lost on people who understand nothing of their content."

"I cannot imagine why some Lord Nesbitt would buy a bunch of old journals." Standing, Christina stretched restlessly in the confines of the tiny cabin. "Perhaps he burned them. Scots have weird notions of witchcraft."

"It's not witchcraft," Felicity said crossly. "It is wisdom learned from experience. If I can find the recipe, I can be normal like everyone else. I can live a full life. I can dance and marry and have babies."

"If that isn't magic, what is?" Christina asked.

Buried beneath layers of protective clothing, untouched by any hand except her family's, Felicity peered upward at her sister with eyes glistening in wonder and anticipation. *Magic* was the world around her—the one she had never experienced.

The one she would never experience if she didn't find the journal.

About the Author

Patricia Rice was born in New York but learned to love the warmer Southeast. She is now California dreaming and working her way West by way of St. Louis. Improving houses and then moving is apparently her hobby. She is married with two grown children who also have settled in warmer climes. She would love you to stop by www.patriciarice.com to see what she's doing now or join her at Facebook at www .facebook.com/PatriciaRiceBooks and on Twitter at www .twitter.com/Patricia_Rice